Peggy
My favourite
literary critic

R. Barker

A STATE OF FEAR

R. BARKER PRICE

Copywrite © 2017 by R. Barker Price

All rights reserved. Published in the United States of America by E.T. Hutchings, Company.

Book design by John E. Oleman
Jacket design by Samuel Foster

ISBN 13: 9781547132751
ISBN 10: 1547132752

10 9 8 7 6 5 4 3 2 1

A STATE OF FEAR

1

More often than not, the run from the Marina District to the top of Filmore Street in Pacific Heights would bring even the most devout jogger to his knees. San Francisco was famously known for its hills, but the Filmore climb was in a league of its own; it was a ribbon-like sidewalk, steeply angled with stretches of concrete inclines, interspersed with narrow, calf-burning steps. It was a four-hundred-foot climb from hell, and that's what runners liked most about it.

Jake Altman was halfway to the top when he swiped his runny nose and sucked in deep gasps of cool, misty air. Long shadows had begun to creep across the iconic city. It was rush hour, and the streets of San Francisco were packed with cars. Jake glared at a woman in a battered Toyota coupe that spewed noxious smoke as the clutch burned at a steep intersection. His tattered gray sweatshirt was soaked with sweat, and his faded Nike running shoes dug ponderously at the precipitous concrete hill. Jake was a purist. For him running was in no way a fashion statement; it was a self-deprecating necessity, something to be tolerated in the abstract pursuit of health and promised longevity. He wore the same running clothes he had worn since college, six years in all, including a political science doctorate and a lifetime of study. His socks fell into an entirely different category. Jake had learned to renew them with some regularity, but only after students in his classes began to complain of an unspeakably pungent odor.

Jake had run Filmore Hill many times before, never without reaching the conclusion that he was a flipping idiot for abusing his body so egregiously. He was grudgingly approaching thirty. Just over six feet tall, more on the lanky side. Jake had found that his irregular running sessions had kept him reasonably fit, and he was still a formidable competitor for the many hilly runs in the bejeweled city. Jake's dark eyes lay somewhat hidden beneath a mop of unkempt, black hair that fell over his forehead; his face was angular and youthful, almost to the point of being boyish. Though he possessed a certain talent for charm, if and when he chose to employ it, Jake would otherwise have been content to go about his teaching duties at U.C. Berkeley with a carefully crafted reticence.

The intersection of Filmore and Union, marking the halfway point of the climb, was just above him now, and with the certainty that the climb steepened dramatically ahead, Jake pulled up for a moment, jogging in place. He spread his arms wide, stretching, trying to regain lost oxygen. As he bounced lightly in place, he turned and gazed out over the glittering bay. A few lights had begun to click on far below. It was, as always, mystically beautiful. Jake could see the thick blanket of fog building just beyond the graceful arches of the Golden Gate Bridge. He knew a great, gray pawl would descend soon.

Jake dug in again and drove his legs forward, climbing steadily through the agony of lactate burn. The top of the hill was in sight. He inhaled deeply and began to sprint, quickly passing a tourist couple and an older woman carrying an overstuffed grocery bag. His lungs felt like they would burst, and he was beginning to see double. But then, with a surge of bounding strides, Jake lunged up the last ten steps and exploded onto the busy corner. Still dancing on his toes to relieve the strain, he let out a yelp of victory and threw a look back at the four-hundred-foot climb. Far below, past rows of quaint shops and Victorian homes clinging to the side of the hill, cars and buses inched along Marina Way. A pick-up soccer game was getting underway on the Green, and several tall sailboats slid closer to the yacht club, lowering their Dacron mainsails as they prepared to land.

At the top of the hill, rush hour gridlock had reached critical mass. A MUNI electric bus turned too quickly onto Filmore Street, and its line-pole leaped from the overhead wires in a dazzling display of sparks. The bus rolled woefully to a stop at the center of the intersection. Horns sounded, people shouted, and several spirited middle-finger salutations did little to relieve the tension. Jake Altman should have been amused. Such displays of social discord only served to reinforce his perception that civility had long-since been displaced by the creeping barbarism of the times. He was a Renaissance man, an academic who was the son of an academic, a man who had benefited from a superior education yet found himself encumbered by a nagging sense of social awkwardness. Some might say that

Jake was a cynic, but he simply preferred to perceive the world, and more specifically the nuances of American society, with a cool sense of detachment, observing everything, often with irreverent humor. It all seemed so predictable to him, most like a record caught in the same groove. Jake understood the game very well, and yet he remained unsettled. He was frustrated that he had yet to find his place in an increasingly fractious world.

Another horn sounded. Cars jousted for advantage; it was a maddening swirl of worker bees, flitting instinctively homeward. If Jake had watched more closely, he would have cocked his head and absorbed the strange urban ritual with wry humor. It would have made him smile, maybe even laugh, but as the growling cars and coughing buses slowly untangled themselves, and traffic inched ahead, it was as if nothing at all had changed. The street corner was empty. Jake was gone.

Far below the tony Pacific Height neighborhood, drifting fog swirled around the Golden Gate Bridge, spilling silently into San Francisco Bay. As it did most afternoons, the mist first filtered through low-lying areas; the Marina District, Cow Hollow, and China Town then swelled around the Seven Sister Hills until only the tips remained unclouded. A container ship, just passing Alcatraz, outbound for some far-East port, was lost in the shroud, its moaning foghorn sounding as if it was a world away. San Francisco was once again wrapped in a silent cloak, muted and dreamlike.

Not far away, a MUNI bus lugged its way along Geary Boulevard. Aaron Scott, a career driver with an impeccable record, was making his last run for the day, delivering tired and largely silent passengers to modest homes and apartments dotting the hillside. It was an ethnic neighborhood, populated mostly by working-class Eastern European immigrants. Known affectionately as Little Russia, the immediate area lacked the glitter and stature of Pacific Heights and other more prosperous enclaves just to the north. It was, however, the last bastion of Russian influence in the city, a tiny community that once served as a magnet to early settlers moving down the coast from Fort Ross and Bodgea Bay where their ancestors had established a hunting and lumber foothold in America in the mid-1800s.

There were only three or four passengers still aboard the bus, as the dull churning of its diesel engine rose and fell with each straining gearshift. Streetlights, just now beginning to glow, defused anemically through the fog. Aaron Scott thought it was an unremarkably normal evening. He was looking forward to dinner and his favorite television reality show. His wife was a lousy cook, but he wasn't really particular. He was content to work, eat prodigiously, and lose himself in cable television madness. Just five more years and he could retire, he thought, as his eyes drifted to the oversized rearview mirror hanging above the windshield. There was something *different* about the old woman five rows back. She was tiny, a mere wisp and vaguely eastern European. Her weathered cheeks were creased with age, while her calloused fingers, gnarled with arthritis, clung to the seatback in front of her. Scott glanced into the mirror again. The woman stared vacantly out the window, even as she coughed deeply with an ominous gurgle deep in her lungs. She was wearing what appeared to be an ancient wool topcoat. No, it was more than that, Scott decided. It was very heavy, faded gray, with deep cuffs rolled back over the sleeves and a short cape layered over her shoulders. There were hooks in place of buttons, as well as faded and torn red piping that dressed the edges. Then it dawned on him. It was military, a Russian Greatcoat, very old and rather threadbare.

One of the other riders, a man still wearing work coveralls marked DeTillo's Meats, tugged the overhead cord, sounding a buzzer farther forward. The bus pulled up to the corner of Geary and 26th Street, and the meat-man edged toward the door, grunted to Scott, and stepped off. Scott was about to close the door again when he noticed the old woman struggling to rise from her seat. She was unsteady and seemed disoriented. Scott kicked the bus in Park and made his way back.

"Need some help, ma'am?" he offered. She was even older than he had first thought.

The old woman looked up but offered nothing in return. Only when she held out her arm did Scott understand the depth of her infirmity. He carefully helped her off the bus.

Outside, the fog parted slightly, allowing streaks of light from a fading sun to wash across the corner. The old woman seemed frail and vulnerable to Scott; she could have been a hundred years old. When she coughed roughly again, he leaned closer. "Are you sure you're okay? It's getting late," he suggested, tugging his MUNI jacket more tightly around his chest. "Cold too." When she didn't respond, he stooped to look into the woman's eyes. She turned away quickly and crept up a series of stone steps leading to a broad lawn and a very unusual building in the distance. Scott's eyes followed her then drifted upward to something looming across the lawn. He had seen it before, and it always seemed very out of place in the working class neighborhood.

The cathedral was a large but modestly appointed stone building, painted entirely white. Its lofty archways were accented with colorful religious murals and lined with burgundy edging. There were very few windows. The broad timber entry door was deeply weathered and massively built; it looked more like an entrance to a Medieval castle. Still, the structure might have otherwise been unremarkable if it were not for the two enormous, gilded onion domes rising high into the mist. Each was topped with a golden cross.

The Holy Mary Cathedral had been completed in 1956, but its religious roots could be traced through early Russian settlers in America, and before that, to the Great Schism of 1064 when the separatists broke away from the Roman Catholic Church. The Byzantine-styled Cathedral was one of the largest Russian Orthodox churches outside of Russia, and beneath its soaring, mist-shrouded towers, the decrepit woman looked small and insignificant.

Marvina Dubrovsky gazed at the cathedral in reverent silence then gathered her strength and limped up the brick walk. She stopped abruptly when she heard music softly filtering out through elevated windows; there was an organ, solemn choral voices, too. Like Marvina, the music was very old. It was as if time had stood still, and a thousand years of Russian tradition lay heavily across the once-grand structure.

Inside the cathedral, evening vespers were just getting underway. A sparse crowd of Russian and Slavic-Americans sat in random wood pews. Many of them were infirmed, with the pain of hard years etched in their hollow faces. The holy chancel spread impressively across the front of the room, much of it still gilded and gleaming. A bishop presided, chanting lethargically, recounting scriptural guidance in a thick Russian dialect as his acolyte gracefully swung the thurible incense burner. At the side of the altar, Archbishop Popov Konstantin sat heavily in an ornate thronos with his gold-headed staff planted firmly on a velvet pillow. His vestments were finer than that of the bishop's, and his purple mitre cap was laced with gold threading. A heavy pectoral cross hung around his neck, offering further evidence of his high stature.

Konstantin had been visiting The Holy Mary Cathedral for nearly a year, a goodwill tour, orchestrated by the church leadership in Moscow. Actually, however, Konstantin fully understood the tacit finality associated with his "appointment" to this church. His was a lifetime of piety and service, dimmed now by advancing age, and despite the regal trappings surrounding him at this terminus, it was obvious, even to Konstantin himself, that he was an aged relic, long past years of meaningful leadership. He was an enormous man, flaccid, bearded, with a finely tapered nose. At the moment, Konstantin was bored and barely awake.

No one seemed to notice when the tall narthex door swung open and Marvina Dubrovsky crept inside. Before her, the incantations continued, complimented by a small choir half hidden behind a lattice curtain. Heads were bowed in reverence, and no one took note as Marvina started down the aisle. Each step, though it brought debilitating pain, was deliberate and unwavering. Her cough had deepened, and she was short of breath.

Heads began to turn. People leaned to see more clearly. The bishop noticed Marvina and faltered in his recitation when she did not stop, as was the custom, at the iconostasis, the low wall across the front of the sanctuary. Strict church protocol dictated that parishioners not interrupt vespers. This was widely understood, but a largely forgotten church dictate allowed that the very old and the very sick could come forward for confession, even during the service.

Popov Konstantin cocked a bushy eyebrow and watched as Marvina tried but failed to climb the last two steps to face the manoualia candelabra. She was spent and could go no further. He gathered his great mass and rose up, undulating purposefully forward. Marvina saw the Archbishop coming. Her eyes bore into him as she offered her hand. He took it and gently lifted her to her feet.

Konstantin understood that Marvina sought confession. He uttered a short question in his native Russian tongue.

She nodded and, as a humble seeker of forgiveness, struggled to her knees in front of the altar then raised her hand and placed it on the manoualia. The confession could now begin.

Konstantin droned through the basic liturgical directives then addressed Marvina with a perfunctory question of her confession. When she failed to answer, he asked again. The choir was singing loudly now, as acolytes fervently rang hand-bells. The Archbishop bent closer, anticipating the required, incanted response. Instead, when Marvina lifted her eyes to his, he was sobered by what he saw. Her face was ancient, contorted in pain but filled with grim resolve, an acknowledgement of an unspeakably anguished secret held captive for a lifetime. Konstantin was fearful of what was to come, but finally he called out softly to her, in broken English this time, "Your sin. It could not be so great."

"You are Russian?" Marvina asked weakly.

"Yes."

Marvina paused then uttered a brief, silent prayer and produced a small gold block from her tattered coat. It was the size of a matchbox, not more than a quarter of an inch thick. She placed it in Konstantin's palm, being careful to keep it covered. Her voice was hushed with age, but the words, spoken in a pure Russian dialect, formed a resolute affirmation that caught him completely off guard. She removed her hand to reveal a shimmering gold ruble. Konstantin gasped; his eyes locked in disbelief on the artifact and its elegant engraving. Marvina's eyes danced with the restorative power of her admission. In English, she slowly spoke, "She was here. She was always here." Konstantin's face was ashen. His knees buckled, and he was about to collapse. A young acolyte grabbed him around the waist, easing him onto a tufted stool. He was too stunned to speak.

Jake Altman had turned west when he topped Filmore Hill, churning along the more gradual incline of Broadway Avenue as it carved a picturesque pathway through the moneyed Pacific Heights district. Breathtaking Victorian restorations lined the side of Alta Plaza Park. Mist-draped trees hung heavily overhead. Jake soon turned back toward the bay, dropping down several blocks to Green Street. Here, along the north side of the street, a number of stately brick mansions perched along the precipitous hillside overlooking the bay. Jake knew the route well, but the exclusive display of wealth never ceased to amaze him. He had regained much of his strength, and while he could have run faster, he began to slow. Ahead, through a veil of fog, an austere brick mansion rose above the tops of conifer and Eucalyptus trees. He passed Pierce Street and crossed to the other side. Then he stopped.

Jake sucked in the sea air and stretched several times against a lamppost. For anyone who might have been watching, he would have appeared to be an altogether average after-work runner. Had they looked closer, they would have noted that, between leg stretches and arm extensions, he was watching a mansion across the street. It was a massive six-story complex that seemed out of place in the graceful residential neighborhood. The building exuded an austere and even foreboding presence. Jake's eyes tracked across the façade, noting the thickly curtained windows. The starkly white, ornamental iron fence surrounding the property only served to accentuate its formidable presence.

Jake stooped down to re-tie both running shoes. Taking his time, he glanced casually at the building, taking in the monolithic-stone first story, topped by a towering brick façade that was uniquely devoid of character. Nothing escaped Jake's scrutiny: the polished Bentley coupe, thick rosebushes, and the deeply tinted security window beside the main entrance. It was particularly hard to miss the numerous television monitors arrayed on the building, providing extensive viewing coverage of surrounding street activity. Jake took it all in, carefully, and not for the first time. He knew there was more, and he was certain *they* were watching him.

Recognizing the risks of conspicuous loitering, Jake straightened and was about to continue his run. With a parting glance, his eyes shifted to the polished brass plaque, riveted next to the main entrance. It was deeply etched in Russian, and just below that in English: *Consulate of the Russian Federation.*

Aaron Scott was in the home stretch. He had dropped his last westbound MUNI riders at Park Presidio Boulevard then turned back at the Cliff House loop. A gang of blue-haired skate-boarders was being unruly in the back, while a young couple, obviously heading out for an early dinner date, groped shamelessly at each other about halfway back in the bus. A black man, impeccably dressed and humming softly, was seated closer to the front. Scott pushed the big MUNI bus a little harder, intent on clocking out a few minutes early when he reached Van Ness Avenue.

Just a block away, Marvina Dubrovsky stood on the sidewalk beneath the branches of an aging Eucalyptus tree. She was half hidden in the fog, softly mumbling an ancient Russian cradlesong, something childlike from long ago, an immensely comforting tune. Another coughing spasm interrupted her blissful recollections; pain racked her chest. Marvina gripped a signpost, taking tiny, sipping breaths until the discomfort eased. She saw the lights of the MUNI bus approaching, and she knew it was time. A silent prayer spilled from her quivering lips as her fingers traced the small crucifix in her hand. The MUNI bus was a hundred feet away, barreling toward the stop. Marvina's eyes sank shut. She stepped into the street directly in front of the charging bus and was hit squarely, and with a sickening crunch she was mowed down and ripped apart.

2

Political activism had been a revered sport at U.C. Berkeley for a very long time. The student demonstrations of the sixties and seventies had elevated the tradition to messianic proportions, and Ludwig's Fountain, just outside the Cesar Chavez Student Union building, was considered sacred ground to environmentalists, revolutionaries, atheists, and die-hard anarchists. Those whose sympathies ran cross-grain to the radical tide were most often relegated to the seamy underbelly of campus life.

Jake Altman was moving fast across the cobblestone courtyard with rolled-up papers stuffed in both pockets of his tweed sport coat. His jeans were frayed at the knees, and his tired Nike's bore a remarkable resemblance to his odious running shoes. He edged through a throng of students that encircled a fire breathing, shaved-head feminist standing defiantly atop the fountain wall. She was clearly at the top of her game. Obscenities and scurrilous accusations spewed from her coal-black lips. Jake pulled up for just a moment, captivated by her biting oratory, as she excoriated every imaginable aspect and body part of humble masculinity.

"Do you know why they have dicks?" she snarled with disgust. "So they can stick it to us! No shit!" Spittle was beginning to collect on her lower lip-ring as she screeched even louder. "It's a penis war! That's what it is, a penis war! And we're the ones getting fucked! Every which way, you name it. Girl, if you want a good job, forget that shit. Equal respect, ain't gonna happen. So I say enough! I say we oust the pigs! Pound their female-slamming, vagina-crazed bubbles." Someone shouted out an expletive-laced vote of support, and then, almost as if divinely inspired, the crazed man-basher began to chant, "Pound the Penis! Pound the Penis!" A gaggle of equally frightening female students took up the chant too, while the mostly-bearded male attendees began to shift uncomfortably in their Birkenstock sandals, effectively emasculated by the vehement penis bashing.

Jake nudged a well-tatted, pencil-thin kid next to him and posited, "Hey, how 'bout that First Amendment. You gotta love it, huh?" He turned to leave and immediately ran headlong into a cute coed who seemed more than a little out of place amid the fractious radicals. She was extremely fit, dressed to kill, wearing an invitingly low-cut sweater top, mini-skirt, and cowboy boots. Not too many books in hand.

"Ooh, I'm sorry," she cooed.

Jake could only croak awkwardly, "My fault."

The girl offered a sweetly vacuous smile, "I guess I'm a little turned around."

"Lost?"

"Yeah, I'm new on campus." She pulled out a rumpled map. "I was cutting across the west grounds so I could find the…"

Jake prophetically filled in the blank, "…Art History building."

"Hey, yeah," the girl beamed.

"Art History would be in Doe Memorial Library."

"Yeah, but how'd you know that's where I was going?" The girl exclaimed.

"Jake shrugged, his eyes lingering on her shapely legs, "...wild guess." He leaned closer, pointing over her shoulder. "Try going that way, between those two buildings. Doe Library is off to the right a little."

"Cool. Hey, thanks," the girl chirped. She seemed to hesitate then expertly dangled an unfiltered invitation, "I'm Bree."

Jake could see it coming; this was not a new phenomenon -- the older professor-guy syndrome. Bree was interested; he was late. Jake allowed a slight smile and edged away, saying, "Sorry. Gotta go. Good luck."

"So, maybe I'll see you in class sometime," Bree offered hopefully.

"Absolutely. I teach an intro Poly Sci class Monday, Wednesdays and Fridays, that's if I can't think of a good excuse to cut class."

"Bet I can help with that," Bree teased. Jake held up his hands in surrender and melted away into the crowd. Bree watched him go, making a mental note to sign up for Poly Sci next semester.

Jake angled past Sproul Hall, hurried along a brick path, then bounded up the cut-stone steps of an older campus building. He nearly collided with a mountainous black kid wearing a Berkeley football jacket.

"Yo, Dr. Altman," beamed the behemoth. "Thanks for the C last semester. It kept me on the team, man!"

Jake exchanged a fist bump with the kid and offered gentle equivocation. "Well, Dante, if anyone ever deserved a C, it was you." Jake eased up the steps and disappeared in the building.

Barrows Hall housed a variety of activist departments. Political Science dominated, but African American, Ethnic, Gender and Women's studies also held considerable sway. The building itself was one of those 1960's mind-blowing architectural wonders; it was a study in simplicity: blockishly symmetrical, tinted a perfect shade of baby-shit yellow, and uniformly boring. The halls were narrow and plastered with handbills. The lighting, though, had been upgraded since the last student uprising when every fixture had been smashed. Jake rounded the second-floor stairway and spilled into the hallway. Ahead was a formidable doorway that looked more like an entrance to a Supreme Court justice's lair. Jake slowed, sucked in a couple of breaths, and shoved his unruly hair back.

They were waiting for him. Three of the Political Science Department's most senior review board members sat somewhat rigidly in Calder-esque swoop-back chairs at a glass conference table. Reprints of mawkish Post Modern art works were pegged to sterile white walls. An ultra-modern, chrome clock hung on one wall, with gears, levers, and balance beams exposed and working in efficient unison.

Dr. Ezra Bonner, the tall, sixtyish African American Dean of the Political Science Department, sat patiently at the head of the table. Clearly the product of the university's go-go years, Bonner had survived the turbulent Anti-War movement and weathered all manner of intellectual fads.

His face was etched in scholarly contemplation, but it was also a gentle face, one that reflected a reasoned sense of understanding. His hair, once explosive in a shocking Afro, was now short and gray. He wore a faded blue work-shirt along with a luminous paisley bowtie.

Dr. Eleanor Hinklen, a roundish and bespectacled middle-aged German transplant, was Dean of Public Policy studies, which meant she singlehandedly imposed a starkly progressive slant to the department's "preferred" texts and course tone. The third member of the triumvirate seemed an unlikely teammate. Dr. Katherine Sexton, Associate Dean of Studies, though a bit severe, was nonetheless a strikingly attractive professor in her late thirties. Her hair was dark, kept long like a much younger woman, and she had brilliant, penetrating eyes and well-glossed lips. Katherine wore glasses, but only in an effort to promote an aura of intelligence. Dr. Ezra Bonner shifted some papers on the table and glanced at his watch. "Well, I suppose we should reschedule."

"Jake is always late. Always," Eleanor Hinklen added crisply. "He doesn't respect the process."

Ezra Bonner offered a couched defense, "Jake is a busy young professor."

"Yes, he's usually busy annoying us," Dr. Hinklen snorted."

Katherine Sexton stifled a chuckle. She knew the rules of academic hierarchy dictated that it was her turn to pounce on Jake, but she resisted. It all seemed so pompously overblown to her.

The door suddenly opened, and Jake Altman appeared. He was the picture of decorum, were it not for his shirttail flapping behind him. "Please forgive me," he offered as formal appeasement. "There's a student rally out front, and I just couldn't help but marvel at the constructive exchange of fresh insights."

"Pound the penis," Katherine coughed sarcastically under her breath.

Jake got it. The others did not.

Dr. Bonner cleared his throat. "May we please proceed?"

Jake eased down in a chair at the other end of the table. He clasped his hands thoughtfully in front of him and offered a sincere smile. "You know, I've really been looking forward to this review."

Katherine rolled her eyes. She slapped a binder open. "All right, Dr. Altman. You are in luck. The semester student reviews are, for the most part, positive."

"That's a good thing, right," Jake teased.

Dr. Eleanor Hinklen wasn't amused. She jabbed a boney finger at another report in front of her. "A number of students also commented that you have recently had a tendency to -- wander, if that's the correct invective."

Jake nodded seriously. "Wander?"

Dr. Bonner weighed in with a measured advisement. "Jake, it's getting worse. We are concerned that you may have lost your focus."

"Oh, I'm very focused, Dr. Bonner," Jake assured.

"Abundantly on the wrong things," Eleanor Hinklen huffed. "Dr. Altman, you have successfully completed your dissertation. You have completed the doctoral program, and you have assumed tenure track instructional duties. Why does there have to be more?"

"I'm not sure what you mean, Dr. Hinklen," Jake questioned.

"Well, let's start with the ponderous annotations to your dissertation," she sputtered. "These unnecessary and protracted appendages just keep coming? Why?"

"Eleanor means you're wasting your time and ours," Katherine Sexton inserted. "Because that *is* exactly what you appear to be doing." She shifted her long legs, crossing one easily over the other, causing Jake to lose his train of thought.

"Your dissertation is complete, Jake," Ezra Bonner added.

Jake chaffed at the apparent ambush. He regrouped and said, "There's more that needs to be documented."

"Hardly," scoffed Dr. Hinklen.

"My original dissertation lacked key insights," Jake protested. "It needs clarification."

Ezra Bonner removed his wire-rim glasses. "No, Jake. All of this work is tangential at best. It is not relevant to your core thesis."

Eleanor Hinklen jumped in again. "Dr. Altman, you seem to be immersed in a frivolous cause of some sort, a higher calling, but it is indeed far beyond the parameters of accepted academic pursuit, and it is distracting from your classroom work at the university."

Katherine Sexton, who seemed to enjoy the confrontation, cut to the chase. "No one cares about your conspiratorial theories about Vladimir Chernov."

"I do!" Jake snapped.

"Exactly," barked Eleanor Hinklen. "But we do not!"

"Vladmir Chernov is the *key* to my whole thesis! The rise and fall of the Soviet Union, as well as the enablement of the new Russian Federation, were the direct result of his covert dealings for the past forty years. Chernov worked in the shadows, always behind the scene, but he pulled the strings! Brezhnev, Yorkin, even Gorbachev to some extent, and now Dmitri Bellus. Every move they made, every policy decision, every inflexion of Russian power, it all stemmed from Vladimir Chernov's Rasputin-like manipulations."

Ezra Bonner took a moment to assemble his thoughts. "This committee recognizes the validity of your thesis, Jake. It is the continued *extension* of this thesis that gives pause."

Katherine Sexton drove to the point in question, "Vladimir Chernov has been named the new consul general to San Francisco. That doesn't make him a terrorist."

"But he is a terrorist!" Jake exclaimed.

"We've covered all this before, Jake," Ezra Bonner said calmly.

"Ezra, my work is well documented and properly cited," Jake countered. "It is critical to defining the broader context of my dissertation and Vladimir Chernov. He's a *bad* guy. He's not coming here to ride cable cars!"

"Your opinion, Jake, not ours," said Katherine Sexton. "It's just a theory that's completely consumed your attention. You teach a class on South African apartheid, but somehow you manage to infuse the discourse with Cold War Russian polemics. And what about your class on emerging Anglo-Canadian economic alliances? Don't you think that post-Glasnost Russian subversion theory, as you have seen fit to include in the curriculum, is a bit out of place here?"

Jake knew an ambush when he saw it, and that meant it was time for a hail-Mary defense. "I was just making comparisons."

"And they are confusing the students," Dr. Bonner wagged tiredly. He held up a stack of student evaluations. "We have complaints, Jake."

Eleanor Hinklen leaned forward with heightened gravity as her boobs spread out across the tabletop like displaced Jello. "Dr. Altman, you must stop pursuing a fractured theory that simply doesn't resonate. Leave Vladimir Chernov to the historians. He is an anachronistic relic. He is history."

Jake had suddenly grown very serious. "You don't understand."

"No, Jake," Dr. Bonner said softly. "We *do* understand." He paused, searching for the right words, and when they came, his compassion was unmistakable. "You know that I deeply regret the tragedy of your loss, Jake. We all do."

"Don't go there, Ezra," Jake snapped,

Bonner fell silent for a moment. He could see the pain in Jake's eyes. "Jake, you have to…."

"No!" Jake shouted. "Don't!" He abruptly leaned forward and planted his palms on the conference table. "I'm right about Chernov." Jake said coldly. "All of you are afraid to confront it. You're all too comfortable floating your PhD credentials around the diplomatic cocktail circuit. Drinks. Polite chit-chat. But you won't face the facts. You're all cowards."

"Enough!" Ezra Bonner bellowed. His eyes flashed with uncharacteristic anger. "Now you shut up and listen. You are treading on very thin ice, Jake, and it is fracturing in all directions around you. This panel has stood behind you; we have consistently supported you and your research. I think you know that. It's why we brought you into this program. You are a bright and talented educator but…" Bonner placed his glasses back on his nose, thought for a moment, then looked closely at Jake. "You have a bountiful future, Jake. Do not throw it away. Can you sense what I am trying to convey here?"

Jake took a moment to absorb the not-so-subtle context of Bonner's threat. The other faculty members watched and waited. Jake stood abruptly. He desperately wanted to say something, but the words would not come. He turned and left.

3

The funeral was over. Marvina Dubrovsky had been buried in the tiny cemetery high on a bucolic hillside overlooking Bodega Bay. It is what she wanted. She was one hundred and four years old.

The handful of mourners, mostly old, were making their way back down the grassy hillside. They were still stunned by Marvina's tragic and unexplainable death outside a Russian cathedral in San Francisco. Below the departing group, the golden land rolled out toward the emerald waters of Bodega Bay and the expansive Pacific Ocean beyond. Not more than fifty miles north of San Francisco, the remote fishing community had not really changed in over a hundred years. A cluster of small buildings hugged on the eastern shore, while a sprinkling of modest homes spread out and away across the opposite peninsula. Fishing trawlers filled the commercial fleet, tugging gently at sun-bleached mooring lines, while a few elegant sailboats, most certainly owned by the San Francisco summer home crowd, bobbed at their anchorages.

The cemetery itself was quite old. It was ringed by a low stone wall. Time and unforgiving elements had collapsed hand-laid sections here and there. The headstones were uniformly simple; the grass was neatly cut. And yet, in its stark simplicity, there was a certain grace to the site, set far above and apart from Bodega Bay but ever watchful in its panoramic solitude.

Mikhail Roman, heavily bearded and fitted stiffly in a worn suit, stood alone beside Marvina's freshly filled grave, his eyes reddened with grief. He was an imposing man, hardened by years of fishing the sea. At seventy-six, he was still strong, probably stronger than any man in Bodega Bay. His eyes were kind, but they were also wise, seeing everything and fearing nothing.

Mikhail was working his tweed cap slowly in his hands. He had known Marvina well. He knew that her body had been ravaged by cancer and that her remaining life could be measured in weeks, not years, but still he could not bring himself to accept the certainty of her grave. Marvina Dubrovsky is dead, he thought to himself. What now? What was he to do?

Mikhail cocked his head, gazing deeply at the simple headstone. It wasn't set properly and had been left leaning slightly to one side. "They should treat you better, sweet Marvina," he growled softly. "After so much, they should treat you better."

Mikhail lowered himself to his knees beside the headstone. He wrapped his massive hands around the marker, and he pulled. At first, the stone refused to yield. Mikhail pulled harder still until the veins in his neck bulged and blood seeped from beneath his fingernails. The ground around the stone buckled and the marker shifted, just enough. This was good, Mikhail thought. The old man stood and dusted his hands. He tamped the upturned earth carefully around the headstone then tucked his cap over great waves of gray and white hair.

Mikhail spoke softly again. "Be at peace, sweet Marvina. For you, the journey is over."

Satisfied, he nodded with a desolate smile then turned and followed the others down the long hillside.

The brothers of Theta Epsilon Tau, long revered as the most ill-mannered fraternity on the U.C. Berkeley campus, were not about to let a soaking rain get them down. It had been pouring all day. Pooling water spread out across the frat house lawn. It must have been a foot deep and thirty feet wide when the first bare-chested brother careened down the sidewalk, launching himself headlong into the pond, belly first, in an enormous splash. Mud and water spewed in all directions, dousing a nest of guys and girls hovering on the front porch. Cheers erupted. Beer was swilled.

A second Tau brother, bigger and broader than the first, and probably a whole lot drunker, hit the water at full speed just as Jake Altman trudged past on the sidewalk. His umbrella afforded little protection as a mini-tsunami cascaded across him. He stopped in his tracks. Raucous voices instantly went silent; the kids knew a professor when they saw one, and they understood the possible ramifications of their indiscretion. However, instead of unleashing a verbal reprimand, Jake calmly folded his umbrella, swiped water from his face, and turned to the revelers. After a moment pregnant with apprehension, he called out, "I went twice as far. Jake Altman. Spring semester, 2008."

Confused Greeks muttered nervously. Then it dawned on someone, who cried out, "Alt-man -- Brother Altman! The *Skid Man!*"

"No way," a stunned brother proclaimed.

"He's a living legend!" another boasted.

"He did fifty feet -- buck naked!" someone else announced triumphantly.

A willowy coed shouted, "I thought the Skid Man died in a knife fight at the Sturgis Motorcycle Festival."

"Naw, he was shot in a London subway!" someone corrected.

And then the cheering began; it was spontaneous, loud, and exuberant. Jake popped his umbrella open, possibly savoring the moment, then moved on. He could still hear the cheers of adulation when he was halfway down the block, about the same time that Dr. Ezra Bonner caught up with him.

"Jake," Bonner called out. "Wait. I tried to call you yesterday."

Jake stopped and looked at the dean. "You let them hang me by my thumbs, Ezra. And then you piled on."

"Yes, I did. It was an unfortunate but necessary display of solidarity with my fellow deans. I'm sorry about that."

Jake started walking again, feigning indignity. Bonner tagged along under his own umbrella. "I believe I've groveled appropriately. I said I was sorry."

"You're supposed to be my friend."

"Yes. We are certainly friends, more perhaps. It is quite probable that I taught you very much of what you know, though the success of that endeavor remains elusive at times."

"I have a doctorate in Political Science."

"And I'm responsible for the department that conveyed that degree upon you."

"What do you want me to do, Ezra? Do you really want me to give it all up? Just quit? You know I'm right about Chernov."

"No," Bonner corrected. "I know you are probing at things better left unprobed. Is that a word, unprobed? Damn, I desperately wish I matriculated with English Language instead of Political Science."

"I don't feel sorry for you, Ezra," Jake noted.

"I'm not asking for your sympathy. I'm asking you to consider some disturbing questions. What if you are wrong about Chernov? What if he is exactly what he appears to be, an aging Russian diplomat who is putting himself out to pasture, most probably to pursue a less complicated and far more bucolic life? That's possible, isn't it?"

Jake stopped to look closely at his mentor. "Ezra, Vladimir Chernov, at age twenty-four, wrote every single speech for Leonid Brezhnev, every one of them. He did the same for Andropov and Chernenko. The man ran the stinking KGB for twenty-two years. He had to swallow the collapse of the Soviet Union under Mikhail Gorbachev, and he damn-well mentored Dmitri Bellus when he clawed his way to the Russian presidency six years ago."

Dr. Bonner set a calming hand on his friend's shoulder. "He's just an old man."

"He's a dangerous, old man, Ezra. There is no way in hell he's coming to San Francisco just to coast through his golden years as consul general of a hilltop Russian mansion!"

Bonner was at a loss for words of support. Jake relaxed slightly and was about to offer something conciliatory when his cell phone buzzed. He lifted it out of his pocket and glanced at the message. "Shit!" Jake coughed out. "He's here. He's on his way to the consulate right now -- two weeks early!"

"Chernov?" Bonner asked. "You're certain?"

"Yes, I'm sure. Look, I know a guy that knows a guy. And he *knows*, okay!"

Jake snapped his umbrella closed and forced it into Bonner's hand. Bonner shook his head, "Jake, you haven't heard a word I've said."

"I have to go, Ezra. It's important."

Jake turned to leave, but Bonner caught his arm and landed hard on him. "Is this for you, or is it for Eryn O'Shea?"

Jake stiffened, stung by Bonner's pronouncement. "That's a cheap shot, Ezra."

"Eryn was a brilliant young political scientist, but she's gone, Jake. We've moved on. You won't let it go. Don't you see? This thing has clouded your vision and consumed your mind."

"Chernov killed Eryn."

"No!"

"Yes, damn it, Ezra. It was Chernov. I can prove it."

Bonner was spent. His shoulders sagged, and his words came more softly now. "I'm trying to help. Don't shut me out."

Jake understood, and in many ways he knew his mentor was right. The numbing agony of losing Eryn had left him utterly impoverished. However, for Jake, there was no other way. He snapped his arm free, and Bonner watched helplessly as he dashed off through the rain.

A steady drizzle continued to fall, and Green Street was all but devoid of traffic. The Russian Consulate, jutting up through the drenched tree canopy and framed against the gray skyline, seemed somehow isolated and uninviting. A San Francisco police car appeared suddenly and sped past with lights flashing but no siren.

There were three or four other cop cars parked near the front of the consulate where a small nest of officers huddled together beneath their raincoats. A large sergeant sauntered up to the group. His hand-held radio crackled with police traffic, as he glanced down the street then addressed the lesser officers, "Five minutes. I want this done right."

The cops exchanged silent nods as they eyed a nest of people that had begun to gather across the street. A news crew slipped closer and set up for a remote report while a fresh-faced reporter nervously scanned her notes. The police sergeant scowled at the crowd then turned to stare down the street again and grumbled to himself, "Fucking diplomats..."

Nearby, the roof of Jake Altman's ten-year-old VW convertible was leaking as he ran the bug through rain-slicked streets. He was driving a little recklessly, clearly preoccupied, as he often was. A blaring car horn went unnoticed. Jake jerked the car around a corner and dropped down a precipitous downgrade. Louis Ottly, riding shotgun, slammed his hands on the dash, desperately trying to keep from being whiplashed to death.

"Hey, Jake, back it down a little," he barked. Louis was a small, wiry man about Jake's age, an ever-feisty artisan dressed in suitably baggy pants, a hip shirt and bright red suspenders. He was trying to load his expensive camera as the car bounced and swayed.

"Are we working on a death wish here?" Louis sniped. "Slow down, man."

Jake shook his head furiously, "No time. We're not going to make it."

"Not the way you're driving," Louis chided as he snapped his camera closed.

Jake tossed a glance sideways. "Why the hell do you still use film, Louis?"

"Because I'm what they call a professional; you wouldn't understand."

The VW bounced hard again and skidded around a corner onto Vallejo Street. Louis leveled a deadpan look at Jake. "So, are we going for mood or detail?"

"You're pissed, aren't you, Louis?

"Me? Naw. What the hell. You need a favor. I'm the favor man," Louis shrugged. "The shoot I was setting up was only gonna pay for a new color corrector, but you call, begging your ass off, and I drop my work and split. That's cool."

"I appreciate it, Louis. You know I do."

Louis wasn't done yet. He said, "I mean, who cares if it took me three months to convince Lauren to get naked in the name of high art?"

"You're a pathetic lecher."

"Sticks and stones, man."

Jake tossed a hard look at him. "Louis, this is important."

"So was Lauren."

The police were getting nervous; there were too many people. The sergeant cursed again. "How the hell did all these tourists find out?" His radio crackled with indiscernible gibberish, but he got the message and shouted to his men. "Two minutes. Move 'em back!"

The drenched cops moved in to clear the street. Cameramen jockeyed for position while several escapees from Berkeley's radical left coalition shoved peace signs in the air and shouted loudly. "Dump the nukes." "Peace with Russia."

Jake's VW bottomed out hard on Green Street. Ahead, the roadway was choked with cops and gawkers. Louis gaped at the crowd and brandished signs. "Shit. Who is this guy anyway?"

"Hold on!" Jake barked. He slammed the bug to a sliding stop, wedging it against a fire hydrant.

Louis nodded with sanguine approval. "This is nice, man."

Jake lunged out of the car and grabbed Louis as he came around the bumper. "Remember. I point. You shoot."

"Whatever you say, boss."

Jake tugged Louis through the growing swell of people. Just ahead, he could see cops clearing the street in the other direction. Louis was still completely perplexed by the impromptu show. He tugged at Jake's jacket, "Jake, who is this guy?"

"Not who, but what," Jake tossed back. "Vladimir Chernov is the new Russian Consul General in San Francisco. He's gonna be here any minute."

"So?"

"So just get some good shots! He's going to be moving slow. He's eighty years old."

"Oh," Louis exclaimed. "Now I get it. You drag me away from Lauren and her extremely-photographic tits just to snap a few pics of some Ruskie dilettante who may piss in his pants if he gets too excited. Jake, who cares about this shit?"

Jake took one last stab at it. "Okay. Listen up. Chernov may be eighty, but he's been wired into the Kremlin forever. He ran the KGB, the Red Guard, and the CIB.

"CIB?"

"Communist Information Bureau."

"Never heard of it."

"Exactly! Wake up, Louis. Chernov is a shadow-man. Nobody really knows him. The man has had people killed. He is not to be messed with. Do you get it?"

Louis was recalcitrant. "Yeah, well he's still eighty, and my money says he's here just to gum-it-up with some other politico relics." Jake stalked away. Louis called after him. "He probably wears Depends too."

Sirens suddenly screamed farther down the street, startling Louis. He hugged his camera and tore after Jake, who had edged in front of a couple of cosmic skateboarders. "Piss ass," growled one of the boys.

Louis noted the kid's enormous nose ring. "Nice gold. You ever get boogers caught in there?" Jake jerked him away by the suspenders. A sleek Bentley limo streaked up and stopped just a few feet away. Water glistened on its finish, as a pair of hood-mounted diplomatic flags fell slack. A black-suited and surprisingly cherubic aide jumped out and reached for the rear door. He was about fifty and looked more like an innocuous small-town baker than a polished aide-de-camp. Jake was almost disappointed, but the diminutive assistant was quickly forgotten when a tall, slender man eased out of the limo. Vladimir Chernov was truly an impressive sight. In his Savile Row, three-piece suit and dark overcoat, he looked for all-the-world to be a Wall Street investment shark. He was refined, dignified, and, as far as Jake was concerned, extremely dangerous. Jake jabbed a fist at Louis.

"There. Him. Wide shots then close up."

Police swarmed in around Chernov, effectively clearing a pathway. Several news reporters shouted impromptu questions. Chernov offered the crowd a measured smile then called out in a thick but eloquent Russian accent, "It is an honor to be in the United States of America. Your people and my people, we have much which can bring us together. Our shared aspirations and hopes are like a light that cannot be extinguished."

Jake was indignant, "Bullshit."

Louis' camera motor whirled. Chernov was moving away now, angling toward the consulate door. Suddenly, a young woman broke from the crowd. She was mostly concealed beneath a hooded, dark blue rain jacket as she dodged past the police thrusting out a small white envelope. A pair of security men from the consulate stopped her only feet from Chernov. Jake strained to see her face, but it was half-hidden beneath the blue hood. He barked at Louis, "Whoa! Her. Get her!"

Struggling to free herself from the two men, the girl called out, "Chernov!" When he just kept walking, she shouted again, "Vladimir Chernov! The Baikal sailed with the tide."

Chernov's head snapped around. He slipped back a few steps, eyed the envelope in her hand, then quickly snatched it. Jake was trying to make sense of the confrontation while Louis' camera clipped off another volley of shots. Abruptly, Chernov turned away and was gone. Jake and Louis saw the two grim-faced Russian security men start for them. Jake pulled Louis' camera down. "Louis, get lost, now!"

Louis was completely bewildered as he was thrown back into the crowd. Jake tossed a look over his shoulder and saw the girl break free and run like hell. Louis was struggling awkwardly with his camera when he knocked an old man down and fell. Jake hauled his pal up, stumbling over the cursing senior. Before they could regroup, they were swarmed by the two Russians who ripped Louis' camera from his shoulder and shoved them down again. The thugs were instantly gone, lost in the crowd.

Louis pulled himself upright, nursing a bloody lip. "What the hell was that all about?"

"We just made the "A" list," Jake replied.

"Yeah, well I got other plans, man."

Jake stood slowly, swiping gutter water from his tweed jacket. Louis was still dabbing at his lip. "Son-of-a-bitch Russians."

"Who says they were Russian?"

"Dude, you've been reading too many spy novels."

"Maybe not."

Louis wasn't through. "Okay, so who was the chick?"

Jake glanced back through the crowd. "I don't know. Don't care. They got your camera. We're screwed."

Louis grinned capriciously. "Untrue, man." He dug in his pocket and produced a tight roll of film. Jake was stunned as Louis slipped it in his hand and said, "This one is going to cost you."

4

A fresh breeze washed across the fishing fleet in Bodega Bay while wisps of high cirrus clouds danced across an azure sky. Several faded trawlers were still chugging into the harbor, but most of the other boats were in already for the day. Seasoned fishermen shifted boxes of Dungeness crab, packed in ice, onto waiting trucks. Several scruffy crewmen were arguing about a baseball game; it was a fraternal gathering of hard men who loved the sea. The fishermen cajoled and insulted each other with colorful accusations and outright fabrications.

A faded Blazer SUV rolled to a stop in the dusty parking lot adjacent to the fleet. The hood was sun-scorched and the doors were rusted nearly through at the bottom. It must have been twenty years old. When the engine sputtered to a stop, a young woman climbed out. Anna Roman pulled her blue rain-slicker over her shoulders and marched to the edge of the wharf. She was dressed for hard work: jeans, low boots, and a heavy wool shirt. But when the wind blew her hood back, her long, auburn hair tossed freely in the wind. She was radiant, with large, caring eyes and full lips. No makeup; none was needed. Anna searched the swarm of fishermen and called out, "Hey, old man! Mikhail!"

Farther out on the fleet dock, Mikhail Roman, looked up from his work. His eyes sparkled as he shouted back defiantly, "A man called me "old" once. He got pitched in the bay. You should show respect."

"And you said you wouldn't stay out for two days any longer. You promised," Anna chided affectionately as she made her way down the dock. By the time she reached Mikhail, he was beaming through his thick beard. Anna, his only child, had been born very late when he was already nearly fifty. Now, she was young and beautiful; he was old enough to be her grandfather. None of this seemed to matter. She idolized him, and he loved her dearly.

Mikhail looked down at Anna and whispered gently, "You were worried about me?"

"Yes. I was worried. Let the young men fish."

"They don't know what they're doing."

"Let them learn," Anna cajoled.

"But what if they take all the fish? Maybe I am selfish."

"So am I," Anna said. "I want you all to myself."

Mikhail broke into a robust laugh, "You are my princess. I think I will keep you." Nearby on the docks, other fishermen shuffled past pushing handcarts. Mikhail lowered Anna and gestured to the iced-down catch. "The crabs came crawling to us when we called, Anna."

One of the other fishermen called out loudly. "Yep, but they were slow to march into our traps. I got a wife that likes me to stay away too long, so she can "go fish" with someone else."

"Don't take much *bait*, either, I hear," Mikhail bellowed.

The fishermen roared with laughter then begin to drift away. Anna looked more seriously at the old man. "Mikhail, I'm sorry I couldn't be there when you buried Marvina. There was a whale grounding in Mendocino. She was suffering. I couldn't leave her."

"This is not a problem. Everyone understands what you do and how important it is." Mikhail hesitated then smiled. "We buried the old girl good. It was a nice day. She would have liked it."

"I know," Anna offered. "Marvina was wonderful. She was so old and wise."

"Wise, yes, once. Near the end, she was very sick and her mind, it was in another place. This was sad too." Mikhail paused, remembering so much, then abruptly he brightened again. "She was like a mother to me. I loved her, and I buried her well."

"Good for you." Then Anna aimed a threatening finger at him. "Dinner is at 7:00. You get "hung up" at the Sea Hag, and I will come after you. Got it?"

The old man nodded with a generous smile, "I will come home."

As wharf-side taverns went, the Sea Hag was really nothing more than a ramshackle timber structure perched on barnacle-encrusted pilings. Its steel roof was only half painted, and the rusting eaves were streaked with seagull crap. Weathered by seven decades of Pacific storms, it leaned precipitously away from the bay; a good wind might knock it down. Still, the tattered bar was, for the most part, the epicenter of life in Bodega Bay, at least for the fishermen. It was rarely empty, and was more often, as this night, overflowing with end-of-the-week revelers.

The dusty parking lot was packed with cars and trucks, and loud music rattled through glass windows. A young fisherman, still stuffed in his hip boots, hurried out the door, effusively tugging a cute but chunky young girl with him. They stumbled up against the sagging shutters and landed in each other's arm, pressed passionately together. Their kisses and groping grew more frenetic, and soon they broke away, racing for the inviting privacy of a two-tone pick-up truck.

Inside the Sea Hag, a large crowd of locals caroused as if the Great Flood was upon them. Beer flowed freely amid raucous honky-tonk music and bursts of cackling laughter. A long, varnished bar top ran through the center of the room and was surrounded by round tables and a few board-back booths. Hundreds of sea-faring artifacts hung from the low ceiling.

Mikhail Roman had settled at a tall bar table. He was sitting atop a stool, nose-to-nose, with a towering, much younger man. Yedor Fedin was rock-hard with massive shoulders. He had been fishing for only about ten years. Still in his early thirties, he already owned his boat, an accomplishment more often reserved for seasoned fishermen. Yedor had a big, boastful smile, and waves of blond hair that spilled freely over his shoulders; he was handsome, and he knew it. At the moment, his eyes were intensely focused on the old man faced-off across from him. Mikhail glared fiercely at Yedor. "I break men thirty years before you wet your mother's arms."

"No more, old man," Yedor growled back.

"Most men know better than to call me old."

Yedor didn't blink, "Most men are pussies."

Mikhail landed his beer mug on the table and began to roll up the sleeve of his work-shirt. "You don't fear me, Yedor. This is a mistake."

Yedor's lips curled into a thin smile. "Maybe we see." He began to roll his sleeve up.

Nearby revelers spotted the coming storm. Chairs went over. Beer mugs skidded off tables. A roaring crowd of fishermen and their women crowded around. Yedor cocked his arm and dropped his elbow on the table. He actually winced, though, when Mikhail's elbow landed with a resounding crash. The table rattled, threatening to collapse. A nearby, old salt thrust up a wad of cash, and the betting began. It was absolute bedlam, yet, at the very center of it all, the two men just stared at each other.

Mikhail flexed his thick hand, extending it fully. Yedor took up the challenge, slamming his fist into Mikhail's. One of the Sea Hag's statuesque, if not a bit sleazy, "regular" ladies entered the fray, fixing the contestant's arms. Voices fell silent around the room. "Ready, Go!" she yelled.

Both men heaved forward. Yedor drove Mikhail's hand down toward the table, but the old man evoked a gut-wrenching howl and inched back. They centered again. Cheers and shouts filled the crowded bar. Money flew through the air. Yedor realized how strong the old man was and, for a moment, a look of concern spread across his straining face. Mikhail pulled as if for his life. Veins bulged from his neck. Yedor gained the advantage, but Mikhail refused to concede. Sweat rolled down his face and arms. He screamed again as if possessed. Slowly, but relentlessly Mikhail drove Yedor's arm downward.

Suddenly, it was over. Yedor's arm crashed to the table. He collapsed, spent, utterly defeated. Mikhail's roar of victory resounded across the room. He leaped to his feet and was cheered, hugged, kissed, and doused with beer. Finally, he looked down at his humiliated opponent. "You are strong, Yedor Fedin. There's no shame in what you did."

A resigned smile fell across Yedor's face. He nodded then rose up, thrusting Mikhail's hand high in the air. He tossed his hair back and boasted for all to hear, "Mikhail Roman! A better man for sure!" And then, as a quick aside to Mikhail, he chided, "…at least for today."

The night air was chilled and damp outside the Sea Hag. Fog and settled over Bodega Bay an hour before, leaving lights to glow tepidly through the mist. Mikhail Roman ambled out of the wharf-side bar and stopped to relish the intoxicating scent of the sea. He found great comfort in the boundless tranquility and the timeless predictability of the tiny fishing community.

Just a few yards away a spindly old drunk was squatting against the side of the building. Mikhail called out to him, "Cold night, Attaboy. You okay out here?"

"Fine and dandy," Attaboy crooned.

"Need a little something to keep you warm?"

"Naw. I got a sack of Jack Black here. I'm livin' large, Cap."

Attaboy, his name derived from his vigilant attempts to know absolutely everything going on in Bodega Bay, was an affable town derelict. "Hey, Mikhail," he called out from the shadows. "You heard about the Monterey II catching fire and sinking out near Noles Sound. Just to let you know, everything's A-okay. Ole Alex got off the boat before she went down, him and his two crewmen."

Mikhail had already heard all about the sinking, but he felt the need to support Attaboy's well-intended account. "It's good they got off the boat. Thanks, Attaboy."

"Not a problem, skipper. That's what Attaboy's for," the old drunk sang out. He tipped his bagged whiskey bottle and downed a healthy gulp.

Mikhail tugged his heavy jacket more tightly around his shoulders then suddenly remembered his dinner promise. He slipped out an old pocket watch, grumbled, and started across the parking lot. Mikhail stopped beside his ageless Ford pick-up and dug around in his pocket for his keys.

Somewhere in the darkness behind him, he heard the crunch of footsteps in the gravel. Mikhail turned to look. Two figures emerged from the fog. One man was tall and lumbering, while the other was squat, bald and built like a bulldog. Neither of them was smiling, and Mikhail felt a certain menace. He offered a cautionary greeting, "I don't know you."

Oleg, the much taller of the two men, was a middle-aged thug of strong Nordic descent. He had thinning near-white hair and cold, darkly sunken eyes. He was an ungainly giant, a misanthrope who had little to say. The smaller man was working class British, black, with eyes that danced with nervous anticipation. He cocked his head, looking smugly at Mikhail then growled, "Mikhail Roman?"

It was more a statement than a question. Mikhail was not intimidated. "You knew this before you stopped me. What is it that you want?"

"You've been hiding for a very long time, Mikhail Roman," Remi remarked casually with a thick, cockney inflection. "Aye, mate. Now it looks like you've been found for sure."

Mikhail looked closely at the two men, carefully measuring them. "Did Vladimir send you?" he asked, though he already knew.

A smirk crept across Oleg's horse-like face. Remi just stared silently, clenching his fist. Mikhail understood what was to come next. He squared his feet in the gravel, but Oleg was faster, lashing out with a short club, smashing it across Mikhail's forehead. Blood spewed from the gaping gash.

Across the gravel lot, Attaboy saw the assault and cried out. He tried to pull himself up but was too drunk to move. He began to bang his bottle on the side of the Sea Hag.

Mikhail staggered, but only briefly. He recoiled and crushed Oleg's nose with a hammering blow. The taller man cried out, grasping at the bloody pulp where his nose had been. Remi sidestepped another blow from Mikhail and landed his own club on the old man's forearm, snapping it with a brittle crack. Mikhail buckled but refused to cry out. He spun around and landed his boot squarely in Remi's groin, sending him spiraling to the ground. Oleg, enraged and crazed, came at Mikhail again, feigning a strike at his broken arm then spinning full circle to land a vicious kick to his neck.

Mikhail's head snapped back. His vision blurred, and he now saw only fractured images of his attackers. He lunged for Oleg and drove his fist into unprotected ribs, shattering at least three of them. Oleg doubled over and vomited blood. Remi descended on Mikhail again, whipping his club with lightning-fast strikes. Oleg came back too, pounding Mikhail with his fist. It was a savage, unrelenting beating. Mikhail went down slowly, first to one knee, then to both, battered, kicked, and gouged. His world spun before him as he hit the ground, blood streaming from multiple wounds that would have killed a lesser man. Oleg staggered, gasping for air. He swiped blood and tissue from his face and kicked Mikhail in the head one last time.

Mikhail could not see the men now, but he heard Remi's voice, echoing as if from some distant place. "You won't be hiding from us no longer, mate." Remi swiped at his swollen cheek and barked at Oleg, "Get him in the truck."

Oleg wrapped his massive arms around Mikhail's shoulders and lifted him up, dragging him toward their waiting SUV. Remi limped after him, cursing and spitting blood.

The door to the Sea Hag suddenly fell open as several well-lubricated fishermen spilled out. Attaboy was howling at them. They saw Mikhail and the two bloodied men, and instantly cried out for help. Oleg and Remi hesitated, at least until four other burly fishermen exploded from the bar.

"Fuck me," Remi sputtered as he grabbed Oleg's arm. "Let it go, mate. Leave him."

Oleg let Mikhail collapse into the dust. The two men hobbled to their truck, piled in, and tore away into the swirling mist.

5

Fishing boats of all shapes and sizes could be found in Bodega Bay. Most were simple crab trawlers, roughly painted and streaked with dried seaweed and fish guts. The two largest vessels, marginally newer than the rest of the fleet, were owned by a commercial fishing outfit in Redwood City. Most of the other boats were quite old, weather-beaten, and family owned for at least two generations.

Mikhail Roman's boat, *The Princess*, a ubiquitous but sturdy thirty-eight-foot trawler, tugged gently at its mooring lines in the placid, fog-shrouded night. The surrounding docks, dimly illuminated by a few wire-strung bulbs, were completely empty. A warm glow radiated softly from inside Mikhail's boat. Classical music drifted across the water: Franz Schubert, a soft, melodic piece.

Mikhail lay motionless in the forward berth of the boat. A small electric lamp swayed gently overhead, while Anna Roman tenderly mopped blood from her father's lacerated face. He was awake, watching Anna closely. "You are a beautiful young woman, Anna. This makes me proud."

"Forget about me, Mikhail. Look what they did to you."

"I hurt them good, Anna," Mikhail whispered.

47

"They broke your arm, Mikhail!" she countered. "Why?"

Mikhail shifted sorely in the berth. "…just a fight. You should not be concerned."

"You're my father. Don't lie to me. What happened?"

Mikhail blinked slowly. "…men work, drink, and sometimes they fight."

Anna could barely restrain her tears. She glanced over her shoulder. Sheriff Lawrence Jackson sat on the entryway steps. Like Mikhail, he was a big man with a thick, protruding brow and intense eyes. As Bodega Bay's first black sheriff, he respected the law and was serious about his job. Jackson had been sheriff of Bodega Bay for eight years, ever since he retired from the Marines. He was fond of the quaint community, its glittering harbor and sweeping, tree-rimmed bay. He had grown up there in one of the only two black families in the town. Jackson was well liked in school and spent many imaginative hours with white friends digging holes in fields with U.S. Army "foxhole" digger shovels for absolutely no other reason than it was a lot of fun. Jackson went to the community high school and married Loretta, a diminutive but feisty woman who put up with his often-cantankerous temperament. She adored him.

As Lawrence Jackson watched silently, he couldn't help but remember how much the old man had helped him. Fresh out of the Marines, he had no discernible job skills, but Mikhail had walked him around town, demanding that businessmen and storeowners take note of the young man's possibilities. With a few added embellishments, trumpeting Jackson's unlimited potential, he was able to secure a job for the young man as a sheriff's department recruit. Now, Jackson was the top-cop in town.

Sheriff Jackson worked his brim-stained Stetson slowly in his hands as he gazed at Mikhail. It was dispiriting. The old man's beating had affected him at a very personal level.

"Does he remember anything else, Anna?" Jackson asked quietly.

Anna looked into Mikhail's swollen eyes then turned back. "There were two of them. It was dark. That's all he's said."

"Mikhail is pretty good at not saying what he doesn't want to say."

"Yeah," she said.

Mikhail's bloodied lips curled into a weak smile. Sheriff Jackson nodded thoughtfully then stood up. He had bad feeling about the attack. "If there's something going on, I mean more than a couple of bar boys mixing it up, I need to know about it."

"Come back later, Lawrence," Anna said softly. "I'll drag the truth out of him."

The sheriff thought about pressing Anna and Mikhail further but, out of respect, he decided against it. He turned and climbed out of the cabin.

When Anna looked back at Mikhail, his blackened eyes were open. He was gazing deeply at her. She sensed something she had never seen before -- fear, certainly not for himself, but rather it was as if her father was holding something back, something that gave him grave concern.

"You've told me everything?" she asked softly.

Mikhail nodded and forced an anemic smile. "I will be fine, Anna. You do not need to worry."

"That's not what I asked."

Mikhail was silent, but his eyes betrayed a far deeper context to his assurances.

Anna brushed Mikhail's thick, gray hair back. Her mind was filled with sobering thoughts and too many questions. "Mikhail, why did you send me with a note to the Russian consulate?"

"It was nothing, Anna," he said.

"Do you know Vladmir Chernov?"

"Yes. From a very long time ago."

"How -- why? I don't understand."

Mikhail shifted his hand, still caked with dried blood, over her arm. His eyes seemed sad now, filled with doleful remorse and an odd sense of defeat. "I am tired, Anna. We can talk of this later." Before Anna could protest, Mikhail closed his eyes and slept.

Jake Altman had pretty much worn himself out, but he was still running hard. The soft Tartan surface on Edwards Track, Berkeley's premier Olympic running facility on the southern edge of campus, was forgiving to his sore knees. Jake ran here often, always wearing his shabby shorts and T-shirt. He didn't mind the monotony of endless loops around the four hundred-meter track. This afternoon he was alone, lost in ruminative thought while the rhythmic sounds of his feet slapping at the track echoed softly off the deserted stadium bleachers.

His visit to the Russian consulate weighed heavily on Jake. While it was not the first time he had seen Vladimir Chernov in person, his new encounter with the austere Russian power broker, if only from a distance, had been a chilling reminder of the importance of his work. He was more certain than ever that Chernov's appointment as the new San Francisco Consul General signaled something far more insidious than a simple end-of-career posting. It didn't make any sense. Jake's mind whirled with unsettled speculation. He knew his research was well grounded. It included a carefully documented, point-by-point evaluation of Chernov's behind the scenes maneuvering for over fifty years, notes from three fact-finding trips to Moscow, countless interviews and incised analysis of obscure Russian texts, as well as a brief introduction to the aging diplomat two years ago.

And then there was Eryn, her work, her disappearance and death, memories still too painful to touch. All of it, like peering into a roughly unearthed crypt, had led Jake to an ominous assessment of Vladimir Chernov.

Jake swiped sweat from his face as he came around the back turn on the track. At first, he didn't notice the woman running fifty meters ahead of him, but as he drew closer, he saw that it was Katherine Sexton, the indifferent but shapely political science department associate dean who had joined his lynch mob the day before. She had a strong stride, and Jake found nothing in her tight running leggings that he didn't appreciate. It was as if the pink spandex had been carefully painted around every taut curve of her amazing ass, he thought. So what if she was a lascivious vamp. Jake picked up his pace and drew alongside her, trying not to gape at the tempting bounce of her breasts. For a forty-year-old woman, Katherine was a complete package. She had it all, and she knew it, he thought.

She flicked a dispassionate look at Jake and picked up the pace. "So, you think you can take me?" she jabbed.

Jake grinned, images of his academic review dismemberment fresh in his mind. "No. I think I already lost that one."

"Yeah, well -- sorry about the meeting."

"At least you and the other inquisition stiffs were consistent."

Katherine was not amused. "The department has standards, Jake. Rules for the tribe, and you're drifting off the reservation."

Jake couldn't think of a crisp reply. Besides, there wasn't any point in pursuing verbal combat with Katherine. He knew he would lose. Instead, he tossed her a generous smile and called out, "Have a great run, Katherine." He peeled away and angled for the locker room as Katherine strode ahead, not bothering to acknowledge his salutation.

The last showerhead on the left in the twenty-head shower room of the Edwards Stadium locker room was the best on campus. It gushed torrents of hot water. When the university dove headlong into a number of Green initiatives earlier in the decade, someone forgot to wedge one of those pissy little flow-restrictors into this one particular head. It was a well-kept secret, a tightly guarded factoid shared by only a handful of observant faculty.

Jake stood beneath cascading hot water as steam billowed up, completely fogging the room. The sound of falling water echoed softly off tile walls; there was simply nothing else. Jake uttered an involuntary groan of relief then took in a gulp of water and spewed it out, allowing the soothing shower spray to massage his shoulders. The soreness was slipping away now, and he found finally himself comfortably lost in mindless lassitude.

Jake was still drifting when the flimsy curtain jerked open. He turned, squinting through water-drenched eyes. Katherine Sexton, spectacularly naked, glanced down Jake's lanky but taut body and pursed her lips expectantly. "That oughta do," she remarked, stepping into the shower.

Jake was speechless, but not at all unimpressed. "Uhm, this might be considered inappropriate protocol," he noted.

She slipped beneath the steaming water. Her lips, dripping and full, were inches from his. She whispered to him, "Inappropriate, indiscreet, debauched, and certainly a heinous abdication of our respective positions at the university. Did I miss anything?"

Katherine kissed him then bit down on his lower lip, sucking it into her mouth. She pushed him against the shower stall wall. Jake's resistance ebbed as she kissed him again, deeply. She was sultry temptress with absolutely no inhibitions.

"Katherine, no," Jake protested as he withdrew slightly.

She shook water from her face and brushed her thick bangs back. "Oh, I think you want it just as much as I do."

"We can't do this, Katherine. Not again."

"Kill-joy," she mocked with amusement.

"No. Look, before, it was -- well, it just happened."

"Yes. It's happened before. Three times so far, but who's keeping score.

"...three times? Really?"

"Not counting that weird thing we did in your VW at Stenson Beach."

"I forgot that one."

Katherine laid a slender finger on his lips, "Are you afraid of me, Jake?"

"No. But I might be lying."

"That's good," she mused. "That's very good, either way." Her hand was already sliding down his chest. He shuttered once and almost begged, "Katherine, no -- please."

She laughed and kissed him again, easing her tongue past his lips. Jake was lost. Katherine cried out only once then hissed in his ear. "Fuck protocol."

6

Vladimir Chernov stood alone in his office, silently staring out a tall window. He was absorbing the breathtaking late afternoon vista of San Francisco Bay and the Golden Gate Bridge arching out and away toward Sausalito. The room was large and ornately decorated, with vaulted bookcases and fragile oriental vases. It was dark too, insular and protective, almost as a centuries-old castle rectory might have been.

Chernov's face revealed little; it was a trait he had mastered over many tumultuous decades of service to the Mother Country. His hair was very white, wispy, with tufts curled back and over his ears. His eyes were the color of Siberian icebergs, radiant blue; they were as menacing as they were piercing, especially for a man of his age. As always, he wore a tailored London suit and Russian red tie. Anything less would have been unimaginable.

Chernov's graceful façade masked a mind that raced night and day; he analyzed absolutely everything at a legendary processing speed. It was impossible for others to comprehend what he was thinking. Adversaries understood that nothing escaped his penetrating insight; they knew with great certainty that that no detail was too insignificant to be overlooked.

The door to the study opened and the cherubic aide slipped in with afternoon tea. Anton Sorokin was much younger than Chernov, middle-aged, probably just on the long side of fifty. He was a small, round man of slight stature. Sorokin had cultivated a keen appreciation for Western fashion, very much befitting an aide-de-camp to a man such as Vladimir Chernov. Outgoing and quite voluble by nature, Sorokin, had, in less than a full year of service, fully earned his keeper's trust. He valued this most of all. As the product of farming-class Ukrainian parents, he understood that his life was far better than most, and he was determined to preserve his hard-earned station through fastidious service and implacable loyalty. "Good afternoon, sir," Sorokin chirped as he set a tea tray down. He looked out the panoramic window. "It is a magnificent view."

Chernov turned slowly and addressed his aide with correct yet detached precision. "Thank you for the tea, Anton. Our American friends unfortunately do not understand the importance of good English tea, which has, in their case, been superseded as far as I can tell by an egregiously misplaced craving for what they call -- soft drinks."

Sorokin nodded solemnly. "Yes."

"Their disgustingly common beverages are so laden with sugar it's no wonder that obesity is epidemic."

"It is a distasteful habit," Anton dutifully confirmed.

Chernov took the teacup when the small man offered it to him. He sipped then glanced at his aide. "You were only weeks away from retirement, Anton, and yet you accepted this new posting, far from your family, and amid a strange society. You could have stayed in Moscow."

Sorokin offered a simple smile. "It is my great honor to serve you, sir. That pleasure far surpasses any minor inconvenience."

"Now you patronize me," Chernov mused.

"Hardly so, sir. What I tell you is true."

Chernov nodded comfortably. "Do you think we will like San Francisco?"

"I do. Yes, sir," Sorokin replied. He reflected for moment then added, "There is much work to be done here, is there not?"

Chernov sipped his tea again then returned the cup to Sorokin's tray. "There is indeed work to be done."

The fact that Jake Altman's respect for Dr. Ezra Bonner was deeply ingrained, made it all the more difficult to accept his mentor's cautionary guidance. Bonner was a realist. He preferred immutable fact to simple conjecture, and his teaching style reflected this belief. He was direct yet perceptive, wise yet encouraging.

Jake had invited himself into Bonner's office atop Barrows Hall; he knew he didn't need an appointment. It was late, and most of the faculty had already left for the day. Ezra Bonner leaned back in his vintage wood recliner, a gift from a small-town banker-friend. It creaked loudly. He was thinking, and Jake, sitting across the desk from him, knew it was best to let his mentor ruminate freely.

Jake was fiddling with a stack of tiny stone building blocks piled on the edge of the desk. Each stone was no larger than a pack of gum. They were multi-shaped, pastel-colored and cool to the touch. Jake smiled to himself, remembering how many times he and stacked and restacked the blocks over the years. Ezra kept them there for his students. Somehow, the smooth stones calmed and soothed fragile young souls who were more often than not overtly nervous in the presence of the "ultimate authority."

Dr. Bonner's thoughtful gaze shifted to the large balsa-wood model of the Wright Brothers 1909 flyer hanging from the ceiling before he leveled a compelling look at Jake. "We've talked about this before, Jake. Is there a reason you think I might have changed my opinion?"

"I was hoping you might have had an epiphany of some sort, like maybe you realized you were wrong," Jake suggested with a hopeful smile.

Bonner leaned forward in his chair. "Logic precludes an epiphany in this case."

Jake waited a moment before continuing. "The Chronicle covered Chernov's arrival at the consulate. Did you see it?" he asked.

"Yes."

"And did you notice the God-awful spectacle of his bloated ego?"

"No. I thought his comments engendered a certain sense of grace. He appeared to be a man who, in the twilight of an impeccable career, was entirely comfortable in his own, fifteen-hundred-dollar Russian Calf Shoes."

"No way," Jake bristled.

Bonner was amused by this. "All right. I realize that your position on this is crystal-clear. You think Chernov is a *bad dude*, if you will excuse the shameful colloquialism."

"He *is* a bad dude."

"That sort of gross oversimplification often leads to a serious miscalculation."

Jake leaned closer, absently knocking over his newly built block sculpture. "Come on, Ezra. Talk *to* me, not *at* me. I can't beat you at wordplay. So, for the record again, I do not think Chernov is a common scoundrel; he's not some has-been political hack. He is a deadly lethal Russian operative who has murdered or had murdered a whole bunch of his own people, not to mention a slew of foreign agents. He's killed before, and he'll do it again."

"We've discussed all this before."

"Humor me, Ezra. Let's try again."

"Is there something new to your theory, Jake?"

"Yes! Chernov is *here*! He's not tucked away in some Siberian rest home for spent Russian oligarchs. He's *here*!"

Dr. Bonner paused to think again; he was not a man who spoke too quickly. Then he asked simply, "Jake, can we talk about Eryn?"

Jake stiffened. "Why?"

"Please. I knew Eryn too. She was a singularly enchanting woman, in *many* ways. Losing her the way you did would be enough to devastate any man."

"I'm not devastated," Jake snapped. "Not any longer."

Ezra nodded, "It's been two years."

"Twenty-eight months. Come on, Ezra. Don't dig this up again. Eryn is dead. She's gone."

"Yes, but you still link her death to Chernov."

"That's because he's responsible! He had her killed."

"You *think* he had Eryn killed."

"NO! He did it." Jake could feel the flush of bile rising up within his throat. He hesitated, fighting to restrain the urge to lash out at his friend. Instead, he took a measured breath. "Ezra, you know that Eryn was six months into her fellowship year in Moscow. Her research about the KGB was brilliant. You said so."

"Yes."

"She was on to something big; but she got too close to the truth about Chernov."

"A theory, Jake. That's all it is."

"I have her research! She sent me letters detailing everything. Eryn was right. I know she was."

Bonner pursed his lips. "And you're determined to prove it, even if it destroys your career?"

Jake's eyes flashed. "He killed Eryn."

"Eryn was walking at the park near Red Square," Ezra reasoned tiredly. "She fell in the Moskva River. She drowned. There were witnesses."

"That's not what happened."

"The State Department investigated. They were extremely thorough. Jake, I read the reports. It was an accident, a horribly tragic drowning accident."

Jake was silent. He couldn't hide the anguish that consumed him as he muttered softly, "She was a beautiful person, Ezra. She was *everything.* Eryn was Irish-American. Did I tell you that?"

"Yes. I know. She was wonderful, so very intelligent too," Bonner offered honestly.

Jake slumped in his chair. His voice was a distraught whisper. "We were going to get married when she came back. It wasn't going to be anything special. She didn't want that. Just a few friends and that boring old Presbyterian minister she liked to talk to when he wasn't full of Scotch. I didn't care. I just wanted her to be happy." Jake was mumbling now, repeating himself, "We were going to be married. Just a simple wedding, nothing special." He looked up at Bonner. "I don't know what to do."

"I'm sorry, Jake. I really am. You know that."

Jake regrouped and sucked in a deep breath. "Can you get me in, Ezra?"

"Get you in where?"

"Chernov. I have to talk to him."

"Jake, no."

"Com'on, You got clout with the State Department."

Bonner was stone faced.

"Please! You can make it happen," Jake urged,

Bonner was still shaking his head wearily as he leaned back in his creaking banker's chair. He could see the pain in Jake's eyes.

"Please," Jake said softly.

"It's insane."

"So stipulated," Jake noted with an encouraged smile. "But can you make it happen, can't you?"

Ezra laid his hands on the chair-arms, saying nothing as he creaked back and forth slowly. His head was shifting side to side – as if to say no, but then he stopped rocking and looked carefully at his young friend. "I'll try."

Jake nodded silently then stood as was about to leave. Ezra knew that Jake was making a mistake, but he desperately wanted to help. His voice was almost hushed. "Let her go, Jake. You will never be able to forget Eryn, but you have to let her go."

Jake turned and walked away.

Evening vespers had ended at the Holy Mary Cathedral. Archbishop Popov Konstantin left before the somber organ sending, slipping out a side door to a narrow hallway behind the altar. Several dim lights were perched on aged stone walls as Konstantin glanced back briefly then trudged away, disappearing into his personal chamber.

The private study was dark. He liked it that way; it was easier on his cataract-encrusted eyes.

The archbishop eased off his heavily adorned robe and hung it carefully in a closet alcove. He switched on a table lamp and deposited his ponderous mass into a soft chair. An ornate grandfather clock, clicking rhythmically in the shadows, seemed to mark the timelessness of the past and the utter inconsequence of the future. Konstantin sat silently for a few moments, listening to the faint strains of the organ music. Consumed with desolate thoughts, he pulled a slip of paper from his pocket, studied the numbers scrawled on it, and lifted a nearby telephone receiver, dialing carefully.

Konstantin displayed little emotion when he spoke. He was tired as he tried to focus on the task at hand. "Hello," he said. "It is Popov."

A moment passed while he listened to the voice at the other end of his call. Then he said, "There is a problem. I have been given a gold bar. It is a Russian ruble." He hesitated then solemnly pronounced, "The minting date is 1897 and it has the Great Seal."

Konstantin listened again as the voice suddenly became more urgent.

"Yes," Konstantin acknowledged. "It appears to be uncirculated." He paused, listening to instructions, then spoke again, "I have it. It is with me now." He slid his fingers into a breast pocket and withdrew the ornately engraved gold bar that Marvina had given him. Konstantin listened again, as the artifact shimmered across his face. "Yes. That is acceptable," he advised with authority. "I will be waiting for your courier."

7

Bodgea Bay lay flat and still, with only an occasional splash from a leaping sea bass to break the mirrored surface. The fishing fleet was in for the night, and the sun was just a thin ribbon draped across the horizon. Anna Roman glanced back at her father as she climbed into her truck. He was sitting comfortably on the long "fisherman's bench" stretching across the upper wharf adjacent to the Sea Hag. She had protested at first when Mikhail asked to sit outside and watch the sunset, but he was adamant. He had recovered more quickly than expected from his beating, and now found the musty confines of *The Princess* to be oppressive. Anna had propped several cushions, hastily borrowed from the Sea Hag's outdoor terrace area, behind his back and under his arm which was still wrapped in a heavy cast. He thanked her and seemed quite comfortable. Besides, she thought, the trip to the grocery shouldn't take more than a half hour. Mikhail could wait at the wharf. The fresh air would do him good.

Anna waved and called out a warning. "You move, old man, and I will lock you in the chain locker on Titus Morgan's boat. And you know what that smells like."

Mikhail called back tiredly. "Titus Morgan's chain locker smells bad because Titus smells bad. Tell him he needs a bath."

Anna waved again and ground away across the dusty gravel. Mikhail watched her depart then shifted his eyes to the spectacular sunset. It was beautiful, he thought, a sight that never failed to inspire warm memories that spread out comfortably in front of him: colorful images of his boat – the focal point of his life, fishing the blue-green swells just off the coast, his friends, many gone but not forgotten. A smile crept across his bruised face when he recounted his youth and his many cherished indiscretions. Most of all, he thought about Anna. He was proud of her. No, more than this, he treasured her. What could he possibly tell her, he wondered. How could she ever understand? Mikhail looked up slowly, sobered by the inescapable morass sinking around him. He quickly realized, however, that reliving the tragic past would do little to assuage new complications. There were certainties to be dealt with. The men that beat him would be back. He needed to be ready.

The old man gathered his strength and stood. The sun was all but gone now, lost beyond the crimson-streaked sea. His legs wobbled and he considered sitting again. Instead, he hitched his broken arm against his side and walked unsteadily across West Shore Road then turned up a tree-studded gravel lane. Mikhail could feel his legs grow stronger as the glimmering lights of the fishing fleet filtered away behind him. He angled past scattered cottages, mostly owned by fishermen like him. All were modest tin-roofed structures, many unpainted and weathered to a fine, extant gray. There was a chill in the air, wet as always, and a gentle night breeze rustled through the outstretched limbs of scattered Post Pine trees.

Mikhail stopped and looked through deepening shadows at a clapboard cottage. It was much like the others, except for the flowerpots. There were hundreds of them: large, small, round, square. Some were gaily painted, and some were simply weathered terracotta. Plants and flowers exploded from the randomly placed vessels. Mikhail thought, as he often did, that the dense clutter of plantings looked more like the remnants of a long-forgotten nursery.

The windows in the cabin-like structure were dark. Mikhail moved across the shell-bed path and forced his legs to lift him up two timber steps to the narrow, covered veranda. Memories flooded back as his fingers traced the wood column supporting the roof. He closed his eyes for a moment then uttered an involuntary whisper, "Marvina."

Mikhail turned the front doorknob; Marvina never locked it. He stepped inside. If the darkness brought with it an unfamiliar aura, the smell did not. Marvina had been a wonderful cook. Crab was her specialty, but the squash and okra from her small garden were incredible too. The faint odor was still there. It was warm and inviting. Mikhail felt through the darkness and clicked on a small table lamp. Nothing had changed, he thought. The room was quite small and the low ceiling almost brushed Mikhail's thick hair. His eyes scanned quilt-draped furniture: a short couch abutted an enormous reading chair, a stack of firewood beside the still hearth. There were books too, mostly imprinted with obscure Russian names. Photos, dozens and dozens of them, aged and fading, were propped on tables and shelves in a simple wood frames.

Mikhail picked up a particularly large sepia photo. It was a very old family picture, a formal presentation of a handsome Russian officer in his red-trimmed military jacket. Beside him was his wife, breathtakingly beautiful, with large, searching eyes and wisps of hair curled around her cheeks. The three children stood respectfully beside their parents: a boy in dress shorts, two younger girls, one of which displayed her mother's radiance.

Mikhail's eyes shifted, circling the room, taking in images and thoughts from a lifetime now ended. He barely noticed a faintly muffled sound that crept out from somewhere deeper in the cottage. A mouse, he thought, but when another sound followed, a hollow – clunk, Mikhail froze. Instantly, he understood that someone else was there. He took two silent steps and slipped a fat log from the pile beside the fireplace. His eyes bore into the darkness of a narrow hallway. With a broken arm, he knew he was at a disadvantage. This didn't manner. There was no fear, as anger swelled inside of him at the thought of looters foraging Marvina's life. Retreat was impossible. He moved forward.

Mikhail stopped halfway down the hall. A rustling sound seeped from beneath the bedroom door. Suddenly, a loud crash broke out; a drawer being flung to the floor. Mikhail charged, slamming into the door. It was locked. He drew back quickly and rammed the door again. The frame buckled and split but the lock held. The sound of breaking glass burst out from the room. Mikhail smashed the door again, and then again, and with one tremendous blow, he knocked the door cleanly from its hinges. Darkness.

Mikhail lunged for the wall-switch and the room was instantly filled with harsh light. It was empty. A tall window beside the bed had been shattered where someone had leaped out.

Mikhail glared at the destruction surrounding him. Tables were overturned, and the bed was ripped apart, with loose stuffing still drifting through the air. Drawers from Marvina's dresser and desk lay scattered and broken on the floor. Mikhail was still trying to absorb the numbing intrusion when he heard another sound; footsteps in the hall behind him. His thick fingers tightened around the log as he waited, then as a shadow rounded the corner, he lashed out, arching the club downward in a powerful roundhouse swing. The shadowed figure ducked as the log smashed a huge hole in the wall. Mikhail recoiled and was about to swing again, when a voice cried out. "Mikhail, no!"

The old man checked his swing an instant before he would have crushed Anna's head. She cowered against the wall, terrified. "Oh, God!" Mikhail wailed as he dropped the club and pulled Anna into his arms, crying out, "I didn't know! Anna!"

Anna steadied herself against Mikhail's towering frame and looked plaintively into his eyes. "I heard noises. I didn't know it was you," she exclaimed.

Mikhail was still holding her when she finally saw the ransacked room. She was stunned. "What happened?"

"I don't know. There was someone here. They went out the window." Mikhail regrouped and held Anna back. "Why did you come here?"

"That's what I was going to ask you, old man," Anna chided with certain relief.

"It doesn't matter."

"It *does* matter! Tell me!" she charged.

Mikhail hesitated. "I wanted to be with her again," he whispered. "I wanted to remember. Anna, how did you find me?"

"Titus Morgan," she explained. "He was at the wharf when I came back; he said he saw you cross the coast road and head this way." She offered a gentle smile. "I knew it was Marvina."

Mikhail grumbled, "Titus Morgan should mind his own business. I almost crushed you."

Anna was smiling now. "He's a good friend, Mikhail, even if he does smell like dead fish."

Mikhail chuckled, hugging Anna again. His sense of relief was quickly displaced, however, by darker thoughts. He was still holding his daughter when she asked, "What did they want? Marvina didn't have anything of value."

Mikhail shrugged. "She is dead, Anna. Gone. People knew where she lived. Thieves came; they took what was not theirs." The old man fell silent again. Anna pulled back and looked into his eyes. She knew he was lying.

At first, Jake Altman didn't understand why his friend, Louis Ottly, had planted his photo studio in the Lower Filmore area. Most San Francisco artists and musicians preferred the Tenderloin District, a large area west of Jefferson Square. The dazzling array of bizarre street people that populated the Tenderloin was very much a part of its endearingly psychotic ambience.

Louis shrewdly chose the more affluent Lower Filmore district, Pine Street to be exact, where his loft's proximity to the big money in Pacific Heights resulted in a steady stream of well-funded patrons. Louis loved money; his affinity for wealth far surpassed his artistic talents. He was a consummate salesman, though, and with little difficulty he had successfully insinuated himself into the rich fabric of San Francisco's elite crowd of luminaries. He shared the four-story white stucco building, which he owned without any debt, with a yoga studio on the first floor. His studio took up the entire second floor, while an elderly, often venomous trust-fund dowager lurked about on the third floor. Louis had wisely not attempted to evict the old woman when he bought the house. She would have cut off his balls, or worse. Adding further to the eccentric ambiance of the hulking landmark was the persistent rumor that someone had once committed suicide in the forth-floor attic apartment; it remained an oddly appealing but unoccupied source of gossip.

Jake stood outside on the small, awning-covered stoop, impatiently tagging the buzzer to Louis' studio. A couple of spandex-clad trophy-wives, tossed him playful glances as they sauntered into the yoga studio through an adjacent door. Jake pegged Louis' buzzer again. There was no answer at first, but another burst of buzzer punches finally brought a gruff response as the wall speaker crackled loudly. "Go away, man!" Louis shouted.

"Let me in, Louis."

"No."

"You're being an ass again."

Another double-buzz brought Louis's voice back, "Beat it. I got a big-ass dog in here."

"Aw, just give it a break, Louis," Jake complained. He was about to ring again when a striking young woman stepped under the awning. She had short, dark hair and a perfect Southern California tan, no doubt obtained at great expense at an overpriced tanning salon. She was good looking and she knew it, and she wore her pale green raincoat like a seasoned runway model.

Jake smiled and stepped aside as the girl checked the names and punched Louis' button. "Look, I told you to take a hike," Louis' voice bellowed back.

The girl was startled. "Mr. Ottly?"

Louis' voice melted, "Jolene?"

"Yes. It's Jolene Betts."

"Well, heck, Jolene. Com'on up!" Louis called back brightly. The door lock clicked open and Jolene slipped in, closely followed by Jake. When she threw a cautionary look at him, he dug haplessly in his pocket. "Forgot my key."

Jake and Jolene climbed the stairway and congregated outside Louis' framed glass door. "Louis Ottly - Style Photography" was splayed across the glass in pretentious script.

"I assume you know Louis," Jolene remarked.

"Best buds."

Jolene knocked, and the door opened. A wiry young man with very straight, bleach-blond hair peered out. Jolene produced a sweet smile. "Louis?"

"Oh, I think not," the man sparkled flamboyantly. "Louis would be that way." He spun lightly on the balls of his bare feet, hiking a delicate finger toward the back of the loft. Hermie glanced disapprovingly back at Jake, "Well, this should be just fab-u-lous."

"Hermie, how's it hanging," Jake retaliated in good humor.

"Wouldn't you like to find out," Hermie quipped as he flounced away.

Louis Ottly appeared around a corner, his unctuous smile evaporating instantly when he saw Jake.

"Louis, my man," Jake offered brightly.

Louis glared at his friend then abruptly perked up when Jolene thrust her hand out. "Louis, I'm Jolene Betts."

"Of course you are," Louis flirted shamelessly. "And you *are* stunning. Your fiancée is a very lucky guy, isn't he?"

"Leland's a sweetheart," Jolene demurred. "This is mostly *his* idea."

"Well, good for Leland, because we are going to have mucho fun today, aren't we?"

Jolene may have blushed slightly. "Sashie said that you are very good, discrete too."

"As always. This is your secret day."

Jake rolled his eyes, numbed by his pal's shameless grandiloquence. Louis glared at Jake then took Jolene's arm and aimed her toward a dressing room. "The dress and make-up are in the fitting room. Everything you need is right there."

Hermie was standing by, tracing his fingernails along his teeth with bored indifference. Louis threw him an impatient look, then patted Jolene on the hand. "Hermie will take care of everything."

Jake watched Jolene's perfect hips as she sauntered into the dressing room. He couldn't help but wonder how Louis pulled off his outrageous charade.

Jake looked back when he heard a door slam. Louis had disappeared into his darkroom. The door wasn't locked, but Jake hesitated as he quickly scanned the cluttered loft, unordered and overflowing with dresses, ruffles and other photographic "props." He rattled the doorknob. "You live like a pig, Louis, a whole bunch of pigs. Let me in."

Louis' muffled voice was clipped. "You brought me a new camera?"

"No."

"Then go away."

A light clicked on inside the darkroom, spilling a deep crimson glow from beneath the door. Jake slipped inside. It took a moment for his eyes to penetrate the opaque shadows. Louis had his back turned. He was working prints through developing solution.

"I told you I would make it up to you, Louis," Jake offered.

"With what? Your professor's salary is worth about squat."

"I can pay you."

"You have debts like a butt rash, Jake. The camera cost over four thousand dollars."

"Ouch."

"It'll cost five to replace it," Louis sniped as he flipped a strip of negatives aside. A bell sounded, and Louis eased a print out of the developing solution. He flicked on a dim wall light, and Jake crowded in for a closer look. Louis was frowning. "It was a tough shot. You rushed me," he crabbed. "Shitty resolution."

"Tell me again why you still use film cameras," Jake quipped.

"Told you before. I'm a professional."

Jake stared at the grainy photograph of Anna Roman pushing through the crowd at the Russian consulate. Her face was mostly hidden by her rain-slicker hood, but he could clearly see the small envelope in her hand. He could also see the truculent look on Vladimir Chernov's face as he reached out for it.

Louis wiped his hands, glanced at the photo, and offered an offhand comment. "I call it a size six. Nice ass."

"Any other pearls of wisdom?" Jake replied.

"What? You want me to give you her address?"

Jake's eyes were searching the photo. He was mumbling to himself, "Rain-slicker -- see the cuts on the arms. What's that all about?" Then he pointed to her neck. "Necklace -- a pendent. No ear rings. No makeup."

"Yeah, so I bet she likes to get spanked."

"There's something about her," Jake noted, ignoring his friend. "Look at the way she's pushing forward. She's not looking for Chernov's autograph."

Louis glanced dismissively at the photo again. "Okay, Sherlock, so she doesn't look like your average political groupie."

"Chernov knew that too. Look at him. He sent his goons after her."

"He sent his goons after *us* too," Louis quipped. "That cost me a four-thousand-dollar camera." He brushed past Jake and marched out of the darkroom. Jake was right on his heels.

"Louis, will you look at the damn picture again," he barked.

"It's a photograph, not a picture. What's with you? You're all wigged out over this thing."

"Fine. Whatever. Now look at your photo -- the girl and Chernov, and tell me she didn't blow him away with whatever she said."

Somehow, their moving confrontation had taken them back to Louis' main photo set. Hermie was staring at them over the top of his purple-framed glasses as he loaded a Pentax SLR studio camera. Jolene Betts, stunning in a flowing white wedding gown that accentuated her shimmering tan, was timidly reclining in a Chippendale chair. Flowers spilled from a large vase on the table beside here.

Louis ignored Jake and moved closer to adjust the flow of Jolene's dress and, of course, nimbly work his fingers around the firmness beneath her daringly low-cut décolleté top. Jolene glanced at Louis and offered a sensuous admission. "Leland said he wanted me to show off what I have."

Louis' smile was sublime. "I think we can work with that." He slipped a quick grin at Jake, "Private wedding photos."

"Pervert," Jake muttered under his breath.

"Hermie, let's rev up the engine," Louis called out. "Give me some illumination here."

Hermie triggered a bank of photofloods and tagged an exotic DVD deck. Music rose up with a pulsing beat. Louis stepped behind his camera, quickly framing the young bride in his lens. "Excellent. Oh, that's *so* outrageous. Perfect," he coaxed, as he clicked off three shots. "Leland is going to be very excited by these photos. Please tell me I can come to the wedding."

"Why not hang out with them on their wedding night," Jake hissed in his ear. "You're halfway there anyway."

"Go away," Louis snapped. He started shooting again, coaxing Jolene with a stream of erotic encouragements. "Love it! There. A little more attitude, please. Now simmer for me, baby. Give it up."

Jake knew his conference with Louis was over. He headed for the door, turning back only once when he heard Jolene giggle as she called out to Louis. "You'll tell me when I should get naked."

8

The intoxicating aroma of fresh pizzas wafted through Jake's second floor apartment just off Hearst Street on the south side of campus. He had rented the studio apartment from Nick Rommel, the very German owner of Pablo's Perfect Pizza's, for almost three years. It wasn't much. In fact, it was pretty much a dump, a gabled storefront attic that was roughly framed and painted a horrible shade of green. Jake didn't mind. It wasn't that he didn't have better taste, but rather that he was perpetually cash-strapped and had far too many other things on his mind.

Still, the warmly appealing odor of fresh pizza crust, sausage, peppers, onions and mushrooms continued to creep into his consciousness as he hunched over a small desk, carefully perusing the six, eight-by-ten photographs that Louis had developed for him. It was quite late. The dim table lamp framed Jake and sent long shadows slanting across the facetted attic roof.

Jake produced a magnifying glass and bent over one of the photos of Anna Roman outside the Russian consulate. His eyes shifted from her partially hidden face to her outstretched hand and the small envelope. He looked closer. There was something about her hand. It was slender and delicately defined; not the hand of a working woman. Jake looked at her blue rain jacket too. With the aid of the magnifying glass he was able to see a number of thin lines, cuts probably, struck randomly across the slicker sleeves. Finally, his eyes shifted to the smeared red marks on the sides and front of the rain jacket. It appeared to be blood.

He leaned back in his chair, trying to remember the exactness of Anna's affront to Chernov. It had happened so quickly; she had broken out of the crowd, and without hesitation confronted the aged Russian operative. Jake considered that she might have been a political activist of some kind, or maybe a reporter, but neither concept felt entirely compelling.

Suddenly, Jake swung forward in his chair. He grabbed the magnifying glass and zeroed in on the cuts on Anna's coat. He had seen this sort of thing before in a magazine. "Fisherman," he mumbled absently to himself. "She's a fisherman."

San Francisco's commercial fishing fleet had survived fires, earthquakes, crooked politicians, and the grim invasion of marauding tourists. Located just off the Embarcadero near Taylor Street, it had long been surrounded by gift shops and over-priced seafood restaurants. Surprisingly, despite the relentless incursion by outsiders, the fleet had remained largely insular, an eclectic collection of fishing boats, smelly nets and grizzled fourth and fifth generation fishermen. The tourist-minded city officials liked it that way, and they kept the dock rental rates ridiculously low for just that reason.

There was a flurry of pre-dawn activity around the fishing fleet. No tourists were out this early, just a few joggers, a noisy street-cleaning truck, and a nest of fishermen downing hot coffee at the edge of the wharf. The city skyline glowed through the mist, rising up steeply to Telegraph Hill and beyond.

Jake Altman stopped atop a long gangway leading down to the boats. He could hear the early cries of hungry seagulls and he could smell the damp sea air. Jake hesitated for a moment, scanning the tangle of fishing boats and their heavily wired outriggers. It was a world that was foreign to him, and though he had jogged the meandering wharf boardwalk many times, he realized that he had never really given appropriate consideration to the tiny outpost, its abundant history, and timeless pace. It was an enigma, an unsolved mystery of survival amid the great sprawl of urban progress that had engulfed it.

Jake walked down the ramp and moved quietly among the boats. Smoke began to cough from soot-stained exhaust stacks. Men were shouting at each other through the mist. A seasoned fisherman hauled a coil of rope from the cabin on his Monterey Skiff. Jake called out, "How's the crabbing been?"

The fisherman glanced up at the dock but continued to work. "You offering something better?"

Jake could only shrug. "Sorry. I teach, write books."

The fisherman scoffed, "Books."

Another mildewed crewman appeared and stepped past Jake without acknowledging him. No slight was intended; Jake understood that these fishermen had seen tourists before, and they simply didn't have much time for them.

Jake regrouped and called out again, "I'm looking for someone." He pulled one of the photographs of Anna from his jacket pocket and held it out. "I'm working on a story about her..." He pointed at Anna. "Here, the girl in the center. She's wearing a blue rain jacket. I saw one like it in a store over there."

The grizzled fisherman wiped sea-moss from his callused hands and took the picture.

"Nice," he replied with a lot of subtext. "She's a crabber. Girlfriend?"

He handed the photo back to Jake, who pressed for more information. "You sure she's a crab fisherman?"

"We fish cod and sea bass down here, maybe some rock crab from time to time. Those cuts on her jacket came from a crabber's knife." He shrugged indifferently and gestured out past the mist-shrouded Golden Gate Bridge. "North coast, Redwood City, maybe north of there, she could work anywhere."

"But not around here?"

The fisherman shrugged again. Smoke belched from his boat's exhaust stack as several other crewmen began to work lines free. Jake nodded and backed away, but just before the boat slid free from the dock, the old fisherman called out. "Hey, writer man, you might try some of the fleets up around Point Reyes or Bodega Bay. Bunch of Russian crabbers up there." He gestured toward the photo again. "Nice looking lady."

As Jake wandered back up the long ramp as he studied the photo of Vladimir Chernov and the mysterious young woman in the blue slicker. The look on Chernov's face was uncharacteristically shocked. Jake was certain that he had been caught completely off guard. He angled back toward his VW, parked illegally in a handicap zone.

As he climbed into the car, he noticed a tourist standing on a promenade walkway above the water. Something about the man seemed out of place to Jake. He was vaguely military, about forty, lean, with close-cropped hair, sport coat and tie. Who the hell wears a tie at six in the morning at Fisherman's Wharf, Jake thought. Still, it wasn't so much the man, but rather his camera that caught Jake's eye. It was an expensive professional rig with a large, searching lens, and Jake had the inescapably uncomfortable feeling that it had been pointed at him, not the placid harbor.

Dr. Ezra Bonner was a punctual if not an overtly predictable creature of habit. He took a morning break every day, most often spending a half hour or so sitting on a heavy cypress bench situated in the shade of a Sycamore tree just outside the student union building. The bench had been a gift of a graduating Industrial Arts major who often played chess with him. Ezra marveled at the exquisitely fit joints and thick dowel locking pins. He was not at all resourceful with his hands and, recognizing this infirmity, he took pride instead with the depth and breadth of his mental faculties.

Ezra looked over the top of his book, watching a couple of students toss a Frisbee. It was an unusually sunny day on campus. Colors seemed brighter, and sharply defined shadows heightened the visual clarity. On the nearby quad, a girl snagged a high Frisbee toss and lofted it back to a jockish underclassman preening shamelessly with no shirt. As he grabbed the disk with an impressive one-hand catch, Bonner couldn't help but observe how innocently, yet physically, the youthful mating game proceeded. Ezra Bonner felt a warm glow of tranquility, and of the satisfaction that, at that moment, all was right in a terribly unsettled world.

Time was short, however. Class would begin in fifteen minutes. Bonner's eyes drifted back to his book for a few fleeting moments of respite. He was quickly consumed by the text and didn't notice when Katherine Sexton appeared. She sat down beside him. He turned to look at her, and she quickly admonished, "Ah, I've caught you again, Ezra. You're obviously embroiled in yet another densely-oblique academic treatise."

Bonner glanced at his book and turned it toward her. "Fly Fishing in Montana," he recited. "…by Homer B. Weed of Billings. The man has a fourth-grade education, but he can cast a fly fifty yards and hit a frog."

Katherine refused to capitulate. "Well, I suppose even that sort of book brings a certain degree of cerebral reflection."

"Not really, Katherine. It's just fun."

"And fun it should be, Ezra."

Bonner looked at her over the top of his glasses. "This isn't a social visit, is it?"

"No. But it is rather important."

"I'm sure it is."

Katherine understood that Ezra Bonner was every bit a match for her. He was smart as hell, and she knew it. Actually, he was quite *wise,* too, she thought. Bonner was widely published, with thoughtful texts covering a host of diplomatic and politically historical events. And while he conveyed a sense of scholarly intensity, he also had the uncanny ability to absorb the many commonplace issues of everyday life.

"You know, you're really quite a renaissance man, Ezra."

"Flattery will get you anything, dear."

"I was counting on that." Katherine took a moment to collect her thoughts. Then she spoke with directness. "Have you read Jake Altman's most recent epistle -- his new chapter dealing with Vladimir Chernov's direction of the ubiquitous Russian plot to seize the planet?"

"He said that?"

"Not in so many words, but the intent is pretty clear. Have you read it?"

"I have."

"And?"

"Well, the piece is certainly precise and surprisingly forthright," Ezra shrugged. "Very well thought out, but a bit long-winded at times."

"It's a train wreck, Ezra."

"That may be a bit harsh."

"It's an un-disciplined indictment built entirely on unsupportable conjecture."

"Really?"

"Ezra," Katherine chirped. "Jake is way off base, and you know it."

"Yes, but he makes some good points."

"No, he doesn't make good points," she exclaimed. "Look, I understand Jake's academic standing around here. You like him. We all like him. But what happens if his accusatory and utterly spurious work reaches the wrong hands?"

"Whose hands might that be?"

"Stop toying with me, Ezra. This is serious, or at least it could become serious. Jake has launched an unreasonable attack on Vladimir Chernov, the new consul general to San Francisco. The Russians won't be pleased. This could very easily have broader implications for U.S.-Russian relations."

"It's just a dissertation."

"Yes," Katherine protested. "A *completed* one! But Jake just keeps tagging on new assertions and claims. He's consumed with this thing, I mean more than before. Some of his material even seems…"

"Paranoid?" Bonner inserted.

"Possibly."

"What's your point, Katherine?"

"He's gonna piss off the wrong people!"

"The Russians?"

"Stop it, Ezra. This institution benefits from relationships with any number of federal agencies. They give us money. We help them. Do you really want some untenured newbie professor hurling potty-bombs at our extremely delicate international relationships?"

"Of course not."

"I don't either," she continued. "But if Jake keeps up with this conspiracy thing of his, he's going to drag us into a big mess."

"Katherine, I sincerely doubt that Jake Altman's appendage-expanded study of an aging Russian operative will prove to be any more than an articulate, well-documented, and marginally convincing academic rendering that will serve two important purposes."

"Such as?" Katherine jabbed.

"First, and foremost, it will provide some measure of closure for Jake. He lost his fiancée in Russia. Two years hasn't done much to assuage his grief. This paper will at least allow him to know that he *tried* for her."

"That's an *emotional* outcome. A dissertation is an intellectual pursuit."

"Which brings me to my second point, Dr. Sexton," Bonner added softly. "As an academic institution, our job is to nurture young minds, to champion intellectual pursuit, investigation if you will, and to encourage the search for answers to big questions. Jake has a big question."

Katherine fell silent for a moment then abruptly stood up. "I think you are wrong, Ezra. But I also think, no I *know*, I'm not going to get anywhere with you on this."

Bonner nodded quietly. "Thank you."

She turned and started to walk away. Bonner called after her, "Katherine."

She looked back, waiting for Ezra to complete his thought. Bonner removed his reading glasses and looked closely at her. "Are you having an affair with Jake?"

"What!" Katherine spat back.

"It's a simple question. You came to me with a question. It seems fair that I should ask one too. Are you having an affair with Jake?"

"Of course not."

"Then why are you having sex with him?"

Katherine glared at Bonner. She wanted to lash out, but something in his eyes told her he did know, and that there was a price for his silence. She spun on her heels and hurried away.

Dr. Bonner watched her depart. His lips tightened, as his voluble good nature was now fully displaced by solemn thoughts.

9

Jake's ten-year-old VW was running flat out at seventy-five miles per hour, top down, flapping plaintively in the wind. This sort of speed would have been unimaginable if it were not for the long downhill grade on Pacific Coast highway north of San Francisco. Only minutes before, he had been snaking his way along the twisted road high atop windswept bluffs overlooking the sea. But Bodega Bay lay before him now, far below in the distance. Jake had been up this way a few times before, and the grandeur of the northern California coast continued to amaze him. The land was large and green and majestic. The sky was beyond expansive; it seemed to reach out forever. Just ahead, the road abruptly straightened as it fell away toward the vast rolling countryside which wrapped protectively around the tiny seaside enclave and its broad, azure bay.

Soon, as the grade lessened, Jake was able to slow the old VW's harrowing descent. He was actually a little relieved. The wheels were still on, as were the doors which had rattled menacingly only moments before. A truck eased out onto the road in front of him. It was tugging a boat trailer laden with a rusting Marin County skiff. Sea gulls swooped through the boat's tattered rigging, crying out as they struck at wires and netting, snaring sinuous remains of the last catch. Jake would have enjoyed the Rockwellian vision if the smell had not been so bad. He was relieved when the truck pulled off again, dropping down toward the southern edge of the bay.

Jake slowed further as he approached the weathered bayside town. He motored past a collection of bait shops, a corner grocery, and Bodega Bay's only bank then noted a nest of pick-up trucks parked next to the Sea Hag, a ramshackle wharf-side bar with absolutely no discernible curb appeal. Jake nosed his VW into the gravel and parked just off the coast road. He climbed out and eyed the trucks laden with crab cages and heaps of soiled netting.

Several hundred yards away, higher on a tree-shrouded back road, a black Yukon SUV glided slowly to a stop in a narrow pull-off area. The windows were darkly tinted, and no one got out. A faint puff of dust swirled up beneath the exhaust pipe, but the engine idled in near silence.

When Jake eased into the Sea Hag, he spotted a couple of old fishermen playing checkers in a corner booth. Several other men were elbowed up to the bar, while a group of aging anglers and their wives ringed a long table, enjoying their weekly breakfast gathering. The bar's lethargic proprietor, Martin Coleman, was cleaning glasses. He was a small man, with puffy cheeks and thin, comb-over hair. Coleman paid little attention to Jake as he slid onto a tall barstool.

"…morning," Jake offered as a perfunctory greeting. "Could I get a cup of coffee, black."

Coleman cocked an eye at Jake, mumbled something to himself, then shuffled to the far end of the bar to tap the morning brew. He returned and slid a cup in front of Jake then allowed a wet finger to aim out the picture window at Jake's top-down Beetle. "Kinda brisk for that, ain't it?" he grunted.

"…top got stuck down," Jake replied as he sipped from the mug. "Hey that's good," he lied as he absorbed the sour bite.

Coleman nodded. He was about to move away when Jake produced several eight by ten photographs and laid them on the bar-top: Anna Roman at the Russian consulate. "So, I drove up from the city this morning. I'm writing a story about fishing. I'm trying to find this lady. It's about my research."

Coleman glanced casually at the photos then allowed his eyes to drift back to Jake. "Sorry."

Jake pressed a little harder, "Yeah, I ran into her a few days ago. Didn't get her name. Would you know who she is?" he said.

"No," Coleman replied flatly.

Jake tapped his finger on Anna's rain jacket. "She was wearing a slicker; it has cuts along the sleeves, see. Maybe they're knife marks. Bodega Bay's a crabbing fleet, isn't it?"

"Crab, Shrimp, Rock Fish, you name it. I don't know your friend though."

Jake noticed the two men farther down the bar, both watching the exchange. Coleman flicked a quick look at them, and their eyes sank back into their coffee mugs. Jake held up one of the photos, half-waving at the barflies. "Anybody know her -- the girl in the blue slicker?"

"Lots of fishing fleets up this way, mister. You better try someplace else," Coleman growled.

"Right," Jake noted observantly. "Thanks for the coffee." He dropped a couple of bucks on the table and turned to leave just as the tavern door opened and Anna Roman whisked in carrying a large thermos bottle. She was wearing her blue slicker. Jake threw a look at the bartender, who remained utterly poker-faced, even as Anna sauntered up and leaned on the bar.

She gave Jake a quick smile then slid her thermos across the counter and called out, "Martin, I'm going to put my life in your hands and try a jug of that three-day-old Columbian you got back there." Coleman snatched the jug and hustled away. Anna felt Jake's eyes on her. She turned to him and forcefully said, "Hi."

Jake knew it was meant more as a polite warning for him to mind his own business. "I'm sorry," he said.

"You were staring."

"...yeah, well, I...."

"It's not polite to stare," Anna noted frankly.

Jake wasn't really embarrassed by her challenge, but he was nonetheless at a complete loss for words. The young woman, who had moments before been nothing but a grainy photograph with little detail, had now revealed herself to be a strikingly beautiful young woman. Even with her wind-tossed hair, Anna radiated a tomboyish natural allure. Her eyes were large and blue, sparkling like the sea at sunrise.

Jake tried to smile, but it came off as a goofy grin. "I could say I was up here giving away free toasters, but then you wouldn't buy that." She just looked curiously at him. "I'm a writer," he continued. "Actually, I teach at U.C. Berkeley."

"That's fascinating," Anna tossed back.

Coleman returned with Anna's coffee thermos. His eyes tracked from Anna to Jake.

"Look, I was trying to find you," Jake admitted, as he pulled out the photograph. "A friend of mine snapped this the other day at the…"

"You have the wrong lady," Anna inserted when she saw the photo.

Jake's face registered confusion. "No, that's you. Right there. You were in the middle of the other gawkers at the Russian consulate. You're wearing the same rainslicker."

Anna's face flushed, "I don't know those people, and I don't know you."

She tossed some bills on the bar and grabbed the thermos. "Thanks, Martin."

Anna marched toward the door, but Jake caught up with her. "Hey," he protested. He reached for her arm but pulled up when he saw Coleman step out from behind the bar with a Louisville Slugger baseball bat in his hand.

Anna quickly waved the squat bartender off. "It's okay, Martin." She pushed through the door, heading outside and across the gravel lot.

Jake was right behind her. He was certain he had the right person. "My name is Jake Altman," he called out. "I know that's you in the picture. You were there. Why? What's your excuse? Why were you there?"

She spun back to him. "I don't know what you're talking about."

"Yes you do!"

"Okay, so I was protesting. Why don't you just run with that?"

"You weren't protesting anything! You shoved an envelope at Vladimir Chernov."

"Hey, if you don't leave me alone, I'll get Martin and his baseball bat to come out here. He likes me, which means he doesn't like you." Anna shoved past Jake and started to climb in her fifteen-year-old pickup truck.

"Aw, com'on. Talk to me," Jake whined.

"I don't have anything to say to you."

"Well, you had a lot to say to Vladimir Chernov! You gave him an envelope and you said something, and then he lit up like a Christmas tree."

She slammed the truck door. Jake slapped his hands on the open window ledge. "My friend and I were taking pictures, just like all the other stiffs. It was a pretty dull group. Only when you showed up, the whole thing turned into a free for all. Chernov was pissed, and my friend and I got busted up by a couple of Russian security guys. They grabbed his camera. *Who are you?*"

"Nobody, Mr. Altman, I'm nobody at all. You've wasted your time." Anna gunned her truck to life and tore away in a spray of gravel.

Jake leaped back but caught a good look at the sticker on her bumper:

CMMA
CALIFORNIA MARINE MAMMAL ASSOCIATION

Jake watched Anna's truck grind away then dusted himself off and hiked toward his VW. He climbed in and angrily slammed the door. When he keyed the engine, it just clicked pathetically. This was not new territory for Jake. He cursed the rebellious Beetle and tried again.

The black SUV was still parked two hundred yards away, high on a roadway turnout. It had not moved, but a rear window was cranked halfway down. A slim silencer, screwed on the end of a very long rifle barrel, protruded from the opening. The tinted lens of a large telescopic gun-sight glimmered in the sunlight. The two men inside the Yukon, the same two men who accosted Jake and Louis at the consulate, remained motionless.

"Take the shot," Remi hissed, but Oleg held his fire, taking his time to zero Jake perfectly in the cross hairs of the powerful scope.

Jake keyed the VW again then smacked the dash in frustration.

An enormous garbage truck rumbled over a rise with seagulls diving-bombing the rig for soggy morsels of fetid refuse. It was heading south on the coast road, and it was doing at least seventy when it hurtled past Bodega Bay.

Watching from inside the big SUV, Remi snapped at Oleg again, "Mate, take the damn shot!" Oleg held Jake tightly in the cross hairs and eased his finger around the trigger. "Now," Remi hissed.

But at the last second, Oleg saw the speeding garbage truck, and whispered, "Better this way." He jerked the gun a fraction of an inch to the right and pulled the trigger.

The right front tire on the semi cab exploded, and the rig raked out of control, careening directly at Jake's VW bug. He saw it coming and leaped out of the car, rolling away in the dusty gravel, just as it was run over, smashed, torn, and crushed beyond recognition. When the dust finally settled, Volkswagen wheels, axles and body parts were splayed out from beneath the garbage truck which had tipped up and over, gouging to a stop.

Jake clambered to his feet and was standing in flat-footed amazement when a pimply-faced young truck driver squirmed out of his overturned cab. Dooley Dodson was a Bodgea Bay hometown product. He had just turned nineteen and had been driving the city's garbage truck for two years, ever since he dropped out of high school. "Man, are you okay? he gasped. "God, I couldn't stop. I...I mean the fucking tire blew and the rig just locked up on me. Wham! I couldn't hold it. Christ!"

Jake looked blankly at Dooley then turned to the tangled and twisted mass of steel that was once his VW. It had been shredded and heaped thoroughly with all manner of disgusting garbage.

Martin Coleman and others from the Sea Hag burst into the sunlight. Everyone was pointing and shouting. Dooley, faint from shock, had to sit down on a rock. He looked at his overturned rig and seemed ready to cry. "Oh, man. I am so fucked."

Jake stooped down and picked up his battered license plate. He was still staring at it when Dooley called out. "Hey, man. It's okay. I think we got insurance."

High on the hillside, several hundred yards away, Oleg calmly withdrew the gun barrel from the cracked window. If he was disappointed that his shot had not resulted in his predicted outcome, he didn't show it.

Remi growled to himself and slipped behind the steering wheel. The black SUV rolled back onto the highway and disappeared.

Sheriff Lawrence Jackson poured another cup of coffee. He always kept two pots brewing in his small office, and he was rarely without a hand-rolled cigar close by. After a smooth sip from his mug, he glanced at Jake Altman, sitting in a chair opposite the desk. "Is that about it?" Jackson asked.

Jake shrugged haplessly. "Yeah. That's it. I really didn't see the rig coming at me until the last second. I just leaped out the door."

Sheriff Jackson picked up the gnarled VW license plate from his desk. "Nice move."

There was a loud flushing sound and Dooley Dodson emerged from a closet-like bathroom, wiping his mouth on his sleeve. "Man, that was some righteous up-chuck."

"Dooley, you been sucking on weed again?" Sheriff Jackson charged. "Maybe I need to make you piss in a cup for me."

"Hey, it's cool, man," Dooley protested. "I don't do that shit anymore. It's like I told you. My tire like exploded, and I couldn't hold the rig on the road."

A deputy sheriff stuck his head in the office. "Sheriff, you got a minute for me out here? "It's the mayor's wife again."

"Yeah, yeah -- it's always one disaster or another," Jackson groaned. He headed out the door with the deputy but paused to look back at Jake and Dooley. "You guys stay put. See if you can't come up with some facts for me."

The door closed behind the sheriff. Dooley offered Jake a meek smile. "This is the shits, huh?"

"...yeah," Jake growled. He tugged his jacket off and laid his head back against the wall. What the hell was he doing in a Podunk police station, he thought. He hadn't done anything wrong, but the hometown super-cop had just kept chewing on him. Jake scanned the cluttered room. It was pretty typical: dusty file cabinets, a clipboard on the wall held a wad of faded Wanted posters. Apparently, the sheriff didn't use a computer, at least he didn't have one in his private office. There were a couple of phones and an old radio transmitter with a hand-held mike. Jake shook his head wearily and slipped the folded photos out onto the desk. Dooley craned his neck for a peek.

"Hey, that's Anna Roman," he gushed.

"Anna Roman?" Jake noted. "That's her name? You know her?"

"Yeah, yeah, that's her. What the hell is she doing in the middle of that crowd?"

Jake realized he had stumbled on to a chatty village idiot. "That's from the Russian consulate last week," he said.

"No shit? She was in the city? Was Mikhail with her?"

"Who's Mikhail?" Jake probed.

"Hell, everyone around here knows Mikhail and Anna. She's his daughter, and he was like Marvina's caretaker. She was a very cool one-hundred-years old." Dooley shoved the photos apart further and thumped Anna with a dirty finger. "She's pretty damn hot, huh? You a *friend* of hers?"

"I don't really know her. Not yet anyway."

"Yeah, well, she's nice to me and all, but you know, she's not really my type. I like 'em more on the chubby side, a little cushion for pushin', you know. Hey, did you shoot this pic before Marvina Dubrovsky got run down by that bus?"

Jake was perplexed, but he didn't want to let Dooley slip away. "I'm not sure. Can't remember the details."

"In the city, man," Dooley squealed. "Talk about shitty luck. Man-oh man." He was tiring of the conversation. "Anyway, Marvina caught the coast bus into the city then got blasted."

"Any ideas what happened?" Jake posited.

"I don't know. Mikhail couldn't figure it out either. Marvina hadn't left Bodega Bay for, hell, musta' been twenty years, and then she showed up at the frigging Holy Mary Cathedral in San Francisco. I heard she went right down front in the middle of a service, kneeled down and gave a confession then walked out and stepped in front of a MUNI bus. Wham. It was really gross, man. What do you think?"

Before Jake could reply, the door opened and Sheriff Jackson walked in. He spotted the photos on his desk and pulled up short. "What's all that about?"

"Just some photos," Jake offered.

"Hell, Lawrence," Dooley beamed. "I told him right off that's Anna Roman, plain as day."

"What else did you tell him, Dooley?" the sheriff asked pointedly.

"Well, shit. I thought I oughta' tell him about...." Dooley suddenly went silent, realizing what he had done. "Nothin', Lawrence, they're just pictures."

Sheriff Jackson looked at Jake then picked up the crumpled license plate and handed it to him. "I'll have your car hauled to the junkyard over in Napa," he advised. "The Trailways bus stops right out there in front of the Sea Hag, usually around noon. I'm guessing you want to catch a ride back to the city."

10

The Princess undulated serenely on afternoon sea swells. Both outriggers were lowered and the trap lines were out. Mikhail Roman stood at the stern of his boat, bracing his legs against a stack of crab traps as he stared out over the vast expanse of Pacific Ocean. A thin line of land lay ten miles off to the east, half hidden in a patchy coastal fog. Mikhail normally would have derived a deep sense of inner peace from the majestic vista. For him, for many years, there was always something incredibly restorative about the sea; it comforted and centered his restless soul. And yet, on this otherwise unspoiled afternoon, Mikhail was haunted by dark memories. He thought about Marvina and her senseless death. He thought about Anna and the danger she now faced because of Marvina's unwitting overture. Finally, he allowed his thoughts to drift to Vladimir Chernov and the portentous secret they both held.

Sooty smoke belched from *The Princess'* twin stacks as Anna pulled the throttles back. Standing at the controls high in the open bridge, she knew the lines would sag at idle speed, but there were things that needed to be said and questions that needed to be asked. Anna leaned over the railing and called down, "You work too hard, Mikhail.

We're going to rest now, and I'm going to fix you a sandwich."

Mikhail shielded his eyes from the sun and looked up at his daughter. "You feed me like you did last night, and I may explode." He shifted his sore arm, still wrapped in a sailcloth sling. Mikhail was immensely proud of Anna; she had been the focus of his life since the day she was born. He had been forty-nine then, really too late in life to have a child. However, his wife of only three months, a widowed Russian translator on vacation in California, had not questioned his passionate request. They loved each other deeply, and she had willingly agreed. For Mikhail, who, for a lifetime, was too afraid to marry and possibly expose himself, it was an act of supreme selflessness. He was determined for it not to end with him. He desperately wanted a child. Even with this, the inherent physical risks of a late in life pregnancy and parenting were eclipsed by Mikhail's instinct to honor what was past and to embrace what could be the future. He consummated his marriage, and his wife was soon to have a baby. All was well, until fate dealt a tragic hand. His wife died giving birth to Anna. Mikhail was devastated. He would never be able to forgive himself; he could only dedicate his life to his daughter.

Anna left the boat on autopilot at a very slow speed. She climbed down the ladder and disappeared inside the cabin. Mikhail stood alone on the aft deck for a few more moments then followed her.

Anna was busy piling thickly sliced ham on a coarse bun. She laid tomato slices and pickles on top of this.

Mikhail sunk down behind the worn mahogany-trimmed table and gazed at Anna in silence.

"You're watching me again," she said.

"Yes. I watch my beautiful young daughter work for an old fisherman when she should be ashore with her own life."

"I'll take care of my life. But right now, I am going to take care of you," Anna mused, as she slid a plate in front of Mikhail and sat across from him. "Eat the sandwich. I put extra pickles on top."

"You spoil me, Anna."

"Actually, it's a bribe."

"As I thought…."

Anna leaned closer. Mikhail sensed what was coming, but he took a moment to devour a huge bite from his sandwich. He tapped his mouth with a paper napkin. "You want to talk," he concluded.

"Tell me about Marvina," Anna said softly. "I know what you have told me before, that she helped raise you when you were small, and then she did the same for me."

"Yes," Mikhail reflected.

Anna continued, probing gently. "I know that you knew Marvina for a very long time, and that you cared deeply for her. But there's much more; things you've never said. I need to know. It's time to tell me, Mikhail."

Mikhail settled back in the narrow settee. He had always known this moment would come. Anna was right. It was time he told her, but how?

"Marvina Dubrovsky was a very special woman, Anna."

"I know that."

"I have told you that Marvina was midwife to your mother.

"Yes."

"Dorna was spectacular, Anna. I loved your mother deeply."

"I know that too," Anna added. "I was born and my mother died. There aren't any remembrances for me to cling to. All I have are a few photographs."

"She was gone too quickly. But she gave me you."

"What's this have to do with Marvina?"

Mikhail hesitated, measuring his words carefully now. "The day you came into my life, Marvina lifted you into my arms. You were so perfect, so beautiful. And then your mother -- she was dead. It was difficult. So long ago. Now Marvina is gone too."

Anna's lips tightened. She took Mikhail's hand, pausing, not yet satisfied with what he had told her. She said, "The envelope, the one you had me take to Vladimir Chernov. What did it say, what did it mean?"

"Just a simple message."

"About what?"

"It was about our life."

"I don't understand."

"I think Marvina told the archbishop about me, your mother, and about you. And if she did, Vladmir Chernov would have learned this too."

"Mikhail, what are you telling me?"

Mikhail's voice was almost a whisper. "Marvina held a secret until she could hold it no longer."

Anna's face seemed frozen. She was confused, angry, and afraid. "I should know these things. Please."

"I thought I could tell you," he said absently, but then he began to shake his head, "But now, even now, it may be too hard."

"Tell me, Mikhail!"

Mikhail was awash in memories and fears. He was determined to speak, but couldn't. Anxious moments passed. Finally, the old fisherman shifted his broken arm so Anna could see it clearly. "They found me, Anna. Now they will try to find you."

Louis Ottly downshifted hard, pegging the engine tachometer on his Porsche 911 Carrera. He cut a corner at Union Street and hammered the gas again. The cherry-red, hyper-powered sports car turned heads wherever Louis went. He liked that. After all, he knew his exclusive Pacific Heights boudoir photography business was built on the wholly unfounded perception that he was an extremely successful photo-artist. The Porsche was a brazen manifestation that only enhanced the image. Besides, it was great for picking up women.

Louis dug into another tight turn then ripped into third gear. Jake Altman was wedged in the hand-rubbed leather seat next to him, trying to study a wad of notes. He threw a look at Louis when the car bottomed out hard. "You're pissed, aren't you?"

"Yeah, well you got some kinda nerve," Louis bawled.

"I lend you things all the time."

"Sure. Absolutely. Your squashed VW for a hundred thousand dollar Porsche."

"Louis, even if I had the urge to *lease* a Porsche, as we both know you did, because I thought long-legged ladies would drool all over me, I'd still lend it to a pal."

"For the record, asshole, it's a business expense. I've got an image to maintain."

"I still need the wheels." Jake's cell phone sounded and he clicked on.

At his end of the conversation, Dr. Ezra Bonner was pacing slowly on a treadmill in one of the university's athletic facilities. The workout room was packed, and he was surrounded by student sweat and determination. Actually, he enjoyed the curious looks he received from students forty years younger. Sometimes he would talk with them, but mostly he just listened. Their thoughts, concerns, and aspirations fed his intellect and helped him understand what life meant to a new generation.

Bonner slowed slightly, holding his cell phone close to his ear. "Jake, I have news," he posited. "I got you in."

"How?"

"I have a friend at the Russian embassy in Washington. He was a professor at the Moscow State University when I met him, and we've exchanged views over the years." Bonner stopped when Jake rattled on about something. Then he overrode his friend with a stern warning, "Jake, this cost some demonstrable favor chips. It did not come easily." Bonner listened again then smiled. "You're welcome, Jake. Did I mention that you should not screw this up? Chernov will know a fool when he sees one." He clicked his phone off and stepped down from the treadmill. He was frowning again, and he knew why.

Louis, with his frustration mounting, was still pushing the Porsche hard. He threw Jake a glaring look. "So, your teacher buddy got you an audience with Vladimir Chernov. Excuse me, but isn't he the asshole that sent his knuckle-busters after us?"

Jake was still trying to figure out how Bonner made it happen. "I didn't think he would be able to do it. Damn. The old bird can still whip up some serious sway."

Louis wheeled up in front of his studio and skidded to a stop. He took a couple of deep breaths then reluctantly climbed out. Jake climbed out too and headed around to the driver's side. Louis was still protectively holding on to the door. "Jake, I swear to God. If you wreck it, I will kill you."

"Not a problem," Jake boasted. "Thanks a bunch." He grabbed the keys, climbed in, jerked the door closed, and hit the accelerator. The 911 could do zero to sixty in four point six seconds. He was gone in a flash.

Archbishop Popov Konstantin had finished his lunch early. He was reclining in his plush armchair in an anteroom just off the sanctuary. This had long been his favorite napping spot; it was a comfortably restful zone where his digestive system could efficiently process copious amounts of rich Russian food. All was well. Konstantin's eyelids drooped, and he fell into an enzyme-induced stupor.

Konstantin had shaken off the startling surprise of Marvina's visit, the gold ruble, and most of all her anachronistic pronouncement. Her claim was astonishing; it simply was not possible. All of this, and more, rumbled uncomfortably amid the old priest's fitful respite. He had done the right thing, he drowsily told himself. He had made the *call* and delivered the gold piece as instructed. The matter was certainly out of his hands by now, he thought. He didn't want trouble. Warmer thoughts of his impending retirement sifted into his consciousness: fishing in the Ural Mountains, strolls along the lakes of the low country. It was enough to bring an agreeable smile to his cookie-speckled lips.

The church choir was practicing behind the lattice façade on the far side of the sanctuary. Tenor voices soared with lofty notes, while deeper bass underpinnings grounded the hymn in solemn reverence. Somewhere in his drifting mindlessness, Konstantin heard footsteps. At first, they really didn't register; the church staff understood that his afternoon nap was not to be disturbed. But there was something less familiar about the tapping on the tiled floor. The great man opened his eyes.

Jake Altman was standing in the doorway of the anteroom. "Excuse me, father," he offered respectfully. "The choir director said I might find you here."

Konstantin managed to rouse himself, at least to a state of semi-comprehension. "Are you orthodox," he mumbled.

"No. I'm not. But I need your help."

Konstantin's eyes were fully open now. He did not recognize this stranger in his church, and this in of itself was reason for concern. "I have office hours beginning at three o'clock," he advised somewhat flatly.

"This won't take long," Jake pressed. "An old woman came here eight days ago, Marvina Dubrovsky. She was run over by a bus when she left."

"Yes, this was tragic."

"Did you know her?"

"No. Who are you, sir? I have already spoken with the police several times."

"Actually, I'm a professor at Berkeley -- political science."

"I'm afraid I don't understand," said the old man. "Why is this matter of interest to you?"

"Honestly, I'm not sure. But Marvina Dubrovsky was connected to a family in Bodega Bay: a young woman, Anna Roman, and her father, Mikhail Roman."

"I do not know these people."

Jake stepped closer. "Yes, but Marvina came to see you, to confess. That's what I read in the papers. Someone in the congregation saw her give you something."

"No. This is a mistake. I told the police that she gave me nothing."

"What did she say to you, father?

Konstantin remained silent. He glanced over Jake's shoulder, nodding to a lesser priest standing at the doorway. Jake pressed harder. "Sir, I believe that the family I spoke of, the young woman and her father, are in danger. I saw Anna Roman pass a note to a high-ranking diplomat at the Russian consulate. This was two days after Marvina was killed. Please, can you tell me anything?"

"A confession is given with the assurance of confidentiality," Konstantin ordained. "I cannot speak of what was shared with me, but I can tell you it had no bearing on the lives of this woman or her father."

"How can you know that?"

"I know."

"No. You're not telling me the truth."

"Enough," barked the archbishop. He rose slowly, steadying his massive body, before lumbering past Jake.

Konstantin was almost to the door when Jake challenged him, "If you are wrong, father, people may die."

The old priest paused but did not turn back. He lifted his polished staff, as if a stern punctuation, and called out pompously, "God's will be done." Then he was gone.

Jake wanted to grab Konstantin and shake him. Instead, he stood dolefully silent then turned and started back toward through the sanctuary. Halfway to the door, a man caught Jake's eye. He was seated near the aisle. Jake wasn't sure what drew his attention to the man, except that he as younger and better dressed than the mostly older working-class parishioners. There was something very familiar about the man too. He had thick, cropped hair and bristling eyebrows. Jake stopped beside the pew. It was the man's sport jacket that gave him away; it was identical to one worn by the man taking photographs of him at Fisherman's Wharf.

"Why are you following me?" Jake demanded. The man looked up curiously. He uncoupled his prayerful hands and leaned back in the pew. Jake moved closer; his voice was sharply accusatory. "I saw you before -- at the fishing fleet. You were taking pictures. What's this about? I know you're following me."

Still the man said nothing. Jake lost control and snagged the man's sport coat. "Tell me, dammit!"

The bewilderment in the man's face only deepened. He finally spoke, but Jake was taken aback when the words came out in a thick Russian dialect: deep words, conditional and almost apologetic. The man had no idea what he was talking about.

Jake released the man's coat and hurried from the cathedral.

After his distressing encounter with Jake Altman, Popov Konstantin retired to his personal office. He normally enjoyed its large windows and proximity to the choral music, but today he just wanted to be left alone. Konstantin flicked a small radio on and settled onto a broad settee as the soothing notes of a classical French horn filled the room. The lilting music washed across him like a gentle summer rain. It was a pleasant experience that quickly dispensed thoughts of the distasteful matter of an old women crushed by a speeding bus.

Konstantin sighed comfortably and allowed an unexpected burp. All was well again, at least until there was a faint knock at the door. "By God's holy grace, what is it now?" he bellowed, certain that Jake had circled back for another attack. "Leave me alone!" But when the door opened and Konstantin saw the two men filling the frame, his brusque demeanor instantly evaporated. Oleg and Remi stepped inside the priest's inner sanctum and closed the door. The archbishop pulled himself up more erectly and made a feeble attempt at defiance. "I told you what I know," he said. "You have the ruble now."

A lupine smile formed on Remi's lips. Oleg, his head nearly touching a dusty chandelier, just stared. His nose was still heavily bandaged.

"What do you want?" Konstantin brayed.

"You just spoke to a man," Remi noted almost casually.

"He came to me! He asked questions, but I said nothing."

"How can we be sure of that, priest?"

"You have no right to question me," Konstantin protested. "This is a house of God!"

Oleg and Remi moved closer, drifting apart, forcing the archbishop to twist his head back and forth to confront them.

"Tell us about this man who came to see you," Remi pressed.

"There is nothing to tell. He asked me about the old woman, the one who died on the street."

"What did you tell him?"

"Nothing!"

"Did you talk about the old woman's confession?"

"No."

"Did you talk about the gold ruble?" Remi hissed.

"Of course not." Konstantin began to blubber aimlessly, "I know nothing of these things. The gold bar was very old. I had seen it before."

"Where?"

"In a book, only in a book. I -- please, I'm just a priest. I do God's work."

Remi's eyes shifted to Oleg. He nodded, and the bigger man lifted an ornate velvet pillow from beside the priest. Konstantin's eyes darted furtively between the two men, but he knew what was to come. Oleg stepped over the enormous archbishop, straddling his slippered feet. Konstantin could only whimper as Oleg wrapped the pillow over his face.

11

When Jake wheeled Louis' gleaming Porsche to the curb a half a block from the Russian consulate, he was surprised to see rows of spotless town-cars parked in front of the austere building. Drivers had gathered in small groups, most smoking and gabbing.

Jake locked the Porsche carefully then crossed the street. Several security agents stood just inside the wrought-iron gates. They watched Jake approach then shifted slightly to block his path. The younger of the two men was entirely polite. "Hello. Do you have business at the consulate today?"

"I do."

Many of the guests attending the brunch hosted by Consul General Vladimir Chernov were attuned to the fineries of diplomatic life. They were dressed expensively, and a number of nationalities were represented. The couples, mainly older, moved comfortably from group to group, exchanging perfunctory banalities. Some even took note of the regal library surrounding them. The room was quite large, with several expensive Oriental rugs framing clusters of Queen Anne antique furniture. Old and obviously valuable books filled the floor-to-ceiling shelves.

The library served as a formal gathering place for many important functions, and Vladimir Chernov was very much satisfied with this, his first, official consulate event. He graciously met arriving guests, soothed inflated egos, and adroitly cajoled good humor from otherwise dull career diplomats.

Anton Sorokin, Chernov's genteel aide, had greeted Jake in the grand entry space. He guided him down a vaulted hallway, gesturing to various noteworthy artifacts. "And that would be a Van Dyck portrait," he offered as he aimed a slender finger at a large painting. "He was of considerable Flemish Baroque influence. The name of the subject eludes me."

"It's a self-portrait, early sixteen-hundreds."

"Really."

"Actually, I have three Van Dyck's in my office at the university," Jake added. Anton's balding head cocked upward with surprise. Jake smiled. "That's not really true."

Anton offered a cautious smile. "Ha, that's very good."

Jake couldn't help but be amused. "I'm sorry," he said. "It's an American thing. We make jokes, mostly about anything."

"Ah, I see. It is good to have humor. Sometimes," he added more carefully.

"Have you been with Vladmir Chernov for a long time?"

"No, no. I came to this position through unexpected good fortune. The Consul General's long-time aide retired. Rather abruptly, I heard. I didn't know the man, but I had strong references and a friend who helped. I was interviewed extensively, and I was selected. It's been a little over one year now."

"And you enjoy working for Chernov?" Jake asked.

"Yes, of course. He is a gentleman."

Jake couldn't resist. "Was he a gentleman when he ran the KGB for ten years?"

Anton pulled up stiffly at a tall doorway opening into the crowded library. The exchange abruptly became perfunctory. "If you would be so kind as to wait here, Dr. Altman, I will let the consul general know you have arrived."

Jake, still dressed in his ratty sport coat, felt decidedly out of place. He surveyed the gathered guests and watched bland-faced men discretely vying for position. He noted the women too, most well-kept, resplendent with jewelry and far too much make-up. It looked like a gathering of funeral directors, Jake thought. His face darkened, however, when he spotted Vladimir Chernov on the far side of the room. The aging diplomat was taller than Jake had remembered, dignified, empowered. His white hair was full, and his eyes still burned with something starkly powerful. Chernov was a scion of Russian military elite. While a step removed from true aristocracy, he embodied the history of a proud country.

Anton Sorokin approached Chernov with appropriate fealty, whispering in his ear. The old Russian's eyes drifted across the room and landed on Jake. It was a dispassionate gaze, and it made Jake feel very uncomfortable.

Anton slipped back through the crowd and stepped in front of Jake. "I'm very sorry, Dr. Altman. The consul general regrets that more pressing matters require his attention today. Perhaps another time."

"I have an appointment."

"I'm sorry, sir."

"Dr. Ezra Bonner was given assurances that this meeting would take place."

Anton worked his moist hands together. He was clearly embarrassed by the situation. "Please, Dr. Altman. This is the way it must be."

Jake looked back at Chernov, who had returned to idle cocktail banter, with no further thought of the young man standing in his doorway. Anton gestured toward the hallway. Jake turned and walked away.

Behind him, far across the crowded room, Vladimir Chernov glanced up from his conversation and watched stoically as Jake departed.

Louis' Porsche swept across the Golden Gate Bridge as Jake angrily slammed the stick shift back, catapulting the car forward. Behind him, the shimmering San Francisco skyline evaporated into drifting fog. Ahead, the densely-treed mountains of Marin County were wrapped in an ethereal shroud of mist. Jake threw a quick look at his cell phone, glancing at the on-screen image of an official seal, framed on a background of sea-blue. It was a blow-up of the image on Anna Roman's fishing parka. The letters C.M.M.A. arched across the top, and the words California Marine Mammal Association spread across the bottom. Jake tapped the screen and a map overlay clicked on, plotting a route north from San Francisco.

Nothing was making any sense, Jake thought. Why had Chernov refused to see him when he had already agreed to do it? Why had the old priest lied to him about Marvina? And what was Anna Roman hiding, or what was she hiding *from*? There were too many coincidences, and Jake was certain that all of them, in one way or another, led back to Vladimir Chernov.

The Porsche screamed over and around the low hills of northern Marin County. Mist had become a dismal fog, and the sun, or what was left of it, was just a diffused orb suspended in the gloom. Jake raced down the winding coast road, finally descending to the flat land and the sleepy seaside town of Bodega Bay. He shot past the Sea Hag and the harbor, glancing only briefly at the fleet of fishing boats. No stopping this time. The Porsche ripped past eighty, as the road straightened and rose slowly again, climbing northward along the edge of the sea.

Jake's world had become surreal and dreamlike; it seemed foreign to him, majestic yet foreboding as he swept through the fog, carving a circuitous path around new curves. Finally, he backed the engine down. The turbo decompressed, and the high-pitched scream quickly became a dull growl. Jake checked his cell phone map again then looked ahead and pulled off the roadway. A wide gravel drive wound past a tiny tugboat, landlocked and perched as a marker on an embankment just behind a largely weathered C.M.M.A sign.

Less than a hundred yards down the roadway, Jake nosed Louis' sports car to a stop next to a hulking dumpster. There were a few other cars parked helter-skelter in a gravel lot. He climbed out of the car and was immediately greeted by a chorus of grunts and barks, as he scanned rows of chain-link enclosures teeming with marine mammals: sea lions, seals, and sea otters. There were dozens of them, all squalling angrily to be fed. A couple of young volunteers were busy heaving slimy fish parts to the hungry animals. Seagulls scavenged tenaciously, screaming as they dove then rose again with prized fish guts clutched in their beaks.

A stocky but attractive young African American woman appeared beside Jake. He noted that she was wearing a blue slicker identical to the one Anna Roman wore at the Russian consulate.

"Hey, this is really something," Jake offered gregariously. He was reaching for something nice to say.

"Our little slice of heaven," the girl offered.

"Super place to hang out," Jake added dumbly.
She offered him a beaming, toothy smile then shrugged. "…it's the rush season. No reservation, no room. Sorry."

Jake waved off the pungent animal odor. "Think I'll pass."

The girl swept her hand across the collection of squawking sea beasts. "They get bashed up on the rocks, shot, maybe hooked on netted. We fix 'em up, the ones we can, then send 'em back to the sea."

"Sounds like a noble endeavor."

"Yeah, we win some and we lose some."

"They don't all make it?"

"Most of them don't make it," she announced. "What brings you to our little nursing home?"

Jake dug his hand in his pocket and produced a U.C. Berkeley staff card. He gave it to the girl then toed the gravel absently. "Actually, I'm looking for a girl. Her name is Anna Roman. I think she works here."

"And you want to ask me if I know her."

"I thought I just did."

"Cute. I like cute." She glanced at his staff card then grinned, "Okay, Dr. Jake Altman, so you nailed it. Anna works here, but she's off today. Tomorrow too."

Jake swiped indifferently at his nose. "I guess she lives around here, I mean close by."

The girl knew he was tooling her around. "Anna lives back down the road, just outside Bodega Bay," she volunteered. "I guess you want her address, too."

"I guess."

The young girl cocked her head, as if waiting for him to say something else. "You got a pen?" she asked finally.

Jake fumbled to retrieve a pen from his shirt pocket. The girl snagged his hand then scribbled Anna's address on his palm. She clicked the pen closed and deftly eased it back in his pocket, patting his chest just to be sure it was secure.

"Thanks," he said simply.

"You're very welcome," she replied softly. "If you can't find Anna, I'll be around here until six."

Jake accepted this as an invitation that he didn't need. He smiled, half-saluted, then backed away. He was climbing into his car when the girl shouted out to him.

"Anna lives alone, but her dad hangs out there a lot." Jake wasn't sure what she meant by this. She called out again, "He's a big guy -- Russian. And he doesn't like stray boars sniffing around his girl."

"I'll remember that," Jake called back.

The girl just laughed. "You better."

Jake was glad that Louis' overpriced play-toy was equipped with fog lights. Darkness had fallen and he could barely see the edge of the highway as the Porsche crawled through the drifting mist. Ahead, he could see muted lights dotting the perimeter of Bodega Bay. Jake held his palm beneath the dash glow, reading the scrawled address. He was close.

If he had blinked, he would have missed the road sign: Breeze Way. It was barely visible in the dismal fog. Jake turned onto the drive and wound his way through a stand of pine trees. There were no other houses, or at least there were no lights visible. When a single mailbox, marked 114, appeared, Jake came to a stop. He clicked the headlights off. Only then could he see the dim glow of a porch light. As he climbed out of the Porsche, Jake noted that there was absolutely no sound or breeze of any sort. Drifting fog enveloped him, begrudgingly parting as he paced up the narrow walkway.

Jake surveyed the tiny cottage through the gloom. It was weathered gray, well maintained, and very old. Mist condensed on the metal roof and dripped evenly from the front edge. The cottage was completely dark, with no hint of activity as Jake felt his way up to the front door and called out. "Hello. Anna Roman?" There was no response.

When Jake turned to look back at his car, his coat brushed the front door, and it creaked open slightly. He hesitated then eased the door back and called out again, "Hey, your door is open." Jake stepped inside and allowed his eyes to adjust to the dim light. A small fire crackled in the fireplace. He could make out furniture and an oval rug but nothing else. He abruptly froze when a faint hissing sound rose up from farther back in the cottage. "Hello," he called out. "Anna?"

The sound grew louder, and Jake inched deeper into the shadows. He felt his way around a doorframe and could see the outline of a long counter, the kitchen he surmised. Without warning, the hissing sound rose quickly, breaking into an ear-piercing whistle. Jake saw the ring of blue flames rolling up from beneath a glass teapot on the stove. Steam spewed out as the shrill sound grew louder still.

Jake grabbed the teapot, jerking it off the flame. He fumbled for a wall switch, and a cord-suspended overhead light snapped on, instantly illuminating the visceral horror of a man, sprawled across a kitchen table, flat on his back, arms spread wide. Mikhail Roman was dead. His eyes were fixed – glazed and lifeless. Blood trickled form his mouth and ears. His shirt had been ripped back, and his chest was a bloody mess. A length of thin wire was stretched tight, cutting around and into his neck, while his hands were pegged grotesquely to the tabletop with steak knives.

Jake gasped and reeled back, dropping and shattering the teapot. He banged into the overhead light, sending it into wild gyrations. It was almost too much for him to comprehend, and he was still trying to process the macabre bloodbath when he heard footsteps behind him.

Jake lunged out of the kitchen, intent on fleeing. A gun roared with a blinding flash of fire, and the wall beside him exploded. He fell to the floor, scrambling to regain his footing. Anna Roman was standing in the shadows in front of him with a twelve-gauge shotgun leveled at his head. "If you move, I will blow your head off," she cried out with an equal measure of anger and terror. She was shaking. Jake was dizzy and too afraid to speak. "Where is he," she demanded, calling out, "Mikhail!"

"He's gone."

"Like hell he is."

"No, I mean he's...." Jake couldn't find the words. "Anna, put the gun down. How did you get here? I didn't see car lights."

Anna shoved the gun barrel closer to his head. "I came the back way. I walked." Then she shouted again, "Mikhail!"

"He's dead, Anna."

"Mikhail!"

Jake tried to reach out to her, but Anna shoved the gun barrel hard against his temple and lunged past him. She stumbled into the kitchen and saw Mikhail. Her mouth gaped open with a gut-wrenching scream. The shotgun crashed to the floor, and her legs buckled beneath her.

Before either of them could think, a pair of headlights flared on outside, glaring through a front window. Jake reacted instinctively, diving into Anna, sending her sprawling on the floor just as a hail of gunfire ripped through the windows. The cottage seemed to explode around them as bullets ripped and shredded everything; walls blew apart, pictures shattered, and a large vase disintegrated. It seemed to go on forever. Jake held Anna tightly against the floor. She was screaming in terror with her hands clutching her ears.

Suddenly, there was silence. A car engine roared to life. Jake leaped up and stumbled to the front door. He thought about the fallen shotgun, but it was too late. The car was careening away into the night. It was large and it was black. Jake was still gasping for air when he turned back to the cottage. The errant mist had begun to sift inside, slinking silently around splintered wood, broken glass, and shredded books. The fire still crackled in the stone hearth as Jake stepped into the hallway again. Anna Roman was gone. So was her shotgun.

Jake grabbed a bookcase for support, his mind reeling with terror. He thought he might collapse but, instead, he suddenly bolted from the cottage and away from the sickening carnage. He ran for the Porsche and was gone in a violent spray of gravel.

Inside the cottage, a log shifted lower in the fireplace. The light in the kitchen was still swaying back and forth, bathing Mikhail Roman's ghastly death mask in a surreal dance of alternating light and shadows.

12

A dreary rain had begun to fall from the night sky in San Francisco. It was late, and the glistening streets were completely deserted as a pair of headlights ripped around a corner. Louis Ottly's Porsche skidded to a stop in front of a well-preserved Victorian home near Washington Park. Jake tumbled out of the car and ran to the front porch. He hammered the doorbell as if it was a broken vending machine. "Come on, damnit! Ezra!"

Jake didn't notice the black SUV that pulled up and stopped across the street.

Lights clicked on inside the house, and the front door inched open, just slightly. Dr. Ezra Bonner, still half asleep, peered out warily. "Jake?"

"Let me in, Ezra! Please. Now."

Chains rattled and the door swung open. Bonner gaped at Jake, standing flat-footed, with wide-eyed fear etched on his face. Hot breath pumped from his lungs as a gush of words spilled out, "There's a dead man in Bodega Bay! Ezra, he was tortured. I was there. I saw him. The girl too…"

Bonner took Jake's arm, "Jake, it's late."

"Do I look like I'm screwing around? The guy is *dead*!"

Ezra Bonner was quick to absorb the gravity of Jake's proclamation. He nodded and motioned for Jake to come inside. The front door closed behind them.

Across the street, there was a flicker of light behind the tinted windows a black SUV. Remi's face was briefly illuminated through the glass as he took a long draw from his cigarette.

Jake followed Bonner across the entry hall into his study.

"Okay," the old dean mumbled as he steered Jake into a plush armchair. "Sit. First, I will make us tea."

"But…," Jake started to protest. Bonner physically shoved him down. "Stay here."

Jake nodded vaguely and allowed his head to roll back against the chair-back. It was raining harder now as he gazed blankly out the rain-splattered window. Jake could hear his mentor rummaging in the kitchen. The warmth and silence of the old house comforted him, and his thoughts began to coalesce as some sense of sanity returned.

"Ezra," he called out. "What the hell is going on?"

"That's what you are going to tell me all about," Bonner said reassuringly as he returned to the study. He sat in a chair directly across from Jake. "The tea will be ready soon," he remarked and then he just sat, waiting.

Jake's heart rate had eased slightly, but Bonner noted that his eyes seemed to dart about reflexively with no clear point of focus. Slowly, the room slowly grew more familiar to Jake. It was filled with books, mostly richly historical academic accounts, as well as numerous photos and documents, each carefully framed and labeled; they were treasured mementos of countless liaisons with scholars and world leaders. Nothing ever seemed to change here, Jake thought. And it was from this reservoir of memories that he was able to regain his footing, remembering his many enlightened exchanges with Bonner in this room. The house had been an oasis of contemplative discourse, and Jake had always found the older man's intellect to be uniquely insightful. Bonner's multifaceted career had been centered on European history and political science. He had seen so much in his lifetime: the tumultuous aftermath of World War II, the partitioning of Germany, the emergence of the Cold War, détente, the collapse of the Soviet Union and, as Bonner had often argued, the stagnation of European enlightenment and will.

Bonner was still watching closely, peering over the top of his reading glasses, when Jake's attention returned to the calamity at hand. "Ezra, I'm not making this up. I'm serious. I found the girl I saw at the Russian consulate, the one that gave the envelope to Vladimir Chernov. Her name is Anna Roman."

"And this woman lives in Bodega Bay? How did you find her?"

"Doesn't matter."

"But this is where you found a man dead, right?" Bonner questioned.

"Yes. I found him in her cottage. His hands were pegged to the kitchen table with steak knives, Ezra. Christ!" The older man grimaced but remained silent. Jake rattled ahead with his disjointed thoughts. "They garroted him and carved his chest up into this mass of bloody pulp. He was on the kitchen table! He's dead!"

"Who is he?"

"I don't know, not for sure. But I think he's Anna Roman's father, Mikhail Roman."

"I don't understand."

"I don't either! It's insane! But I saw it all. Then Anna showed up and saw it too."

"She saw her father dead?"

"Yes!"

"Jake, you're sure about this? All of it, I mean, it's not just something that you…"

"Made up?" Jake shouted. "Gimme a break, Ezra. I'm not insane! I was there. They almost killed me too! What don't you understand about that?"

"Okay, I believe you," Bonner advised. "Now you need to understand this. A man is dead in Bodega Bay. You found him, and then you ran away. You left a crime scene, Jake. I have to call the police."

"No!" Jake roiled. "No police!"

Bonner absorbed this then suddenly reached for the telephone. Jake lurched out of his chair and ripped the phone from Bonner's hand. He heaved it to the floor.

"I said, no!" Jake spat out.

The old man recoiled, strung by the voracity of Jake's bizarre outburst. He was frightened. Bonner laid his hands on his desk and leaned back in his chair, studying his young protégé with new concern. Jake knew he had over-reached. He slid back into his chair, and stared blankly at the table.

Bonner allowed the moment to pass, then stood slowly and slipped into the kitchen. He returned with hot tea, and poured two cups. They both drank.

Jake collected his thoughts and tried again, "Ezra, all I know is that a girl named Anna Roman went to see Chernov. I got photos of them together, and someone mugged Louis and me to get them back. When I found Anna in Bodega Bay, she lied about who she was, at first anyway. I found out where she lived, but when I got there, I found an old man dead. Then Anna showed up with a big-ass gun stuck in my face, and that's when all hell broke loose."

"There's more?" Bonner sputtered in disbelief.

"Yeah. When the girl pinned me down with her gun, someone outside opened fire. It was like a goddamn Fourth of July celebration. They sprayed bullets all over the place, tore the cottage apart."

"What about the girl, Anna?"

"She's gone -- again."

"Then we *have* to call the police, Jake."

"No! Look, it's all closing around me too fast. I already had a run-in with the local sheriff. The guy would love to hang this on me."

"How do you know that?"

"I know!" Jake shouted. "I don't trust him, or the San Francisco police either." He leaned closer to the desk. "Someone has been following me, Ezra."

"Who?

"I don't know, but I think he's a cop, or something like that." Jake hesitated then somberly announced, "Ezra, they're trying to kill me."

Bonner was stunned. He went silent as he considered Jake's outrageous proclamation. He couldn't help but wonder if Eleanor Hinklen had been right. Jake wasn't making good sense, and his postulations had become increasingly paranoid.

He asked, "Why would someone want to kill you?"

"I'm not sure. Maybe I saw too much, knew too much. Chernov has to know that I have copies of Eryn's research, all the stuff she sent me before they killed her."

"Jake…" Bonner countered. "Please. Listen to what you're saying."

"Ezra, don't shut me out!" Jake cried. "People are dead! I know what I saw. It all happened, just like I said. And then, when Anna took off after the fireworks at her cottage, I didn't know what to do. I was scared, so I ran."

"You realize that this will complicate things," Bonner advised.

Jake ignored the warning. He leaned heavily on the edge of the desk and almost whispered, "Ezra, what do you know about a hundred year-old woman named Marvina Dubrovsky?"

"Nothing. Who is she?"

"Actually, the question should be, who *was* she," Jake noted. "About a week ago, she was run over by a bus outside the Holy Mary Cathedral in San Francisco."

"That's a Russian orthodox church," Bonner observed.

"Exactly. Marvina Dubrovsky, who, I learned from the locals, had never been to the church before, but she went inside, confessed, then walked out and threw herself in front of a bus. She was from Bodega Bay and she knew Mikhail Roman. Probably Anna Roman too."

Bonner nodded silently. He stood up and paced across the room. His next words came more difficultly, "Jake, there was a high-ranking Russian archbishop visiting the Holy Mary Cathedral. The police found him dead. They think he was murdered, smothered by a couch pillow. It was all on the evening news."

"Ezra, I met the man!" Jake gushed.

"When?"

"I was there today, earlier. I wanted to find out more about Marvina Dubrovsky."

Bonner abruptly held up his hand. "Jake, I've heard enough. Don't you see how dangerous this is?"

Jake sensed subtext in Bonner's advisement, "It's because of Vladimir Chernov, isn't it? That's what you're telling me?"

"No. You can't jump to that conclusion."

"Two Russians are dead, and they both knew the same old woman who gave her confession then killed herself. You tell me Chernov's not involved!"

"It doesn't matter if he is or isn't," Bonner protested. "You're too caught up in this thing. You've lost your perspective. Can't you see that? Jake, let it go! Get out of it. Forget about your photograph of Anna Roman, and all the rest too. People are dead. I don't want you to be one of them."

Jake hesitated then threw a hard look at his mentor. "Vladimir Chernov refused to see me today."

"But you had an appointment. I pulled strings…"

"Well if he agreed to it earlier, something changed his mind," Jake snapped. "And I think that something was Marvina Dubrovsky." He pulled his coat around his shoulders and moved toward the door.

"Jake," Bonner called out. "Please. You have to take this to the police. This is not worth your life."

Jake lowered his head but did not turn back. "It wasn't worth Eryn's life either."

Bonner's face tightened. He could see the debilitating tentacles of paranoia curling around Jake and could only watch helplessly as he went out the door and disappeared into the rain-washed night.

Business was slow at Pablo's Perfect Pizza. The foul weather had kept normally ravenous Berkeley students sequestered in their dorms. Nick Rommel, the German-American proprietor, shoved his thinning blond hair back and checked his watch again. "Scheisse," he cursed, as he watched his three-person kitchen staff idly tossing dough balls at each other out of sheer boredom.

Jake had just pulled up directly in front of the pizza shop. The Porsche's engine was still rattling beneath the hood, while Jake stared blankly at Anna Roman's address, penned on his palm. He thought for a moment then killed the engine and climbed out stiffly. All he wanted to do was to take a shower and get some sleep, but before he could lock the car door, he noticed a man lingering in the shadows next to the building. He said nothing and seemed to be swaying slightly from side to side. Jake thought about running, but when Louis Ottly stepped out of the darkness, he gave a sigh of relief. "Louis. You look soaked."

Louis ignored Jake, wobbling closer to his precious car. He was drunk with gin and grief as he gawked with bleary-eyed remorse at the Porsche. It was covered with mud. Gravel nicks peppering the front hood. The engine, run to exhaustion, hissed and popped erratically. Louis laid his hand on the door. "You just wrote yourself out of my will, man. Look at this. Muck. Fuck. Aw, Jake, will you look at it."

Jake slumped down to sit on the stairway leading up to his apartment. He was too exhausted to argue.

Louis prattled indignantly as he ran his hand over the car, discovering one ding after another. "The guy gets his oil-can VW bug squashed, and good ole Louis hands over the keys to the goddess. No problem, says Jake. It'll only be a couple of hours. What the heck, I'll be back by five."

"I thought it was supposed to be five-thirty."

"It's eleven o'clock, man!"

"I'm a little late."

"You think this is funny? It's not. This is a serious breach of friendship. Aw, look -- tar. I don't get it. You really screwed me good." Louis steadied himself against the car and wagged an accusatory finger at Jake. "You're supposed to be a pal."

Jake knew it was time to grovel. "Louis, I'm really sorry."

"Keys," Louis snapped.

"Com'on."

"Gimme the keys."

Jake dug the keys from his pocket and Louis snagged them forcefully. Drunk and destroyed, Louis tumbled into the Porsche and tore away.

Jake climbed the rickety outside stairway and unlocked the door of his apartment. Inside, the message light on his desk phone was blinking. Jake didn't care. He was exhausted. The wafting smell of Pablo's Perfect Pizza sent pangs of hunger racking through his body, but he didn't have enough energy to climb back down the stairs for a carryout. Jake glanced at the phone again then tapped the message button. Katherine Sexton's voice was as edgy as ever, "Hey, Altman. I read the third section of your dissertation revision today. It's pretty shitty, full of your usual prosaic mewling. But the thing is, despite all the dreadful pandering, I kept seeing you in the narrative. Good ole Jake. My Jake. Actually, I kept seeing you naked in my bed. Call me. Tonight."

The invitation, such as it was, failed to rouse any lustful urgings. Sex with Katherine never failed to invigorate, but it was not going to happen tonight. Jake knew Katherine was using him, but in a sense, he was using her as well. He understood that their torrid affair would not smooth the way to approval of his dissertation annotations, but rather, the unabashed sexual encounters fed a more immediate need. He was lonely. Two years without Eryn had left him hollowed out and introspective. Katherine was there, eager, and outrageously uninhibited. If ever there was a friends-with-benefits relationship, he thought with a momentary chuckle.

Jake dragged into the kitchen and hauled a beer out of the refrigerator. He took a hard swig. It helped, but not a lot. He pulled off his shirt and was about to head for the shower when he heard the crappy music rolling up from the pizza patio directly below. The window was open, and this puzzled him, at least until he saw her in the shadows across the room. "I have a gun," Anna Roman hissed. He heard the pump action slam a shell into the chamber.

"How did you find me?" Jake asked carefully.

"CMMA. You gave your dinky Berkeley I.D. card to April when you were snooping around," she noted wearily.

Jake slumped down in a chair. "What do you want from me?"

Anna moved silently out of the shadows. She was rain-soaked, muddy, cut, and obviously terrified. Her eyes were fixed on Jake. She held the shotgun low but right on target. Anna dropped his card on a table. "Are you with them?" she asked quietly.

"With who?"

She shifted the gun higher. He could see that she was shivering and very pale. Even through the muck and cuts, Anna could not hide the fact that she was remarkably beautiful. Jake had absolutely no idea what she would do next. She was a pitiful sight, but he knew she was not to be messed with.

"Are you with them?" she asked again.

"I'm not with anybody."

"Don't lie to me. I'm sick of being lied to."

Jake stood up and stepped toward her. "Look, I know you're afraid."

"Stop -- there," Anna hissed. She steadied herself against the wall, barely able to hold the shotgun up. "I went to the sheriff, to Lawrence. He called the state police. Then they grilled me."

Jake cocked his head curiously. "If you told them what happened, they would have already come for me."

"I didn't tell them everything."

"Why not?"

Anna faltered, and Jake sensed that she wasn't sure herself. "I could have told them about you," she said.

"But you didn't. You don't believe I had anything to do with the murder."

"...maybe not, but you know a lot. You know about Mikhail, me, Chernov too."

Jake tried to redirect Anna. "What did you tell the police?"

"They asked questions. I told them what I saw. There wasn't anything else to say. I don't think Lawrence bought it, but he told the State cops to back off. He said he would take care of Mikhail -- his body." Anna's eyes seemed to sink wearily. Jake took a step toward her, but she jerked the gun up again. "Come any closer, and I'll shoot you."

"Jake regrouped. "I'm not what you think I am."

"You were there," Anna gnashed. "Mikhail is dead. I saw you. He didn't tell you what you wanted to know, and you killed him."

"No."

134

"You wanted him to tell you something. He warned me. Now it's my turn. You want me."

"No! I mean, yes, I want to talk to you," Jake offered. "That's all. Just talk. Look, I'm a researcher. I saw you at the consulate with Chernov -- with the envelope. I just wanted to know more."

"Why?'

"Put the gun down. I'm not going to hurt you."

Anna hesitated. The shotgun was heavy and she was tiring. She eased it lower, just slightly. "Why did you want to talk to me?"

"My dissertation. I've been on to Vladimir Chernov for two years, or really for a lifetime -- his. He's not a good guy."

"He's just an old diplomat."

"No. He's more. I can prove it."

Anna sank lower to sit on the arm of the couch. She swiped mud and water from her face. Jake watched her blink wearily. He knew he could probably take her, but he waited instead. "Chernov did not come to San Francisco just to retire," Jake said firmly.

"I wouldn't know. I don't care. Mikhail told me to take the note to him."

"You didn't look at it."

"No."

She began to shiver violently, barely able to stay upright. Jake was concerned. "You're cold," Jake said. "Let me get you a blanket."

"Mikhail told me to go to the consulate," Anna rambled absently. "Take the envelope, put it in his hand, and tell him…" She faltered, dazed and light-headed.

"Tell him what?" Jake probed. "What did you say?"

"Who are you?" she slurred. "I…why…No…."

Anna's large, searching eyes rose up and stared blankly at Jake. Her lips moved, but words would not come out. She keeled over sideways and collapsed. Jake broke her fall, but she still hit hard. Blood oozed from behind her head, as Jake lifted her limp body from the floor.

13

Consul General Vladimir Chernov preferred the solitude of darkness. He was alone in his study, seated comfortably in an ornate English chair. His tailored suit coat had been replaced by a generous Cardigan sweater. Spread out before him, on a small meeting table, were a number of meticulously kept coin collection sleeves. A table lamp cast an angular glow across Chernov's face, but the study was otherwise steeped in shadows.

Chernov removed a coin from a small envelope and studied it under a stationary magnifying class. It was silver, and the etchings were worn and tarnished. A slow piano concerto played softly somewhere in the background. Chernov paused, smiling slightly as the notes soared. His mind drifted to another time and place. Proud memories flooded back, wrapping warmly around the old man like a dense quilt. He turned the coin over in his hand, admiring its age and authenticity. It was Dutch, eighteenth century, a nice piece of modest value.

The door to the study opened, spilling light into the room. Chernov looked up, perhaps a bit put off by the sudden intrusion, to see Anton Sorokin standing attentively in the doorway. The aide's generally jocular temperament was restrained now as he gestured apologetically, "I am sorry, sir. But you asked that I tell you when they had arrived."

Chernov glanced out the broad bay window, taking in the rivulets of water meandering down the glass. "Show them in, Anton. And please remain with us."

"Thank you, sir."

Anton disappeared for a moment then returned leading the two loutish security agents, Oleg and Remi, into the room. Chernov did not get up, and the two thugs knew better than to take a seat. Anton shuffled aside but remained in the room, watching nervously.

Oleg and Remi were uncomfortable with the splendor of their surroundings. Remi, the prickly Brit, remembered his cap, and swept it off his blockish, bald head.

Moments passed as Chernov carefully noted the coin's inscription in a ledger. His eyes never left his work, even when he finally spoke. "Tell me about the archbishop."

Oleg and Remi exchanged cautionary glances. "I'm not sure what you mean, sir," Remi offered.

"Popov Konstantin was a comrade, a special emissary from the Cathedral of Christ the Savior in Moscow. The newspaper accounts posited that he may have been murdered, suffocated. How could this be?"

Oleg's thick mind struggled for a reply. "The police investigated. They're not sure. They think he might simply have died."

"He was a fat man," Remi sneered. "Fat men have heart attacks."

Chernov looked up from his work, allowing a smug smile to ease across his face. "Yes, I suppose they do, but the newspaper accounts point to an unexplainable death, possibly murder."

Anton shifted his stubby legs nervously. His eyes darted from Chernov to the two malefactors. Moments of excruciating silence followed, punctuated only by soft music and rain tapping against the window.

"Tell me about Mikhail Roman," Chernov said evenly as he returned to his coins. "The old man in Bodega Bay. From the news, I learn that he was murdered most brutally; something distasteful about torture and steak knives."

Remi hesitated then gestured with his soiled cap. "I read about it too. Bad shit. I mean, excuse me."

"What do the police do about such atrocities?" Chernov probed.

"They dunno anything," Oleg shrugged. He felt the need to elaborate. "They think it was probably robbers, maybe addicts looking for money and fun."

"Fun?" Chernov noted. "This man's chest was eviscerated and a wire around his neck had slit his throat."

No one spoke. Anton Sorokin seemed faint; it was all too graphic. Oleg and Remi glumly stared at their feet. Finally, Chernov swung his magnifying glass aside and leveled a penetrating gaze on the two thugs. "My arrival in this country presents an opportunity to promote trust between two very powerful nations. Trust is important. That there has been extended news coverage of two recent and very unfortunate *incidents* within the local Russian-American community is of obvious concern to me. People ask questions, and questions do not coexist well with my goal of fostering good will." He paused for a moment then added with great forbearance. "Scabrous events, however they may have occurred, must not in any way detract from my endeavors. Do we understand each other?"

Anton Sorokin watched nervously as the two thugs absorbed the pointed directive. They nodded silent acquiescence and Anton led them out.

A wet, impenetrable shroud still hung heavily over the glowing San Francisco skyline. There was an odd stillness in the night air; it was breathless, almost menacing. Jake Altman, wearily leaning against his kitchen counter, poured a fresh cup of coffee and raked his hair back. He sipped the hot brew but didn't really register the taste; his mind was elsewhere, lost in a surge of conflicting thoughts. He was confused and admittedly concerned about the pain and destruction that seemed to be enveloping him. The fervor with which he had taken up Eryn's crusade seemed clouded now. Had he pressed too hard, he thought. Had he overreached by unearthing and highlighting the enigma of Vladimir Chernov's sudden appearance in the city? He was certain that Chernov was somehow complicit in the deaths of Mikhail Roman, Marvina Dubrovsky, and quite possibly the corpulent archbishop at the Holy Mary Cathedral. But to what end? What was Chernov looking for? What could possibly make it worth the lives of three people?

Amid the tumult of his thoughts, Jake reached back to hold Eryn close, remembering what had been between them and what they dreamed of doing together. Somehow, she was a port in the storm. Even Eryn's death had not dimmed their intractable love.

Jake, coffee cup in hand, padded down the short hallway then pulled up short when he saw that Anna was awake, looking fearfully at him from beneath the covers of his bed. She glanced quickly at the shotgun, leaning in the corner then allowed her eyes to shift to a chair, where her clothes hung neatly over the back. She looked at the covers and her bare arms.

Jake interceded. "You were soaked, half frozen. You were shaking."

Anna pulled her thoughts together, her eyes locked on him now. "You took my clothes off?"

"Yes. Sorry about that."

"No, you're not. Did you get a good look?"

"I didn't look."

"Liar."

"Okay, so looked, just a little. You would have done the same if it was me."

Anna went silent and turned away. Jake pulled a chair closer and sat. He said, "...back in Bodega Bay, why did you run from me? Why are you here?"

When Anna looked back to face him, he could see tears in the corners of her eyes. He also saw fear and abject distrust. "Tell me, Anna. Please," Jake said softly.

"Mikhail is dead," she muttered blankly. "What they did to him, it was so awful. I couldn't comprehend it. So, I ran and I hid. Then I walked to a friend's house,"

"Sheriff Jackson?"

"Yes. He called the state police, and then we went back." She looked up, bewildered and lost. "Mikhail -- he was..." Anna sucked in a quick gasp. "They said it was a robbery -- someone looking for drugs or money. They asked me questions me for two hours, but I couldn't tell them anything."

"And then you came here?"

"No. Another man came to see me first. He was with the FBI or CIA I think. I really don't remember."

"What did he want?"

"He showed me a badge and asked more questions." Anna's eyes fell hard on Jake again. "He asked me if I knew you."

"Me!"

Anna nodded tiredly. She was slipping again and was barely audible, "...that's why I came here. You..."

Anna was desolate; her eyes fluttered and sank shut. Jake tried once more. "You gave a note to Chernov, and you said you didn't read it. I still don't believe that."

Anna's voice was empty, echoing from some distant realm, "Mikhail told me to take the note -- take it to Chernov..."

Jake reached for her arm. It was warm and smooth. "There's got to be more. Tell me."

Anna's eyes broke open but only briefly. They were beautiful eyes, indescribably blue, but they were distant now, haunted by a terrible secret. Then she was gone, asleep. Jake held her arm gently; he could not take his eyes off of her.

Morning sunlight spread slowly across Jake's face as he slept soundly, quilt-covered in an overstuffed chair next to his bed. Anna was gone. The window beside him was cracked open, and a cool breeze gently inflated Walgreens' snap-in curtains. It was too early for Pablo's Pizza crew to show up, though the sweet, breaded scent still floated faintly in the air.

Anna Roman peered around the hall corner. She was more or less dressed now, moving silently on her bare feet, as she inched toward the front door. Anna was about to reach for the doorknob when it clicked slightly, turning first one way, then the other. She froze. There was another click, and then another. She could see a shadow beneath the door as she backtracked carefully. Her eyes desperately searched the tiny apartment for a way out. The door clicked again.

Jake was dead to the world. He slept deeply, peacefully, with dreams as blank as cloudless sky. Exhaustion, both physical and mental, had cascaded over him, leaving his senses dulled and unfocused. That changed in an instant, when he heard the sharp snap of a shell being chambered into a gun. Jake's eyes jerked open. He was staring into the large bore of Anna's shotgun.

As the rest of the room came into focus, Jake could see the man behind the gun. Dennis Luger looked a lot like he did when Jake had confronted him at the cathedral. There was nothing striking about his physique; he was only average in height and build, but his eyes were dark and darting, peering out at him from beneath his thick, boyish hair. Luger was wearing the same tweed sport coat, and he was smiling. "My, but what a big gun we have," he chided playfully. Jake's eyes flashed across the room and saw that the bed was empty. "She's gone," Luger noted. "She gave us the slip. Tricky little treat, hmm?"

Jake watched as the shotgun barrel drifted from side to side, inches from his face. "Who are you?" he said.

Luger grinned, "Well, for starters, I'm not a regular bells-and-smells worshiper at the Holy Mary Cathedral. Da? That means, I speak Russian, just a little."

"It was enough," Jake observed. "You fooled me."

"Yeah? You really shouldn't have been so quick to give me a pass."

Not more than ten feet away, Anna Roman hid in an ironing board cabinet so impossibly narrow that no one would have thought to look there. She could see Luger, but not Jake, through a slit of light.

Jake inched upright in the chair, lowering his feet to the ground. "What do you want?" he asked more pointedly.

"You. The girl. The truth. I want it all." Luger dragged a hardback chair closer, placing it directly in front of Jake. He lowered the shotgun and laid it crosswise on the floor, equal-distant between them. Luger could see Jake looking at the gun. "That really wouldn't be a smart idea, would it?"

"Probably not."

Luger could see that Jake was still looking at the gun. "Of course, you might get lucky."

Jake's eyes shifted from the gun to Luger, but he didn't move.

Luger stretched and took a deep breath. "All right, let's start with names. You are Jake Altman, untenured political science professor at Berkeley. You are thirty-one years old, a decent runner and author of all sorts of inflammatory political conspiracy theories. You live alone. You enjoy sex with a department head at your school but manage to hide your affair from the university stiffs. You live on top of a pizza parlor, though we're not exactly sure why."

"That's more than a name."

"I'm not finished," Luger said, lifting a cautioning finger. "You have no brothers or sisters. You're a non-smoker and proficient social drinker, and you're reported to be infatuated by kangaroos."

"What?"

"Okay, so I made that one up. And, well, let's see -- both parents are dead." He cocked head oddly. "But then, so is your fiancée, Eryn O'Shea."

Jake's face tightened.

From her narrow closet perch, Anna took this in. She was more perplexed than ever.

Jake scowled at Luger. "Who are you?" he demanded.

"Oh, my turn? Well, I suppose so. My name is Dennis Luger." There was nothing else. Luger went completely silent.

"That's it," Jake noted, more as a statement than a question.

"Doesn't really matter, does it?"

"It does to me."

"What matters, Jake, is that we're friends. That's important for you to know, because that's how we feel about it."

"Who is *we*?"

Luger allowed a slight smile. "I work for the government."

"Who's government?"

"Ah, you're asking if I'm a *bad* character?"

"Something like that."

Luger beamed then let out an unrestrained laugh. He had a broad, toothy smile, maybe some restorative work in there, Jake thought. He was still waiting for an answer, but Luger just shifted his chair closer. "You were with a young woman last night. Anna Roman. We want to talk to her -- and to you. So, let's drop the horse shit get something done here. We're on the same side, for Christ sake."

"Look, I don't know you," Jake protested. "You break in here, shove a gun at me, and act like some sort of CIA spook."

"I didn't say I worked for the CIA."

"I haven't seen squat for identification!" Jake asserted.

Luger paused then slipped several photos from his sport coat and held them out. In the first picture, Jake is perfectly framed at the center of two crosshairs, probably from a telephoto gun sight. He is pulling Anna's blouse off. In the second photo, Jake has Anna, naked, in his arms, laying her in his bed. Out of context, the photos are extremely erotic.

"I'm not playing games, Jake," Luger noted. "The girl, she came and she stayed. Did she tell you about the Baikal?"

"The Baikal?"

"Don't play stupid. It offends me."

"You got the wrong guy."

Luger's hand lashed out, slapping Jake hard on the cheek. Jake instinctively lurched toward Luger but another warning finger stopped him. "Don't. Don't even think about it, Jake." Luger stood up abruptly and began to pace. Jake's eyes snapped to the shotgun on the floor, but then he saw the sleek Glock in Luger's hand.

Luger seemed frustrated. The words came faster now. "This is important, so pay attention. I want straight answers. Why have you been stalking Vladimir Chernov?"

"He's a Russian diplomat. I study political science."

"And you just happened to pick Chernov? Why not some lousy middle-east dictator or sub-Saharan king with thirty wives? You could have picked on someone else."

"I prefer Russians."

"Why?"

"They wear funny hats."

Luger moved menacingly toward him, but Jake held up a consolatory hand. "Look, I don't have to...."

Luger cut him off quickly. "Why the Russian? Chernov?"

"I told you. It's what I do. So what?"

"So, you're a bit of a history buff too, aren't you? Is that why you are in this?"

Jake didn't respond, but his eyes widened when he saw a cabinet door slip open slightly across the room. Anna was wedged inside. She couldn't get the door closed again.

"Are you working with the girl?" Luger probed.

Again, there was nothing from Jake. Luger lurched over, shoving his face inches from Jake's. "You are expendable, Jake Altman. Do you understand the term? Expendable. That's a lousy place for you to be right now."

Jake absorbed this then suddenly sat back. "You don't know anything, do you? You're fishing. Anna and I don't fit your narrative; we don't make sense, do we?"

Luger paused, loosening his tie. He sat down again, his dark eyes boring into Jake. "All right. You're a no-nonsense guy. Tell you what. Let's swap stories," he began. "Vladimir Chernov didn't come to San Francisco to drink champagne or pick up choir boys. The man is on a mission."

"No shit," Jake scoffed.

Luger thought for a long moment then nodded with a smirk. "Your poster boy wants out. Chernov has tossed in the towel with the Ruskies. He's quitting."

Jake was incredulous. "Nobody *quits* Russia."

"He's coming across. He's defecting."

"Bullshit!"

Luger watched Jake closely. "You didn't know that, did you? You really didn't know."

"I don't believe you, if that's what you mean," Jake spat back at him.

"Okay, this is good. We're making progress here. You didn't have a clue that Chernov wants out. I'll buy that. So, what is it with you? What makes your clock tick?"

Jake didn't say anything. Luger's face tightened. He holstered his handgun under his coat and slowly lifted the shotgun from the floor, aiming it squarely at Jake's face. Instead of firing, he suddenly jerked hard on the gunstock, quickly ejecting five shells, the entire load. Luger dropped the gun on the floor then stood up and moved for the door.

Jake called out to him. "That's it?"

"No Dr. Altman. I'm afraid there's more, and it's not going to be pretty. I want you to think about the situation we have here. It's a bit involved, extremely dangerous too.

You can run the bases on your own if you like, but you'll be dead before you tag second. Or, you can play ball with us. We're actually not very nice either, but the odds of surviving are a heck of a lot better on our team."

Luger disappeared into the hall, closing the door behind him. Moments ticked by as Jake listened to the intruder's footsteps clumping down the stairs. Finally, there was silence. The ironing board cabinet door swung open. Anna just looked at Jake.

"Do you want to explain that?" Jake asked.

"I don't know what that man was talking about," Anna quipped as she stiffly pulled herself out of the cabinet. "I don't know anything."

"What is the Baikal?"

"I don't know."

"I don't believe you."

"And I can't tell you how sorry I am about that," Anna snapped.

"If Chernov is trying to defect, like Luger said, then the CIA or whoever the hell he works for will pull out all the stops. Chernov would be a prize catch."

Anna was unimpressed, "He doesn't mean anything to me."

"Well he meant something to your father. Was Mikhail his go-between with the American CIA spooks? Was he working for the government? Why?"

Anna turned quickly toward the door, but Jake grabbed her, blocking her exit. "You're not walking away from this thing."

She jerked free from his grip. "Actually, I'm not walking anywhere, I'm *running* away. My father is dead! I don't know why. They pegged his hands to a table and butchered him! Who would do something like that? It's just pathetic. Mikhail was very strong. He wouldn't have given in easily. So, they tortured him."

Jake let this sink in. "That's why I don't think he told them what they wanted to know."

"I don't care! Do you get that? Mikhail is dead. He's all I had, all I cared about, and he's *gone!*"

Anna was weeping now. Jake released his grip on her wrists, and she sank down to the floor. He slid tiredly down the wall to sit beside her. Neither spoke for a long time.

Finally, Jake whispered softly to her. "Anna, listen to me. Please. Chernov isn't going to stop. I don't know why, but he wants you dead."

"You don't know that."

"It's a reasonable assumption. His goons almost killed you at Mikhail's cottage."

Anna wiped her nose on her sleeve and offered a vacant smile. "They didn't want me dead."

"I wouldn't be so sure of that."

"I am."

"Why?"

Anna turned her sharp eyes on him. "Whoever it was at Mikhail's cottage, they knew you were in there."

"Okay, so they knew I was there. So were you."

"They didn't know that. I came in through the back way. No car."

Jake started to protest, but then it hit him. She was right. There was no way the shooters could have known Anna was in the cottage. *He* was the target, not her. The logic of the assumption was simple, but the reality was bone chilling.

Jake fell silent again. Anna sensed his deep introspection. She quietly asked him, "That man, Luger; he said you had a fiancée. He said she died."

Jake took a few minutes to piece his thoughts together. "There was a girl, Eryn," he began. "We were going to be married."

"Yeah, I got that already."

Jake face was drained. He was slipping away to another time and place. "We'd been engaged for three months, but the wedding had to wait until she finished a fellowship in Moscow. Six more months. It was all set, but she never came back. They killed her."

"I don't understand," Anna said softly.

"Eryn was studying Chernov. He was her doctoral topic, three-years-worth of work. She knew everything about him, every seamy deal, every murder committed on his order, every lie and every dreg of espionage and subterfuge."

"What happened to her?"

"They drowned her in the Moskva River. Of course, the official investigation said it was an accident, but it wasn't. By the time I got to Moscow, to her apartment, it had been stripped clean. Her computer, papers, cell phone and photo file, all of them gone."

"I'm sorry, Jake," Anna allowed softly.

He looked up and offered an anemic smile. "But the thing is, Eryn wrote me letters, every day, long letters. She told me everything she had found out about Chernov. All of it, it's all there in the letters. When I told the State Department, they didn't want to see them. They blew me off. So, there I was with nothing. Eryn was dead, gone. And there wasn't a damn thing I could do about it."

Anna had listened to every word Jake said, and in some small measure, it had moved her. She still could not bring herself to trust him, but his admission seemed genuine; his pain was palpable. Anna thought about Mikhail again, what he had asked her to do, and the unspeakable chain of events that followed, and then she understood. "Jake," she said. "That's it then. If Chernov is as dangerous as you think he is, then you need to let go of Eryn; let it all go."

Jake's head sagged. Anna could see the tears on his cheeks.

Jake's voice seemed tired and doleful now. "I can't let go. I tried, and then I tried some more." He looked up at Anna. "I can't forget what Chernov did to Eryn, not any more than you can forget what he did to Mikhail."

Anna understood. She knew he was right. Even more importantly, she was certain now that Jake was inexplicably part of her expanding dilemma. She closed her eyes and laid her head back against the wall.

14

Katherine Sexton always saved her swim workout for the evening. She preferred the Hearst Sports Complex' outdoor pool. While it was somewhat less fashionable than the newly built indoor Spieker pool, it offered a spectacular view of the hills surrounding Berkeley. More importantly for Katherine, the facility was also home to a regular clientele of hyper-buff male graduate students and health conscious faculty. They were serious swimmers, but even the most dedicated were often stupefied when confronted by Katherine's simmering sexuality. She was amused and aroused by the poorly concealed glances, peeks over fogged goggles, and involuntary head-turns. She was an exhibitionist. Her penchant for revealing swimsuits, always undersized and leaving little to the imagination, was more than enough to captivate the lustful attention of the testosterone-charged male herd circling her like blood-crazed sharks. None of her gaping young admirers would have guessed she was nearly forty-years-old, nor would they have cared. She exuded a raw sexuality that was alluring as well as compelling, and while her dalliances were most often brief and unrepeated, they were always explicitly intense exercises, balancing perilously on the edge of pleasure and pain. It was all a game to Katherine. She usually won.

Katherine sliced cleanly through the water, touching the end of the lane. She tossed her hair back and raised her goggles. At first, she didn't notice the man moving closer on the deck of the pool, but when she looked up, she was surprised to see Dr. Ezra Bonner peering down. Katherine offered her department co-chair a smoldering greeting, "Ezra, what a treat."

Bonner looked out over the water and sea of churning bodies. "You know, I used to do this a lot."

"You were a swimmer?"

"No. Not at all. But we seemed to regularly congregate around fire hydrants when we were kids. The fire department appeared most any day it was over ninety. They opened the hydrants and let the water spray. There must have been about a thousand black kids going crazy in the gutter."

"Maybe you should try a real pool," Katherine flirted as she flicked water in his direction.

Bonner smiled slightly then sat on the end of a bleacher nearby. He removed his tam and scratched his graying temple contemplatively. He wasn't one to beat around the bush. "Katherine, tell me about your sex games with Jake Altman. It's true, isn't it?"

"...and I thought you were here for an evening swim, Ezra."

"I'll take that as a yes."

"You may take it however you like."

"What do you want from him?"

Katherine grinned again. "I think you may have that turned around."

Now, even Ezra chuckled. "Yes, I can see how he might find you attractive. The sex, I assume, is good?"

"Sex is always good."

"What do you talk about, Katherine, you and Jake?"

"Uhm, let's see. Oh, now I remember," she chirped coyly. "There isn't much talk, Ezra. We sort of bypass all that noise."

"You know that he's still disconsolate about the loss of his fiancée."

"It's a reasonable, even predictable, reaction. What's your point?"

"Jake has a lot on his plate right now. The sex thing with you only complicates matters."

"We try hard to keep it simple, Ezra."

Bonner was tiring of the banter. He leveled hard eyes on her. "I think Jake has become involved with people he shouldn't be engaged with."

"Present company excluded?"

"Knock it off, Katherine. I have little interest in your salacious sex games. I do care about Jake, however. And I just can't help but question if the thing between the two of you might be a bit more involved than a spirited exchange of bodily fluids."

"Meaning?"

"I will ask you again. What do you want from him?"

"Nothing, Ezra. I already get exactly what I want from Jake."

"What about Vladimir Chernov? Do you find Jake's obsession with an aging Russian diplomat to be a distraction, or perhaps you might even find it *helpful*."

"I don't know what you're talking about."

"I think you do."

"Jake Altman is a bore," Katherine confided. "His life is consumed by a decrepit Russian diplomat he really knows nothing about. It's pathetic. Do I find Jake's insights useful? Hardly. Do I do find him to be -- stimulating? Yes, in ways that might be difficult for you to appreciate."

Bonner rose slowly to his feet. "I don't think your motives are as transparent as you present them to be." He stepped closer to the edge of the pool but said nothing as he looked down at Katherine. Water lapped temptingly around her breasts, and her smirk turned sour as she felt his eyes boring into her.

"Do you like what you see, Ezra? Do you like the view from up there?"

"I've already seen what I wanted to see, Katherine. I should have accepted it before, but for some regrettable reason, I held you in higher regard."

Northwestern Siberia was a forbidding expanse of tundra, permafrost, and fir forests. Uninhabited, it was windswept, inhospitable, and unfathomably dangerous. An azure sky arched endlessly overhead; it was a frigid blue expanse, punctuated by sheer cirrus clouds, streaked and torn by racing stratospheric winds. An eagle soared high overhead, slipping effortlessly upward on a faint thermal. Moscow was four thousand miles away. The nearest rail line was two thousand miles away. There were no roads whatsoever.

A Kamchatka grizzly bear sat heavily in a small clearing at the base of a stubby tree, slowly scratching its massive back across the trunk. It was hungry too, as it tore berries off a tangled bush and devoured the sweet treats with gluttonous bliss. The Kamchatka was a distant relative of the Alaskan Kodiak bear, but it was larger and meaner.

Almost exactly one hundred yards away on an expanse of scrub-dotted tundra, the wind tittered relentlessly through the prickly branches of low hemlock and juniper saplings. Stunted by the cold winds, the trees were squat and gnarled, most resembling a scattering of gnome-like terrestrial creatures. There was nothing else but the wind and the sky, at least until a tiny LED light flashed somewhere deep inside a nest of scruffy branches. There was no sound, just a LED light, blinking, repeating. But then the sapling moved, just slightly, as if uprooted from the bleak soil, it inched sideways several yards until it was next to another clump of hemlock-green.

A man's voice, young and very Russian, whispered softly from the foliage. "Sir, I have the sky-link." His eyes could be seen now; he was completely hidden amid the branches, tentative, even afraid.

The adjoining bush shuddered slightly as a hand and bare arm slid out to receive a small microphone from the whispering bush. The young communications officer, carefully peeled back a branch and called out softly again. "It is Vladimir Chernov in San Francisco -- in his car with Remi and Oleg; Anton Sorokin is driving."

The microphone disappeared into the bushy tree. A gruff voice hissed from the undergrowth. "Da. Vladimir. So, we speak now."

Ten thousand miles away, Vladimir Chernov sat comfortably in the back seat of his black, tinted-window limousine. Remi and Oleg were deposited in the jump seats facing him. Anton was at the wheel, squinting through his thick glasses, terror-stricken by the tumultuous center-city traffic. He jerked the steering wheel one way, then the other. Chernov cursed him once as he grabbed for an armrest. He shoved the phone back to Remi and tagged the speaker button. "Mr. President," he offered deferentially. "Thank you for speaking with me. This is generous of you."

Inside the Siberian bush, Dmitri Bellus, president of the Russian Federation, had one eye glued to the scope of his Mosin-Nagant M-91 hunting rifle. Bellus knew there were more expensive European guns, but he preferred traditional Russian equipment. Loaded with a two-hundred grain SP plug, the Mosin-Nagant was capable of bringing down just about anything short of Godzilla.

Bellus lay motionless in the thick bush. Across the rubble-strewn field, the Kamchatka grizzly was squarely framed in his scope's crosshairs. "Comrade Chernov," Bellus calmly began. "Are we secure? Security is important, especially in America. Are Remi and Oleg listening?"

"Yes, they are in the car with me, as you instructed," Chernov replied from the other side of the world.

"Good. And what of Anton? I'm not sure he is entirely comfortable with his new arrangement."

"Anton is fine, Mr. President. He is here, driving us back to the consulate, but I'm afraid he has lost his way, again."

Bellus chuckled under his breath, "Tell me, Comrade Chernov, are you enjoying the fine aspects of San Francisco? Good wine, rich food, and perhaps a lithesome, willing American woman?"

Chernov shifted in the plush car seat. "My posting is going very well, Mr. President. I feel that affairs here are in order and manageable. We are making progress."

"I understand that there have been unexpected developments -- discontinuities," Bellus noted as he adjusted the range setting on his rifle. "An old Russian woman at a church, I understand she threw herself in front of a city bus not far from the consulate."

"That is correct. It was most unfortunate."

"One wonders what makes people do what they do."

Chernov hesitated, measuring Bellus' comment. "This is true."

Bellus nodded to himself and picked an errant branch away from his face. "This woman's death in-of-itself may not be noteworthy to our efforts, but I now I learn that Archbishop Popov Konstantin has been murdered."

"This I have heard about as well," replied Chernov cautiously.

Bellus steadied his arm beneath the rifle. "Unfortunate."

"Yes. He was a revered archbishop, Mr. President. It is most distressing."

"Konstantin was an old fool. He was a corpulent pig."

Chernov fumbled to reach the telephone receiver, but another errant steering movement by Anton sent him sliding against the door. "Should we go off the speaker phone, Mr. President?" Chernov stammered warily.

"Actually," Bellus began calmly. "Oleg and Remi have a very high security clearance, comrade Chernov, and while it is true that Anton may be a poor driver with an even poorer sense of direction, he understands the importance and consequences of security. Isn't that right, Anton?"

The meek aide cleared his throat and coughed out a response. "All is well here, Mr. President. Quiet. The dead sleep with the dead."

Bellus laughed as his cheek settled into the gunstock. "There, Comrade Chernov. Your driver, our friend Aton Sorokin, is ever vigilant. He can be trusted in his discretion about our affairs in America."

"The American authorities are asking questions about the two deaths," cautioned Chernov. "First, the old woman and now Konstantin. I must also inform you that a Russian man, who was very close to the old woman, has been murdered in Bodega Bay. He was old too, but the authorities feel that the coincidence is -- unusual."

"Is this inconvenient for our plans?" Bellus interjected rather pointedly.

Chernov hesitated. "No. Not at all, sir."

"That is good. Very good." Bellus settled in more tightly behind his gun. The smooth walnut stock was cool against his cheek, and the barrel did not waver. Without losing focus of his quarry, he spoke to Chernov again, softly. "Are you being treated well, comrade?

"Yes, yes. The Americans have been quite hospitable. I am actually quite taken by the city."

"I have heard this too."

Chernov did not respond, though he couldn't help but sense something duplicitous in Bellus' comment.

Deep in the shadows of the limousine, Oleg and Remi exchanged glances as they listened to the conversation. Anton Sorokin could hear too, though he was concentrating hard on his driving and the fractious traffic that swirled around the car.

Bellus was still watching the bear as he smoothly chambered a shell into the rifle breech.

At his end of the conversation, Chernov leaned closer to the speaker. "Would it be prudent to ask our people in Moscow to make inquiries regarding the deaths in our community? Perhaps they could evaluate the impact on our plans. They might be able to tell us something that we should know about."

Bellus' face suddenly went cold when he saw the grizzly twist its enormous head around, sniffing the wind, searching the bleak landscape. "He knows we are here," Bellus whispered.

"Sir?" Chernov replied.

"The bear. It is time." Bellus had only a few seconds to react before the bear lunged to its feet and spun toward him. Without warning, it charged, and absolutely nothing stood in its way. Rocks sprayed in the air, hemlocks trees were uprooted. Birds scattered. The bear was careening toward Bellus with no fear or hesitation. Bellus heaved the satellite transmitter aside and bolted upright, standing resolutely with branches of his camouflage falling away. His rifle instinctively jerked against his shoulder. He fired, but the bear didn't slow.

The camouflaged young soldier carrying the radio stumbled to his feet, slipped and fell again. His eyes gaped wide with fear, as the bear loomed closer. "Derr'mo!" he exclaimed, stumbling backward in abject terror. Several other camouflaged soldiers leaped up too. It was as if the landscape of gnome-trees had suddenly come alive. Several men ran. Others were too afraid to move.

Bellus leaned fully into his gun then marched forward, directly toward the enraged bear. He fired, chambered and fired again. The bear was only a hundred feet away. It roared with defiance and pain. Bellus roared back, stalking forcefully forward. Firing, again and again.

The bear lunged over a rotten log then collapsed, tumbling and gouging through the brush, sliding to a stop ten feet away from Bellus, dead. The Russian president sucked in great gulps of air, his chest heaving beneath his thick hunting vest. For just a moment, he eyed the dead bear. Then he spun on his boots and marched back past the stunned aide, who lay collapsed on a pile of rocks. Bellus looked disdainfully down at him, sniffing the wind. "Derr'mo," he hissed then moved on.

A nearby, brush-enshrined soldier elbowed his companion, gesturing toward the fallen radioman. "Derr'mo," he repeated, and then in rough English he announced, "He *shit* his pants."

Far away in the Emerald City by the bay, Vladimir Chernov waited for President Bellus to respond, but there was only the faint crackle of static.

15

Anton Sorokin eased the big limo into the consulate drive. It was a narrow entryway between the two stone columns, and he was able to navigate the passage with nothing more than the sound of bushes scraping along the side of the car. Vladimir Chernov reached for the door, even before the car had stopped. He climbed out into the damp night air. Oleg and Remi spilled out behind him.

Chernov was still replaying his conversation with President Dmitri Bellus as he paced quickly toward the consulate entrance. At first, he didn't see the man step out of a deep shadow.

"I think we need to talk," Jake Altman advised.

Sleek nine-millimeter handguns instantly appeared in Oleg's and Remi's fists.

"You are trespassing," Chernov growled. He turned away.

Jake hesitated then took a step forward and called out, "We should talk about the Baikal. The girl too, the one with the note."

Oleg's handgun jerked up, aimed squarely at Jake.

Chernov waved his hand dismissively, truncating any messy gunplay. For just a moment, the stillness of the night lay oppressively over the four men. Finally, Chernov cast a wary look in a broad circle, taking in the rows of cars parked on the street. Anna's Blazer was parked in plain view under a streetlight.

Jake gathered his courage and spoke firmly. "I'm Jake Altman."

"I know who you are, Dr. Altman."

"Is there a reason you refused to see me the other day, even after Ezra Bonner cleared it?"

Chernov's eyes continued to search the darkness. His voice was quite low. "You came alone, Dr. Altman?"

"Do you mean, where's Anna Roman?"

Chernov said nothing.

"Anna," Jake continued, "You know, the woman who gave you a note when you arrived at the consulate. Her name is Anna Roman, but you already know that."

"I think not."

"I'm alone, Mr. Chernov, and Anna is in a safe place."

Chernov threw Jake a quizzical glance. He barked at his bodyguards, "Bring him into the library." And then he was gone, disappearing in a wash of cold fog. Oleg holstered his gun. Remi did as well, but he kept one hand on the stock inside his jacket. He motioned for Jake to go inside.

Jake stood alone in the spacious consulate library. He gazed at a floor-to-ceiling mirror, sensing faces staring back. No doubt, it was one-way glass, he thought. Moments passed, as Jake moved along the wall, absorbing a display of historic photographs: diplomacy at its grandest, pomp, ceremony, all providing a seamless accounting from early Russian aristocracy to the Revolution, the Soviet years, and then onward to the new Russian Federation. Jake's face tightened when he saw Chernov in a ceremonial photo.

The library doors abruptly swung open. Vladmir Chernov entered silently. His aide, Anton Sorokin, followed dutifully. Jake remained motionless, his eyes never leaving the austere Russian statesman. He found himself suddenly tense with a toxic mix of disdain and vengeful animosity; he was finally standing face to face with the man that had orchestrated his fiancée's murder.

Chernov glided across a thick oriental rug. He was taller than Jake had remembered, a slender man who easily carried the mantle of a serious and intelligent diplomat. Chernov stopped beside a Victorian armchair, and when he rested his long fingers comfortably on the embroidered fabric, Jake was surprised by how youthful his hand appeared. There were no age spots or signs of arthritis. Jake noted the ring on Chernov's finger too. It was smallish gold coin, set plainly, a Russian ruble turned down somewhat in circumference.

Chernov did not seem the least bit uncomfortable with silence. His gaze revealed nothing, no hint of what the man was thinking. Jake took several steps forward, squaring himself in front of the resplendent Russian. He felt it best to let Chernov make the first move, and finally, the old man spoke. "Would you like something to drink, Dr. Altman?"

"No."

Chernov nodded and Anton slipped away. Jake felt Chernov's eyes land on him again. "Dr. Ezra Bonner told our people about you. He mentioned your interest in

Russian political history, about my history in particular. I understand you are writing a book about me."

"Actually, it's a doctoral dissertation."

Chernov smiled slightly. "Perhaps I should be flattered."

"Not if you read it."

Chernov only stared back blankly. His smile had disappeared. "You know very little about me."

"I know that your family dates back to the last Imperial Age, even before the Romanovs."

"You purport to be a scholar of Russian history, Dr. Altman, and yet you provide me with facts that can be found in the first paragraphs of Wikipedia. I am not impressed."

"All right." Jake began again with a quickening pace. "You were sent to military boarding school at the age of nine. The Second Saint Petersburg Gymnasium; it's still highly selective. There you excelled at sports, horsemanship in particular. I believe your first horse was named Standard."

Chernov waved his had dismissively. "Work of a high school student…"

Jake interrupted him, quickly spewing out information. "Your second horse was Caliber, followed sequentially by Charlotte, named for your niece who was blind in her right eye, then Rotan, your favorite." Jake's eyes were flaring now. "The limp you now compensate for so well was caused by a fight in high school at the N.G. Kuznetsov Military Academy. It was a knife wound just below your left knee. You killed the other student, Serge Brezhnev."

"An accident," Chernov interrupted.

Jake would not relent. "Okay, well you broke his neck. He was a mean-spirited boy, son of an infamous Russian submarine captain, Leopold Brezhnev, who swore vengeance on you, at least until you killed him too in an illegal duel. Matched, rim-fire Carboline pistols. Very aristocratic, very accurate. Your weapon misfired, but his shot only grazed your cheek. You calmly reloaded as he begged for his life, and then you shot him dead. "

Jake detected a faint smirk on the old man's face. "That was not a mistake."

Jake bore in. "Is that why you took Brezhnev's sixteen-year-old daughter from her father's funeral in Vladivostok? It was at the National Naval cemetery, gravesite number six-twenty-three. The girl became your concubine and the mother of your only child who died of tuberculosis after a three-month stay in the hospital, which, as far as I can tell, you attended exactly two times before departing for a new command in Siberia with the newly formed Soviet Central Command. Would you like me to go on? There's really quite a lot to tell."

Chernov paused for a moment. "Better," he allowed.

"Tell me more about your father, Consul General Chernov. There are actually a few holes there. He was an Imperialist."

"My father served the Czar. I served the party."

Jake stepped closer. "Yes. You served the Soviet Union until it collapsed under its own ponderous, corrupt weight, and then you nimbly morphed into a loyal Russian Federalist."

"Dr. Altman, I could not see you yesterday because I was quite busy. That situation has not changed."

"But you let me in after I mentioned the Baikal and the girl with a note."

"Anna, I believe you said."

"Anna Roman," Jake repeated. "What is she to you?" What was Mikhail Roman to you?"

Chernov paused, but Jake could see that something was burning inside him. The old man cocked his head slightly, lowered his voice, and said pointedly, "Are you here to bring me inside?"

Jake was confused by this. "I don't know what you mean."

"It's a simple question, Dr. Altman."

Jake was still processing the ambiguous question. In the context of three recent deaths, it made no sense. He realized that Chernov was watching him keenly, measuring each facial movement, as if searching for a subtle indication, an encouragement. Jake had none to give. Recognizing this, Chernov abruptly terminated the conversation. "There's been a mistake, Dr. Altman. Goodbye." He turned quickly and headed for the door.

Jake shouted angrily after him. "Why am I involved? What do you want from me?"

Chernov stopped at the double doors. He turned back with a look of distain. "There's been a *misunderstanding*."

"Are you afraid of me?" Jake spat back at him.

"No. Dr. Altman. In you, I see impertinence, not intelligence."

"The Baikal! What about the Baikal?"

Chernov offered a perfunctory nod then took several steps toward a large floor-standing globe. He spun it forcefully and landed his finger on a dark body of water in eastern Siberia. "A lake, Dr. Altman, here in the eastern frontier. Lake Baikal. It is a resort of sorts. It's long, narrow, and I presume wet. I've never had the opportunity to visit it."

"Now you're patronizing me," Jake charged. "There aren't any secrets at the lake. And actually, you've been there dozens of times. Other than being a retirement community for decrepit Soviet party bosses who sit around sucking up Vodka, lamenting the great collapse, and recounting past days of glory for the Communist Party, it's really not so special. The Baikal is just a name of a lake, but it means something more, doesn't it? It's important. But is it really important enough that a doddering Orthodox priest and a grizzled crab fisherman should be killed for it?"

Chernov paused, carefully weighing his next words. "The girl, Anna Roman, why did you not bring her with you? She seems to know quite a bit about all this."

"Anna is in a safe place."

Chernov's smirk had returned. "…and what is *safe,* Dr. Altman? Is she hiding in a trusted friend's home, or a threadbare motel? Or could she simply be waiting for you outside in your car?"

"Oh, hell. You got me. Anna's right out there under a blanket in the back seat. We didn't think you would suspect that."

Again, Chernov hesitated, considering Jake, probing for a crack in his surprisingly durable veneer. Finally, he wrapped his knuckle on the towering library door and Remi instantly appeared. Chernov nodded at Jake and allowed a parlous smile, "Show Dr. Altman out."

At first, Anna didn't move when the door to her Blazer jerked open. She remained motionless under the blanket in the back seat. The door slammed shut, and Jake growled at her. "Let's get out of here."

Anna tugged the blanket away and sat up. Jake was already wheeling the car away from the curb. "What happened?" she asked.

"Nothing."

"He wouldn't talk to you, or was he a total jerk?"

"Both."

Anna clambered over the seatback and dropped down beside Jake. She could tell that he was still simmering. "I told you not to try that," she jabbed. Jake didn't respond. Anna continued, "Hey, look. We're a little mismatched here, don't you think? Vladimir Chernov is a smart guy, right?"

"He's an asshole," Jake grunted.

"We already established that."

"Chernov pretended not to know who you were, and when I asked him about the Baikal, he jabbed his bony finger at a globe, Lake Baikal. Did you know about the lake?"

"Yeah. It's not a big secret or anything. It's the biggest lake in Russia, so what?"

Jake was still glowering. "Chernov thought he was cute, and he didn't give me squat."

"Maybe that's all it is, a lake. Something could have happened there to Mikhail a long time ago. Maybe he saw something that Chernov wants to forget."

"Do you think your father was blackmailing him?" Jake theorized.

"Not really, but do you have a better idea?"

Jake's eyes were riveted to the rearview mirror. A certain sense of paranoia had set in. "Chernov has two thugs hovering around him. They're back there."

Anna peered over the seat. "Just looks like regular traffic."

"Hold on," Jake declared. He hit the brakes, sending the Blazer skidding sideways, then he gunned the engine and tore down a side street. Anna was tossed across the seat, crashing into him. He pushed her away and nailed another skidding turn into a dark alley.

"Hey, cut it out!" Anna protested.

Jake ignored her and sped down another narrow alley. When he finally cleared a row of dumpsters, there was no one behind him. He brought the Blazer back on course, motoring quietly into the graveyard-like west entrance to the Presidio, San Francisco's sprawling military reserve.

Fog instantly engulfed the car, as it swept beneath dense eucalyptus trees, circuitously winding down a mist-shrouded roadway. There were no streetlights, and only an occasional car passed by going the other direction.

They glided down through the forest and streaked out onto Mason Street heading directly toward Fort Point, the haunting Civil War era fort that once protected the entrance to San Francisco Bay. Its massive stone breastworks loomed above them, completely silent now, but with many of the original cannon barrels still protruding menacingly from narrow gun ports. Sweeping high over the imposing edifice, the south entrance to the Golden Gate Bridge arched out into the night with its dazzling lights muted now by a drifting veil of fog. But the fort, nestled below in dark shadows, crouched protectively against the wooded hills, its north face spreading out across the entrance to the bay.

Jake wheeled the Blazer into the empty parking lot and stopped. He gazed out over the roiling waves that crashed past the bridge piers and slammed against the embankment protecting the fort. The deep moan of an unseen foghorn cut through the night, a forlorn cry in the emptiness. Anna leaned silently back in the car seat. Jake turned the engine off and sat drearily behind the wheel. He was still trying to piece fragmented images and thoughts together in his mind; the old Russian woman's suicide, Mikhail Roman's grisly murder, the runaway garbage truck that demolished his VW, and most perplexingly, Vladimir Chernov's icy countenance and his utter refusal to acknowledge any culpability.

Jake glanced at Anna. Even in her brooding sobriety, she was far more striking than he had first thought. The abject fear that gripped her could not mask her soft, natural allure. She made him think about Eryn, how beautiful she was, how much he loved her, and how much he desperately missed her. Eryn's image was like a reflection in a still pond, wavering, ephemeral, something so near yet so far away.

It took a few moments for Jake to realize he was still staring at Anna. She didn't enjoy his spectral gaze. "What?" she snapped at him.

Jake refocused and offered a subdued reply, "Sorry."

"Look," Anna posited. "You and I both want Chernov. We may want him for different reasons, but the end result is the same. I know he orchestrated Mikhail's murder. I don't care why. He did it, and he's going to pay for that. You, on the other hand, have it in your head that Chernov is wrapped up in some sort of international conspiracy that your fiancée discovered. Then he had her killed. I get that. It's wigged you out, but I think you're seeing shadows at midnight. What you really need to understand is this, whatever it is that drives you, whatever it is that's crushing you -- I don't care. If I thought the police would do anything at all for either of us, I'd be there in a flash, but the way things are, we still don't have proof of anything. Nothing!" She paused for a moment, thinking hard. Then, as if an epiphany, she kicked at the floorboards and blurted, "Get out of the car."

Jake just looked at her.

"Go on. Get out."

"And that would be because?"

Anna was adamant, "Look, we can do better on our own, okay. I have to go somewhere?

"Where?"

"The public library."

"Oh, well, that really explains things."

"Jake, get out. I mean it."

Jake measured her carefully. She *was* serious. He weighed his options then shrugged gamely. But instead of relinquishing the Blazer, Jake suddenly slammed it in gear and spun away into the night with Anna, astonished, hurling insults at him.

Pablo's Perfect Pizza was winding down for the night when Jake pulled up in the Blazer and stopped. Anna eyed at the teetering old building then glared at Jake. "This is pretty shitty. I told you to go away, but you steal my car instead and drag me to your pizza dive apartment."

Jake snagged the keys from the ignition and jerked the door open. "I need the photos Lou took of you and Chernov at the consulate."

"Impressive detective work," Anna sniped as she surveyed the ramshackle structure.

Jake took a retaliatory swipe at her. "You know, you ought to work on that little chip on your shoulder."

"That, or you can give me my keys and I'll just disappear."

Jake thought for a moment then held the keys up, dangling them tauntingly in front of her. He abruptly pulled them back and climbed out, marching away, crossing the street, hiking toward the stairway to his loft apartment. He didn't make past the first step before he heard the Blazer engine grind over and cough to life. Jake spun around, only to see Anna behind the wheel, ripping a squealing one-eighty in the street. She threw Jake a look of amused contempt and called out, "Spare key."

Jake watched haplessly as the Blazer streaked away into the night. Deflated and resigned, he sidestepped a discarded pizza box and trudged up the precipitous stairway. At the top, he let himself into the apartment then froze in the doorway. Even in the dim light, Jake could see that the place had been ransacked: books ripped from the shelves, sofa torn apart, furniture overturned. From down the narrow hallway, a shadow drifted silently across the wall.

Jake carefully picked up a stool, like a circus lion tamer, and crept closer. The shadow shifted again; someone was in his bedroom. Louis Ottly sauntered around the corner, and Jake checked his swing, smashing his stool into the wall instead of Louis' head. The terrified photo artist howled and slammed against the wall. Jake screamed at him, "Louis! Goddamnit! Shit!"

Louis shoved the stool away from his head. "Man, you sneak around here like the a stinkin' troll! Why didn't you say something?"

"I live here, Louis! You don't! What the hell are you doing?"

"Oh, well, let's see. I call my good friend, Jake Altman about four times. He doesn't answer, so I hike over here to see if he's okay. You know, like a really cool random act of kindness. But when I get here, no Jake. The place is frigging trashed, and then my buddy nearly cracks my head open with a with a shitty stool. Did I miss anything?"

"You're an idiot, Louis."

"You're welcome, asshole. What the fuck happened here?"

Jake grumbled then picked up a fallen drawer. Louis gingerly lifted a woman's bra from the floor. "Okay, so I think I got it."

Jake recognized Anna's bra. "Give me the bra. A friend left it here."

"Nope. That's a lousy story. Look at this mess. It's got pissed-off girlfriend written all over it."

"You ought to know."

Louis ignored Jake. "Oh, yeah. She was tweaked for sure. I mean, can you blame her for wreaking unholy retribution on your philandering ass?"

Jake lifted the bra from Louis' fingers and tossed it aside. "You are *so* wrong."

"Yeah, well, I call 'em like I see 'em."

"Louis, I found the girl, the one in the photo at the consulate."

"*She* did this?"

"No. I don't think so. But Anna knows about Chernov; she knows more than she's telling me, like the real reason he had her father murdered in Bodega Bay."

"Murder?"

"Yeah, he was spread out on the kitchen table, garroted, with steak knives stuck through his hands."

"Aw, man. That's so nasty!"

"Louis, the girl is the key. Anna is right in the middle of it all. She may not know everything, but she's the key."

"To what?"

"I don't know!"

"You're crazy, man. Take a pill. Shit, take a fistful of them. You gotta get a life."

Jake was already rummaging through his scattered papers. "Crap. They found them."

"Found what?"

"The photos you took at the consulate. They're gone."

"The photos?"

"Yes! The goddamn photos."

"Aw, man. The bad guys took your photographs. That sucks." Louis chirped with a mischievous glimmer in his eye.

Jake caught the sarcasm. He spun around. "What?"

"You remember asking me why I used film?"

Jake's face lit up. "You've got the negatives, don't you?"

"What do you think?"

Jake sighed with relief. "You're a good man, Louis."

"It's just some lousy photos. Girl in a rainslicker, stiff-neck Russian corpse posing as a diplomat. It doesn't mean squat."

"It did to the two strong-arm guys that tried to bust us up," Jake noted.

"Bupkas. It's nothing." But then he stopped suddenly. "Hey, what about the nutty professor hovering in the background, back behind Chernov? What was that all about?"

"What you're talking about, Louis?"

"The black dude! Your professor friend from campus coo-coo land across the bay."

Jake was stunned. "Ezra Bonner?"

"Yeah. He was there, slinking around behind the crowd."

"I didn't see him."

"Then you weren't looking very hard. He popped up in one of the shots. I thought he musta' been there to meet you."

"Louis, you're sure about this. You're absolutely *sure* you saw Ezra Bonner in the photo from the consulate?"

"Gimme a break, man. What, you think I'm an idiot? Don't answer that."

Jake wasn't laughing.

16

Dr. Ezra Bonner often stayed up late; it was his designated personal time. The library in his Washington Heights home was nearly dark, with just one small reading light casting deep shadows across the bookshelves. Bonner was comfortably ensconced in his favorite high-back chair. He often wondered if Supreme Court judges, who practically lived in chairs like this, enjoyed the tufted tranquility as much as he did. However, on this particular night, he shifted sorely in the well-worn chair. His deeply shadowed face hung wearily downward, almost as if he was sleeping. The C.D. player had just changed discs, and a soft jazz piece began.

When the telephone rang, Bonner seemed in no hurry to answer. Only after the fourth ring did his hand move slowly to pick up the receiver. He did not speak.

At the other end of the call, Jake Altman was pacing in the street in front of Pablo's Perfect Pizza. "Ezra, I need to see you."

"Not tonight, Jake," Bonner said tiredly.

"It's important."

"I can't talk right now, Jake."

There was something in his mentor's voice that Jake found unfamiliar, even unsettling. He stopped pacing and glanced at Louis who was waited impatiently in his Porsche. The street was completely empty. Jake kicked at the wet pavement. "Ezra, why were you at the consulate the day Chernov arrived?"

Bonner, sat motionless in his high-back chair. He did not respond.

Jake pressed, "You were in one of the pictures Louis took, you were standing there in the crowd. What was that all about, Ezra?"

"It was a personal matter," Bonner carefully allowed.

"You should have told me."

Bonner thought for a moment then leaned forward into light. His voice was low and strained. "Jake, you know I wear a number of hats at the university. Not the least of which is the one I put on to look out for the interests of my careless graduate students."

Jake was confused. "You're saying you were at the consulate for me?"

"Yes. It was my decision. Your passion for exposing Vladimir Chernov has become dangerously self-destructive. You're picking on the wrong guy."

"So, you took it upon yourself to slink around the Russian consulate spying on Chernov yourself?"

"I went to the consulate to watch *you*, not Chernov."

Jake was silent. From across the street, Louis tapped his horn and called out. "Are we going somewhere or not?"

Jake waved him off and turned back to Ezra. "I don't need to be mothered, Ezra, if that's what you think you were doing."

"Well, that's precisely what I was doing."

"You're not telling me everything. There's more, isn't there? Chernov, Mikhail Roman, Anna, Lake Baikal. I can't make the pieces fit, but I think you can."

Ezra Bonner took a slow breath and leaned back in his chair. "Jake, I want you to listen carefully to me. The Baikal was a Russian war ship, a little-known steam frigate. She was lost at sea. The Baikal sank off the coast of California in 1918. They never found it." He hesitated then spoke more pointedly. "Did you know about the ship, Jake?"

"No." Jake was more perplexed than ever. "What does a sunken Russian warship have to do with all this?"

"The Baikal went down with all hands, including its captain, Vladimir Chernov's father."

It took a moment for Jake to absorb this. Then he stopped suddenly. "What was onboard the ship, Ezra?"

"Leave it alone, Jake. Back off." Bonner's voice was strained but direct. "That's advice from a friend who doesn't want his friend to be hurt."

"What was on the ship, Ezra?"

Bonner's eyes wearily drifted closed but his voice resounded with caution. "I taught you well, my friend. You listened to me. Now you need to listen to me again. Forget about Chernov. Cherish your memories of Eryn, but let her go, Anna Roman and all the rest too. *Let it go*. You see, I fear, for you, there is only great danger if you don't."

Jake was about to protest when the line went dead. He stood in the cold night air, his mind racing with thoughts swirling in convoluted circles.

Anna Roman closed the thick book in front of her, being careful not to tear its aging binding. She slid it aside, along with a number of other, equally dusty tomes she had already perused. All were history books, or to be more exact, Russian naval history books. It was late. She was thirsty and her eyes were strained. She wasn't even sure she was making much progress, and there was a stack of at least ten other books looming in front of her. Anna glanced up from her poorly lit table. The fourth-floor reference stacks in the San Francisco Public Library were vacant, seemingly forgotten by time. The study-alcoves at the end of each bookshelf were musty, disorganized, and largely unvisited.

A nearly inaudible intercom speaker broke the silence, crackling softly, followed by a nasally pronouncement that the library would be closing in fifteen minutes. Anna was lucky. Most nights, the facility closed at six o'clock. Wednesday, it remained open until nine.

Anna had always been a voracious reader. When she was very young, Mikhail seemed to have a new book for her every night when he tucked her in bed. He wasn't a particularly good reader, but for what he lacked in phonetics, he more than made up for in enthusiasm. Mikhail loved adventure stories. Anna liked the stories too, but mostly she enjoyed just listening to Mikhail's deeply resonate voice. His eyes always seemed to sparkle with excitement as swarthy characters were cast away on desert islands, flew amazing flying machines low over snowy glaciers, or braved Piranha-infested whitewater rapids in the Amazon. The stories, like Mikhail himself, had always seemed so much larger than life.

Anna blinked, realizing she had been lost in her memories. She sighed and pulled the next book from the stack: Imperial Russia Naval Reserve Fleets: The Baltic and South China Sea Incursions.

Anna wasn't sure what she was looking for. It was just a hunch, actually. The cryptic message that she delivered to Vladimir Chernov for her father had not meant much to her at the time: *The Baikal sailed with the tide*. However, from this slim antecedent, she had deduced that the Baikal may have been a ship. She had no idea if it was the name of a fishing boat, a sailing yacht, or even a deep-sea freighter, and only recently had she considered the possibility that the Baikal might be a naval vessel. She suspected that Vladimir Chernov may have been in the Soviet navy, and that consideration had been confirmed by a journal she had unearthed in other jumbled and undervalued history texts. She learned that the Baikal was a steam-powered Russian frigate. Built in 1901 and lost at sea in 1918, she had a displacement of thirty thousand tons, was powered by triple-condensing, coal-fired Pratt engines, and had a cruising speed of fifteen knots. The reference material was sketchy beyond that; it was little more than a simple compilation of long-forgotten, early Russian war vessels.

Despite this curious bit of nautical trivia, Anna could not adequately explain what it had to do with her father. As an American citizen, he had served in the army after World War II in the reconstruction of Europe. Anna recalled that he disliked the regimentation of military life and mustered out as soon as his commitment had been met. For a few years after that, he had been a stonemason. But, to the best of her knowledge, Mikhail's love of the sea was nascent even then. It had grown slowly but steadily, fueled by colorful weekends he spent relaxing at the fishing fleet in Bodega Bay. He had told her about the cool autumn winds and searing blue skies, the intoxicating sights and sounds of the fleet, laughter, and the comradery of strong men who drank hard and loved to fight. The stories the fishermen brought home from the sea seemed so grand and heroic, and they always lifted his spirits. By the time Mikhail was in his mid-thirties, he had bought his first trawler, and for the next four decades, he fished. It was the love of his life.

Anna regretfully withdrew from these fond memories. Mikhail was gone now, murdered for some reason that was utterly beyond her grasp. But what was the connection to Vladimir Chernov? Why had Mikhail sent her to him, and why had Chernov acted so aggressively? She simply could not find an answer. Now, all she had to guide here were musty books filled with vague references to a long-lost naval vessel. The Baikal was a Russian warship, and that was clearly noteworthy, but otherwise the trail had run cold. Anna pulled another fraying book open and began to search again.

The rows of book stacks were darkly silent. There was only the faint hiss of an ancient steam radiator, a vestige from much earlier construction found only in this wing of the library. It was like a tomb, Anna thought. Even when she heard a new sound, a faint rustling from deep in the shadows, she didn't bother to look up. Then she heard it again, louder now, and her eyes snapped up from the book. She steadied herself, but she did not call out.

Fearing the worst, Anna rose up with a thick book in her hand. It wasn't much, but she could throw it if needed. The sound drew closer. Anna held the book back and was ready to heave it when Jake Altman stepped around the end of a tall bookshelf.

"Jake, Jesus!" Anna exclaimed.

Jake jerked back, eying the book in her hand. "Hey! Back off! Why didn't you say something?"

"Asshole."

"What is it with you?" Jake shot back.

"With me!" she snapped.

Jake reached out to sweep the book from her hand. "What, you were going to whack me with this?" He glanced at the title, *Second World War Naval Engagements in the Baltic Sea.*

"Gimme the book back."

Jake offered it to her but jerked it back when she reached for it. "You knew about the Baikal. You knew it was a boat."

"No I didn't. Not at first"

"Bullshit. You told me the name meant nothing to you. You lied."

"I didn't lie! I may have *suspected* it was a ship, but I wasn't sure until I found the reference here. Obviously, you already knew about it. Why didn't you tell *me*?"

"I just found out."

"Now who's spreading crap?"

Jake waved a dismissive hand. "What else have you found?"

"Nothing. Just nothing." Anna poked Jake with a sharp finger in the chest. "Look, none of this is your business. Not really. You think Chernov killed your fiancée, but you're not sure, and that gets you about nowhere. Why can't you just drop it and leave me alone?"

Jake didn't respond. Instead, he abruptly cupped his hand over her mouth, motioning her to be quiet. He eased Anna backward around the end of a tall bookshelf. Somewhere down the aisle, footsteps tapped softly, closer.

Not far away, Oleg and Remi stopped amid the musty darkness. They were listening carefully and could see the faint lights of study alcoves through the bookshelves. Oleg held a sawed-off shotgun, tucked just inside his black raincoat. Remi brandished a sleek nine-millimeter handgun. They moved forward, stopping to peer around the end of each stack. Sensing a kill, Oleg lifted his shotgun expectantly and lurched around a shelf corner. Books lay scattered about on the study table, but Anna and Jake were gone.

Jake slammed through the stairway exit door, tugging Anna with him. They careened down the switchback steel steps, their clanging footsteps echoing loudly off concrete walls. Somewhere above them, an exit door banged again. Oleg and Remi were coming after them.

"Go! That way," Jake hissed, shoving Anna down another flight of stairs. Together they stumbled wildly downward. At the first floor, Jake crashed through the exit door, pulling Anna outside into the misty darkness.

The Civic Center Plaza spread out in front of them. It was a vast, fog-shrouded expanse of open park ground, punctuated by decorative landscaping, subdued lighting, and a veritable sea of sagging cardboard homeless shelters. Jake pulled Anna with him, racing across the courtyard and into the neatly rowed stand of pollarded sycamore trees. As revered icons of the plaza, the mini-forest of perfectly aligned trees spread out like the columns of the Parthenon. For decades, the trees had been trimmed each year, cutting away any new growth, so that they were topped by gnarled branches so snubbed that they looked like arthritic and blackened knuckles. The foliage was dense and close, covering the deformed branches like a 1960's Afro.

Jake and Anna raced through the trees, using them for cover as the careened toward the other side of the plaza. Suddenly, the darkness was pierced by headlights streaking through the trees. A car was racing across the center of the plaza, straight through the tree park. Its headlights flashed across Jake and Anna in a staccato dance of blinding white and tree-shadowed darkness. A gunshot rang out, slamming into a tree beside Anna's head. They leaped over a makeshift cardboard shanty, ignoring the drunken caterwaul from the terrified inhabitant.

Oleg powered their black Yukon SUV through the leafy maze then skidded to a stop. Both Oleg and Remi leaped out, spreading apart quickly, guns drawn, racing through the corridor of trees. Jake and Anna cut across one tree lane, then back again. Oleg and Remi saw them and fired several rounds, but the gnarled trunks absorbed the hits, splintering wood in all directions.

Jake knew they were approaching the other side of the park. He also knew that beyond the tree stand, there was only open space all the way to the far side of the plaza. They would be sitting ducks, but without recourse, he charged ahead, breaking free of the tree line. Anna lagged back, gasping for air. Jake was about to pull her ahead again, when a dark sedan, seemingly coming from out of nowhere, suddenly tore across the plaza. It skidded to a stop inches away from them. Dennis Luger leaped out, screaming at them, "Get in the car! Do it, or you're dead!"

Jake hesitated. Luger was waving his service revolver in the air. "They'll kill you!" he bellowed.

Jake jerked the rear door open and shoved Anna in. Luger dove back in the car as a bullet slammed into the trunk. He hammered the gas pedal and tore away in a spray of water and gravel. "Get down!" he ordered. "On the floor!"

Another shot rang out and Anna could hear it shatter the side mirror. The car bounced and swayed as Luger drove it hard, smashing through a low hedge, skidding sideways, almost overturning, before landing on McAllister Street. Jake and Anna couldn't see a thing. They were bounced and slammed as Luger tore around the block, evasively skidding and cutting down another narrow street.

"Did you tell them anything?" Luger shouted.

"About what?" Anna protested.

"The Baikal! Damn it!"

Anna was rattled. "Who are you!"

"Why does Chernov want us dead?" Jake shouted.

"Just you, Dr. Altman. Chernov wants you dead. He wants her alive. What did you tell them?"

"Nothing," Anna protested. "They came after us in the library and we ran!"

Luger slowed, just long enough to cut into a dim alley. Jake jerked the rear door open and was about to haul Anna out with him. Luger cut back hard, and the door slammed shut. "Look, Chernov is bailing out!" he cried. "I told you that!"

"That's bullshit," Jake retorted.

Luger was still shouting, "No! It's true! Chernov wants political asylum, but he thinks there's a leak -- someone on our side. He's afraid. He won't commit. It's my job to plug the leak and get Chernov to come across. Those two guys work for Chernov, but they're double dipping! They're not going to let him defect."

"What's Chernov have to do with Anna's father, Mikhail Roman?" Jake demanded. "What's this have to do with her?"

Luger bounced the car over a curb and cut down another street. He shouted back at Jake and Anna. "Mikhail Roman knew everything! People thought he was dead. But then the old Russian woman spilled the beans. She was crazy, but she knew things; she knew *everything*!"

"What are you talking about?" Jake bellowed.

Luger was still driving hard. "Look, Vladimir Chernov wants asylum, but there's more. It's about the money, rubles, lots of them. Chernov is Russian aristocracy. But when the Communists took control, he played the party man. He was smooth. He never skipped a beat. We knew he was doing it for years. The Soviets are gone now, and Demetri Bellus has an iron grip on the country. He sees Chernov as old school, odd-man-out. So Chernov is cashing in his chips. He wants out of the system, but he also wants the money!"

"What money!" Jake yelled.

"Gold rubles! Thirty-billion-dollars-worth!"

"What!" Anna exclaimed.

Luger was still shouting, "The last Czar, Nicholas -- he knew the Bolsheviks were closing in on him early in 1918. He cleaned out the Russian treasury and the rubles disappeared. Gone, forever, but not really. It's all about rubles for Christ sake! Chernov thinks the Czar shipped the rubles out of the country on a boat!"

Finally, it hit Jake. "The Baikal."

"Yeah," barked Luger. "The Baikal. But first the Czar had to get the rubles to the damn boat; twenty tons worth. It all went out of Moscow on the Trans-Siberian Railway, east then south, all the way to Beijing and the East China Sea. The rubles were loaded on the Baikal, and she steamed toward California."

Pieces were beginning to fall in place for Jake. He said, "Bodega Bay. The Russians had a trading center near there."

"Smart boy. Only the ship never got there. It sank somewhere off the coast of California."

Anna was trying to grasp it all. "What did that have to do with my father?"

"Everything!" screamed Luger. "Mikhail Roman knew where the boat sank!" He threw a furious look over the back seat. "Quit fucking with me! The old man *knew*."

Jake was incredulous. "Why would Mikhail Roman know where the ship went down?"

"He knew," Luger screamed. "He told you! Where did it sink? Tell me about the goddamn boat!"

"I don't know!" Anna spat back at him.

"I can help you!" Luger bellowed. "Tell me!"

"I don't know!" Anna shrieked, slamming her hands protectively over her ears.

Luger cursed and cut around another corner. He slammed on the brakes, skidded the car to a stop then jumped out. Jake peered over the seat. Oleg and Remi were standing in the headlights as Luger marched up to them. "She doesn't know," he snapped angrily."

"She wouldn't talk?" Remi growled.

"She wouldn't tell me shit," Luger shouted. "Take her. Kill him."

Oleg and Remi exchanged glances, weighing Luger's order.

In the car, Jake spied the keys dangling in the ignition switch. He took a chance, lunging over the car seat. Jake jammed the car in gear and hit the gas. Remi and Oleg dodged aside. Luger jerked his Glock up, but the car tore past, slamming into him, sending him flying. Remi and Oleg were firing now. Jake swerved one way then the other. A spray of slugs thumped into the car's trunk, but Anna and Jake were already speeding into the night.

Dennis Luger lay bleeding on the ground. He was hurt badly, wheezing and coughing up blood. "Help…me," he sputtered.

Remi was watching the car's taillights fade into the fog.

"Help me," Luger pleaded again.

Remi turned to survey Luger's broken body. He glanced at Oleg and remarked, "He's done." Oleg understood. He swung his gun around and fired a single shot into Luger's head.

17

A tiny old lady climbed the five steps to the front entrance of Louis Ottly's studio building. She was surprisingly nimble and mean as a snake. Louis had wisely allowed her to remain in the third-floor apartment when he purchased the building. She was still fumbling with the rebellious door lock, cursing freely, when Jake and Anna slipped up behind her. When the lock opened, allowing the old lady to enter, Jake and Anna were right behind her. The venomous dowager whirled around and snarled at them, "I carry mace and kick ass."

Jake held up his hands defensively, "Oh, it's okay. Louis is waiting for us. Wedding pictures."

The old woman clucked dismissively. "I know what kind of pictures that man takes."

"Sorry about that," Jake offered.

Anna hissed at him, "What the hell are we doing here?"

But the old lady was already on a roll. "Wedding pictures, my ass. He shoots porn. It's indecent. Naked bodies. Kinky stuff. He should be arrested!"

Anna was confused. "What's she talking about?"

The old woman snorted and hiked up the stairs. Anna slugged Jake's arm. "Tell me why we're here."

"Because Louis made copies of the photos."

"So what?"

"The photos are the only thing linking us to Chernov. We need them to keep him off of us."

"Well excuse me, but isn't that what the police are for?"

"Not a great idea. Remember Dennis Luger, our government tough-guy?" Jake posited tightly. "He rode us around in circles then dumped us right back in front of Rocky and Bullwinkle! Look, if we go to the police, and they tell Luger, we could be right back where we started, or worse."

Anna started to object, but Jake was already bounding up the stairway to Louis' second floor studio. She followed grudgingly. At the landing, Jake reached for the doorbell, but he pulled up short when he saw that the door was cracked open. Jake hesitated then eased inside. The room was fully lighted but completely empty.

"Louis?" Jake called out, but there was no reply. Blaring rock music was playing farther back in the studio. "Stay here," he directed Anna then moved across the studio lobby. He threw her a foul look when she appeared right behind him.

"Louis?" Jake called out, louder this time. He and Anna slipped around a corner and into the photo set. It was ablaze with work lights: studio floods, photo soft boxes, and even a couple of bounce umbrellas. Anna spied the array of skimpy "wedding" dresses, boas, and negligees'. Poster-size pin-ups of past clients adorned the walls: brides-to-be, dressed and undressed. There were even a few guys, too, mostly promoting their own wedding "dowry."

"Oh, this is really nice," Anna quipped.

"Louis is into high art," Jake retorted.

"…and low morals."

Jake spotted a trickle of water running from under the bathroom door. He jerked the door open, but it was just an overflowing washbasin, clogged with a rag. Anna slipped in beside him. She turned the faucet off, but it was Jake that noticed the odd, yellowish liquid splashed across the counter top. He touched it then jerked his hand back, his fingers stinging furiously. "Acid!" he cried out.

Anna's eyes shot up to the wall mirror and she screamed. They both whirled around to gape in horror at the horribly disfigured body slumped in the tub. Louis, or what was left of him, was covered with acid; he was a bloody, oozing mass of burned flesh and seared bone. He was completely unrecognizable except for blood-soaked fragments of his red suspenders. Dozens of acid-eroded photos and negatives were plastered to his chest. Jake could just make out the front of the Russian consulate in one fragment; cars, people, but nothing recognizable was left.

Anna jerked away, revolted and terrified. She stumbled back into the studio. Jake took her in his arms, but she was thrashing hysterically. "God, Jake! What was *that*!"

Jake was still reeling. "They knew about Louis! How? It's crazy! How! They know everything we're going to do before we do it!"

"We have to go to the police!"

"No!" Jake shouted. "It's not safe."

"You call *this* safe?" she shouted back. "Jake…." But she stopped struggling when the studio lights suddenly clicked off, all of them. There was only a wash of a streetlight sifting in through the tall windows. Jake backed Anna toward the lobby then froze when he saw a flashlight beam sweep beneath the front door.

Jake eyed a tall window; there was a fire escape outside. He reached carefully for a window lock, but it was stuck. Anna gasped when the doorknob began to twist slowly. Jake dove for the door, shoving a thick bolt shut. He pushed Anna back, grabbed a freestanding photoflood light rack, and heaved it through the window.

Someone slammed against the front door, once, twice. Jake jerked Anna close, furiously pointing at the shattered glass. "Out! Now! Go!" Together they leaped through the opening and tumbled onto steel fire escape then scrambled to their feet and raced away, around and down, dropping the last eight feet to the top of a dumpster.

When Oleg and Remi finally crashed through the front door, they saw the shattered window and lunged through to the fire escape. Remi clung to the railing, searching below, but there was only an over-stuffed tourist bus chugging past.

Dr. Ezra Bonner balanced three foam cups of ice cream precariously as he navigated the nest of tightly packed tables at The Big Moo Ice Cream Shop just below the Berkeley campus entrance on Bancroft Way. Family owned for fifty years, the shop occupied the first floor of a sagging timber-framed building. Its worn wood floors, creepy display of old wall clocks, and ancient, tiny tables added to the colorful ambiance. There was even a reverently framed poster of *Dilbert* from the comic strip, signed by Berkeley alumnus artist Scott Adams.

Ezra Bonner's unabashed passion for ice cream was legendary, and The Big Moo was his absolute favorite shop. Incredibly, it remained open most nights until midnight, probably an accommodation to the many insomnia-challenged students and faculty. The place was packed. Conversation was loud and animated. Bonner nearly upended one of his three overflowing cups of ice cream when he edged past a pack of poly-sci majors vociferously championing the merits of the Far Left political agenda.

"Excuse me," Bonner interjected, "Don't young people have something better to do than paste smiley faces on a Communist Manifesto calendar?"

Bonner nodded politely then moved on, finally settling at a minuscule table that wobbled on misaligned legs. His two ranking staff directors were waiting for him; Dr. Katherine Sexton and Dr. Eleanor Hicklin knew they had better things to do than slurp ice cream but, nonetheless, they had convened at The Big Moo because Ezra Bonner asked them to do so.

Bonner slid cups of ice cream in front of his team. "Carmel-swirl," he said, gesturing to the treats. "Totally new here. It is marvelous."

"My doctor told me to avoid ice cream," Eleanor Hinklen noted stiffly. "It's laced with wood pulp cellulose."

"Well then, let's all be eager little beavers and dig in," Bonner countered cheerily.

Katherine Sexton discreetly edged her cup away. Bonner noted this but said nothing as he dug into his ice cream. "Yum…" he murmured. "That's damn tasty."

Eleanor Hinklen's will had been broken. She delicately swept up a tiny scoop and savored the sweet passion. Her next spoonful was much larger.

"Ezra," Katherine began. "What's this all about? It's past ten o'clock. That's late in my book. Besides, we already had a department party, the spring thing in Sausalito, remember."

Bonner dabbed his mouth with a napkin. "I wanted to talk to you both, privately. It's about Jake Altman."

"I'm so surprised," Katherine groaned.

Eleanor Hinklen, having succumbed to the temptation, had a mouthful of ice cream, but she downed it quickly and rose to the challenge. "I will support a department reprimand, if that's what you are proposing."

"No, that's not it," Bonner announced.

"Well someone needs to get his attention."

"I have Jake's attention, Eleanor," Bonner continued. "Unfortunately, he's chosen to ignore my advice."

"Lock him up!" Eleanor chirped. She was somewhat giddy from the sugar rush.

"I'm afraid it's more pernicious than that. Jake may have stepped on some very big toes."

"The Russians?" Katherine queried.

"I think so, but there's no way to prove it. Here is what we *do* know. A very elderly Russian woman from Bodega Bay found her way to the Holy Mary Orthodox Church on Geary. She offered a confession to the visiting archbishop then walked outside and threw herself in front of a MUNI bus. Five days later, the archbishop was murdered in his chamber."

"What's that have to do with Jake?" Katherine snapped.

"There's more," Bonner interjected. "Jake has found the young woman in Bodega Bay who delivered a cryptic note to Vladimir Chernov the day he arrived at the Russian consulate. He drove out there to talk to her, but he discovered her father murdered instead. If you will pardon the frankness, I should add that he was pegged to a kitchen table with steak knives stuck through his hands."

Eleanor Hinklen stopped mid-bite. She eased her spoon back into the cup. Bonner continued, "Now, I'm not at all certain these events are directly connected. Neither is Jake, but something is terribly askew, and he's managed to insert himself right in the middle of it."

"Where is he now?" Katherine questioned.

"I don't know. He's hiding somewhere, probably with the girl."

"Why doesn't he go to the police?" Eleanor added.

"Jake is certain the police are connected to this, and not in a constructive way. He told me there's a man who has been following him. He confronted Jake, claiming to be a government agent."

"So, Jake's flipped out," Katherine posited. "I told you he's turned into a conspiratorial nut case."

Bonner was shaking his head, "That may be a bit rash."

"No, it's not. Jake's lost it."

Eleanor Hinklen seemed perplexed. "What do you want from us?"

"First, that you would share my consternation. I'm very worried about Jake. He's in trouble. Both of you have ties to government agencies, both here and abroad. I would hope that you could make some inquiries, find out who knows Vladimir Chernov well enough to convey the certainty that Jake is not a threat to anyone. I don't want him to be hurt."

"Look, Ezra," Eleanor Hinklen noted. "My specialty is Latin American affairs. I don't think talking to Brazil's minster of Carnival would do much good. Besides, I only met Chernov once during the San Francisco exchange visit three years ago."

"Isn't that enough?" Bonner asked.

"No. No, Ezra. I'm not going to advance this nonsense based on Jake Altman's half-baked theories."

Bonner was disappointed. He turned to Katherine, who immediately threw her hands up. "Don't look at me," she quipped.

"I *am* looking at you."

"Why? I don't have any influence with the Russians."

"No. but you certainly knew the Ukrainian consul general?"

"Okay," Katherine deflected. "Look. I don't give a damn if you believe all those smutty rumors."

"There was even one about you and the past Russian consul general," Bonner added.

Katherine was getting mad. "People spin their own webs. It stinks. But, com'on, Ezra. That was total bullshit. I don't know any of the Russian delegation, so can we drop the innuendo?"

"Then you won't help? I'm only asking you to make a few calls to the Russians, just to ease their trepidations. Is that an unreasonable request?"

"No," Katherine announced, "It's entirely reasonable, but I will say again, there is *nothing* I can do."

Bonner leaned back. His ice cream was melting as he thought. Katherine and Eleanor exchanged glances as the moment became more pregnant. Finally, Katherine couldn't stand the tension. She blurted out angrily, "Ezra, Jake is a big boy. If he's embroiled himself in a bad situation, it's his problem. There's no reason on earth you should involve yourself. Jake's just your student!"

"No, you see, Jake *was* my student. Now he's my friend," Bonner announced solemnly. "I'm not going to let him get hurt."

Bodega Bay was still enveloped in a murky shroud of fog when the MUNI bus glided off the coast road and stopped in the gravel lot next to the Sea Hag. Inside the bus, most of the passengers were sleeping. The portly driver wiped his runny nose then clicked the air-release, and the front of the bus sank lower. He unscrewed his thermos and poured a cup of steaming coffee. Six rows back, Jake Altman roused himself slightly, his eyes scanning the dormant bayside enclave. A row of smoke-yellowed lights over the center aisle blinked on, and people began to stir. Jake glanced at Anna; she was still sleeping soundly beside him, her head gently laid against his shoulder. He thought that, despite her smudged face and rumpled jacket, she was astoundingly beautiful. At the same time, she seemed so completely out of place, living a life with no apparent congruence to the world of coarse fishermen and an unforgiving sea. As she slept, her lips were parted slightly with a youthful fullness. She was utterly captivating. Anna didn't belong here, Jake thought. She had given a good accounting of herself in the face of sweeping terror, but her brash assertiveness conflicted with the woman that slept beside him now, vulnerable, lithesome, and helpless.

Jake tried to recall their escape from San Francisco. They had ditched Luger's car at a Seven Eleven Food Mart and hiked eight blocks to a MUNI bus station. Jake had paid for the tickets with cash. They boarded the red-eye coach with a dozen other dozy travelers and had quickly fallen asleep as they slipped across the Golden Gate bridge.

Jake looked out the window again. A bone-thin dog trotted across the parking lot, sending a bevy of fat seagulls fluttering into the dark sky. A single Bud Lite promo light flickered errantly in the window next to the entrance to the Sea Hag. The parking lot was mostly empty except for a pick-up with a flat tire and a salt-bleached, pink Toyota that Jake surmised belonged to some local girl who got lucky that night. Beer bottles littered the parking lot, tossed aside in random clusters, marking spots where girlfriends argued with boyfriends, probably about sex, shipmates ranted outrageous claims about their fishing prowess, or maybe a couple of old geezers gabbed late into the night rather than to go home to their nagging wives.

The bus driver clicked the intercom and announced their arrival in Bodega Bay. Anna's eyes opened, slowly at first. She didn't move, at least until she realized her head was still nuzzled protectively against Jake's shoulder. He forced a smile when her eyes found his. "You slept most of way up here," he said softly.

"I was wide awake," she countered as she pulled herself upright. "Where are we?"

"Bodega Bay."

"What time is it?"

"Eleven-thirty." Jake watched Anna as she tried to wake herself. He said, "Are you going to tell me now why we came back here? I mean, it's not like they won't think of looking here."

Anna's eyes widened. She shifted uncomfortably as an enormous Chinese man brushed past in the aisle. "Com'on," she said to no one in particular.

"Where are we going?" Jake questioned.

"If I told you, you wouldn't want to go."

"Why would I want to go with you in the first place?"

"I don't know. Why *are* you here?" she asked pointedly.

Anna stood up abruptly, slipped past Jake and started down the aisle. He watched her for just a moment, dissecting her comment, realizing that she was right. He was there because he wanted to be there. She was the key to everything, and though he wasn't quite sure how or why yet, he knew with great certainty that she was in as much danger as he was.

When Jake climbed off the bus, he expected to find Anna waiting for him. Instead, he could barely see her in predawn gloom as she hiked across the Sea Hag's gravel lot. He stopped suddenly and spun around when he heard someone singing. Attaboy was lying on his back on a timber fish-gutting table near the edge of the lot, waving a bagged bottle of whiskey wistfully in the air. He was singing a fractured rendition of the Battle Hymn of the Republic.

"My eye have seen da glory of da comin' of da Lord
He's done swiped the devil with his terrible, great
Sword. He has...has...aw, shit. And da truth is truckin'
on..."

Attaboy couldn't remember the rest of the words, so he just hummed between swigs. He stopped, though, when he spotted Jake standing at the top of the long boat ramp. "Dock's closed for the night," he slurred, determined to keep peace and order in his tiny harbor. "Ain't nobody around."

Jake dug a few dollars from his pocket and stuffed them in Attaboy's pocket as he started down the ramp.

"Hey thanks, Cap," drooled the old drunk.

Jake could hear Attaboy start the song over as he slid his cell phone from his pocket. He knew that a call could be traced, but, he felt compelled to talk to Ezra Bonner. He could only hope the police and Luger had not put a trace on his cell phone yet.

Ezra Bonner had just left the Big Moo in Berkeley and was watching Katherine Sexton and Eleanor Hinklen disappear into the darkness across the street. He wondered if they really couldn't help or if they simply didn't want to get involved. When his cell phone rang, he saw Jake's name appear and snapped the phone to his ear. "Jake, where the hell are you?"

"I'm safe, Ezra. You don't need to know more."

"The police have been here asking about you. They aren't fooling around."

Jake fired back quickly, "Was there a CIA type guy with them, Ezra? He might have been wearing a sport coat; he has dark hair, trim, forty-five or so -- doesn't look like a cop."

"I don't know, Jake. Is this important?"

"It matters, Ezra!"

"There may have been someone like that. There were three of them."

"Three!"

"Jake, the police were blathering about a murder in Bodega Bay, the same one you told me about. I think they've linked you and that girl to it somehow."

"Oh, we're tied to it alright. Like up to our necks. They murdered Louis."

"Your photographer-friend?"

"They killed him at his studio, dumped him in the tub and tried to dissolve the body with acid."

"Oh, God."

"They destroyed the photos too, the shots of us at the consulate with Chernov. We've got nothing to show the police now. We're screwed."

There was panic in Bonner's voice. "Jake, where are you? Tell me."

Jake hesitated. He could hear a boat engine fire up below in the misty harbor. "Ezra, if I don't tell you where I am, they can't involve you."

"But I want to help!"

"I know, but…" Jake suddenly went silent when he heard a faint tone in the background. "Ezra, are you recording this call?"

"Of course not."

The tone sounded again. Jake cursed and clicked the phone off. He couldn't believe the police had picked up wire-tap authorization so quickly. Jake heaved his cell phone into the harbor and ran down the boat ramp only to be swallowed up by a swirling mist.

Jake was wrong about the traced call. It wasn't the police. Instead, Remi and Oleg, parked alongside the Pacific Coast Highway, just south of Bodega Bay, were sequestered comfortably in their SUV, carefully monitoring a compact yet powerful cell-intercept device. They had heard everything.

Oleg grunted, "He thinks he is smart not saying where he is."

"Maybe not so smart," Remi replied as he tapped a finger on the equipment. The screen on the wire-tap unit lit up with a map of the San Francisco Bay area. Jake's cell phone registered nothing on the screen. Remi adjusted a zoom feature and the coverage expanded. A clear blip appeared directly at the northern end of Bodega Bay. Oleg looked at Remi, but he didn't need further instruction. He started the engine and pulled out onto the highway.

18

The American Secretary of State tried to hold himself erect and square-jawed as he stood waiting in the opulent anti-room of the Grand Kremlin Palace. Hayward Fillcock was an unimpressive man with thinning hair and thick glasses. For what he lacked in stature, he more than compensated for with a carefully crafted mantle of flinty malevolence. Fillcock was widely viewed as a callous manifestation of political patronage. He liked it this way. Long ago, he had the good fortune of serving with the current President of the United States when they both received plumb intelligence assignments in Germany as young Army captains late in the Vietnam War. The bond had been formed. Ambitions had been explored. Fillcock went on to become a narrowly-elected Senator from a lesser plains state. Ultimately, his friendship with, and loyalty to, the president had been duly rewarded. He had been tapped to run a variety of government agencies, and now he was the new Secretary of State of the United States of America. He liked this too. Fillcock liked the power and prestige of the position most of all. Yet, as he stood waiting for his audience with the most dangerous man in the world, his steely veneer seemed thin and feckless. He was afraid. The prospect of meeting Russian President Dmitri Bellus for the first time had left him with a chilling sense of what was to come. Bellus was not to be discounted. He was brilliant, calculating, and openly vicious.

Secretary Fillcock glanced at the spit-shined Russian military detachment that surrounded him. Somehow, his own Secret Service security team, clearly overpowered in the waiting room, seemed anemic and far less formidable than their Russian counter-part. Fillcock swallowed hard and flexed his delicate fingers, trying to relieve the tension. Even the fat cigar he had smoked away on the way over to the Kremlin had failed to calm his anxiety.

Fillcock was tired. He just wanted to go home. He and his negotiating team had just concluded a difficult diplomatic intervention with the Russians. It had been a bruising confrontation, far more technical than he had been prepared for. What the hell did he really know about North Atlantic satellite rotational symmetry, he thought. The Russians had wanted something they called a "comparative umbrella," which they described as three-dimensional parity for their spy satellite deployments. That didn't help either. Fillcock was still flummoxed. His pencil-thin MIT advisors, with an average age of no more than thirty, had pushed him to make concessions. Give a little, take a little, they had advised; the Russians had to think they maintained the upper hand. That's the way the game was played. The strategy they had laid out sounded logical, even insightful at the outset, but Fillcock was unsettled now as the blur of agreed-upon details clicked past in his mind. The acrid taste welling in his throat told him that something wasn't right. Something deep in his homespun, mid-western intellect was screaming at him now, and then it dawned on him. He had been fucked.

The Russian color guard appeared first, their boot heels clicking crisply on the marble floor of the adjacent processional hallway. Fillcock's keepers offered tight smiles as they nudged him from the anteroom. Lights blazed overhead, and the stirring sound of a Russian hymn rose up, echoing through the alabaster parapets and deep stone arches of the long hallway. President Dmitri Bellus walked crisply toward Fillcock, flanked at a deferential distance by ribbon-adorned Russian military officers and a cadre of youthful political operatives.

The procession stopped when Bellus stopped. No one moved. Bellus tilted his head slightly, perhaps dismissively. But then his hand shot out stiffly, and he offered a perfunctory pronouncement, "Mr. Secretary, this is a good day."

Hayward Fillcock countered with an equally meaningless salutation, "Thank you, Mr. President. It is certainly a good day when diplomacy prevails."

"You have been treated well while you have been with us?" Bellus asked.

"It has been most pleasurable. I thank you for your hospitality."

Bellus leaned closer. "Yes, but did you try the Vodka I sent to you? It was quite old."

"Yes, of course. It was an excellent choice. I'm afraid there is very little left for the housekeeping staff to cart away."

"Ha. Good. This is a good thing," Bellus boasted. He threw out his arm, gesturing that they should proceed.

The vast corridor was lined with honor guards and massive flags. Its gleaming floor was polished to perfection, but otherwise the yawning canyon seemed eerily empty. There was only the sound of music and marching footsteps of the spit-shined color guard.

Desperate to advance the diplomatic discourse, Fillcock leaned closer to Bellus and coughed out a useless note of condolence. "Mr. President, I wanted to express my sympathy, and that of my country, for the unfortunate death of Archbishop Popov Konstantin in San Francisco. It is tragic. I understand that he was revered in your country."

"Yes," Bellus lied without glancing over. "Konstantin was a great man and a trusted friend."

Fillcock nodded appropriately. "Our investigation is certain to lead to an arrest of those responsible."

"One would hope."

"We take these sorts of things very seriously."

Now Bellus looked over with a chilling gaze. "So do we."

They were only a few yards from the beginning of a waiting red carpet runner, and beyond that, a set of towering gilded doors. Though Fillcock was disturbed by the subtext of Bellus' statement, he was certain that his sidebar conversation would play well on the evening news. He couldn't resist a quick follow-up whisper. "We will get the men responsible."

Bellus allowed a bilious smile. "Actually, I doubt that."

"Why?"

Bellus stopped and looked over. "Because America is weak. You are weak, and you negotiate like a crying woman. You have no spine."

The massive chancellery doors suddenly swung open. The entire Russian Federal Assembly, hundreds of dignitaries, and international media representatives were waiting in the resplendent St. George Hall. Fillcock was stunned and completely unprepared for the reception. Cameras flashed. Music rose up, swelling with the powerful notes of the Russian National Anthem. The gold-trimmed hall, used only for momentous state occasions, was far grander than the pictures of it that Fillcock had seen. It was regal, electrifying, a dazzling testament to Russia's storied place in history. The ceiling arched sharply up forming an enormous vaulted canopy with massive chandeliers. Each was easily twenty feet in diameter, fully abloom with thousands of candelabra lights.

Fillcock felt the unexpected enormity of the moment. He thought he was going to throw up. Bellus' cold eyes were still on him, as he moved forward again, seeming to glide over the narrow red carpet with solemn rectitude. Waiting for them, was a speaker's platform, ringed with throngs of Russian statesmen and an abundance of stiff military officers.

Fillcock could feel the sweat creeping down his neck. He was panic-struck. This was a set-up, he cursed to himself. His stupid advisors were dead wrong. He had signed a crappy deal, and now Bellus was hosting a celebration in honor of taking America's pants off. Fillcock was devastated.

Bellus stepped forcefully onto the speaking platform and raised his hands to his cheering countrymen. He gestured magnanimously for his honored American guest to join him.

Sunrise was nothing more than a gentle, flaxen trail creeping slowly over the landward horizon. Somewhere well away from Bodega Bay, Mikhail Roman's tiny trawler pressed slowly ahead, northbound up the coast in a sea so vast that that the boat seemed utterly insignificant. *The Princess* had plied these waters hundreds of times before. Seagulls trailed behind the boat, swooping through the outrigger cables, hoping to snag a scrap of bait or a forgotten fish head, whatever luck would bring them. It was a habitual flocking of shameless scavengers that followed almost every boat sea-bound from Bodega Bay.

Anna Roman braced her knees against the main control console as she held *The Princess* firmly on course. A cold wind blustered across the open main deck cabin, lightly tossing her auburn hair. Anna pulled her C.M.M.A. jacket more tightly around her shoulders. She glanced landward where the low hills of northern California appeared as an ethereal blue-gray shimmer at the edge of the ocean, framed by dense storm clouds brooding farther to the east.

Jake Altman stood far forward on *The Princess'* heaving bow. He clung to the bow-sprit railing, flexing his legs to absorb the thrust when the boat sank deep into a wave trough then straightening again as the trawler climbed up the next wall of water. Wave crests, buffeted by the wind, shattered into a roiling spray. Somehow, Jake found the uncompromising power of the sea to be singularly comforting. It was as if the world ashore, distant now and racked by ungly human frailties, seemed entirely meaningless amid the majesty of a far greater force. Jake's hands were wet and cold, and his face stung from the bite of the frigid sea. He didn't mind. For him, the moment was both an extant reminder his own impermanence as well as a conditional celebration of his life. He was completely overwhelmed.

Jake swept dripping water from his face and turned back to look at Anna behind the wave-splashed windshield. She was watching him. No, he thought, she was measuring him, applying dark questions and assumptions that only she understood. Her wind-chafed face revealed absolutely no hint of her true feelings; there was no sense of trust or reconciliation, only a starkly unspoken acknowledgement that their lives were now inexorably linked.

Liam McGeorge had hosted countless shooting parties during his fifty-year tenure as Shooting Master at the famed Merced Rod & Gun Club. Long ago, he was considered, by any reasonable standard, to be extraordinarily young to hold such an esteemed position, but when the club changed ownership in 1964, he was the only logical choice. Just a couple of years before, McGeorge, at age twenty-two, had won the Olympic trap shooting gold medal for Scotland. At six feet four, he was a powerful young man; fresh-faced, handsome, and confident. He was an altogether dazzling specimen for the front-page of newspapers around the globe.

The famed sportsman's club, located on Lake Merced, just south of San Francisco, had not been doing well. It desperately needed an infusion of competence. McGeorge's Olympic shooting conquest and his newfound celebrity had not gone unnoticed. Several powerful San Francisco industrialists had moved swiftly, sponsoring Liam's move to the United States. They shepherded him through the daunting naturalization process and installed him as the Merced Rod and Gun Club's youngest Shooting Master in the organization's history.

All of that was so very long ago, McGeorge thought as he stooped down to load one of the three portable clay target launchers wedged into the hardpan sand. In his mid-seventies now, he was still an imposing man, erect, with broad shoulders and a dashing Scottish mustache. Had it really been over fifty years, he thought: a lifetime, his lifetime? But then it had all ended when the club abruptly shut down, terminating his career and perpetuating his retirement. Both it and he had been casualties of an unprecedented environmental witch-hunt that culminated two years ago, when the club was shuttered permanently.

Liam's doleful gaze drifted out across the windswept and mostly overgrown shooting range that had once hosted a daunting array of notable sportsmen. It was a broad strip of sand and scrub-brush, punctuated by the shimmering surface of Lake Merced. The environmentalists had brought in expert witnesses that claimed the underlying ground had been irrevocably polluted by spent lead shot to a depth of at least *two feet*. McGeorge couldn't help but scoff at this. He knew very well that lead shot and spent casings were imbedded in the sand at least *four feet* down. But dammit, this was the Merced Rod & Gun Club, fabled playground for the rich and powerful. He had instructed Cary Grant at this very sight, teaching him how to lead his target properly. He had even made a valiant attempt to ease Marlon Brando's rigidly mechanical shooting posture, though the old bastard resolutely rejected his sound instruction. Now it was all over, just a vague tapestry of distant memories.

McGeorge had used his spare key to bring the illegal shooting party past the barred gate. The rustic clubhouse was lifeless and overgrown as the cavalcade of limo-SUV's wound past like a stately funeral procession. A roost of pigeons took to the air, and there was nothing else besides the wind in the trees. They had set up a bright tent top, sporting chairs, a fully tended bar as well as three racks for a variety of McGeorge's valuable trap guns. His traps-men, mostly Hispanic holdovers from the club's grander days, had hiked about fifty yards to the west and east to set up the mechanical throwers, discreetly angling them for not-so-challenging fall-away shots.

Liam rubbed his beard-stubbled jaw and glanced at his shooters. Naoyuki Owada, the Japanese consul general to San Francisco, stood with a wide stance, with his gleaming side-by-side Purdey shotgun aimed toward the horizon. The narrow-shouldered man swallowed hard and shouted out, "Pull." McGeorge signaled left and a single clay target shot skyward. As it sailed out and down-range, the tiny Japanese diplomat muttered anxiously then jerked the trigger. He missed badly.

"Ah, you'll be getting the hang of it now, sir," McGeorge shouted out with a rousing Scottish brogue. "Try coming up a wee bit smoother into the target then give it a good nudge!"

Owada, ever short of patience, had had enough. He cursed in Japanese then stiffly shoved the gun to the next shooter, Vladimir Chernov. "You shoot the gun. I want you to show me," he instructed, as he crossed his arms and stood back. Chernov was dressed impeccably in a casual tweed sports coat and neatly pressed corduroy slacks. He had decided not to wear a tie, but a brilliant purple handkerchief burst expressively from his coat pocket. Chernov surveyed the shotgun in silence. It was an expensive, hand-tooled classic.

Liam McGeorge offered an explanation, "That's an English Purdey, sir, a classic trap gun. It's said that only few of this model were ever crafted."

"Very nice," Chernov called out. "Excellent tooling."

"Aye, sir. The very finest."

Chernov offered a hint of a smile. "I've heard of this weapon before. It is known to us. The gun has a similar balance and fire pattern to our Russian MS-9."

"That would be correct, sir," Liam called back, impressed with Chernov's shooting acumen. "She's a wee bit heavier on the muzzle but very responsive when properly coaxed."

"So I've heard," Chernov noted as he carefully felt the balance of the weapon.

The host of the event, U.S. Consul General, Cotton Hearst, stood a few paces away under a wind-tossed tent-top. He was a career diplomat, an uninspiringly dumpy man who appeared to be perpetually rumpled. Hearst surveyed the assemblage and was pleased by the impressive rank of his guests. He had been able to capture the diplomatic heads of five consulates: Russia, Japan, Germany, Argentina, and Nigeria. A table had been set up under the tent top, ringed with plush-pillowed cane chairs. Two young waitresses served champagne to the near-sportsmen. Deitman von Mirbach, the acerbic German consul general, was drunk already and far more interested in the two lithesome and clearly underage waitresses. Raul Servanti, the Argentinean representative had busied himself forcing unsolicited instruction on the disgruntled Japanese marksman. The Nigerian stood alone, largely uncomfortable with the event.

"Are you ready, sir?" McGeorge called out to Chernov.

The venerable Russian diplomat nodded and lifted the shotgun smoothly to his shoulder. He called out, "Two please, the hard way."

McGeorge, surprised by the request, signaled the trapsmen on either side of the field of fire, two clays on the same pull. The men swung the launchers around setting up an intersecting target arc. When all was ready, McGeorge glanced at Chernov. "On your call, sir."

Chernov responded calmly, "Pull."

McGeorge signaled, and the two launchers sprang simultaneously, hurling clays out and almost directly toward each other. Chernov sighted the first target then fired. The clay exploded. A millisecond later, the shotgun belched flames again and the second clay disintegrated.

Naoyuki Owana yelped enthusiastically. The German and Argentinean marksmen shrugged indifferently.

Liam McGeorge was honestly impressed. "A fine spread, sir. Nicely done."

Chernov lowered the gun and inhaled the lingering smoke. He had always loved the smell: its robustly virile scent never failed to impart an intoxicating reminder of battles past.

Liam McGeorge watched the old diplomat carefully. Chernov might even have been a professional shooter at some point, he thought; that or he came from an aristocratic background that afforded the necessary time to become proficient with the sport's finer nuances. He called out enthusiastically, "You've got a sharp eye, sir, and a steady hand to go with it."

Chernov surveyed the Purdey, turning it from one side to the other. "Yes, you are correct. She's somewhat full on the muzzle; needs to be caressed on the up-swing."

"Aye, sir. That is most true."

Chernov's gaze shifted from the roguish Scottish marksman to a dusty SUV that had just pulled up a few yards away. Remi and Oleg climbed out and simply stood beside the car. Anton Sorokin climbed out too, standing at rap attention beside the driver's door. He stiffened slightly when Chernov seemed to ignore him, instead allowing a quick nod to the two loutish journeymen.

Liam McGeorge studied Chernov carefully. He was trying to unravel the unmistakable enigma that enshrouded him, but the eighty-year-old Russian abruptly handed the gun to an attendant and paced away across the desiccated sand. Cotton Hearst was cajoling the German ambassador when Chernov laid a hand on his shoulder.

"Mr. Hearst, I must excuse myself. My car has arrived."

Hearst's face sagged with disappointment, but he adroitly recovered, "Yes, of course, we understand if you need to go." He hesitated then struck a hopeful note, "But maybe we could convince you to…."

Chernov lifted a halting palm, offering a pointed benediction. "Thank you for hosting us," he said. "It has been a pleasure. Perhaps we can do it again."

"Absolutely. I understand," the American fumbled. He forced an amicable smile then spoke more softly as if a secret was to be revealed between two close friends, "Hate to see you go, Vladimir. You know, our other guests here might have learned a thing or two from you." He leaned closer still and confided, "None of them can shoot worth a shit."

Chernov smiled then paced away toward his waiting SUV. Remi and Oleg approached in silence. Anton accepted an instructive glance from his boss then stepped aside a few paces.

Remi waited. When he surmised that Chernov was not going to speak first, he removed his cap and muttered under his breath, "All is well."

Chernov's lips tightened. "Three inexplicable deaths, all Russian. And none of the gruesome events took place more than fifty miles from the consulate. Do you consider that *all is well*?"

"The police got nothing," Oleg grunted.

"Got nothing?" Chernov scoffed.

Remi interceded, "Our sources are good, sir. The police are just chasing their fat arses."

"And so are the media roaches," Chernov scoffed reproachfully. "Murders sell newspapers. The American press wants answers, and if they don't get what they want, they will simply make up something suitably unseemly. Now please explain to me what the Russian consul general is supposed to say when he is inevitably forced to comment on the killings. Do you see my point? Do you understand the implications?" Chernov caught himself, reining in his temper. "You are experts in these matters. Professionals. Listen carefully to me. I *do not* wish to be confronted by a herd of misanthropic, flat-footed American reporters. You have a job to do. Do it."

Chernov turned away quickly. Anton dutifully swooped in and jerked the rear door open. He forced a smile and advanced a calming platitude, "Did you enjoy the shooting session, sir?"

"No. But these things must be done."

"Precisely, sir."

Chernov threw a cold glance at Remi and Oleg then eased into the back seat. Anton closed the door. At first, the elderly Russian stared straight ahead, his mind fixed on a swirl of distasteful issues. He triggered the privacy screen and was quickly sealed behind dark glass. Finally, he sighed and seemed to regroup. Then, smiling slightly, he said to no one in particular, "It's been some time since we have -- visited."

Chernov turned to look at Katherine Sexton, who was seated demurely next to him. His eyes flashed with the lascivious gleam of a far younger man as he spoke softly. "Did you miss me terribly?"

Katherine's tantalizingly short, black dress rustled slightly as she crossed her stunning legs. The tip of her tongue traced her lips, as she teased, "You're not as young as you used to be, Vladimir."

"I could prove you wrong very easily."

"Perhaps," she replied.

"But first you have something to say to me," Chernov observed as his glacial eyes searched her face.

Katherine hesitated then leaned closer to kiss him blithely on the cheek.

19

Jake Altman carefully made his way back along *The Princess'* narrow gunwale. The boat was rolling steeply as waves slapped at his legs. The previous night's foreboding fog had been replaced by a bright sun and expansive sky. Jake swung around the backside of the cabin and dropped down onto the main deck. He steadied himself by latching on to a life jacket rack overhead under the cabin roof.

Anna's eyes were fixed on the broad sweep of ocean in front of her. She could sense Jake watching her, and she knew he wanted answers. Without looking over, she lifted a finger, pointing at some unseen object off the starboard side of the boat where gulls swarmed overhead. "See the churn in the water? They're Black Backs," she noted. "They make their way down on the coastal current then congregate off that point. The gulls dive and snag the small ones."

"Black Backs," Jake offered flatly. "Just fish, right?" He wasn't interested in talking about seafood.

Anna glanced sideways at him. "It would have been a good day to fish."

Jake said nothing as Anna checked her compass heading and made a slight course adjustment. "Mikhail was happy here," she offered. "Hell, he was happy anywhere, the old goat."

Jake ignored her poorly concealed obfuscation. "How far are we going?" he asked.

"Noyo, just north of Mendocino. Three hours from here, maybe four."

"Why Noyo?"

"We need supplies. They have a little harbor."

Jake's eyes drifted to the vast, undulating sea. "We can't hide out here forever."

"It's a big ocean," Anna replied. Her eyes remained fixed on the horizon as she shoved the throttles down all the way. *The Princess* coughed a noxious puff of smoke into a perfect California sky and rumbled ahead.

For a long time, neither Jake nor Anna felt the need to speak. Each was lost in thought, conflicted and confused by the merciless snare of events that had engulfed them. Jake searched the sea, ubiquitous in its utter immensity, as if it might somehow hold answers to unanswerable questions. The fresh breeze in Anna's face did little to assuage her doubts and fears. Without Mikhail, she was entirely lost, with little hope of finding a way forward.

The sound of a ship's horn caught them by surprise, and when they turned to look back, they saw another fishing trawler closing fast.

"Who is it?" Jake asked tensely.

"Yedor," Anna announced as she recognized the blue striped hull.

"A friend?"

"Yes, he was close to Mikhail, almost like a son."

Yedor's boat, the *Flying Spruce*, was newer and more powerful than *The Princess*. It cut neatly through the waves then slowed as it pulled alongside. Jake could see Yedor, Mikhail's arm-wrestling partner. He was a big man, handsome and chiseled, with a full mane of tousled blond hair. He was Nordic, or more probably Russian, Jake thought. He wasn't exactly sure why, but he didn't like him.

Anna slowed the engines to a bumpy idle. She called out to Yedor, "Why are you this far north? I heard on the marine radio that the salmon had moved down the coast."

"No fishing. Not this trip. Theo Kuzmen ran aground up at Point Sage. I gotta go pull the old bastard off the shoal."

"Did he ground-out at low tide?" Anna asked.

"High tide. Theo should have known better than to come in here, even then. The water ran out from under him. He's stuck hard."

"Anna cast a quick glance out over the water then shouted again to Yedor, "Is anyone going with you?"

"The Desoto brothers are already there in their boat."

"Two boats," she called out. "That's not enough to pull Theo off."

"Maybe not. We'll see."

Anna thought for a moment. Jake, who had passively watched the exchange, cast a cool glance at Yedor. He nudged Anna. "We gotta go. Too many people have seen us out here."

"Theo Kuzmen is in trouble."

"So are we."

"This is different. Theo's one of us. He's mean as hell, but he's a great fisherman."

"It's not our problem," Jake cautioned.

"He's old," Anna reasoned. "All he's got is that boat."

"Let it go, Anna. We've already pressed our luck."

Anna steadied herself as waves rocked the hull. She knew Jake was right, but, for her, it wasn't that simple. Anna and Yedor looked at each other across the water. She knew he was too proud to ask for help.

Jake broke the silence with sharp warning, "We have to go -- now."

Anna seemed to be nodding a silent acknowledgement that she understood. Yedor's face registered disappointment when Anna turned to look at her controls. He offered a slight wave and was about to press ahead when Anna suddenly called out to him. "Yedor. Tell Theo we're coming too. Tell him we'll be there."

Yedor's face lit up. Jake sagged with resignation.

Yedor shoved his throttles down and the *Flying Spruce* lurched ahead. There was no way that *The Princess* could keep up.

Jake turned away and moved to the aft deck, where he steadied himself with his hand tightly gripping the port side outrigger. He was certain this was a mistake, but he also understood Anna's determination. He watched her carefully, allowing his thoughts to drift back to Mikhail, Konstantin's murder, and Marvina's bizarre suicidal leap. Jake wondered how deeply Anna's involvement with Chernov really went. She couldn't possibly be telling him the truth. And while Anna's grim resolve appeared unshakable, Jake could still not accept her consuming focus as being entirely real. She was an enigma, a stunning young woman who seemed completely incongruous with the raw visage of Mikhail's world.

Less than fifteen minutes later, Anna realized she had pushed *The Princess* too hard. The port engine had begun to clatter erratically. It had to be the intake valves, she thought; they were hot. Not enough water was flowing through the cooling system. The heat and backpressure was just too much. Anna reached for the engine throttles and backed them down, first to a slow idle, then to a complete stop.

Jake was confused, but he didn't say anything at first as Anna marched across the aft deck and hefted the engine room hatch covers open. Steam and smoke billowed up from the oily bilge. It smelled as if the engines were completely burnt up. Anna slid a battered toolbox from beneath the gunwale railing and popped it open.

"Problem?" Jake asked.

"The cooling lines are clogged. Probably calcium deposits in the diverter valve."

"And the translation of that would be?"

"No water -- the engines are getting too hot."

"Got it," Jake acknowledged. "So, what do we do?"

Anna pulled a box-end wrench from the tool chest and tossed it to Jake. "I'm going to radio Yedor. You're going to free up the water pump intake hoses and clean the diverter valves." She stooped down and pointed to a nest of hoses circumnavigating each engine block. "Take that clamp loose, then the hose. The intake end of the water pump housing has a diverter valve that's going to have a bunch of calcium build-up. Right there, just in front of the thermostat. You gotta take it out and clean it on both engines."

Jake cocked his head reproachfully, but Anna just snapped at him. "See that hose clamp? Right there. Just loosen it up, okay?"

"Hey, I'm all over it," Jake announced as he climbed into the narrow space below deck between the two grimy diesels. His fingers gingerly traced the snarl of hoses on the port engine then found the suspect fitting. He looked up, anticipating at least an approving nod from Anna. She was gone. He could hear her tuning the radio farther forward.

A half an hour later, bearing scraped knuckles as evidence of his handiwork, Jake had the two lines loose. He had disgorged thick calcium deposits from the steel fittings on the water pumps. Anna was sitting on the toolbox just above him sipping a cold Coke. When she held out the can, offering Jake a drink, he simply tossed the greasy wrench on the deck at her feet. Anna picked up the tool, observed it slightly and handed it back, noting, "You gotta put the hoses back on before we can go anywhere."

Jake nodded tightly. "Yeah. I probably knew that." He bent over the engines again, prostrating himself over the exhaust manifolds as he wedged his upper chest and head into the dank below-deck space.

Anna sat stoically on the tool chest. She could hear him banging around below, cursing floridly. "Are you done, down there?" she called out. The expletive that returned to her was unrepeatable. Anna was amused, but her tenor matured quickly when she took note of Jake's strong thighs and tight butt writhing atop the engine.

With his head and shoulders entombed below in the blackness, Jake adjusted his flashlight and strained for full purchase on the hose clamp nut, turning it no more than a quarter-turn at a time. When he paused to rest, Jake's eyes scanned the cramped space, oily bilge water, and a series of numbers gouged into an overhead deck beam. He called out to Anna. "Somebody carved numbers in a timber down here. What are they?"

Her muffled voice replied, "Coast Guard documentation I.D. Every commercial boat is marked. Aren't you finished yet?"

Jake wiggled his way out of the bilge. He held the wrench out to her again with certain finality. "I'm done."

Anna offered a disinterested shrug. Actually, she was impressed with Jake's plucky sense of determination, if not his attractive physique which she failed to recognize earlier.

Jake dumped his repair equipment into the dented toolbox then turned an eye toward Anna. She was busy firing up the engines again. He said, "You know if we go up there and get involved in some sort of salvage operation for a stuck fisherman, someone could slip up and tell the wrong people about us."

"I owe Theo something."

"…enough to risk your life."

"You might be surprised," Anna offered vaguely as she shifted the boat in gear and shoved the throttles forward.

Jake was still unsure about Anna, but when she looked over at him, ready to deflect another objection, he acquiesced, "Okay, what do you want me to do?"

"It's not much farther. When we get there, you can try to help out. Whatever Yedor tells you to do, just watch out for him."

"Why?"

"Why do you think?" Anna chirped with a knowing smirk.

"Boyfriend?"

"Not really. Not unless you ask Yedor."

Jake was frustrated and he was tired of wordplay. Anna threw a contentious look at him. "Why were you writing about Chernov?"

"He's a bad actor."

"I was hoping for something a little more specific."

"You wouldn't understand."

The boat surged and Jake almost lost his balance. When he straightened up, Anna was still looking at him.

Jake relented, "Chernov is a corrupt Russian operative. He floats with the political wind. Always has. First, he was a loyalist to the old guard -- the aristocracy, then he was a Soviet, an avid Communist party guy. But when the shit hit the fan and the communists gave up, he switched again. For the past twenty-years he's been a background guy in the Russian Federation. Out of sight but just as powerful as before."

"Okay, so Chernov's a player. He knows how to work things to his advantage. What else would you expect?"

Jake's face tightened. "Chernov's killed people, Anna. Lots of people. And it's never mattered to him if they were foreign adversaries, political liabilities, or even lousy Russian peasants. They're all expendable. They're pawns in a chess match where he's a dirty knight. It's just a game, but Chernov plays to win."

"Why did he come to San Francisco?"

"That's what I was trying to find out. But then you showed up in the rain and stopped him dead in his tracks with your note and a cryptic warning."

"The Baikal sailed with the tide," Anna repeated softly to herself; she was replaying the nightmare in her mind: the shockingly visceral images of life and death, her father's gentle voice and strong arms, blood, horror, but when it all began to swirl into an incomprehensible collage of disjointed images and thoughts, she simply shut down. Her mind went blank, and her eyes fell on Jake. "You should have backed off when you still could; your lousy book, your dissertation, why does it matter to you so much?"

Jake was silent. He had no answer. Instead, his thoughts drifted to Eryn, what she had told him, and how she had died. He had tried before to explain it all to Anna, but he knew she could not possibly understand the depth of his loss or the bite of his rage. Jake turned away and sunk down the ladder, disappearing inside the old trawler.

Fishermen had known for a hundred and fifty years that the waters off Point Sage were treacherously shallow. The point itself blocked easterly winds and created a seductively calm stretch of water that appeared to be much deeper than it really was. The fishing was good here, however, and smaller boats were usually able to maneuver over the hidden shoals at high tide. The intangible threat came from the thick bottom sands that often shifted unpredictably.

Theo Kuzmen's weathered trawler lay healed over at a twenty-degree angle, its keel securely embedded in the sandy bottom. Its name, *The Chum*, painted haphazardly on the stern, was cracked and faded, barely readable. The tide had peaked several hours earlier, and Theo had assumed he had enough time to haul in his nets and slip away before the shallows were no longer traversable. It was a calculated risk, and Theo had considered the consequences. Now, he slumped on an empty beer keg on the aft deck, morosely watching the two other fishing trawlers standing off about fifty yards in deeper water. One was Yedor Fedin's boat, the *Flying Spruce*, while the other was the *Pelican II*, owned by Alexi and Zorka Desoto, two brothers who smoked a lot of dope and rarely said a word to anyone.

Theo was resigned to the indignity of his bad judgment. He was a small, angular man with dirty gray hair that exploded thinly from his sunburned scalp. Theo was wearing the same blood-streaked fishing apron that he always wore but rarely washed. His face was creased and weathered, while his teeth were stained a nasty shade of brown from his steady consumption of cheap cigars. Theo had been married to the Bodega Bay librarian for forty years, though no one was quite certain why she stayed with him. He never hit her, but he had a quick, often sarcastic tongue; it was simply accepted that he was disagreeable, inflexible, and unrepentantly foul-mouthed. He was also one of the most skilled fishermen in the fleet.

Yedor Fedin rowed his skiff closer to *The Chum* then stowed his oars and lifted a coil of nylon dock line. "Hey, old fool," he called out to Theo, his face beaming with an unctuous grin. "My half-dead dog has better sense that to get caught in here."

Theo's consternation spilled out as he growled back at Yedor "Cut the bullshit. Just toss the line, Yedor. You can have your fun later, once you get me off this turd-pile."

The Desoto brothers bellowed with laugher but did not join the roasting. Alexi DeSoto, short and chubby, was easing himself over the gunwale, climbing into a small tender.

"Hey, this is hard work!" Yedor shouted at Theo. "What are you going to pay us for this sacrifice?"

"I pay you the same thing you paid me last year when you caught a snag and had to get towed back to port," Theo crowed. "I pay you nothing, asshole. Not a penny. Now are you going to throw me the crappy line?"

Yedor laughed heartily and heaved the rope. Theo grabbed it with one hand and quickly made it fast to his forward towing bitt.

"Two boats," Theo groused loudly, "Two boats are not enough to pull me off. I'll be stuck here like a pregnant whale until the winter swells bash me apart." He could hear Yedor and the Desoto brothers caterwauling, and this only made him madder. When he looked up again, he saw *The Princess* chugging closer.

Yedor saw the approaching boat too and was pleased. He called out to the stranded fisherman, "Three boats, Theo. For sure that should be enough to haul that rust bucket of yours off that shoal -- the shoal that everyone but you knows about."

"Blow me," Theo shouted back.

The Princess slowed and drifted to a stop in the sheltered water. Yedor barked at Anna as he rowed toward her, "Anna, get me a good line to use. Theo Kuzmen doesn't have a single spare line on that tub of his."

Jake scooped up a neatly coiled rope from the aft deck, but Anna waved him off. "No. Get that one," she said as she gestured to a thicker braided line.

Jake grabbed the other hank of rope from beneath the narrow gunwale. Yedor was just off the port side. It was an easy toss for Jake to land the rope in the bobbing skiff. Anna moved in to tie their end off on a stern cleat. Yedor's skiff was directly beneath *The Princess*. His eyes were still on Jake; it was a hard, penetrating gaze.

This was an easy call, Jake thought. The bigger man was jealous, and that was enough to evoke a knowing smirk. Jake actually enjoyed Yedor's frustration, though he didn't fully understand why, at least not yet.

Yedor held his position in the skiff, working the long oars expertly in his hands. His gaze shifted to Anna. "How come you brought him, Anna?"

"Well, Yedor, it just seemed like the right thing to do," she called out. "Is there a problem with that?"

Yedor accepted her pronouncement stoically. He gestured to Jake. "Get in. I need you with me."

Jake cast a quick look at Anna who offered an offhanded nod of approval.

"You coming?" Yedor scoffed.

Jake quickly slid over the gunwale and dropped into the bow of Yedor's boat. He tensely squared himself in front of the man mountain, and Anna was certain that the encounter would not end well. Instead, Jake simply advised. "This was her idea, not mine."

"Got that," Yedor replied without flinching.

"Okay, so I'm lousy with a hammer and worse with a saw. What do you need me to do?"

A crooked smile crept across Yedor's face. "First, you need to sit down so we don't capsize."

Jake sat. Yedor took up the oars again and stroked across the water, heading back to *The Chum*. When he pulled alongside, he heaved Anna's line up to Theo Kuzmen.

"I got water in the bilge," Theo whined. "Musta sprung a couple of leaks when I grounded."

Yedor was clearly frustrated he hadn't been told this earlier. "How much water you got, Theo? It's sort of important, you know."

"I got *lots* of water down there, asshole. You want me to measure it?"

"You got a bilge pump, don't you?" Yedor snapped.

"Hasn't worked for two years."

"You're stupid, Theo, ugly too." Yedor swung the skiff around broadside to *The Chum*. He shouted at Jake. "Get on the boat."

Jake took a moment to absorb the order. "What am I supposed to do on the boat?" he griped.

"Get a bucket. You and Theo gotta get some water out of the hold so we can pull the boat off the shoal."

Jake looked up at Theo, who was grinning through tobacco-stained teeth. "Yedor's a smart boy," he announced. "Get your ass up here."

Anna had maneuvered *The Princess* around so that the towing line played out more or less parallel to the *Pelican II*. Zorka Desoto, missing most of the fingers on his left hand, was at the controls of his boat. His brother, Alexi, was on board Yedor's *Flying Spruce*, slowly bringing the boat and its towing line in line with the other two boats. There were three of them now, *The Princess*, *Pelican II* and the *Flying Spruce*, each with a stout line played out about a hundred feet to the stern of Theo Kuzmen's rust bucket trawler.

Yedor was standing chest-deep in the water, pressed against the slimy side of Theo's boat. He had a long timber pole wedged under the boat's keel and was trying to rock it free. The boat barely moved. Yedor waved his hand at Anna and shouted out. "Go on. Put some pull to it!"

Anna shoved the throttles down and the towing line snapped taut. Alexi and Zorka powered their boats up too, sending a rush of prop wash from beneath the hulls. All three lines were straining now. Theo's boat shifted slightly but didn't budge. Yedor leaned into his timber pry bar again, pressing his massive muscles into the work. The boat rocked, but settled back quickly. Yedor waved the towing boats off and shouted up to the gunwale where Theo Kuzmen was peering over the side. "You stuck her good, Theo."

The old sea dog spat a wad of tobacco into the water. "Told you three boats weren't enough."

"Get more water out of the bilge," Yedor sniped. "You gotta lighten her up."

Theo nodded vaguely then turned to the open aft deck hatch. Jake was four feet below hauling his bucket out of the oily water. Theo grabbed it, emptied the water overboard then tossed it back to Jake. "Yedor says you're a pussy. Bail faster."

Jake glared at Theo then dug the bucket into the nasty bilge water again.

Anna looked up at the hostile sun. It was getting late, and the burning orb was sinking quickly toward the horizon. She made a small adjustment to *The Princess'* controls, carefully keeping a small amount of tension on the towing line. The *Flying Spruce* and the *Pelican II* were still pulling too but only hard enough the keep slack out of the lines.

Jake shoved another bucket of water up to Theo. He was exhausted as he sank back against the engine while Theo dumped the gruel overboard. When the bucket landed beside him with a splash he threw a look up at Theo. "The water's down four inches," he protested. "That's a lot of ballast."

"Four inches?" Theo noted. "Why didn't you tell me you had it down four inches?"

"Aw, give me a break," Jake exhaled.

Theo leaned over the side of this boat and sniped to Yedor, "Your man has got the water down over *eight* inches. What are you waiting for?"

Yedor cocked a distrustful eye overhead. "Eight inches? Are you sure?"

"Probably more like a foot," Theo boasted. "Get me off of here."

Yedor waved at Anna and the others again. "Give it all you got!" he cried out.

Engines roared and black smoke belched into the afternoon sky. The lines whipped tight again, strung out like tightropes over the churning prop wash. Jake pulled himself out of the bilge and collapsed against the gunwale; there was nothing else he could do.

Yedor leaned into his timber pole again, screaming out as he put all his strength into it. Finally, the boat shifted and slipped back several feet, only to grind to a stop again. Yedor cursed in Russian and yelled out to Theo. "Get your bucket man over the side! I need him here!"

Jake heard the order. He was almost too tired to stand, but Theo gave him a calloused hand up. "You'll be okay," he confided. "The water's too stirred up for sharks."

"What about you? You can get wet too," Jake charged.

Theo let out a belching laugh. "Me! Can't you see that I'm old?"

"Maybe not so old," Jake charged.

"Old enough. Get over the side. Yedor needs you."

Jake reluctantly swung himself over the side of the boat and splashed into the cold sea. He coughed up water as Yedor's enormous hand swung out and grabbed his shirt. "Stand up," he barked. "Put your feet down."

Jake settled and sank his feet into the sandy bottom. "No sharks, right?" he sputtered to Yedor.

"No big ones. Lots of little ones," Yedor grumbled. "Here. Help me push."

Before Jake could protest, Yedor waved at Anna and the others again. As soon as the towing line took hold again, Yedor shoved Jake low in the water, beneath his massive arms.

Somehow, Jake found the timber pole in the frigid water. He wedged himself into the sand and shoved upward. He could feel Yedor's legs leaning against him, pushing from above.

The pole moved and the boat shifted, but Jake wasn't ready. He was roughly tugged under water. It was dark and cold, and Jake struggled to gain footing. His head banged against the pole and he expelled a burst of air, sucking water in behind it. Choking and sputtering, Jake found the pole again and heaved upward. He was running out of air, but he continued to push. Yedor's knee slammed into his back, and it was all he could do just to hold on. Finally, the boat shifted again then abruptly slid backward.

Jake exploded from beneath the waves. He let out a great whooping yell when he saw the old trawler drift comfortably into deeper water, bobbing lightly as if it had been anchored for the night in a safe harbor. Yedor was standing beside him, leaning tiredly on the pole, not quite sure what to make of Jake's euphoric yelps. Jake caught a wave in the face and coughed out water. When he wiped his face, he could see Yedor watching him carefully. He wasn't smiling, but the sneer of disrespect was gone. Yedor nodded, "Jake Altman, you are not much use on the sea."

"Sorry about that. You can dock my pay."

"...not much use, but I think maybe I like you better now."

Jake understood the backhanded compliment and was glad to accept it. He picked a wad of seaweed from his hair and looked across the water. Anna was looking back, watching him too.

20

The Curb Club, located on a trendy stretch of Filmore near California Street, had only been in business for one year, but it had already become a favored haven for San Francisco's glamorous young motorcycle crowd. It was a new-age biker bar, where a line of outrageously sleek bullet bikes could be found out front every night, glaringly displayed beneath mist-shrouded streetlights. High-end Triumph Bonnevilles, Ducatis, and Suzukis all preened for dominance. There was even an Icon Sheene weighing in with a price tag of over one hundred seventy thousand dollars. Without a doubt, the Curb Club was the epicenter of affluent decadence in San Francisco; it was brash, loud, and garishly unrepentant in its overstatement.

The bar itself was dark with multifaceted glass partitions and broad sliding glass doors, normally left open to the street-side cabana area. Stylish young bikers, adorned in two-thousand-dollar, multi-hued riding leathers, spilled outside, brandishing pink and blue twenty-dollar cocktails. The men were gorgeous, most with sweptback hair and uber-tight riding pants, while the girls all seemed to be drop-dead beautiful. All were obscenely rich, and if not fully endowed with superfluous spending cash, they certainly knew how to make a credit card scream for mercy.

The early evening crowd was completely caught up in revelry when a lone motorcycle rolled up and stopped. A stunning biker-girl turned to watch curiously as a black, shit-stomper boot hit the pavement and knocked the kickstand down. The bike was an enormous Harley twelve hundred, vintage 1969. It was a monster relic, fully accented by a modified, chrome rake in front, upturned monkey handlebars, and Spartan accenting of chrome sprockets and exhaust system. It was a Hog.

Another head turned, then another. The chopper rider eased off his machine and stood motionless, eyeing the glittering motorcycle scene. He was a big man, dressed in jeans and a worn leather jacket with fraying fringe coursing down each sleeve. He most resembled a degenerate outlaw biker.

Dr. Ezra Bonner slipped his helmet off, unzipped his jacket, and adjusted his paisley bow tie. His well-starched U. C. Berkeley persona had been miraculously replaced by a rebellious alter ego dating back to the heady, free love 1960's. Ezra loved his Harley, but he largely kept its restoration secret and was even more elusive with his sporadic weekend rides. It wasn't that he was ashamed of his passion for unfettered freewheeling on the open road, but rather that his age and station in academic circles seemed to dictate a more conservative persona.

Ezra strapped his helmet to his bike and moved off into the fresh-faced curious crowd. His appearance as a mysterious nightrider, a sixty-year-old, gray-headed black man wearing throwback biker gear and a paisley bow tie, was certainly noteworthy, but the revelers soon returned to their inconsequential banter.

The bar was crowded three deep. Drink orders were shouted out and money flittered through the air. Ezra Bonner found the back corner of the bar and was able to slip past a GQ poster-boy biker in lime green suede riding pants. A little farther back, a spindly and rather plain young woman, dressed well beyond the necessity of her looks, peered over the top of her bookish glasses, motioning to Bonner. Liza Strommer had made it her goal in life to find a place for herself in the glitzy, too-cool biker crowd. It had been a struggle. Her position as a not-yet tenured communications systems instructor at Berkeley left her with a discernible disadvantage. Liza had known about Bonner's biking passion but had discreetly avoided the subject on campus. When he had contacted her, pressing for a bit of questionable assistance, she had not given his biking passion any thought. But when he suggested they meet at the Curb Bar, she knew something was up.

Bonner navigated past the last line of bar-hounds and slipped up beside Liza. He was pretty much taken aback by the scope of narcissism surrounding him. "Interesting ambiance," he noted.

"Nice leathers," Liza tossed back at him.

Bonner was still surveying the crowd. "I'm reasonably certain that Hunter Thompson would have been disappointed by all this."

"Times change," Liza shrugged. "Look, Ezra, you've got no business riding around on that hog relic of yours. It's beneath you."

"Not really, Liza. I enjoy the redemptive exhilaration."

"Ezra, you're a shameless product of the sixties. Worse still, you are an academic. That should make you a card-carrying radical. Instead, your politics are something right of Attila the Hun. Why do you insist on flaunting that bike of yours as the last vestment of your wild years?"

Bonner allowed a warm smile. "Guilty as charged. What shall we talk about now?"

"Beats me. You're not going to ditch the bike?"

"Hardly."

Liza threw up her hands, "Okay. So, where are we? Oh yeah, you called, I'm here."

Bonner didn't answer, but rather he paused to survey the boisterous crowd again. Liza noticed his cautionary gaze. "Why couldn't we have met on campus or somewhere over in Berkeley?" she asked.

"This is better."

"Great. It's also a thirty minute drive."

"Hmm. Well then I supposed my next question should be to ask if you have had any luck?"

"Of course I did. Cell phone records are about as safe as a piggy bank." She slipped a cell phone from her pocket and slid it across the table to Bonner. "Here's your phone back."

"You were able to trace the call, the one from Jake?"

She was grinning. "Ezra, there are no secrets in electronic communication."

"Especially if you are Liza Stommer, multi-talented communications systems professor."

"No *professor* yet, Ezra," she corrected. "You're well aware of that. But the way I see it, you're gonna lay a little quid pro quo on me for tracking Jake Altman for you."

"That would be outside the boundaries of department protocol."

"But I am going to get my research grant, aren't I?"

"Only if you qualify."

"Do I qualify?"

"Of course you do. Now, tell me. What did you find out?"

Liza cautiously dug in her leather vest and produced an over-folded index card. "Jake was in Bodega Bay when he called you last night. The data places him at a dumpy little bar by the commercial wharf."

"Excellent."

"The girl, what's her name?" Liza added.

"Anna Roman."

"She was with him," Liza continued. "Or, at least there was a girl with him. I could hear her talking in the background."

"Well, that's insightful."

"No, not so insightful. They're gone already."

"Oh." Bonner was clearly disappointed.

Liza seemed put out. "Ezra, have I ever short-sheeted an assignment from you?"

"You know where they went, don't you?"

"I made a few calls myself. They got on a boat, *The Princess*; I think her father owns it."

"Her father was murdered two nights ago."

"Whew. Okay, that's awful. But it doesn't have a whole hell of a lot to do with me. So, back to Jake and the girl -- they got on the boat and left the harbor."

"Right or left?"

"Pardon?"

"Once they exited the harbor, did they turn north or south, right or left?"

"Right. They went north, Ezra. Does that mean something?"

"Yes, of course. We now know with great certainty that Jake and his new friend did not go south."

Liza groaned with frustration. "Why is this so important? It's not like you to go slinking around trying to track down one of your young professors and his girlfriend."

"I don't believe that Anna Roman is Jake's girlfriend."

"But you don't know, do you? What if she is? What's going on? Look, I'm a little worried about you, you know."

Bonner hesitated then leaned over and gently patted Liza's hand. "Thank you."

"You're welcome."

Bonner rose up and melted away into the crowd.

The sea was dead calm as the last rays of light spilled across the placid water. It was as if life itself had been sucked from the ocean, leaving only a smooth, reflective shimmer, still and immensely deep. Amid the wet, chilled air, Jake sat tiredly on a coil of rope on the aft deck of *The Princess*. It was uncomfortable, but he was far too exhausted to stand. He rolled a cold, longneck bottle of beer in his hand, soothing his blistered fingers. Anna sat nearby on an ice chest with her head tilted back against the cockpit side. She sipped her beer then closed her eyes, lost in a myriad of haunting remembrances.

"I did good, didn't I," Jake offered tiredly.

Anna didn't bother to open her eyes. "Yedor didn't tear your head off, if that's what you mean."

"Yeah, what a guy. Did you see him pull nails out of the hull with his teeth?"

"Funny." Anna's eyes cracked open. "You did okay, okay?"

"Thanks."

"How are your hands?"

Jake surveyed his blistered palms. Blood oozed from several ruptured wounds. "I should have used gloves."

"Yedor didn't need gloves."

Jake chuckled then took a swig of beer. His eyes fell on Anna again. "What now?"

"I thought we were resting."

"I mean after that. You said we were going somewhere."

"You see, that's the thing, with you, Jake Altman. You jump to conclusions. All I said was that I was getting on Mikhail's boat and going out to sea. That's all I said, just going out to sea. You invited yourself to go along."

"Then we're not going anywhere in particular?"

"That depends."

"On what?"

Anna tilted her head over and looked deeply at Jake. Her gaze was focused, boring into him, searching for something worthy of her trust. She wanted, no needed, to tell him more. Jake was certain of this, but the unspoken barrier between them remained, a near impenetrable cloak of distrust and apprehension. Anna set her beer bottle down. "I smell like bilge water. You smell worse. It's time for a shower." She rose abruptly and started down the steps into the cabin. "Get another beer if you want it. I don't plan to leave any hot water for you."

"Love you too," Jake sang out as she disappeared below.

Darkness and a shroud of incoming fog had thinned traffic on the northbound lanes of the Golden Gate Bridge. The halogen road lights had become diffused in the swirling mist, forcing cars to navigate the two-mile bridge slowly, guided for the most part by the blurred tail-lights of the vehicle in front of them. Nothing at all could be seen of the twin, three-hundred-foot support towers; they were completely lost in the drifting, gray pall.

Ezra Bonner was doing seventy-five, speeding his motorcycle somewhat recklessly past more-cautious drivers. He swiped condensing mist from the faceplate of his helmet and squinted to bring greater resolution to the surreal milieu. His mind raced even faster, reviewing, organizing, and calculating his options. Bonner fervently believed in the comforting structure of calm, dispassionate evaluation. Even when he was much younger, just another poor black kid from Oakland, he had the good sense to recognize necessity of obtaining a good education. Bonner had studied hard, being careful to cultivate relationships that might lead to opportunities in the future. It was a measured, even predictable path; there was nothing circuitous about it. He knew what he wanted and had a clear plan to get there, but somehow, along the way, Bonner's nihilistic conception of life had been sidetracked. He discovered his own humanity, and along with it, he began to embrace a worldview that recognized the intrinsic value of langauge, the arts, and political history in particular. It was a true epiphany for Bonner. He finally grasped the connection between the past and present, as well as the permanence of the many historic and political antecedents he had studied; he finally understood the impact these events had on the world. Ezra Bonner was certain that he had discovered an invaluable truth; it was this same truth that he had shared with his classes for over forty years, consistently postulating how the actions of a *few* defined and impacted the lives of *many*.

Bonner's big Harley roared with throaty, guttural bombast as he shot off the north end of the Golden Gate Bridge, climbed past the quaint, harbor-side community of Sausalito, and disappeared into the darkly serene Marin Headland foothills.

Katherine Sexton stood in the shadows of the narrow stairway leading up to Jake's apartment as a damp breeze filtered past. She was certain that he would have forgotten that she knew where the key was hidden.

How long had it been, Katherine thought, a year, probably more. They had both been drinking freely; Jake, as compensation for his reservations about having a torrid fling with a senior department head, she, simply because wine was always preferred before sex. It had been very late, and the pizza shop had been closed for an hour. They had stumbled up the steps, groping urgently, aroused by what they both knew was coming. It had been their first time together. Katherine had orchestrated the encounter, seeing Jake as yet another conquest in her insatiable quest for risky liaisons. She remembered that he had been adverse initially, most probably hesitant to tarnish the memory of his beautiful fiancée. Katherine knew that she would win, and she did. They had stumbled to the top of the stairway, oblivious to a spitting rain. She bit his lip hard as she tore his shirt open, and it was all he could do to fumble blindly along the window ledge, upturning a porcelain frog to retrieve the key.

Katherine was hidden in the murky shadows now, as she slid the sun-bleached amphibian statue aside and lifted the key. She glanced over her shoulder then unlocked the door, leaving the key in it, and stepped into Jake's apartment. A light glowed softly over the sink, but the room was otherwise wrapped in darkness. Katherine produced a small flashlight and snapped it on. The disarray of the overturned apartment surprised her. It had been ransacked, and now she was afraid. She looked around quickly then made her way to Jake's desk. Katherine wasn't certain what she was looking for, but she instinctively assumed that he was not the sort of man to rely on complicated security measures.

Papers were strewn across the desk, spilling onto the floor. The main desk drawer had been yanked out and overturned on a chair. The smaller drawers revealed little, but then Katherine noticed that a stack of three or four yellow legal pads had fallen off the back of the desk and were stuck against the wall. She dug them out and studied the rumpled, note-filled pages. A quick survey of Jake's cursive ramblings yielded little except a crude sketch of a foul weather slicker with the letters, C.M.M.A. inked on the back. Katherine mouthed the letters to herself; C.M.M.A., but nothing registered. She tore the page out and stuffed it in her pocket.

"Who are you?" a gruff voice suddenly called out.

Katherine spun around. Nick Rommel, proprietor of Pablo's Perfect Pizza, was standing in the doorway, fully adorned in his flour-splattered cooking apron. He wasn't wearing a shirt; his flaccid and very hairy shoulders bristled like a brutish Neanderthal hunter. Nick held a menacing rolling-pin in his hand.

"I asked you who you were," he repeated.

"I'm a friend, Jake's friend."

Nick eyed the roughly ransacked apartment then glared suspiciously at Katherine, "Did you do this?"

"No, of course not." Katherine offered a disingenuous smile, "Jake gave me his key. He asked me to check on his place while he was away."

"He didn't say he was going anywhere," Nick retorted. "Maybe I oughta check with him."

"Sure. If that's what you need to do. But it's not really necessary."

"Because you're Jake's friend?"

"Exactly."

Nick allowed his eyes to trace down her firm body. He noted her long legs and pouting ass. "Yeah," he grumbled. "Jake could go for someone like you. But that doesn't make it right for you to be in here, not with the place tossed like this."

"I told you I didn't do it," Katherine snapped.

"Yeah, heard that too," Nick growled. "But I think you and me, we're gonna go down stairs and call the cops." He stepped aside and motioned with the rolling pin for Katherine to go first. "Ladies first."

Katherine sighed and slapped her hands on her hips. "Okie-dokie." She sauntered past Nick, and he couldn't help but gawk at her shapely, swaying hips.

Katherine had no more than cleared the doorjamb, when she suddenly slammed the door behind her and flipped the key over, locking it.

Nick was still inside, incensed, and he grappled with the door lock. It took a few seconds for him to realize she had locked it. He angrily flipped the inside lock tumbler over and the door popped open.

Katherine was already halfway down the stairs, racing away. Nick treaded after her, but the sub-standard wooden stairs quivered ominously as he shoved his considerable weight downward. By the time he had reached the bottom, Katherine had already leaped across a puddle of water and bolted away into the night.

Nick bellowed a stream of obscenities and heaved his rolling pin after her.

21

Jake took a slow swig of beer and settled back on the rope coil on the aft deck of *The Princess*. He was in no hurry to get up. Darkness had fallen, silent and protective, as a spectacular explosion of stars swept across a coal-black sky. Jake didn't know what lay ahead; he was still trying to sort through the disjointed collisions of the past several days. He was afraid; of that reality, he was certain. Beyond that, the deluge of violence and death had come so fast, and from so many directions, that it was impossible to think strategically. Anna wanted and needed to take him somewhere, but for reasons he could not fathom, she was hesitant to trust him. Jake felt as if their aimless wandering across the sea had become a subjective dance, an oblique and uncertain probing, that left him with more questions than answers. Jake understood her recalcitrance, but he sensed something deeper, something more calculated.

Jake assumed that Bodega Bay's starchy sheriff, Lawrence Jackson, had linked him, via Anna, to Mikhail Roman's murder by now. That meant the San Francisco police were probably involved too, and were now probing his relationship with the Berkeley faculty, Ezra Bonner in particular. Jake was unsettled by this. Ezra was a scholar, a lover of all things historical and of nothing relating to bleak human infidelities.

Jake heard the boat's shower pump kick on below deck. It vibrated softly, oddly complimenting the sound of creaking hull planks and the lazy play of *The Princess'* rudder against the current. He rose stiffly and navigated the steep steps leading below deck. Squeezing into the galley, Jake downed the last of his beer and opened the tiny refrigerator, withdrawing a second bottle. He called out through the narrow, varnished door to the head, "Am I allowed to get drunk?"

"What!" Anna called out above the shower spray.

"Never mind. I'm going to get drunk anyway," Jake retorted. His stomach was growling offensively. It had been at least eight hours since he had eaten, and he began muttering to himself as he made his way forward, peering in various cabinets, searching for some noteworthy snack. "Hard work, a steady sea," he crooned. "Honest blood on an honest man's hands." He toasted himself and sipped his beer, calling out to no one in particular, "Give me a tall ship and a star to sail her by." Jake burped ferociously. "To hell with the sea. Give me cab-fare back to the city and dinner at Valentti's."

The shower stopped. Jake was busy searching the cabinets for food. He opened another door, but hesitated, looking closely. It was filled with common staples: corn meal, dry soups, a few cans of tuna. But there was something else there too. A large album was wedged sideways between a sack of flower and the cabinet wall. Jake slid the book free. The cover was blank.

Somewhere nearby by the haunting call of a whale rose up and echoed through the night; it was a baleful moan, deeply toned, a primordial cry. Jake listened carefully, touched in an unexpected way. He was about to slide into the narrow, Formica-topped dinette when a gentle swell lifted and rocked the boat. Another moaning call reverberated across the still water, followed immediately with second shifting swell. The whale, Jake thought, must be very close.

As *The Princess* rose and fell, the door to the head creaked open, presenting Anna, naked and only partially wrapped in a towel. She was stunning, Jake thought. Her shimmering hair was still wet, flounced playfully over her shoulders. Jake was no more than five feet away, and he could not bring himself to look away. Anna's eyes met his. It was a strange gaze, focused yet unrepentant; she was neither embarrassed nor lustful. And as the boat's sturdy oak hull creaked softly in the subsiding swells, the whale sounded for a third and final time. Then it was gone. Anna closed the door again.

It all happened in an instant but to Jake it seemed like his entire life had soared past in one sweeping rush, framing the moment with a sense of clarity he could not hope to describe or explain. Jake was awestruck. He sat motionless for a moment, failing to find any sense of logic for his feeling.

Behind the heavily varnished mahogany door, Anna stood motionless. Water dripped from her graceful cheeks and ran in meandering rivulets down her slender shoulders. She started to towel her hair but was forced to stop again. She tried desperately to realign her thoughts. Jake had roughly intruded into her life, immeasurably complicating it, and ultimately catapulting them both into the crosshairs of international assassins. Damn him, she thought. He had no right to involve himself, dragging her into his conspiratorial suppositions. But, as she gently pressed the towel to her hair, she could not suppress the sensation that her heart was calling out to her with an entirely different perception, one that she found frighteningly unexplainable.

Jake had collected his thoughts. Still seated in the dinette, he peeled the album open. The contents proved to be the second shock of the night. Jake's eyes froze on the first page, but he quickly flipped to the second and the third. It made no sense at all, but then suddenly, as a blinding epiphany, it really *did* make sense. The album was filled with photos of Anna. Slick eight by ten professional shots, each one presenting Anna in yet another dazzling outfit: Anna at a gala museum opening, draped seductively in a sleekly sequined evening gown, Anna atop the aft deck of an opulent motor yacht in a flirty and daringly low-cut cocktail dress, Anna in a near-nothing bikini, playfully cavorting across a virgin sand beach. Jake turned the pages quickly at first then more slowly. He was astonished by Anna's stunning, natural beauty. She was at one moment gracefully elegant then, with a mere flip of the page, she became provocatively seductive, impish, urbane, simmering, or reflectively introspective. Anna was a professional, a top-tier runway model. She was almost too beautiful to comprehend. Finally, Jake understood.

Anna wasn't paying attention as she eased out of the head, wrapped snuggly in a white robe. Determined to place their visual encounter in context, she said, "Look, about the bathroom door thing, let's just let it…." But she caught herself when she saw the album. "Hey! Put it down!"

Jake purposefully looked up at her, "You were a model. You should have told me."

"Put it down!" Anna cried, "Now!"

Jake shook his head and held the album back, pressing harder, "When we were on the photo set at Louis' studio, I should have known it then. There was something about the way you moved, the way you looked. You've been on a photo set before -- a lot of them."

Anna was furious. She lunged for the album. "Give it to me! Let me have the damn book!"

Jake hesitated then held it out. Anna jerked it from his hands and clutched it tightly. She tossed her hair back defiantly. "You're a bastard."

Jake took a moment before responding. Then he smiled slightly. "You were good, weren't you?"

"It was a long time ago. I've forgotten."

"Why?"

Anna's mind was racing. She wanted to scream, but she was just too tired. Instead, she sank heavily into the dinette opposite Jake.

"Why would you forget something that elegant?" Jake said earnestly.

"Because it wasn't me. Not really. I thought it was, and for a very long time I made myself believe it was." Tears ringed Anna's eyes, and a tiny drop laced down her cheek. "I believed it all -- all the hype, the adoration, the money. But it was all crap, and I bought into it."

Jake took a sip from his beer. He was quietly thrilled that Anna was talking, really talking, for the first time. Determined not to press too hard, he waited a few moments then gently asked her, "Will you tell me about it? Please."

Anna looked up and forced a faint smile. "I ran away, wanted a life of my own. I was seventeen."

"Tough way to start out."

"Tell me about it. Mikhail was furious, but he let me go."

"Was it hard, getting started?"

"Not at first. I got jobs pretty quickly. It was easy. Then it started to get complicated. I was traveling constantly. Name a city. I saw it -- and it saw me. New York, Rome, Paris, Madrid, and so many I've lost count. It was fast and furious. Then I suppose it got out of control."

"That would mean drugs," Jake observed.

"Yeah, drugs, booze, money -- anything to get a thrill, to make it seem better than it was. I was a mess."

"So you bailed out. You broke free from it."

"Not really. Mikhail got me out. All the parties, the cocaine, more -- I didn't know which way my head was screwed on, didn't care either." Anna stopped for a moment and wiped a tear from her eye. She tried to smile again, but it didn't feel real. "I was in San Francisco for a shoot," Anna continued. "Might as well have been Madagascar; it didn't matter. Mikhail showed up. He broke the photographer's jaw and beat my drug-pumping boyfriend senseless. That old man could get really pissed."

Jake set his beer down. His hand moved carefully toward hers and their fingers fell together.

Anna took a deep breath and went on. "Mikhail took me here, to *The Princess*. He fed me, cleaned up the puke; I was really good at that. It seemed like it took forever when I crashed, but even when it hurt so bad I couldn't stand it, I knew that Mikhail was there. He took care of me. He saved my life."

"What about your mother?"

"She died when I was born."

"So, it was just Mikhail?"

A deep smile spread across Anna's face. "Jake, don't you see. It was *always* Mikhail. He put me together again. He made the pieces fit. The man didn't have a high school education, but he understood so much. He always understood."

"I wish I had known him."

"I wish I had known him longer."

The tears came more freely now, but Jake held her hand tightly. He was overwhelmed and could say nothing. All he knew, what he knew with great certainty now, was that he wasn't going to let Anna be hurt again. He wasn't going to let her go, ever, and now he knew why.

22

Anton Sorokin was sitting in his closet-sized office at the Russian consulate when he took the call from the security intercom at the gate, wondering why someone would be arriving so early in the morning. The man identified himself as Mr. Liam McGeorge. He said he was there to see Vladimir Chernov. At first, the name didn't register, but then Anton remembered the shooting party at the Merced Rod and Gun Club. McGeorge was the Scottish guy, a big man with a thick handlebar mustache.

Anton crossed the foyer and opened the front door. McGeorge filled the doorway with his broad shoulders. He was holding a heavy shotgun, broken open at the breech. It was an expensive weapon, old, ornately engraved and beautifully polished. The security guard appeared behind him, nervously feeling for his concealed Glock pistol.

McGeorge offered Anton a roguish grin then chirped brightly, "Good morning to you, sir. I've come to see Consul General Chernov. I'm Liam McGeorge, from the gun club event the other day."

"I remember you, sir," Anton announced without allowing his eyes to leave the open shotgun. "Did you have an appointment with the Consul General? He's still getting dressed."

McGeorge cocked his head apologetically, "Well, of course I should have known better than to call so early, but

I really had hoped that Mr. Chernov could help me understand this fine shotgun. I mentioned it to him at the shooting party. He seemed to know a lot about guns of this period, and I'm having a devil of a time properly categorizing it. Ah, but if now is too much of an imposition, I can certainly come back another time."

Anton was relieved. "Well that would seem to be better because...."

He was cut off abruptly when Vladimir Chernov appeared at the door and called out, "It's all right, Anton." He was still adjusting his tie as he extended a hand to the highland Scotsman. "Mr. McGeorge, it's good to see you again." He gestured to the shotgun. "Did you come to shoot me?"

"Ha," bellowed McGeorge. "That is most assuredly not my intention, but I thought you might be interested in this piece. She's a bit of a mystery, sir."

Chernov took the gun and traced the stock with his fingers. "German -- a Merkel 200E, I would think."

"Aye, that she is. Fine as they come. I think this one came from the Suhl factory, sometime after the East German communists took control."

"Yes. This is probably the case. The gun was banned from export to the United States during the Cold War. It shouldn't be too difficult to trace its history."

"Well, you see, that's the thing, sir," McGeorge advanced, "The shoulder stock and the trigger-guard don't match other guns of this class. See the engraving, there and there. I had hoped you could shed a wee bit of light on the subject."

Anton interjected, "Sir, you have a meeting with the Vietnamese trade delegation in thirty minutes."

"Hmm," Chernov grunted. "Well, I think this shouldn't take very long."

"Certainly. As you wish, sir," Anton acknowledged.

Chernov handed the gun back to McGeorge and waved a dismissive hand at his aide. "Mr. McGeorge and I are going to the library to have a look at this fine weapon."

McGeorge beamed, and Anton could tell he was thrilled by Chernov's accommodation. He stepped aside and allowed the big man to ease past, following Chernov across the hall. The two men disappeared into the library and the door closed behind them.

The Princess rounded Todd's Point and angled across Noyo Bay around two in the afternoon. San Francisco was now many miles to the south. Anna and Jake stood in awkward silence at the helm. Conversation had waned long before, but the sight of the harbor and its tightly clustered boat docks farther up the narrow inlet river seemed reassuring to Jake. He knew that the tiny seaside town of Noyo lay just over the crest of the hill and that they would probably walk into town for supplies.

Half a mile away, Remi was watching. Actually, he was sitting on the front hood of the black SUV, roughly consuming a sloppy deli sandwich he had bought at the local grocery. Remi held a hunting telescope in one hand, peering through the eyepiece, while shreds of ham and mayonnaise dribbled down his chin. He had *The Princess* focused in his scope and could see Anna and Jake fairly clearly as the boat churned steadily through the waves just off the coast. Remi allowed a thin smile, realizing they were coming in.

Oleg appeared, climbing roughly up from a brush-covered ravine. He was carrying a roll of paper towels, as he hitched his belt tight and zipped his pants. "Goddamn burritos," he griped, "Fucking cat meat."

"All better, mate?" Remi chided. "You look like shit."

Oleg suddenly grabbed his stomach, spun in his tracks, and shuffled back down into the ravine.

Anna eased the throttles and brought *The Princess* down to wake speed. A party fishing boat passed by, heading out to sea. Jake could see the scattering of seniors and kids lining the side decks, hopefully setting up fishing rods with large casting reels.

"Do they ever catch much of anything?" he asked. It was more of a statement than a question.

"Rockfish are pretty easy to catch up here, maybe some Black Backs," Anna noted flatly. "But the day-fishermen don't get much into King Salmon and Lingcod."

"Looks like they're having fun."

"Yeah, it doesn't really matter to them if they catch fish or not, they just like being out here."

"It is sort of peaceful," Jake added, mostly to himself. Anna gave him a sideways glance.

The double arches of the Pacific Coast Highway Bridge loomed high above *The Princess* as it motored into the mouth of the Noyo River. Anna slowed the boat again, and held the ship's wheel over to the port. Jake scanned the rag-tag fleet of fishing boats, bobbing at anchor or tied off in narrow slips just in front of them.

"Grab the line on the bow," Anna instructed. "Make it off to the port cleat. I'm going to nose *The Princess* into that slip on the end. Hold me off the wall until I get a line off the stern then you can haul up from the bow." She could see that he was frowning, confused by her instructions. She jabbed a finger toward the bow. "Just go out there and keep me from running over the dock."

"Got it. Simple English. Works every time."

Jake climbed back around the narrow cabin walkway and made his way forward to the bow deck. Anna slid *The Princess* into the boat slip and backed down on the throttles. The exhaust stack coughed up black smoke as the boat lurched once then came to rest. She hurried to the stern deck cleat and tied off the mooring line.

Anton Sorokin squatted on a stool in the consulate kitchen, nervously watching the clock. He was halfway through a large piece of pecan pie, ruminating about McGeorge's unexpected intrusion. Anton knew that Chernov loved guns, but it seemed strange that he would afford such hospitality to an old master shooter. Gun people were an odd lot, Anton thought. They talked about their weapons as if they were their children, and the pursuit of accurate categorization of a gun's history, in excruciating detail, was almost a religion. Anton shook his head disparagingly and shoved another wedge of pie in his mouth. He was still chewing when he heard the front door open and close.

Anton stumbled off the stool, gumming voraciously at his mouthful of pie. He shoved the plate into the sink then swung the cardboard pie box closed.

By the time Anton had emerged from the kitchen, the foyer was empty. "Consul General Chernov?" he called out. "Sir?" But the estate was suddenly quiet. Anton slipped his sport-coat on and hurried back down the hall, angling toward Chernov's personal office.

Vladimir Chernov was heading in the other direction. After saying goodbye to Liam McGeorge, he had slipped through a door at the far end of the foyer leading to the staff quarters. Chernov was preoccupied and in a hurry as he rapped on a heavy door then opened it. Unlike the ornately decorated public spaces in the consulate, this room was dark and cluttered. It was an office of some sort, where two metal desks opposed each other. Volumes of papers and files lay scattered about. Electronic surveillance equipment bristled from three different steel racks, with scores of tracking lights twittering errantly. Discarded bags of fast food surrounded an overflowing wastebasket, while a pair of ceiling-hung work lights cast a harsh glow down in two intersecting circles.

Chernov moved quickly to the first desk. A nasty tray of chewed cigar stubs left little doubt this one belonged to Remi. The old Russian shoved papers aside, quickly sifting through the accumulated documents. He found a large map nestled in the disarray. Chernov looked closer at the notes scribbled obliquely across it. He could see San Francisco, the bay, and the coast for the next hundred miles north. Inked-in lines vectored across the map, web-like, with no apparent purpose.

Chernov's eyes tracked across the data, absorbing everything, missing nothing. He suddenly called out loudly, "Anton!" Moments passed as Chernov swung around behind the other desk where piles of wadded-up food bags trailed down to the floor, filled the wastebasket and spilled over. Oleg's deplorable eating habits were of no surprise to the consul general. "Anton!" he bellowed without looking up.

The door burst open and Anton, completely out of breath, staggered in. "Sir, I am sorry. I thought you were back in the...."

"No matter," Chernov interrupted. His quick eyes landed on his cherubic aide's cheek. "Is that pie?" he queried disdainfully.

Anton was mortified as he swept his sleeve over a glob of pecan filling. Chernov's gaze had returned to the surrounding clutter. He picked up the map again. Pieces were beginning to fit together. Remi and Oleg had been absent from the consulate more than once recently: their reports had been vague, even unfocused. Chernov assumed they had been effectively doing his bidding, but now the mistakes had begun to take a toll.

"Where are they, Anton?" Chernov demanded.

"Uhm, I'm not certain, sir. You told me they wouldn't be needed this morning. They left."

"Call them."

"I did, sir. Just ten minutes ago. They didn't answer."

Chernov's face tightened. He quickly began to fold the map. "Get the car, Anton."

"But, sir, you have the meeting with the trade delegation."

"Get the car. Now."

23

The small seaside enclave of Noyo, California had, for a very long time, been overshadowed by its more popular sister-town of Mendocino, the beguiling get-away retreat about twenty miles farther down the coast. With a resident population only slightly less than Mendocino, Noyo had simply never been able to grow. It was a nice town though, with a sweeping bluff, crescent-shaped beach and spectacular sunsets. Its sheltered harbor, tucked safely around the first bend in the Noyo River, had long been an oasis for fishermen working their way along the coast. There was a chandlery, several boat shops, and at a couple of raucous bars lining the hillside above the flotilla of fishing vessels.

Just a little farther inland, Anna Roman backed out of the tiny Pic-Pac Grocery at the north end of Woodward Street, loaded with a large box of supplies. Melba Torez, the tiny storeowner, held the weathered screen door open for her. Melba had owned and operated the shop for thirty years, never once closing the doors, even when her husband's fishing trawler disappeared forever twenty miles off the coast. No one was really quite sure if Melba enjoyed her work. She was pleasant and had a generous smile, but she carefully avoided any sort of meaningful engagement with her customers. Today was different. As Anna edged past her, she could not hide her concern. "Anna, you know how I felt about Mikhail. He was so special."

"Yeah. That and more. Thanks, Melba," Anna replied, refusing to let herself sink into the debilitating morass of her father's death.

"Have the police found anything yet?" Melba pressed.

Anna hesitated, racked with at least some measure of guilt in the fact that she knew absolutely nothing. She offered Melba a faint smile. "Someone is bound to know something about his murder."

"I suppose these things take time," Melba added guardedly. "You must be working closely with the police."

Anna realized that Melba was subtly questioning her presence in the tiny town. "No," she replied. "There's not much I can do."

Melba nodded sympathetically then glanced at Jake, who was easing out the door, carrying an even larger box of groceries. She turned back to Anna and offered a confiding assessment, "I suppose it's good to have a man around, hmm?"

Anna set her box on a bench and put her hand on Melba's arm, lowering her voice to impart a sense of gravity. "You didn't see me, Melba. I wasn't here," she whispered, more as a sincere request for help. "Do you understand? People are looking for me."

"The police?"

"Probably, but I can't talk to them right now. Even that's not safe. Please. Just let us disappear. Can you do that?"

"Of course," Melba said reassuringly. "Is there anything else I can do?

"No. Thank you."

Melba was uncharacteristically somber. "Anna, you know that for Mikhail, I would do anything. You must know that."

Anna wrapped her fingers around the storekeeper's tiny hand. "We have to go now."

Anna lifted her box of supplies and turned to the steps. Jake was waiting on the sidewalk below the timber veranda. He knew they needed supplies, but the fear of being seen and reported was inescapable. Anna could see the frustration in his eyes as she slipped past him.

Melba watched Anna and Jake carefully as they turned away, her thoughts probing for the truth that she knew was being kept from her. When Jake glanced back, he was more certain than ever that it had been a mistake to be seen like this.

Without warning, sharp gunshots rang out, a rapid-fire burst of loud cracks. Jake dropped his box and slammed into Anna, knocking her roughly to the ground. Groceries scattered across the sidewalk, as a second volley of shots broke out, louder and closer than the first assault. Anna cried out in terror, as Jake tried to shield her body. Then there was silence. Jake could see two figures darting away through a cloud of dust and smoke. The boys couldn't have been more than ten years old; they giggled hysterically as they raced through the remnants of the fireworks they had just set off. They were gone in an instant.

Jake pulled Anna upright as he waved at the drifting fireworks smoke. "Are you okay?" Jake asked. Anna was still shaken but her eyes were wide with gratitude. Melba stood on the veranda above them, mystified by their kneejerk reaction to simple hometown pyrotechnics.

"Kids," Jake called out offhandedly. "The little bastards."

Anna shoved her hair back and dusted her blouse off. She was watching Jake very closely. Something had changed, and he sensed the depth of her gaze. "What?" he asked.

"You covered me, why?"

Jake had to think for a moment. "I thought it was gunfire." Then he said nothing.

Anna accepted his silence, but any doubts she had about Jake and his true intent had been instantly washed away in a spray of kids' fireworks. Anna had not expected it, but knowing, finally, that Jake was to be trusted, meant more to her than she ever would have thought possible. She pulled herself up. Jake rose up too, dusting himself off. When he looked at her, Anna was still gazing deeply at him. After a moment, she called out over her shoulder. "Melba, could you hold these groceries for us for an hour or so?"

"Well, I supposed I could," Melba announced cautiously.

"Let's go, "Anna announced softly to Jake, "There isn't much time."

"Hey. Where are you going?" Melba called out.

Jake was confused too. "Yeah, where are we going?"

"Sometimes the truth is closer than you think," Anna responded, but Jake couldn't tell if it was an answer or a warning.

Anna led Jake back down Woodward Street then angled toward the bluffs hovering over the harbor. She didn't seem to want to talk, and Jake was okay with this. He sensed, even in her silence, that he had somehow broken through Anna's guarded façade, but when the sparkling water came into view, Jake thought for a moment that he had been wrong, and that she was simply leading him back to *The Princess*. But why? Why leave the groceries behind?

Jake became even more puzzled when Anna turned abruptly to the east, veering off on a narrow gravel lane. The town and harbor were quickly left behind. Towering Eucalyptus trees arched over the winding roadway, bathing it in cool shade. Beyond that, up a slight hill, Jake could see tall, dry grass undulating over the rolling countryside.

"Well, this is nice," Jake noted acerbically.

"It's not far," Anna offered as an appeasement.

Jake was tiring of Anna's reticence. He was about to press harder when she veered off the roadway and stopped beside a pair of neatly-built stone columns and a handsome copper plaque marked the entrance and proclaimed this to be the Saddle Peak Home.

Jake looked down the long lane, where an old Victorian home stood alone, prominently perched atop the verdant foothills. "What's this? I don't understand," he posited.

Anna gestured toward the rambling structue, "That's why we're here."

273

"What do you mean?"

Anna stopped and turned to Jake. "I don't have the answers you're looking for, Jake. If I did, I wouldn't have told you before. I didn't trust you."

"But now you do?"

Anna's eyes fell on the old house in the distance. "I think the answers to our questions are in there. At least I hope they are." Anna moved on without explaining. Jake followed, and he soon spotted a group of people on the lawn in front of the house. They were old; some were playing croquet, while others simply basked in the sun, reclining comfortably in weathered yard chairs.

"This is a retirement home," Jake observed.

Anna had fallen silent. Memories flooded back. Finally, she took a breath and looked at Jake, "There's a woman here who knew Mikhail. She knew Marvina Dubrovsky too."

"Marvina? That's the woman who jumped in front of a bus at the cathedral in the city."

"Yes. Marvina Dubrovsky."

"She's dead," Jake noted flatly.

"Yes, but her sister isn't."

Tarvina Dubrovsky was still dressed in her robe and heavy slippers. She was very old and tenuously frail. The remnants of her birthday cake, two days old now, sat on a side table. Three number-candles stood atop the icing, proclaiming, incredibly, one hundred and four years.

Soothing morning sunlight flowed through a tall window, warmly caressing Tarvina's second floor bedroom suite. She sat in her favorite chair, very still, staring out across the golden countryside. Tarvina was nearly blind, but the sun bathed her face and cheered her spirits. Her memories, all but gone now, came to her only in disassociated images, confusing fragments of a very long life.

Anna and Jake appeared in her open doorway, but she didn't see them. For just a moment, Anna looked at the old woman, remembering so much. "Tarvina," she whispered softly. "Tarvina, it's Anna."

Tarvina's head turned slowly, but her clouded eyes showed no sign of recognition. Anna threw a quick look at Jake, shaking her head to confirm that this would be difficult. She moved closer and sat in the chair beside the old woman. Jake stayed in the doorway, waiting, watching. There was something about Tarvina that was very familiar. Finally, it dawned on him. She looked *exactly* like her sister. Anna saw Jake's look of amazement and said, "Twins."

Anna put her hand over Tarvina's frail fingers. "Tarvina, I'm Anna, Mikhail's daughter."

Tarvina's voice was vacant and weak, "Anna."

"Yes, I'm Anna. Do you remember?"

"Mikhail," Tarvina said more strongly. "I remember."

"Mikhail is dead, Tarvina. So is your sister. Marvina is gone."

Tarvina's eyes grew wide as she struggled with faint remembrances. "Marvina – Mikhail --dead?"

Jake knew there was a deep and interwoven history here, but he was still struggling with the unexplained intersections. "Anna, why are we here?" he asked softly.

At first, Anna ignored him as she gently brushed Tarvina's hair with her fingers.

"Anna," the old woman recounted with a spreading smile.

Anna smiled too then turned to Jake. "Marvina and Tarvina raised Mikhail. They were there when he was born. They were devoted to him and his mother. They *knew* the secrets Mikhail kept from me, from everyone."

"Is that why Marvina confessed then threw herself in front of a bus?"

"I think so, but it's also very complicated."

A tall black man had appeared in the hallway behind Jake. "It *is* complicated, but not impossible to discern," Ezra Bonner announced.

Jake spun around, stunned to see his mentor. "Ezra? What the hell?"

Jake noted Bonner's riding leathers and the helmet he carried in one hand. The professor smiled warmly and edged past Jake, pacing purposely into the room. He set his helmet on a table. "I suppose I should explain."

"That would be nice, Ezra, considering you have absolutely no business being here," Jake snapped.

Anna was watching too, completely perplexed and even afraid. Bonner eased down on the side of the bed and scratched at his white hair. "Marvina and Tarvina were midwives to Mikhail Roman. Anna knows most of this, but not everything. That really doesn't matter now. What is crucially important is what happened *before* Mikhail was born."

Anna was shaking her head, "I don't understand."

Jake moved closer. "Ezra, stop playing games. What do you have to do with all this?"

Bonner's eyes flickered with an intensity that Jake had not seen before; he went on to reveal a strangely convoluted story, "You both know about the Baikal, the ship that sailed from Russia in 1918. And by now you most probably know that the ship was carrying a vast amount of gold rubles, the last of the Romanov dynasty's treasure."

"The gold is a fantasy," Jake scoffed. "You've read the accounts. It's a myth."

Bonner patiently continued, "The Baikal and the gold are real. The ship sailed from the South China Sea with over thirty billion dollars-worth of uncirculated gold rubles aboard."

"Bullshit. Ezra, you don't have any way of..."

But Bonner cut him off quickly. "Listen to me, Jake! The Baikal sank off the coast of California. It was lost. This *really* happened."

Anna had had enough. "What does it have to do with Mikhail, Marvina, and Tarvina?

Bonner eyed both Jake and Anna carefully, measuring them. "Mikhail's mother was on the Baikal. She survived the sinking."

"No," Anna choked. "That's not possible."

She looked quickly at Tarvina, but Bonner intervened, laying his hand on the old woman's arm. He leaned closer and said one word, "Anastasia."

Tarvina gasped. She snatched Bonner's hand. "Anastasia," she repeated.

Jake was stunned. "Ezra, what are you telling us?"

Bonner hesitated then spoke with calm resolve, "Anastasia was the eldest daughter of Nicholas the second, last sovereign of the Russian empire. Everyone thinks they know what happened to her, but the historical record is incomplete. It's wrong. Anastasia didn't die with the rest of her family at the hands of the Bolshevik rebels in the basement of the Romanov country estate. She escaped on the Baikal, and she survived when the ship sank."

"More stories, Ezra," Jake barked. "There have been at least a dozen disenfranchised European blue-bloods who claimed to have been Anastasia. They were all fakes!"

Jake threw a look at Anna, but she had suddenly become silent, lost in distant memories. She looked deeply at Tarvina. "Tarvina, is it true? Was Mikhail's mother the princess Anastasia? Please. Tell me."

Tarvina's eyes narrowed and her brow wrinkled. She looked away again, searching the spreading California countryside.

"Tarvina, please!"

The old woman bowed her head, lost, then suddenly rose unsteadily to her feet. With Anna supporting her, she crept to her dresser, pulling out a weathered wooden box. Tarvina allowed her fingers to trace the surface of the container. Then she sat down again and opened it, peeling back a lace coverlet to reveal a multi-jeweled cross, boldly emblazoned with the Romanov family crest.

"A gift. To me from her," Tarvina whispered.

Tarvina clutched the bejeweled cross in her hands and rocked back and forth in her chair. She was muttering something, but Jake couldn't make it out. He knelt down beside her and spoke very softly. "Tarvina. Who gave this to you?"

The name rolled ever so sweetly from Tarvina's lips, "Anastasia."

"Oh, my God," Anna gushed.

Ezra Bonner turned to Jake. "It's true, Jake. Anastasia was Mikhail's mother, and then he…"

Jake finished the sentence for him. "Then he married and they had Anna."

Bonner added solemnly, "And that makes Anna the last of the Romanov's."

Tarvina continued to rock. Her eye sank shut as a radiant smile spread across her face. She whispered again, "Anastasia."

Anna was shaking her head in utter disbelief, but Bonner pressed her. "Anna, I want you to listen very carefully to me. Mikhail kept the secret all of his life. Marvina and Tarvina, midwives to your father and to Anastasia, kept the secret even longer. There were people who would have come and taken you if they knew. Mikhail, Marvina and Tarvina protected the Romanov lineage for a lifetime."

"But Marvina went to the archbishop! She killed herself!" Anna protested.

"She was old and sick," Bonner continued, "Her mind was gone. We will never know why she went to Konstantin or what she told him, but it seems plausible that her pilgrimage was a simple act of contrition for a lifetime of lies."

"How do you know all of this?" Anna charged.

Bonner sighed and settled back. "I wasn't born when the Russian empire collapsed and the Communists seized power, but I saw what they did. They destroyed a proud country. I watched them tear down the foundations that had built a richly textured culture and grind it into the ground. I've studied this all of my life."

Jake had not spoken for a few minutes. Bonner looked at him and asked, "Jake, do you understand?"

When the reply came, Jake's voice was hollow and even reproachful as he quickly drilled to the heart of the matter. "Are you trying to kill us, Ezra? Is it you?"

"No."

"Then it has to be Chernov."

Bonner was unsure. "I don't know, not anymore."

Anna had found her voice again, "Well, you're here, and you know an awful lot," she charged. "There has to be a reason; it's something very personal for you, isn't it?" She hesitated, her eyes fixed on Bonner as she accused, "You think Tarvina knows where the Baikal went down. You want the Romanov gold."

"Hardly," Bonner scoffed. "I'm an academic. I have no use for gold."

"What do you want?" Anna demanded.

Bonner fell silent. Jake grabbed him. "Answer her, Ezra! What do you want?"

"For myself, nothing."

Jake jerked at Ezra's coat again, but his old friend slapped his hands away. "Get off it, Jake. Don't be stupid. I've taught you better than that. Anna is a Romanov. There are dangerous people in Russia who want her. Her very existence is enough to turn the country upside down. That she knows where the Baikal sank, makes her all the more valuable -- and desired."

"Then it *is* Chernov," Jake posited.

"I think not," Ezra allowed. "But it would be hard not to believe that the Russian president, Dmitri Bellus, is involved."

"Bellus?" Jake retorted in surprise.

"There have been attempts to reconstitute the royal family before," Bonner explained. "Dmitri Bellus publicly supported the idea, as long as he could retain real power. But if you think carefully about it, with the rise of new nationalistic fervor, a resurgence of the Romanov family could utterly destroy him. He's not going to let that happen. Bellus has to control the situation."

Jake and Anna fell silent, each immersed in a flood of confused thoughts; they were angry and afraid, searching for answers to a one-hundred-year-old enigma. Tarvina was still mumbling to herself as she rocked and rocked. A handmade Russian clock ticked loudly on the dresser.

The silence was finally broken by the sound of Remi's roughly clapping his hands. Jake and Anna spun around to find Remi and Oleg looming in the doorway. Oleg lifted a sawed-off shotgun from beneath his coat, while Remi continued to smack his hands together sardonically. He was staring at Ezra Bonner. "That's just really special, mate,"

Remi chided. "You're a friggin' whiz at flapping your gums. What a story. And to think, this is all about the girl after all."

Jake stood quickly and stepped in front of Anna. "She doesn't know anything," he spat back at Remi.

"Aw, now Dr. Altman, I'm thinking we know better than that."

Ezra was on his feet too. "You are making a mistake. Anna doesn't know about the gold. You effectively ran this thing into a dead end when you killed her father." He gestured toward Tarvina. "Any remaining knowledge of the Baikal was with her. It's gone now."

Remi withdrew a sleek Glock handgun from his jacket. "Well, now that everybody's had their yap about things, let's quit jacking off and get going." He motioned for Jake and Anna to come toward him. "This way."

Jake hesitated, blocking Anna's movement, but Oleg chambered his shotgun and Remi grinned again. "Not a good alternative, mate. Move. Now."

Jake relented. He shifted cautiously toward the door with Anna. Ezra cast a look back at Tarvina, oblivious to the confrontation, still mumbling to herself. He stepped forcefully forward. Remi threw a quick nod at Oleg, who shoved his shotgun in front of Ezra, blocking the way. "Not you, old man," he growled. "You're not invited."

Ezra blustered, "Look. If you're taking them, you're going to take me too. I think it's…" But he didn't get to finish. Oleg slapped the shotgun barrel hard across his face. Bonner went down and stayed down; he was unconscious.

Remi punched Jake in the ribs with his weapon and snarled, "Go."

As the group eased into the upstairs hallway, Jake and Anna moved silently toward the stairway. Jake could see four or five senior residents watching anxiously from the lobby below. "Go away," Jake shouted. "Get out of here!"

"Very well said, mate," Remi chirped. "Smart idea." He was fully in charge now, and he was enjoying it.

Jake and Anna started down the steps with Oleg and Remi just above them. When Anna glanced back, her eyes widened and her hand shot out to Jakes arm. He turned to look. Oleg and Remi were still there, but Tarvina was behind them all now, standing unsteadily in the open hallway. She held a rusting Colt 45 revolver in both hands. The weight was almost too much for her, but she managed to keep the gun trained on the two thugs.

"Tarvina! No!" Anna screamed.

Oleg spun quickly. He jerked his shotgun up, but Tarvina pulled the trigger first. The gun cracked angrily, bucking her backward. Oleg shuddered from the impact as blood exploded from his head. He lurched over the stairway railing and crashed to the floor below. An instant later, Remi's revolver belched fire, and Tarvina slammed into the wall with a gaping hole in her neck. Her gun went off, clipping Remi in the skull. Blood splattered the wall as he careened into the railing and tried to fire again. Tarvina, probably more dead than alive, toppled over the edge of the stairway and crashed into him.

Jake tugged Anna aside, barely avoiding the two tumbling bodies. Tarvina ricocheted down the flight of stairs. She landed hard, sprawled across the floor face up, her dead eyes gaping open. Remi crashed down on top of her; he was dazed but alive, and although he could hardly see through his bloodied eyes, he spotted his fallen handgun and he struggled to reach it.

Jake saw the gun too. He leaped down the stairs three steps at a time, but he was too slow. Remi's fingers curled around the gun and he fired, missing Jake by inches. Jake kicked Remi hard in the face and the pugnacious Brit skidded sideways. Somehow, he was able to hang on to the gun, cursing and spitting blood as he tried to pull himself upright. Anna flew past him into Jake's arms, and they tore out of the old house, stumbling away down the narrow lane.

Midstride, racing down the road, Jake and Anna passed the thugs' SUV, but they were far more focused on putting as much distance as possible between them and Remi. Anna could barely keep up. She fell once, gouging into the dusty gravel. The road seemed to go on forever, until finally they could see the bluffs ahead. When Jake and Anna broke into the open field high over the tiny harbor, they saw the car, not the black SUV this time, but rather it was a sleek limousine with darkly tinted windows.

Anna threw a furtive look back and saw Remi limping down the long roadway. Jake saw him as well. Remi was too far away to shoot, and he seemed to be struggling more with each stride. Jake grabbed Anna's arm and lunged over the hillside, streaking down the switchback trail leading to the boat docks. Both of them fell near the bottom and tumbled roughly into the marshy flats.

Jake pulled Anna up and shouted at her, "The boat, get to the boat!"

She ran ahead while Jake sucked in air, fretfully watching the hillside, waiting.

Remi, swiping at the bullet crease on his forehead, struggled to the top of the bluff. He could see Jake below and Anna scrambling aboard *The Princess*. He swiped blood from his face and hauled the gun up, knowing full-well that he was too far away to hit anything. Remi fired off three quick rounds then cursed and sank to his knees in the tall grass. He tried to think, but his head was throbbing. He was still sucking in air when he heard the car door open.

Remi twisted his head around to see Anton Sorokin climb out of the limo. He was carrying a neatly scoped high power rifle, as he strode over, set the rifle stock down, then let the gun fall into Remi's lap. Something was very different about Anton now. There was no sign of his diminutive meekness, or even his correct sense of deference. He glared at Remi and said, "Do you think maybe you can do this without screwing it up again." He gestured to the gun. "The first round is chambered. Seven others are in the clip. Take the shot."

Far below, Jake rocketed across the marsh and then the dock. He leaped aboard *The Princess* just as Anna fired off the two smoking diesels. "Get the lines," she shouted. But before Jake could move, the cabin hatch opened and Vladimir Chernov stepped up onto the deck. He was wrapped in a dark cashmere topcoat, and his face was set in an intense gaze. Anna's eyes flashed from Chernov to Jake. Finally, Chernov spoke, "Are you going to bring me inside?" It was the same oblique question he had asked Jake at the consulate, and it made no more sense now than it did then.

The powerful crack of a rifle echoed across the still harbor. An instant later, a section of the boat's console exploded in splinters. Jake and Anna ducked down below the aft deck coaming, but Chernov didn't move. He cocked his head and hissed at Jake again. "Remi is going to kill you. There won't be any second chances." He paused then asked again, "Are you going to bring me inside?"

Another gunshot rang out and the windshield exploded. Jake spotted the cleaving machete buried in its sheath under the coaming. He lunged for it, screaming at Anna, "Go. Hit it!"

Anna leaped up and shoved the engine throttles down. The mooring lines snapped taut, holding the boat back. Jake snatched the machete and dove for the aft mooring lines. One whack severed the line. He swung around and chopped the second line. The boat surged under full power, and the remaining lines snapped free. *The Princess* lurched backward.

High on the hill, Remi tried to shake his blurred vision. Anton kicked him in the side. "Shoot, you idiot! Kill him!"

Remi threw his cheek into the gunstock, sighted, and fired again.

A round screamed past Jake, slicing neatly across his shoulder. He fell back, clutching at the wound. It was just a crease, but it hurt like hell. *The Princess* had spun around and was moving away, picking up speed, throwing out a heaving wake. Chernov had never moved from the cabin doorway. His dispassionate eyes fell on Jake then angled upward to the edge of the bluff. He could see Remi and Anton clearly. But when his cherubic aide suddenly snatched the rifle from Remi's hands, Chernov knew in an instant he had been very wrong.

Anton whipped the rifle up, leveling it with a marksman's precision. He clicked the site adjustment once then laid his cheek into the stock. The scope's crosshairs fell squarely across Jake. It was an easy shot. Anton sucked in a steadying breath then flicked the gun to the right, putting Vladimir Chernov dead in the sights.

Anna saw the floating stump at the last second. At the speed they were going, it would have holed the hull and sunk them. She jerked the ship's wheel, just as another shot rang out from the bluff. The bullet, traveling at three thousand feet a second, slammed into Chernov's side. The old man doubled over and sank to the deck. He was immobilized by the hit, but his eyes shot up to the bluff. Anton was chambering another shell. Chernov could only watch in stunned disbelief; he was racked by the portentous deception finally revealed and, in an instant, he understood. Anton was in charge of everything; he had been assigned to watch Chernov, to monitor everything and to kill him when it was finally time.

Anton swept the scope's crosshairs across Chernov's forehead. He wouldn't miss again. He paused, just for second, when he saw the disbelief in his charge's eyes. Then he pulled the trigger. The shell jammed. Anton cursed and feverishly tried to clear the round, but it was too late. *The Princess* cleared the coast highway overpass and churned hard toward a thick fog bank building just off shore. It was almost dark when the trawler was swallowed up and lost.

24

Ezra Bonner awoke slowly; his head was throbbing. He was disoriented, and it took a few moments for him to realize that he was lying face down on the floor in Tarvina's rest home room. He heard voices too, distant yelps of surprise and fear, hurried footsteps, and shouts from even farther away. Bonner pulled himself upright. The side of his head was bleeding, but he was more concerned by the pronounced lump on his scalp. Bonner saw old men and women, most in robes and slippers, stuttering past the doorway. They were calling out anxiously to anyone who would listen.

By the time Bonner steadied himself and made his way into the hall, to the broad landing at the top of the stairway, a large crowd of terrified octogenarians had gathered, both on the stairs and at the bottom. They dumbly surrounded the two lifeless bodies crumpled on the floor. Tarvina's eyes gaped open, a frozen gaze, lifeless and hollow. Oleg lay face down next to her. The back of his head had been blown away, leaving a ghastly trail of brains and blood flowing to the floor.

The police and EMS had just arrived, and it was utter pandemonium. The medics crouched attentively over Tarvina, but they knew she was dead. At the top of the stairs, Ezra Bonner peered out from behind a rotund old man wearing nothing but his stained underwear and black knee socks. Everyone was pointing and whimpering. Bonner could see that he had no escape option down the stairway. Instead, he backed away and spotted an exit sign at the far end of the hall. Before anyone took notice of him, he slipped through the door and disappeared down a back stairway.

Anna set the autopilot on a north-by-northwest heading then turned to look back. Jake was slumped on the deck, sitting half-upright against bulwark. His shoulder wound wasn't deep, but it was bleeding profusely as he clutched it with his other hand. Vladimir Chernov was collapsed in exactly the same position directly across the cockpit. His wound was more severe, but Anna ignored him and dropped to her knees beside Jake, carefully peeling back his blood-soaked fingers. Jake forced a weak smile. "Bad?" he asked.

"I've seen worse," Anna replied.

Jake was somewhat deflated. "It hurts like hell."

"You'll live," Anna advised. "I'll get bandages from below. She scrambled to her feet, threw Chernov a quick glance then disappeared down the cabin hatchway.

Jake closed his eyes wearily and laid his head back against the bulwark. He heard Chernov speak but didn't bother to look.

"She is right. You will live," the old Russian said flatly.

Jake sucked in a deep breath and opened his eyes, staring directly at Chernov. He could see the old man's hand laid protectively across the wound in his side. There wasn't as much blood, and Jake surmised that the bullet had entered and exited cleanly. He couldn't help but wonder how many vital organs had been pierced.

Jake was confused. He tried to replay the attack, the hail of gunfire from Remi and then Anton Sorokin's appearance. Slowly, he absorbed the reality of what had just happened. Chernov was still looking at him. He showed no sign of pain or fear, though Jake could sense a certain pall of resignation had sunk over the old man. "Do you have a gun?" Jake growled.

"No."

"Why should I believe you?"

"Believe what you want."

Jake took stock of Chernov. It was incredible. The old man seemed completely ambivalent; he was slumped on the deck of a dumpy crab trawler with a gunshot through his side. His trusted aide had turned on him, and he knew he was now a marked man. Yet despite all this, and excruciating pain, he showed absolutely no emotion.

"He shot you," Jake noted.

Chernov shrugged. "Remi is not such a marksman as he thinks he is."

"Not him," Jake corrected. "The other one, he was your own man. He shot you. Why?"

Chernov's didn't speak. Jake's eyes probed his dark features. "Your man, Anton, went bad on you, didn't he? You're not as in charge of things as you thought."

"Perhaps."

"How does that make you feel?"

"Somewhat insecure," Chernov replied with a wry smile.

Jake couldn't help but smile too. Chernov's self-effacing comment seemed so far out of character that it made things even more confusing.

Anna clambered up the cabin steps and sunk down again beside Jake. She had bandages, several tubes of ointment, as well as a wicked-looking fishing knife. "I'm going to cut your sleeve off so I can clean the wound."

"You're going to make it hurt more."

"Probably," she noted flatly.

Jake scoffed then stopped her. He nodded toward Chernov. "Him first."

Anna was perplexed, but Jake nudged her again. "He's an old man with a hole in his side. I don't want him to die, not here, not like this."

"I am resolutely touched," Chernov opined. "But dying does not have a proper place or time. It simply occurs."

Jake's face turned dark again. He gripped Anna's arm and grimly repeated his directive, "Him first."

She rose slowly from the depths of the black Pacific Ocean, a menacing leviathan nearly six hundred feet long. The Novgorod was a Delta class Russian submarine built in the early 1990's. Originally configured as a first strike ballistic platform, she was armed with a threatening array of both intercontinental and early-generation cruise missiles. The sub had been quietly withdrawn from service fifteen years ago to be rebuilt and re-tasked as a stealth surveillance craft. When she emerged from her retrofit, the thirty-thousand-ton monster was more powerful, faster, and arguably more silent than many of the newer Russian

Boomers. Her missile silos and cruise missile launchers were gone now, carefully replaced with hyper-sophisticated eavesdropping electronics, including both sonar, side beam, and a newly developed pulse-wave detection array. The advanced computer systems filling the forward section of the hull represented the Russian navy's most sophisticated cyber-attack technology.

All told, the Novgorod had a frighteningly invasive spy capability. She had ventured across vast expanses of the oceans, and her clandestine missions often took her perilously close to major U.S. military ports where, by international law, she could approach no closer than within twelve miles of the coastline. Of course, the Novgorod ignored these restrictions and slipped closer, sometimes slinking within ten miles or less of the shore.

The Americans were well aware of the Novgorod's existence and of her demonstrable capabilities. What they were *not* aware of, was that a Russian mini-submarine, another tactical vestige of the Cold War, had secretly been mated to the mother ship, piggyback fashion. Much like a pilot fish, leeched to the back of a great white shark, she rode atop the Novgorod's forward main deck. The *MS521* was one of only two Losos-Class subs built under the Russia's sophisticated Piranha Spy Program. She was a mere ninety-two five feet long but had proficiencies far in excess of her inconsequential size. The mini-sub was built entirely of titanium. Virtually undetectable by the Americans, she was the ultimate stealth ship, with the proven capability of running soundlessly in extremely shallow water to penetrate even the most advanced detection systems.

Two decks below the Novgorod's conning turret, Captain Illia Lavrov stood firmly at the con, quietly absorbing the mind-numbing barrage of navigational, propulsion and communications information. He was a thirty-year veteran, with fifteen years spent at the helm of the Novgorod. At first, he resented his reassignment to the aging ex-Boomer. Many of the officers who graduated with him from the prestigious N.G. Kuznetsov Naval Academy in St. Petersburg had long since moved on to the more challenging attack submarine commands. It was only with time that Captain Lavrov understood the vast responsibility that he had been given. He was a prudent man, cautious and intelligent. Lavrov was proud of his ship and his men, and they in-turn revered him, his steely nerves, and his prescient sense of combat tactics.

The Novgorod glided southward down the California coast, propelled by the relentless tug of the North Pacific Gyre current and her own nuclear reactors, where hyper-hot steam pulsed through thermal turbine engines to spin stealth-like spiral propellers. She climbed up from the vast abyssal plain like a frightening apparition from the deep; time was of the essence, secrecy was paramount.

Captain Lavrov was accustomed to the cryptic and often demanding directives fed to him over the ship's sub-sonic communications system. He understood this and saw no reason to question the guidance that arrived in millisecond bursts of encrypted code. And yet, when a new tasking directive came through twenty-three hours ago,

Lavrov was confused. His current mission was barely half completed, but now he was being asked to depart immediately from his posting near the major U.S. Naval base at Tacoma, Washington. The Novgorod was to establish a new surveillance position just a few miles north of the intersection of the San Francisco Bay approach lanes. This in itself was of no substantive concern to Lavrov. However, the directive also specified that he take up position southwest of the Cordell Bank, and this puzzled the captain even more. With a water depth of over twelve hundred feet, the area was more than adequate for ship maneuvers, but it was the proximity of this new posting to the coastline, and San Francisco Bay itself, far inside of the United States' twelve mile territorial limit, that seemed perplexing; six miles from the Golden Gate Bridge was close -- too close.

Anna had been able to help Jake down the cabin hatchway and into an uncomfortable position on one side of *The Princess'* galley table. She had sliced off the left side of his jacket and shirt and had bound his shoulder wound as best she could. Jake was still in a lot of pain, but the bleeding had subsided. He had propped his right arm on the Formica tabletop and laid his head back to rest. Anna was topside again. After a few moments, Jake cranked his head over when he heard the cabin hatchway slide open again. Anna backed down the steps, trying to support Vladimir Chernov. He was doubled over in pain but refused to cry out. Anna had removed his topcoat and cut his shirt free in order to wrap a wide band of gauze around his chest. He had not said a word, and Anna was in no mood to converse with the parlous Russian diplomat.

Jake watched silently as Chernov slumped into the galley seat opposite him. He didn't utter a sound, though his lips were pulled tightly together in grim defiance. The two men stared at each other, both ignoring the gently rocking hull and the low drone of the diesel engines.

Finally, Chernov swept his palm across the table, as if to clear away unseen obstacles. "You see, Dr. Altman," Chernov began. "Had you not found it necessary to plunge into matters beyond your purview, you might not be here now with a bullet wound to your shoulder. This was entirely unnecessary."

"The death of my fiancée was unnecessary."

"Ah, the girl."

"Her name was Eryn O'Shea."

Chernov shrugged indifferently. He knew exactly what Jake was talking about but found little need to rehash matters that were no longer germane to his immediate needs. Jake accepted his equivocation; he really didn't expect more.

Anna had gone topside again to check their course. The old trawler rocked gently as it rose and fell on dark swells, its thick oak planking groaning occasionally, singing a mournful kinship with the sea.

Jake and Vladmir Chernov continued to stare at each other. The old man's gaze was impossible to interpret; he was neither afraid nor threatened. Each man was cautiously measuring the other. Only when Chernov winced slightly, did Jake sense a fracture in his façade. "Does it hurt?" Jake asked, gesturing to Chernov's side.

The taciturn Russian reflected on the question before stiffly advising, "Pain is matter of perception."

Jake nodded flatly, "I hope it hurts a lot."

"I suppose you would," Chernov replied. He gestured toward Jake's shoulder. "Yours?"

"Hurts like hell."

"I'm sorry."

"No, you're not," Jake countered. "Tell me why your man shot you."

"Perhaps he was aiming at you and missed."

Jake didn't buy into Chernov's tact. He said nothing.

Chernov continued, "I suppose that, given the probable reality that Anton was shooting at me and not you, there appears to have been a modest shift in loyalties. Should we make that assumption?"

"You're the one with a bullet hole through your side."

"Yes, it would seem so."

"So, it looks like I'm a target too," Jake said. "What about Anna?"

"Hardly," Chernov scoffed. "Anna adds intrinsic value to these proceedings. You do not."

"What about *your* intrinsic value?" Jake posited. "It looks like you just got booted from the first string team."

Chernov shifted again, not bothering to hide the pain in his face. "You have heard rumors about me, why I came to San Francisco?"

"Some."

"And I suppose you don't believe that I want to defect, to disassociate myself from certain scabrous failings, both of my making and those of my country."

"Bullshit."

Chernov smiled thinly. "When you came to see me at the consulate, I was disappointed that your research had missed intrinsic elements of importance. You saw, in me, the man you wanted to see."

"I saw a killer."

Chernov's face clouded over. He remained silent for a few moments then shrugged offhandedly, "Did you know that I once met your fiancée? She came to my office and refused to leave without speaking to me."

"Eryn was headstrong. She didn't like you either."

"She was breathtaking," Chernov allowed almost wistfully. "She was beautiful and brilliant, and for this I could look past her misplaced fervor. She was wrong, of course."

"I don't think so," Jake growled.

"Then you are wrong, too." Chernov hesitated then smiled through his pain. "So, you see, Dr. Altman. We were both wrong. I trusted Anton, not so much Oleg and Remi. I saw them as inconsequential."

Jake's hand traced his shoulder wound, and Chernov noted his stiffness. The aging diplomat shifted again, edging closer across the table. "Are you going to bring me inside, Dr. Altman?"

Jake was impressed by Chernov's resolve. It was as if all past matters were irrelevant; this was a new issue, one of paramount importance.

"Are you here to help me?" Chernov repeated.

"What do you think?"

Chernov leaned back suddenly, put off and angered. It was Jake's turn now, but before he could speak, Anna shoved the hatchway open and dropped into the cabin, tightly clutching the topside cleaving machete. Her restrained veneer had collapsed, as her terror-stricken eyes shot from Jake to Chernov. She lashed out, "Okay, so we're pretty much screwed. What happens now?"

Chernov looked at Anna for a moment then offered a chilling admission, "I have no idea."

"Liar," Anna hissed. Something about her seemed different to Jake. Any pretense of control had been overtaken by indignant rage. She was still glaring at Chernov as her fingers wrapped still tighter around the machete handle. "He's a liar and a murderer," she shouted at Jake.

"I make no excuses for what I have done for my country," Chernov scoffed. "But of the death you speak, of your father's murder, I was not involved."

"They butchered him on a kitchen table!"

Chernov callously deflected the charge. "I've seen this done. It is an unfortunate way to die."

"Unfortunate?" Anna coughed out.

She jerked the machete into the air, but Jake caught her arm. "Anna, no. Not this way," he warned.

Chernov's hand slid to his bandaged chest. The pain was excruciating, but he refused to cry out. Anna's eyes were transfixed on him. Jake realized that the horror surrounding her had finally set her off; she was being driven entirely by instinct now, with no sense of fear or allowance for considered judgment.

Jake spoke more softly, asking, "Anna, where are we?" She looked blankly at him. "Where are we now?" Jake asked again.

"Northwest of Mendocino," Anna mumbled absently, "We're maybe ten miles away."

Chernov's cheek twitched slightly. "Have you turned off your electronics?"

Anna glared at him, but Jake quickly interceded, "He's right. You need to turn everything off -- everything."

"The radios are off. So is the satellite phone," Anna announced mechanically. "We need the radar. They can't track that."

"Most people can't," Chernov allowed. "But there are people who can."

"I don't have to listen to this, Jake," she warned menacingly.

Jake knew the Chernov was right. It wasn't safe to power up *any* of the electronics. If they were listening, which they probably were, Anton and Remi could easily track them. "Anna, turn off the radar," Jake advised.

She didn't budge.

"You would be wise to listen to him," Chernov noted. "If you don't, they will find us, and you will face a knife at your throat as you father did."

Anna exploded and lunged across the table, swinging the machete back and then down. Jake's hand shot out, blocking the blow, and sending the weapon clanging to the deck. Anna landed on Chernov, raining blows across his face, thrashing and tearing at the old man. Jake tried to pull her off, but his shoulder burned with pain. Chernov cried out as Anna's blows found his bloodied chest. She was sprawled across the table, dragging herself closer to Chernov's throat. Jake lunged out again, half-crippled by his wound. This time he was able to reach her, slowly curtailing the withering blows.

Anna wept deeply as Jake dragged her off Chernov. She was shaking with anger and fear, disconsolate in her anguish, enraged by Chernov's inhumanity. Finally, she collapsed, crying. Jake held her, whispering gentle words of comfort.

Suddenly, Anna cried out with a primordial scream. She broke free of Jake's arms, swept up the machete and jerked it high above Chernov's head. When it came crashing down, it dug deeply into the tabletop. Anna had desperately wanted to kill him, yet, even in the depths of her catharsis, she could not. She leaped back and raced up the companionway. Moments passed before Jake turned to Chernov and said, "She doesn't like you very much."

Chernov offered a tepid smile. "And is that supposed to upset me?"

Jake was seething now too, but he constrained his anger and remained silent. Chernov shifted uncomfortably; blood was soaking through his bandages again. He was thinking, quickly and efficiently reconstructing events and players. He understood the murders now, but he was unable to reconcile why Oleg and Remi had turned on him. The depth of Anton's subterfuge was more difficult to comprehend. He had trusted these men. Had something changed, or had he been set up all along? Chernov cursed himself for his lassitude. The girl, Anna, was safe, at least for now, but he knew they would come for her, and for him. And what was he to believe about Jake Altman? There was a story here, but that narrative was stubbornly elusive and lacked any degree of clarity.

Jake was still staring at him. "Do you want to talk about it?" he asked.

Chernov shook his head tiredly. "No."

25

The world saw Dmitri Bellus, President of the Russian Federation, through a constant stream of well-orchestrated media releases covering state events with influential world leaders. Bellus understood the need to maintain a very public presence, but he generally preferred solitude, especially when contemplating deeply complex issues. To him, the political milieu was all a grand game; it was an intricate chess match, propelled by calculated moves, political head fakes, and boldly preemptive actions, all with the singular purpose of reestablishing Russia's rightful position at the very top of the world order. As a young technocrat, an inconspicuous cog in the KGB's sprawling network, Bellus had been crestfallen when the Soviet Union collapsed around him. The implosion hurt him deeply. He had sworn to right the indignity and had relentlessly pursued that agenda for the next three decades.

Bellus' aide had left him alone at his desk in the private study adjacent to his formal State Office in the Kremlin. It was a spacious room, purposely arranged with no windows. Thick Siberian walnut paneling covered the walls, and a plush burgundy carpet effectively muffled extraneous sounds. A cup of hot tea sat on the corner of Bellus' desk, simmering with an intoxicating aroma. It soothed his nerves and helped him think more clearly.

Bellus was dressed in a neatly tailored, black suit. His tie was expensive though not ostentatious, and his gold cufflinks glistened in the dim lamp light. He was not a man who found informality appealing. Shaking hands was an effort, while disingenuous and often awkward hugs left him sick at his stomach. For Dmitri Bellus, there was no distinction between the man and the office he held. Protocols were met; perfunctory statesmanship coexisted with supercilious accommodations. It was all a front, of course, a deadly charade, but it was one that he managed with a polished confidence. However, when he found time to slip away, to be truly alone to reflect and analyze, Bellus often found himself lapsing comfortably into a state of self-aggrandized rapture. Here, the shackles of pomp and ceremony were easily eclipsed by a sense of duplicitous purpose bordering on messianic reverence to the far greater god of power.

Bellus carefully sliced the security seal on the thin diplomatic pouch lying on the blotter in front of him then inserted his fingers and withdrew a single small gold ingot, a shimmering Russian ruble bar. He laid it down beneath the lamplight and, with one finger, delicately rotated it ninety degrees, carefully assessing the fine edges and bold engravings. His eyes found their way to the embossed stamping year, 1898. The years and decades instantly collapsed backward in Bellus' mind; 1898, so much had happened. It was as if a lifetime of memories had been locked away in the cool gold bar. When the call light on his encoded satellite phone flashed, Bellus eased the receiver from its cradle and waited without speaking while a man's distant voice gushed gratuitously in a thick Russian dialect. Finally, the caller paused and Bellus said simply, "Da," The voice at the other end blathered faster now, but Bellus roughly cut him off. "Is the girl safe?" he demanded.

The apologetic voice continued in Russian. Bellus shifted slightly in his chair. He sensed an unpleasant subtext and cut the man off again, "There is more, yes?" But before the voice could find the courage to speak again, Bellus shouted, "Is she safe!"

Now, the caller slipped into halted English. "Yes. She is safe. I think. But she is not with us. Not at this moment."

Four thousand miles away, Anton Sorokin stood beside his dark limo, mopping sweat from his forehead as he clutched his satellite receiver. He threw a glance at Remi, injured but standing on the other side of the car, then half-covered his mouth, meekly confessing, "Anna Roman has eluded us, Mr. President. She is on a boat, just a fishing boat. They are somewhere off the coast in thick fog."

Bellus' face tightened. "Chernov?"

"He is wounded, but not dead, I think."

"Derr'mo!" Bellus cursed. "Tell me!"

"Oleg is dead, Mr. President, and so is the old woman, Marvina Dubrovsky's twin sister. Anna and the American professor escaped. He is wounded too, but they were able to get on their boat. Chernov is with them."

"Find her," Bellus commanded. "You have the resources you need. Find her. Take her." He hung up, paused, then cursed under his breath and shoved the gold bar away.

Jake held tightly to the side rails as he climbed up *The Princess*' companionway steps and swung the door open. A rush of cold sea air engulfed him, as the old diesels rumbled softly beneath the deck. Anna was at the helm, staring blankly into the fogbound night. At first, she didn't look over. Jake understood. He steadied himself against the shifting swells and waited. Anna's face, already blushed from the cold, was bathed in the glow of console instrument lights. She knew he was looking at her. Finally, she nodded toward the hatch leading below and spoke without looking at Jake, "Sorry about that. He's a murderer, but I'm sorry I cracked."

"Nothing to be sorry about. I understand."

"I don't think you possibly could," Anna lamented. Her lips tightened and she turned to look at him. "Jake, what the hell is going on?" she whispered. "What do we do now?"

It took a moment for Jake to assemble a coherent answer. "I'm beginning to think that the same people who want you also want Chernov."

"That's crazy."

"I would have thought so too, but the gunshot that took Chernov down back there, that wasn't an accident. It seems like Chernov's little Russian aide has a special agenda, or more probably he's part of someone else's agenda."

Anna was utterly perplexed now; she couldn't fit the pieces together. "Jake, the whole thing was because of Chernov. He already knew about the Baikal, and Marvina led him to Mikhail and me. That's what happened. Chernov wants the rubles and he thinks I'm the key."

Jake shifted his shoulder, searching to relieve the discomfort. "All of that makes sense, at least until you consider that Chernov's own man tried to put a sniper round through his head."

"But you know what Chernov is! You know what he's done and what he's capable of doing!"

Jake was shaking his head slowly. "It's possible, just possible, that we're stuck between two separate factions. What if Chernov only thought he was in charge? What if they just let him think he was calling the shots?"

"Who's *they*?"

Jake could only shrug. Anna's mind was racing. So many people had been killed. It all seemed so hopeless. "Jake," she whispered, "What happens now?"

"We have to go back in," Jake announced quickly, "We have to find someone that can bring us in safely."

"Who?" Anna cried. "They found us once; they can do it again. They're listening for us now. You said so. So did Chernov."

Jake's shoulder ached and he was cold, but he also believed that staying out on the water would result in a very bad outcome. His eyes ticked to the control console. "What's our heading?"

"Northwest – three hundred twenty degrees."

"Turn us around," Jake said.

Anna realized that it was neither a request nor a command, but rather a simple statement of the need facing them. She hesitated then slowly began to turn the vessel southward. "Who are we going to get to help us?"

"I'm not sure."

"…your friend from the university, Bonner?"

"No."

"Because you don't trust him any longer?"

Jake's face tightened. "Not Ezra. Not this time."

"Then who?"

A flicker of hope spread across Jake's face, "Tell me about your sheriff friend in Bodega Bay."

"Lawrence Jackson?"

" You've known him a long time?"

"All my life," she allowed. "But I can't call him, not on the radio. They'll hear it."

Jake nudged her aside and thumped the de-energized marine radio. "That's because they'll be listening for this, a marine band VHS transmission, right?"

"Yes."

"Okay, so we can't do that, but what about that one?" Jake pointed at a smaller radio unit wedged in the roof structure overhead. It was dusty and lifeless.

"That's just an old shortwave unit. Mikhail used to bug ham operators with it when he was bored. One time, he nearly set off a riot in Bodega Bay when he convinced a couple of old lady ham operators that a Russian invasion force had landed. The state almost jerked his license."

"But they didn't take the radio."

"What are you talking about?"

Jake moved closer. "I saw a radio like this in your sheriff's office in Bodega Bay."

"Yeah, that's his hobby. He's got a bigger one at his house." Then it dawned on her, and she smiled. "Lawrence has about zero social life. He works, goes home, and diddles with his wife. At least that's what he claims. But when the urge hits, he fires up the radio and gabs with people all over the world."

"What's he talk about?"

"Anything. Everything. It's like his escape. He's scared to fly, so he travels all over the place on the radio."

"So, he's probably at home right now, cold beer in hand, running his trash past some Gisha Girl on the other side of the world."

"That would be a reach. He's pretty devoted to Loretta, but it doesn't matter anyway. We can't call him. They're out there, listening."

"Not for ham short wave radio transmissions. It's a totally different frequency."

Anna eyed the old radio with great trepidation.

"That's a lousy bet, Jake."

Jake nodded, allowing Anna to weigh their limited options. He gave her a faint smile then reached up and punched the radio power button and handed the mike to Anna.

The Novgorod had trimmed out, zero bubble, at a shallow fifty feet. She was nosed into the southern coastal current, with just enough power to maintain dynamic positioning. And it was there that she went dead silent, a thirty-thousand-ton predator from the deep, waiting less than one mile off the northwestern edge of the craggy, undersea plateau known as Farallon Island. The mound rose steeply from deeper water, with its crest less than thirty feet beneath the surface. It was a known, deadly hazard for mariners coming out of San Francisco Bay. It was also the perfect place for a Russian submarine to hide. The undersea landmass baffled the ship from the ever-present American sonar bursts emanating from the Navy's surveillance station to the east.

Captain Illia Lavrov was in the officer's ready room, drinking his second cup of black coffee in less than an hour. He was still chaffed about his cryptic orders. Lavrov understood that Command often adjusted sub deployments. Re-tasking, especially for a reconnaissance ship, was to be expected. But something felt inconsistent about the Novgorod's new orders. They lacked specificity and gave the captain no sense of his true mission.

An aft watertight hatchway suddenly ratcheted open and Lieutenant Nikita Gorke stepped into the room, presenting himself rigidly in front of Lavrov. The older man looked up but said nothing. He didn't like Gorke; as far as he was concerned, the young KGB officer was an ill-bred snot.

Lt. Gorke was a small man, but his taut body was hard and angular. He was wearing a dark turtleneck sweater and combat pants. Gorke's hair was close-cropped and his eyes were narrowly set.

"Captain Lavrov," Gorke spat out crisply in his native Ukrainian dialect, "We have a new communiqué." He thrust out a folded slip of paper.

Lavrov eyed the message distastefully. "And why was this message not delivered, unopened, to me?"

Gorke could not suppress a churlish grin. "It is a KGB matter, Captain. And in these details, I have authority,"

Lavrov growled then took the note. He unfolded it and read the message, only to flippantly toss it aside. "This tells us nothing."

"The directive is quite clear Captain," Gorke explained. "We are to remain here, unobtrusively, and we are to prepare the Losos and my advance team."

"Yes, yes," Lavrov sniped as he stood abruptly, towering over the young KGB officer. "Prepare and wait. And we are to prepare for what? What is the mission?"

Gorke pointed at the discarded message. "For the moment, *that* is the mission."

26

The Princess lurched ahead through the damp night, slicing through the fog and ocean chop two miles off the northern California coast. There was only a slight wind, but the boat's steady advance sent mist curling around the upper deck.

Jake was at the helm now, carefully watching their southern heading on the marine compass. The dimmed console lights wrapped him in a subdued glow. When Anna emerged from the companionway she was carrying a fleece parka. It took a moment for her eyes to adjust to the darkness, but she closed the hatchway door behind her and handed the jacket to Jake. "Here, put it on," she said.

As Jake slipped into the coat then pressed Anna, asking, "How long will it take to get back to Bodega Bay?"

"Two hours, maybe a little less with the current."

"Seems like your sheriff friend has a good head on his shoulders."

"What do you mean?"

Jake shrugged. "He's meeting us outside the harbor at the entrance to the bay. That's smart. If anybody's watching from the shore, they won't think much of a police boat on routine patrol."

Anna nodded absently, and Jake could tell that she was adrift with bleak thoughts. She seemed drained, somehow less vital than before. Jake sensed she was grieving Mikhail, as if the lull in the furious chain of events had only now allowed her to fully comprehend the depth of her loss. He regretted that there was nothing he could do to ease her pain. When their eyes met in the dim light, he nodded toward the hatchway and asked simply, "How's Chernov doing?"

"Sleeping."

"Is he still losing blood?"

"Does it really matter?" Anna said flatly, as she edged in front of him. "Let me take over."

Jake was frustrated now. "I think I can run the boat."

She took the wheel anyway. "Not when it's my boat."

Jake stepped aside then took a jab at her, "We can't just throw him overboard, you know."

"Who?

"Chernov."

Anna didn't respond. She swiped at her hair and adjusted the course slightly. Jake dropped the subject and settled back against the console. He watched Anna in silence, trying to reconcile her many ambiguities. She was beautiful, yet seemed oblivious to her radiance. She had graced exotic fashion covers and run with the international high-profile crowd, yet she felt more at home in jeans and a hook-raked fishing parka. And then there as Mikhail, his mysterious past, which she now understood to be her past as well. Anna was a Romanov, last of a royal lineage that traced back to the tenth century. It all seemed surreal to Jake. She was a princess without a kingdom, and she may well be the key to an enormous fortune in sunken Russian gold.

"Tell me about Eryn," Anna said softly.

Jake was shaken by the question, as much for its suddenness as by the reality of Eryn's death crashing down on him again. He said, "I told you."

"Tell me again."

Jake instinctively withdrew; it wasn't easy for him to think about Eryn, and it was even more difficult to talk about her. Anna was still looking at him, however. He relented. "Eryn was in Moscow doing research on Vladimir Chernov. She got too close. He had her murdered."

"I heard that part before. Why was she chasing after Chernov? Why him?"

"Eryn couldn't handle hypocrisy."

This puzzled Anna. "And that would mean…?"

"Chernov is a paradox; he always has been. The world saw Brezhnev, Chernenko, Gorbachev, and now Dmitri Bellus strutting on the world stage, but Vladimir Chernov was always there too, just out of sight. He was a phantom, never in the public eye; he lived in the dark shadows of Soviet realpolitik."

"Eryn wouldn't have been the first to have discovered him."

"No, U.S. intelligence knew he existed, and they knew how powerful he had become, but it was Eryn who dug deeper, much deeper. She went to Moscow as part of a graduate student exchange program to study political evolution of the respective countries. The Russians didn't expect Eryn to land on Chernov, to peel back the onion."

"She was smart?" Anna asked.

"Brilliant," Jake whispered. "Once she realized that Chernov had a far greater role in Russian policy, there was no stopping her."

Anna thought for moment, musing about Jake and Eryn, two policy wonks, desperately trying to do what the entire intelligence community had failed to do. "How did you meet her?" she asked.

Jake had to think for a moment. A faint smile spread across his lips. "She found me."

"What, like at a campus bar?"

"No. We were on two different graduate tracks at Berkeley, so we never really met at the university. But somehow, we both ended up across the bay one day at a presentation at the San Francisco History Museum. A visiting Russian historian was giving a presentation about something or other I can't even remember now. But Eryn was there."

"Is that when you realized she was brilliant?"

"That's when I realized she was extremely hot."

"Academically speaking?"

Jake couldn't help chuckling. "Yeah, sure, it was all about academics." His mind drifted to vivid images of Eryn and their time together. They had talked incessantly, about everything. Hours became days, then weeks. They lay on their backs in Golden Gate Park, caressed by the not-so-faint scent of pot wafting south from Haight Ashbury, watching clouds drift past and listening to cheesy seventies-music squealing from ageless head-shops nestled along Lincoln Way. Jake thought about the sex too. It was as if they were two fireflies careening out of control through backyard trees on a simmering summer night. Their dance was passionately intense, and when they were in each other's arms, the rapture of the moment shook him in every fiber of his being. He remembered everything: her scent, the smooth fullness of her body, her gentle Irish lilt, and probably most of all the taste of her sweetly inviting lips.

Jake withdrew from his memories and was surprised to find himself earnestly asking Anna, "Why did you ask about Eryn?"

Anna did not speak, but Jake could see it in her eyes; there was something that had not been there before. It was an unfiltered and wholly honest aura that, for the very first time, revealed a tragic sense of vulnerability. The corners of her lips curled upward, just slightly, when she finally answered his question, "I just wanted to know."

It was a simple statement, but a thousand meanings raced through Jake's mind. Anna hesitated then spoke again, "I wanted to know what it was like."

"What it was like to what?"

"To have someone you cared that much about," Anna admitted softly.

Jake fell silent, stunned by the realization that swept over him like an unexpected rush of sea air. Anna was alone, so very much alone. There had *never* been someone in her life to love. Mikhail was different, of course, and Jake knew how much she cherished him. But there had been no other man, no love or true passion. The depth of her emptiness and longing had now been laid bare. And in that one moment of brutal honesty, both for Anna and for himself, Jake finally understood what she meant to him. He knew that she would lead him back; she would save him from the spiral of remorse and self-guilt that had strangled him for so long. Anna was now his hope and his future.

"You okay?" Anna whispered. Her voice collided violently with Jake's epiphany. He took a deep breath then nodded with the realization that she had seen deeply into his soul. She smiled; it was an impetuous gift, a release from her probing eyes, "Want to drive?"

Sheriff Jackson had been more than a little surprised when he received Anna's shortwave radio transmission. Loretta was out for the evening, something about quilting at church. He had just finished a hefty Marie Callender pot pie and was tuning his ham radio system up for an evening of cavorting with faceless, yet fascinating fellow operators in Istanbul, Caracas, or even Singapore.

Anna's transmission had jarred him. They had been close for many years, and there was even a time when his feelings for her had matriculated to something beyond warm respect. He had flirted with Anna, and, at least at one point, she had flirted back. Still, always, there was something about their relationship that never guided them to anything more. He had loved her, of that he had always been certain, but in many ways he knew it had been a love deeper than romantic involvement.

When Anna's radio transmission had come through, Jackson instantly knew she was in trouble. He had put on his uniform and sidearm then squared his broad-brimmed hat on his head and slipped out of his seaside cottage.

Anton Sorokin was parked just off the coast highway, near the entrance to the Sea Hag in Bodega Bay. He was both tired and bored. Remi was beside him, nursing his bruises with a pint of whiskey. His face was still blood-caked, and the side of his cheek was swollen badly.

It was very late, and there was virtually no traffic on the roadway. Twice in the last hour, Anton had received conflicting instructions by cell phone. He wondered if anyone really knew what the hell was going on. Remi groaned then cursed and took a long draw from his cigarette. The local sheriff's pick-up cruised past and turned into the gravel lot near the Sea Hag. Anton and Remi were watching carefully as Lawrence Jackson parked and climbed out. He seemed to be in a hurry as he trotted across the expanse of gravel and slipped down the marina ramp, only to disappear among the flotilla of empty boats.

Attaboy had slept for nearly an hour. He was just beginning to rouse himself from a blissful whiskey stupor, as he lay sprawled across Sea Hag's timber stoop, mumbling softly to himself. He had barely noticed when Sheriff Lawrence Jackson appeared and immediately disappeared down the boat ramp, and he had only snorted loudly when Anton Remi passed by him. With Herculean resolve, Attaboy managed to swing his stubby legs over the stoop and stand.

Ezra Bonner brought his big Harley down the hillside outside Bodega Bay. It struck him how isolated and lifeless the town seemed at night as he rumbled slowly into the lot beside the Sea Hag. The bike's twin exhausts popped and chortled, sending dust whirling into the damp night air as he footed the kickstand and killed the engine.

The lot was almost empty, and the lights inside the Sea Hag were muted and uninviting. Ezra Bonner climbed off his Harley and searched the blackness, distrusting the palpable calm surrounding him. A trash can lid clattered to the ground somewhere in the service alley beside the tilted tavern as a figure moved silently in the shadows.

Bonner cocked his head and stepped closer. He heard a faint tinkling sound and then a man's voice humming The Battle Hymn of the Republic. Finally, he spotted a scruffy bum beneath a feeble backdoor light. Attaboy was standing splayfooted, with one hand resting heavily on a low roof overhand, pissing on a trash container. He suddenly stopped singing, but not pissing, when he saw Bonner in the darkness. He grinned toothlessly, certain that he knew the large black man gaping at him. "Hey, Lawrence, my main-man sheriff."

"Sorry, I'm afraid I am not the sheriff," Bonner explained, stepping cautiously closer.

Attaboy's red nose wrinkled. "Then who the hell are you?"

"I'm a friend of Anna."

"Yeah? Ain't that somethin'. You look sort of familiar." Attaboy had finished pissing now but was still shaking off. "Hey, you look like Sheriff Jackson. You his brother?"

"No."

"You look like his brother, I mean the way you are."

"You mean black."

Attaboy chuckled again. "Yeah, hey, it's dark out here. How 'bout you smile, so I can see where you are." He blurted out a belly laugh and farted. Composing himself, Attaboy confessed. "Sorry, brother. I use that one on Lawrence all the time. He ain't smacked me yet."

Bonner accurately surmised that Attaboy wasn't in any shape to help, but he was all there was. "Can you tell me where to find Sheriff Jackson?"

"Well, now that's not so hard to figure. See I pretty much keep tabs on things around here. That's why they call me Attaboy."

"Ah. Of course. What's your real name?"

"Attaboy."

Bonner knew he wasn't making much progress. "I believe you were going to tell me about the Sheriff."

"Oh, yeah. Brother Lawrence. Well, see, most any night this late, he'd be at his house down there at the end of that road, the gray one with white shutters."

"Good," Bonner replied.

"But he ain't there tonight."

"That would be because?"

Attaboy pushed his chest forward proudly, certain of his command of the tiny harbor's affairs. "Lawrence is out on his boat. Big ole kick-ass police rig with lights and such."

Bonner pointed toward the sea of boats in the marina. "Do you mean he's down there somewhere?"

"Naw. Hell, he come bustin' down here all in a hurry a while ago. He took off for his boat. Then I sorta, uhm, well

I guess I drifted off a little. And then I musta woke up when I heard a bang or somethin'.

"A gunshot?" Bonner probed.

"Naw, probably a car backfiring or somethin'. We got a lotta shitty cars around here. But when I woke up. I saw ole Lawrence's boat was chuggin' way out that-away, making for open water. He had her all jacked up, runnin' hard."

Bonner's eyes flashed across the still water of Bodega Bay and stopped on the distant harbor entrance and black expanse of ocean beyond. There was no sign of the police boat. Somewhere halfway out in the marina, the lights on a single boat flicked on and a pair of engines coughed to life.

"Who's that?" Bonner asked.

"Shit, that just ole Yedor Fedin," Attaboy cried out, gesturing with a wave of his bagged bottle. "He gets out there fishin' hours before anybody else around here."

Bonner hesitated, thinking hard. Then he turned back quickly to Attaboy. "Thanks for your help," he called out as he hurried away.

"Well, yep, glad I could...." Attaboy caught himself then shouted at Bonner, demanding, "Hey, you forgot somethin'. Ain't everybody knows what I know. Cause I know just about everything around here. Go ahead say it."

"Say what?" Bonner called back.

"Just say it!" the old drunk bellowed as he pulled himself upright and threw out his chest.

Bonner caught on and shouted emphatically, "Atta-boy!

"Yeah, man," Attaboy gushed as he watched Bonner hurry down the marina ramp.

27

Jake was concerned about the steam sifting out from around the engine hatches on the aft deck of *The Princess*. He knew the old diesels had coolant issues, but he had thought his makeshift hose repairs should have held better than this. Anna was pushing the trawler hard, due south. The fog had abated, and Jake could see the dark line of the California coast off to his left. Stars had emerged and a crescent moon drifted out from behind rim-lit clouds.

"You're pushing the engines too hard," Jake cautioned.

"They'll hold," Anna replied vaguely. She was thinking about what lay ahead. Sheriff Lawrence Jackson had accepted her clipped radio transmission calmly. She had said very little, but Jackson understood the urgency of her message. He would meet them, he told her, but Anna had balked at his suggestion that she come ashore at the police boat dock at Bodega Bay. *"Too risky,"* she had warned. The Sheriff had gone silent for a moment, before he suggested, "Ice Cream Island, lee side." This meant nothing to Jake, but Anna had to smile. Ice Cream Island didn't really exist. It was a name that Anna and friends had given to a tiny island just north of Trail Head point, a remote and uninhabited coastal area due west of Bodega Bay. When they had been much younger, Anna had taken Jackson and group of five other friends out to the island for an afternoon crab bake. It had been an unforgettably debauched event. The beer had flowed freely. Copious amounts of fresh crab were consumed, only to be followed by mounds of homemade ice cream. Inhibitions waned, and at the zenith of the revelry, Zeek Hoffman simply took his clothes off. No reason; it just felt good, he said. Soon the entire group was stark naked, cavorting around the beach like crazed castaways. Someone had taken pictures, and from time to time for years afterward, an embarrassing photo or two would surface. Ice Cream Island was the perfect place to meet.

Jake had lapsed into deep introspection as the cold night air rushed past his face. He rehashed their options, but the solution didn't change. They had to go in, to find someone who could protect them until they could tell their story.

"Do you trust your sheriff friend?" Jake asked Anna without looking over.

"I've known Lawrence all my life."

"But do you trust him, now, with all this?"

"Yeah," Anna mused. "He's a solid guy." She couldn't help but wonder if he had secretly kept any of the beach party photos.

The ten-year old Sea Crest police boat surged past Doran Beach and the North Jetty at the outfall of Bodega Bay. It wasn't much to look at, but it was extremely fast. Sheriff Jackson had pulled some funding strings and repowered the boat two years ago with a pair of four hundred horsepower diesel engines he salvaged from a yacht that sank in the harbor. Now, it was running without lights, shrouded in darkness as it swung around the south end of the peninsula then broke toward the north and the opaque expanse of Pacific Ocean.

Vladimir Chernov watched Jake rummage through a narrow cabinet next to the galley. The pain in his side had eased, but he was still unable to move. Chernov knew that Anna was topside, driving the boat southward, though he wasn't exactly sure of their intentions.

Jake pitched a couple of towels from the cabinet then hauled out a gigantic box of cereal and angrily tossed it aside. Chernov zeroed in, "Not your brand?"

Jake ignored the jab. He was about to move to another cabinet when he found what he was looking for, right where Anna had told him to look. The bright orange flare gun was unimpressively stubby, with three fat shells sheathed in a plastic holder attached to the handle. Chernov was amused. "Now that's a fine firearm. Three whole shells too."

"I don't want to hear it," Jake snapped. He ripped a shell free and crammed it into the flare gun then shoved it in his belt.

He was about to head topside again, but Chernov held out a halting hand. "When are you going to tell her," he asked pointedly. Jake refused to take the bait. He started for the hatchway again, but the old man called out, louder this time. "They're coming for her, and they will find her. It doesn't seem fair not to tell her that there's no hope."

Jake stopped in mid-stride and glanced back. "You don't know what you're talking about."

"Oh, but I do. In these matters, I'm quite certain of what is to come."

Jake took a step sideways and eased into the dinette across from Chernov to address the provocation. "Okay, maybe you're right, but you're not infallible. What about Anton Sorokin and his two gangsters -- what happened there? One minute they're guarding you, and the next they're trying to kill you. Now, I don't really know whose team you're on, not anymore, but you missed the call on your loyal staff. That's sloppy work. So, maybe you really don't have such a good handle on this thing after all."

Chernov simmered, distilling Jake's charges. It took a few moments before a sneer appeared on his lips. "It will happen this way," he announced. "If by some divine intervention you are able to make land and find protection, the tactics will change, but the result will be the same. They will find her. They will recalculate, then act. There will be a lapse in security, something so inconsequential that no one could be blamed. But Anna will be left unattended, unprotected, if only for a few moments. Then she will be taken, and she will not be found again."

Jake absorbed Chernov's prophecy but was unable to refute the possibility that he was right. "What about you? Absent divine intervention, your fate may be sealed too."

"As it must be," Chernov allowed stoically.

"And me?"

"You, Dr. Altman, are entirely inconsequential. That means you will be the very first to die."

Jake thought for a moment then rose abruptly and leveled a declaration at Chernov, "Keep your opinions to yourself, old man. Maybe once they held sway, but not any longer." Jake bent over suddenly and grabbed Chernov's coat lapels, dragging him roughly to his feet as he advised, "It's show time. We're going topside."

Anna scanned the low hills lying beneath a simmering moon just off *The Princess*' port side; craggy peaks punctuated the night vista, but the land was dark and lifeless.

Jake emerged from the cabin, hauling Chernov with him. He deposited the wounded diplomat on a tool chest then threw a look at the steam hissing from the engine hatches. It was getting worse. "How much farther," he asked Anna.

Anna gestured toward a pair of coastal peaks, one slightly taller than the other. "That's Stewart's Ridge. We're close."

Chernov was growing weak from loss of blood, but he still refused to acknowledge the pain. Instead, he lifted a bloody finger, pointing at the rising coolant steam. "That's not good."

"I know it's not good," Jake barked.

"The engines are too hot. They will seize up and stop," Chernov growled back at him.

"No. No, they're not going to stop, right Anna?"

"Sure," she tossed out breezily. "Whatever."

Jake was tense. Anna and Chernov weren't helping. "Okay, "Jake noted. "So, we're a go with the plan, right?"

"Works for me," Anna announced somewhat less than enthusiastically. "We meet up with Lawrence then he radios the Coast Guard station and requests an emergency intercept."

Jake continued, "The night watch at the station will have to scramble a crew. That's what you said. But they could get out here within an hour, right?"

"If we're lucky."

Chernov was chuckling sardonically. He seemed to enjoy the shroud of menace that surrounded them. "What do you do if this plan fails?"

"I told you to drop it," Jake snapped angrily; he knew there really wasn't a back-up plan. "How much farther?" he snapped at Anna.

"You just asked me that," she replied. "That's Ice Cream Island dead ahead."

Chernov was grinning again. Jake collapsed on a lashed-down buoy on the other side of the cockpit. His eyes bore into the wounded Russian, but neither man spoke. *The Princess'* engines churned as the boat undulated in the sea.

Chernov laid his head back, relishing the breeze. His eyes were fully closed when he called out, "Do you have a preference for the weather on the day you die, Dr. Altman?" Jake refused to engage, but Chernov's thought had landed hard. The old Russian continued philosophically, "I prefer clear skies -- night. Yes, there's something intangibly uplifting about the prospect of your soul drifting sublimely aloft into the great starry beyond." Chernov glanced at Jake, aware that his allusion had fallen on deaf ears. "Actually, I rather hoped that you might somehow craft a suitable escape for us. Death is a highly-overrated certainty. It's the *timing* of one's departure that remains ambiguous."

Jake was looking at Chernov now. "You're as afraid of dying as I am," he observed.

"Yes, of course. But death in of itself is not as fearful as the prospect of not living any longer.

"There's a difference?"

"Of course. The former is a state of nothingness, but the latter is a loss that cannot be replaced." Then he was silent. Chernov's eyes suddenly seemed impoverished. Jake was disarmed by this, and, if only for a moment, he sensed the probity of the old man's admission.

Anna suddenly pointed ahead and called out over the engine rumble, "There!"

Jake clambered to his feet and leaned around the side of the cabin, thrusting his face into the wind. Directly ahead but at least a mile away, the dark, low form of a boat pounded across the moonlit sea. There were no running lights, but Jake could tell it was moving fast. "Is that him?"

"Maybe," Anna shouted hopefully. She stretched across the control console and flashed *The Princess*' running lights three times. The approaching boat did not respond. "That's got to be Lawrence," Anna brayed.

The big powerboat was closing fast now, and finally Anna could see the distinctive hull stripes. "That's Lawrence," she exclaimed as a blue police light blinked on then off again.

Anna felt a surge of hope. Jake threw a look at Chernov, who allowed an indifferent shrug that morphed quickly into a faint smile of hope.

"He's slowing," Anna advised. She pulled *The Princess*' throttles back too, and the trawler settled into the sea. There was a light breeze skittering across the surface of the water. Just ahead, the police boat's searchlight snapped on. It was intensely bright, nearly blinding Jake and Anna. She held her arms up, waving.

Jake was leaning around the side of the cockpit, searching the silhouetted vessel for Sheriff Lawrence Jackson. Anna still could not see clearly, at least until the searchlight drifted off to one side and she spotted the sheriff standing at the center console. He was mostly hidden in the shadows, but there was no mistaking his broad sheriff's hat. "Lawrence!" Anna cried out.

The two boats drifted closer. Jake could see Jackson more clearly, as the stone-faced cop lifted a hand in a welcoming wave. He turned back to Chernov. "Looks like lady luck just smiled on us."

"Yes," Chernov allowed. "But you should be careful who you trust."

Jake was about to toss something back when the police boat's engines suddenly roared. The sleek vessel lurched forward and plowed headlong into the side of *The Princess*. Both Jake and Anna were thrown to the deck, but they could hear the beaklike bow of the police boat ripping through *The Princess*' hull planking. They had been speared like a bulbous tuna, run through by a charging sailfish.

Jake stumbled to his feet. The companionway hatch had flown open, and he could see water running across the floorboards. "We're taking water!" he shouted at Anna.

The police boat spun sideways, ripping its way free from *The Princess*. It slammed alongside, sending its glaring searchlight raking across them. Anna shielded her eyes, and Jake whirled around too. They could see Sheriff Lawrence at the helm. He was dead, roughly lashed upright against the center console. Blood seeped from the bullet hole directly between his glazed eyes.

Remi stepped out from behind the corpse, allowing the dead man's hand to slump down. His Glock handgun hung loosely in his hand. "Hello, mate. How's the fishing been?"

Anton Sorokin appeared now too. He was cold and somber, wrapped tightly in a dark overcoat. He had a sleek handgun. Vladimir Chernov looked directly at his diminutive aide, allowing an unctuous smile. "Anton, congratulations, well done. Deception is sweet, is it not?"

"Fuck you," Anton snapped back at him. The little man gestured toward Anna. "Get her," he growled at Remi. "The rest of you stay where you are."

Remi, limping now, started for the gunwale, but the police boat suddenly sagged and heeled sharply. Water burst from beneath the console. Anton threw a look over the side of the boat. "We're sinking!" he shouted. "You rammed them too hard, you idiot!"

Remi had one leg across the mated gunwales; he was at a complete loss for what to do. Anton brushed past him, swinging quickly over to *The Princess*. Remi toppled into the boat too, landing with a thud on the aft deck.

Jake moved toward him, but the pug-like Brit snapped his gun up with a crisp warning, "Aye, you don't want to do that, mate." Remi peered into the lower cabin. "She's leaking, but she should hold," he called back to Anton. He clawed to his feet and found the bilge pump switch on the console.

Chernov seemed oddly amused by the dilemma, "Two ships sinking in the night," he called out. "It's almost poetic. I assume you have a spectacular contingency plan in place, Anton."

"Shut up," Anton snapped. He turned a full circle, thinking quickly. "All right, Remi, we'll take this boat." He waved his gun at Jake, pointing at Chernov. "Get him up. Get him to the police boat."

Jake didn't move. Remi angrily shoved the barrel of his weapon against Anna's head. "Do it," he yelled.

Jake lifted Chernov's shoulders and hauled him up, leaning him against the coaming. The old man groaned once; his lips were tightly drawn. With one great heave, the crippled Russian slid over the gunwale and collapsed on the deck of the police boat. Jake tumbled in too. Anna started across, but Anton screamed at her. "No!"

Remi snagged Anna's arm and jerked her back. Anton fired *The Princess'* engines then threw the single holding line free. The boats separated, and the old trawler ground away slowly, wallowing under the weight of incoming water. Jake and Chernov were left alone on the sinking police boat. They could hear Anton shouting at Remi, and Jake could see the plaintive look on Anna's face as *The Princess* slipped away, disappearing into the night.

The police boat shifted again, sinking hard at the stern. It was going down fast. Chernov was resigned to his fate. His eyes swept across the aft deck. Water was pouring in and washing around Lawrence Jackson's boots. The dead man would go down with his ship.

"We shall be under in another minute," Chernov noted calmly.

Jake staggered as the boat shifted again. The engines failed. Chernov was unable to stand. He half-floated across the deck, sloshing into deeper water at the stern. Jake's mind raced. Suddenly, he leaped through the hatchway beneath the control console. It was nothing more than a cramped cuddy-cabin. He gasped as the frigid water swept around him then shoved floating debris aside and snagged two lifejackets. When he emerged from the space, the stern was going under, and Chernov was about to be sucked into the sea. Jake lunged for the old man, snagging him by the coat collar. Somehow, he wrestled a life jacket around him then tugged his on as well. Chernov floundered haplessly as the sea rushed in from all directions now. It only took a few seconds. The police boat slipped from beneath them, sinking ignobly down, leaving only the very tip of the hull protruding skyward like a lone iceberg. Jake sputtered and thrashed through the water. He grabbed Chernov's life jacket and held it tightly as he searched the horizon. The coastline was shrouded in darkness, an unachievable goal over two miles away. There was nothing to do. Jake hauled Chernov through the water to the slender bow of the police boat rising up from the surface. Both men grappled for a handhold amid the jagged shards of broken planking. When Jake caught his breath, he looked into Chernov's eyes and was stunned by the old man's ineffable sense of calm; it was a stoic capitulation to the frigid darkness swelling around them as surely as death itself.

28

Five miles to the south, *The Princess* plowed ahead more slowly, weighed down by the steady inflow of seawater through fractured planking. The boat's oscillations were more pronounced now, as each heave sent a surge of oily water slamming across the bilge.

Topside, Anna was behind the controls. Anton Sorokin steadied himself nearby, leaning heavily against the coaming. He kept his gun adroitly aimed at Anna, but the boat's sluggish roll had taken a toll on him. He was seasick, and though he was not yet incapacitated, each dip of the hull sent nauseating waves through his stomach.

Remi limped up the companionway steps and spat a wad of blood on the deck. His head hurt like hell and his pants were soaked. "Friggin' water just keeps gushing in," he complained.

"Is the pump keeping up with it?" Anton demanded.

"Barely. Looks like the water's up a little, even with the pump."

Anna could see the concern in Anton's face. "The hull planks are shattered," she advised. "They're working against each other now. The leak's going to get worse."

"Shut up and drive the boat," Anton sniped. He suddenly lurched halfway over the coaming and vomited into sea. He was still heaving pitifully when the satellite radio chirped from inside his pocket. Anton hauled himself up, roughly wiping his mouth on his sleeve. He tugged the radio receiver out and clicked it, "It's Sorokin."

A distant voice chastised him. Anton ratcheted to attention as he listened carefully, then stuttered, "Yes, sir. I understand. There will be no mistakes." The signal went dead, and Anton stuffed the radio back into his coat. He anxiously glanced at the compass and checked wristwatch.

Anna waited for Anton to relay instructions to her, but he only grumbled to himself and pulled his coat more tightly around his shoulders.

Afraid, but equally frustrated, Anna pressed him, "Where are we going?"

Anton thrust a pudgy finger into the wind and called out, 'San Francisco is that way, correct?"

"Yes."

"Then keep driving."

The Losos mini-sub decoupled from the Novgorod with a solid clang of release bolts. At first, she drifted upward slightly then leveled out, levitating thirty feet above the Boomer's main deck. Inside the stubby craft, Lt. Nikita Gorke surveyed his crew of four sailors as they carefully adjusted leveling planes and powered up the electronics system. The four man KGB detachment was crammed together just forward of the command center. Like Gorke, they were dressed in black combat fatigues. Compact ammunition packs lay nearby, as did a small arsenal of deadly weapons. The men were applying lampblack to their faces.

Satisfied with his preparations, Gorke laid a hand on the chief helmsman's shoulder and called out softly. "Bearing zero-three-zero, one half-speed ahead."

The helmsman crisply repeated the command and began to work the rudder to port. The tiny craft came around to the new heading and slipped away from the mother ship without a sound. Gorke watched the telemetry and monitored the engine harmonics. "We are too loud. Feather the props two degrees." The helmsman complied, though he glanced questioningly at his navigator. Neither of them had heard a thing.

Gorke paused to think about Captain Lavrov. He was certain that the seasoned submariner was well past his prime; he had grown cautious and overly protective of his position. Gorke sensed that, with anticipated success of his highly-classified mission, he would soon reverse the roles of the commander and the commanded. He was young, aggressive, and impatient for advancement. This was to be *his* mission, and he was determined that it would be brilliantly executed. "All ahead full," Gorke barked at the helmsman. He spun around and called out to a lanky armament mate further aft, "Load both forward torpedo tubes, but deactivate the tips first. No explosives. I want the fish to run dead in the water."

The mate was confused by the order; what good is a deadhead torpedo, he thought. His ruminations were quickly cut short when Gorke snapped at him again. "You have your instruction. Do it!"

A few miles behind the Losos mini-sub, the much larger Novgorod hovered motionlessly in deeper water. Captain Illia Lavrov was monitoring the Losos' progress. Having not been provided with details of Gorke's mission, he could only watch the tracking screen in silence as the tiny vessel ran straight and true, rising closer to the surface as it quickly picked up speed. Lavrov was perplexed. What could be of such importance as to risk putting the mini-sub on a trajectory that ran directly into the coast just north of the entrance to San Francisco Bay? Gorke was only five miles from land now; soon he would be within three or less.

Jake's fingers had grown numb as the trenchant chill of the Pacific Ocean bled into his body. Chernov was silent, his lips blue, and his head drooping to one side. Jake threw his good arm higher on the beak-like bow of the police boat, grasping at the splintered wood.

They were utterly lost in the shifting sea, nothing more than inconsequential drift, barely float and hopelessly captive to the biting cold. It wouldn't be light for another four hours, Jake thought; they would never make it until then. He considered the abyssal grave that awaited him, the cavernous ocean that would slowly take them under and down, one thousand feet to blackness and nothingness. Jake's benumbed mind drifted to Eryn, and he remembered how much he had loved her. Even in the delusional fog of his failing consciousness, he knew he would always love her; this was immutable. But in some unfamiliar dimension, the vision of Eryn, once so sharply defined, had now become ephemeral and far more distant. Almost at the same instant, he saw Anna. He felt her near him, as a warm rush of life coursed through his body. It was a strangely insular manifestation, carefully enveloping him and bringing great comfort.

Jake's eyes were beginning to blur, and he could only assume the worst when a loud, guttural hum began to ring in his ears. He shook his head and coughed out frigid water. The hum was still there; it was growing louder. It was only when an angry shaft of light swept across his face that he realized the sound was not in his head. Jake struggled to lift himself higher against the police boat's protruding bow. The light came again, raking across the scene, then quickly returned to land directly on the astonished survivors.

The boat had come out of nowhere. It churned closer, slipping alongside, but Jake was too weak to cry out. He could hear shouts of encouragement then recognized Ezra Bonner's voice.

The *Flying Spruce*, Yedor Fedin's powerful trawler, loomed above Jake and Chernov, its wake slapping hard against them. Jake could see Ezra now, fretful and astounded. He saw Yedor too; his cocksure smirk was eclipsed by sober concern and hard-set determination in his eyes. A ladder dropped over the side of the *Flying Spruce*. Jake reached out and clung to it with his bad arm while used his other hand to work Chernov's fingers free from *The Princess'* fractured hull planks. He tugged the old man closer. Ezra Bonner's arms appeared overhead. He grabbed Chernov's coat, slowly hauling him up and into the boat. Jake was next. He tried to climb unassisted but only fell back in the water. Yedor was shouting at him, commanding him to fight and to live. Jake tried again, first catching then inching up the swaying ladder. This time, Yedor's powerful arms snatched him from the sea and brought him roughly over the gunwale.

Both Chernov and Jake lay slumped on the aft deck of *Flying Spruce*. Yedor and Ezra Bonner dug blankets from below deck and covered them as best they could. Only then did Jake begin to realize that they had been saved. He rolled over on his side and spat up seawater. Chernov's eyes fluttered and opened. His lips began to move, but no words came out.

Bonner had ducked below again to grab a coffee pot from the stove. He scrambled up the hatchway ladder and dropped to his knees beside Jake, quickly filling a mug. A faint smile spread across Jake's face as he hoarsely whispered, "I hope that's not decaf."

Bonner helped Jake pull himself up against the cockpit coaming then held the cup up to his lips. Jake drank, a little at first then more. His fingers, still stiff from the cold, wrapped around the steaming mug as he looked up at Bonner. "Thanks," he whispered.

With great relief, Bonner quipped, "Do you mean for the coffee, or for extracting you from the frigid brine?"

"Both," Jake muttered. He tried to stand up, but Bonner held him down when he spotted blood seeping from Jake's wound.

"You've been shot, Jake. Don't try to move."

Jake roughly shoved Bonner's arms away. He was determined to stand but couldn't find the strength.

Yedor was working on Chernov, furiously rubbing his chest through the blankets. "This one's not so good," he called out to Bonner. "Hypothermia. I can barely find a heartbeat."

Ezra leaned closer to Jake. "What happened to your boat?" he pressed.

"They rammed us," Jake sputtered.

"Who?"

"Chernov's aid from the consulate. His thug was there too. They were on the sheriff's boat. We didn't know until it was too late. They holed us, but they were done too. Their boat sank. They took Anna with them on *The Princess*."

"What happened to the sheriff?"

"Dead. They killed him," Jake said as he staggered to his feet, still clutching the blankets tightly around him. An ocean swell hit the side of the boat and sent him lurching against the coaming. He almost fell again. "Yedor," Jake barked, "Anna is on *The Princess* heading south. We have to stop them."

Ezra Bonner was on his feet now too. He quickly interceded, "I'll radio the Coast Guard. What channel?"

"Use channel sixteen," Yedor called out.

Bonner hurried across the deck and steadied himself against the control console. Yedor was shouting at him again, "Put us on a one-eighty heading and get us going!"

Bonner shoved the throttles down and spun the ship's wheel. The *Flying Spruce*'s engines roared and the boat lurched forward. As soon as the gimbal-mounted compass swung around to reflect the new heading, due south, Bonner snapped up the radio mike and clicked on. "Mayday,

mayday," he exclaimed. "This is the trawler *Flying Spruce*." Static-laced voices crackled back.

"I think I've got someone," yelped Bonner. He clicked on line again and continued. "This is an emergency. We've recovered two men from a sinking boat. We're two miles off the coast of Bodega Bay."

Yedor had been able to revive Chernov, at least to the point that he could see and mumble incoherently. "I've got him!" Yedor boasted. He looked up at Bonner, still tweaking the radio and was impressed by the old man's calm resolve. Had he looked closer, however, he would have seen that, while Bonner held the radio mike tightly, his other hand methodically spun the volume control to OFF every time he spoke. No one could possibly hear the distress call.

"Tell them about Anna!" Jake coughed out.

Bonner clicked "on line" again, calling out loudly, "A woman has been abducted. Anna Roman, she is on board her father's trawler, *The Princess*, heading due south toward San Francisco. She is in great danger, I repeat, great danger. The men that took her are heavily armed. Do you copy?" Again, static echoed back, masking faint, broken voices in the background.

Yedor pulled himself up and made his way to the control console. Bonner saw him coming. He adroitly slipped his hand around the back of the radio and unplugged the antenna lead. When Yedor took the radio mike from him, he could find nothing but static on the tuner. "Shit!" he cursed.

"I think they heard me," Bonner lied hopefully. "I think I heard them repeat our position."

Yedor edged Bonner clear of the controls. He pushed the throttles all the way down then shoved harder still. The *Flying Spruce* streaked across the moonlit water as wind whipped around the forward cabin. Yedor had always prided himself on having the fastest boat in the fleet. Now it was going to pay off; he was certain it would.

Jake slumped down next to Chernov. He lifted his cup to the old man's lips, but the coffee mostly dribbled down his chin. Chernov was shivering. Jake gave him one of his blankets. "Where will they take Anna," he pressed.

"I don't know," Chernov wheezed.

Jake snagged his collar and slammed him against the gunwale. "No more games, old man! Tell me!"

Chernov coughed and sputtered, managing to growl out a reply. "They will take her away, out of the country."

"What?" Jake exclaimed.

"Anton and Remi have lost her twice before. They can no longer be trusted."

"Trusted by whom?"

Chernov was certain, "Ultimately, that would be Dmitri Bellus."

Jake was speechless. He released Chernov's collar and sank back, staring blankly into the night. "Why would the President of the Russian Federation want Anna?"

"Surely, you must already know the answer to this."

"Enlighten me. Is she a threat to him? How? Can the Romanov name still be so powerful that he would be afraid of her?"

Chernov managed a derisive wave of his hand, "The news of her lineage will almost certainly leak out. Dmitri Bellus will, of course, welcome her back to Russia but only as a figurehead, a curiosity really. She will be treated as royalty, paraded before the public in a shameless display of pomp and circumstance."

"Then what?" Jake asked cautiously.

"Then she will be tortured. She will die but not before she tells Dmitri what he wants to know."

Jake absorbed the grim dictum then took a deep breath. "Will it matter at all if she really doesn't know where the Baikal went down?"

"No," Chernov remarked flatly, as his eyes sank shut.

Ezra Bonner emerged from the lower cabin, carrying an unwieldy stack of clothes. He dumped them on the deck and wrung out a floppy sweatshirt for Jake. The front was emblazoned with a large, gold fishing hook and two, underscribed words: Bite Me.

Chernov smirked, at least until Bonner tossed a sweatshirt at him. It was fronted with an enormous pair of puckered red lips with a gaping space between them, boldly inscribed with the word: Vacancy.

29

Anna was exhausted and chilled by the rush of damp sea air as she continued to steer *The Princess* southward. It had been over an hour since she had been abducted, and she was still reeling from the horrifying dilemma that enshrouded her. She fully understood that time was running out.

As moonlight danced obliquely off the waves in front of her, Anna allowed a peripheral glance at Anton Sorokin. He was an operative, she thought; he must work for someone quite powerful. She also realized that, once *The Princess* had gotten underway, the smallish man had recovered somewhat from his sea sickness. He was watching her closely. She noted that he did not blink; it was as if he was totally immune to extraneous distractions and was unalterable in his focus.

Anna was certain that Jake would have succumbed to the frigid water by now. He was dead. Chernov was gone now as well, though this was of little consequence to her. Still, despite her stoic resolve, Anna could not escape a pressing awareness of loss. She didn't understand it, and certainly could not explain it, but, without Jake, she felt more alone than ever. She missed his pugnacious spirit, infuriating as it was; he was meaningfully different from other men she had known. He had an agile mind and was not disposed to accept failure, and to that end, he was strong in a very complete sense. These attributes were easy for her to identify and value, but Anna knew there was more and that she knew she could not hide from it. A faint smile appeared on her lips when she recounted how impossible it had been for Jake to mask his growing affection for her. He had cared, really cared. Anna was moved and deeply saddened. Without him, she wasn't sure she had the will to fight any longer. Still, driven by an unexplainable need, Anna regrouped, searching for a plan. Finally, she slipped her hand to the top of the console and clicked the radio on. Anton had not seen her do it.

Remi emerged from *The Princess*' cabin again. He was bruised and disheveled, gnawing aggressively at a stale roll of French bread. He was starving, and the treat he had found below had done little to ease his hunger pangs. Remi cursed at the cold, noting that nothing had changed since he left to warm up. Anna was steering the boat, while Anton stolidly watched her. The silence grated on Remi. He flung the bread overboard and wiped his mouth, growling. "Why don't you tell me again where we are headed."

Anton wasn't in the mood to talk. "South," he remarked lethargically.

"Ooh, well I like South. South American, South of the border? South Pacific?"

"Shut up."

Even in his battered condition, Remi enjoyed incisive word games with his handler. He gestured toward Anna. "Is she that special? I mean, she's a delicate little bite, right, mate? A tad on the skinny side, but I'd do her just for fun."

344

"Shut up and do your job, Remi," Anton snapped.

"Naw, I'm thinking she's more than a poster-girl," Remi teased, "Maybe a whole lot more. She must be pretty *valuable* to someone, or else we wouldn't be chasing all over the stinkin' ocean for her."

Anton shifted his gun to his other hand but did not respond. Remi chortled then pulled a pint bottle of whiskey from his coat pocket.

"Where'd you get that," Anton barked.

"Compliments of the house," Remi held the bottle up to the moonlight then took a hard slug. As he was screwing the cap back on the bottle, he casually reached across in front of Anna, being careful to brush lasciviously against her, and snapped the radar on.

"What's that for?" Anton called out.

"Nothing. Just thought it might be fun to see who else is paddling around out here tonight. Hell, we might find us a…." But he abruptly stopped chattering and looked closer at the screen. "Someone's coming up from behind us," he snorted. "Look here."

Anton moved closer and glanced at the glowing radar screen. A boat of some sort was running about a mile behind them but much closer to the shore. There were other random "blips" too, farther away. "Fishermen," grunted Anton, "There must be dozens of them running up and down the coast."

"At night?" Remi questioned.

"Yeah, at night. Turn it off."

"Fuck you, mate."

Anton's hand twitched and his gun roared with two quick blasts. The radar display exploded in a spray of glass and sparks. Remi was still gaping at the destroyed unit when Anton nudged him with the gun. "Don't push me, Remi."

Yedor Fedin had already spotted *The Princess* through his binoculars; the classic rake of the hull was unmistakable, silhouetted by the moon against the black sea. Jake was watching too. He was grateful that Yedor's boat was so fast. Anton Sorokin could not have anticipated that they could narrow the gap so quickly.

When he first spied *The Princess*, Yedor had slowed his trawler and shifted course to run closer to the shore. He was determined to maneuver as close as possible before being detected. The plan seemed to be working. Ezra Bonner had withdrawn to the recesses of his thoughts, and Jake knew he was analyzing every aspect of the situation, weighing every contingency.

Vladimir Chernov rested on a crab trap, but he had a clear line of sight over the gunwale now. Both he and Jake had changed into Yedor's stored clothes. They looked like a couple of Greek sardine fishermen in baggy pants and drooping, obnoxious sweatshirts.

"Take the helm," Yedor ordered Jake. "Keep us well off her port stern."

Jake complied, stepping over to take the ship's wheel. Yedor ducked below, but he was only gone for a few moments. When he reappeared, he had a high-powered hunting rifle in one hand. "This is all I've got," he advised warily.

Jake dug in his coat pocket and produced the flare gun. "I got this," he added.

Yedor scoffed at him. "You know, they make those little things so the flares sort of squiggle all over the place when they go up. Makes it easier to see, but it doesn't do much for accuracy. You couldn't hit the side of a supertanker if you were nosed into it."

Jake was offended by Yedor's jab but, instead of challenging him, he simply checked the shell in chamber and snapped the gun shut.

Ezra Bonner was less vocal with his concerns, though Jake knew the old man put little stock in a miniscule flare gun.

Chernov's indifferent eyes remained on *The Princess*, well off to the starboard. Then he called out to no one in particular, "What makes you think you can get close enough to the boat without being shot dead?"

"What makes you think I won't put a round in your head if you don't shut up?" Yedor offered politely.

"Anton is no fool," Chernov coughed. "How do you plan to get from your boat to theirs?"

"An invitation would be nice," Jake called out.

"Ha." Yedor chortled.

Jake abruptly hoisted Chernov from his seat. "Com'on, Mr. Consul General, you're going below."

Chernov grimaced from the pain as Jake edged him carefully down the companionway steps.

Yedor snapped up the radio transmitter, but all he heard was static. He cursed himself for having lost radio service and was about the re-clip the mike. Instead, he instinctively reached behind the radio and felt for loose wires. The disconnected radio antenna fell into his hand. Yedor studied the fitting for a moment then simply reconnected it. The static disappeared. "Well, son-of-a-bitch," he exclaimed.

Ezra Bonner looked over, covering quickly. "Well, that certainly explains things."

Anton Sorokin had moved closer to the forward end of *The Princess'* cockpit. Anna was just off to his right, still manning the vessel. She noticed that Anton had relaxed his scrutiny of her and was searching the open sea expectantly. There was nothing out there, she thought, just an endless expanse of dark water shimmering beneath a low-hanging moon. Anton flicked a glance toward the shore then back to sea; it was as if he was measuring their position, lining up the point of land to the east against some unseen point toward the west.

"Pull up here," he demanded. "Slow your engines."

Anna complied, knowing that whatever Anton had planned, it would not be good for her. She had seen the radar marker of an approaching vessel, but she held out little hope that it might be help. With the display now destroyed, even that hope had evaporated. Her assessment changed quickly when *The Princess'* radio crackled to life. A man's powerful voice broke in, "This is the trawler

Flying Spru*ce* calling the southbound vessel just north of San Francisco Bay. Do you copy?"

Anton spun around to glare at the trawler about a mile to their landward side. Anna's heart leaped when she saw the blue-striped hull. It was Yedor Fedin. She was about to reach for the mike when Anton knocked her hand away. "Don't respond."

After a few moments of silence, Yedor's voice came back again. "Flying Spruce calling on channel 16. Southbound trawler, do you read me? We are in need of assistance."

Anna's eyes flashed at Anton. "I have to pick up. It's a distress call."

"He will stop transmitting," Anton growled.

"Southbound trawler," Yedor's voice pressed harder. "I repeat, we are in need of assistance. We are nearly out of fuel. Do you copy? *Please.*"

Anton watched the strange trawler steadily moving closer. He didn't respond at first when Anna called out to him, "If we don't answer, he'll report us to the Coast Guard. It's illegal to ignore a distress call."

Without a viable alternative, Anton relented and gestured for Anna to receive the transmission. He laid his gun barrel on her lips and motioned for her to be very careful.

Anna snapped up the mike, "Flying Spruce, this is the Princess, returning your call. Go to channel 22." She knew that marine radio protocol dictated that they stay off the universal frequency hosted on channel 16. Anna flipped the dial over and waited.

Yedor's voice returned quickly. "Princess, this is Flying Spruce. Do you copy?"

"I'm here, Flying Spruce." Then, carrying on with the charade, she called out, "What is your home port? I've not heard of you before."

There was a long moment of silence then Yedor's voice came back, "We are out of Spokane, Washington."

Anna almost burst out laughing, knowing that Spokane wasn't on a navigable waterway. "Got that, Flying Spruce. Do you want fuel?"

"Affirmative. We only need about twenty gallons. Can we approach and breast-up."

Anna looked at the approaching boat and at Anton. Remi was on deck now too. He was scowling, distrustful of any intrusion. "Tell 'em to shove off," he growled.

Anna wasn't listening to Remi. She clicked on line. "Come ahead, Flying Spruce. Best to meet us on our leeward side." She had no more than clicked off-line before Anton hit her in the face. It was a glancing blow that knocked her aside. He barked at Remi, "Stay out here with her. I'll go below." Anton shoved his gun barrel into Anna's quivering lips. "Get him his fuel then get him out of here -- fast. He'll be a dead man if you mess this up."

Anton withdrew silently, sinking down through *The Princess*' hatchway door. Remi made sure that Anna saw the gun he had beneath his coat.

Yedor wheeled the *Flying Spruce* around the leeward side of *The Princess*. Ezra Bonner was handling the deck lines, but he was wearing a deeply hooded parka that effectively hid his face. There was no other crew visible.

Ropes were tossed over, and Remi awkwardly tied off so Bonner could pull the boats together.

Anton Sorokin was just below and behind the hatchway door. His gun was chambered as he peered through a narrow crack.

Yedor bounded across the aft deck of the *Flying Spruce*, beaming with a self-depreciating grin. "Thanks to you, captain. We were sure to run bone dry in another couple of miles."

The fierce twinkle in his eye told Anna that help was at hand. "Glad to do what we can. I'm Anna Roman."

"And I would be Edward Teach," Yedor boasted.

Again, Anna could barely repress her smile. She knew that Edward Teach was Blackbeard's real name.

Only Yedor could make light of a treacherous situation. He gestured to Ezra Bonner, "My man here will hand you over some fuel cans. Do you have a hand pump for the diesel?

"We do," Anna called out. "Let's do it."

Bonner began to haul an unwieldy group of plastic fuel containers across the gunwale to Remi. Anna pitched in, helping to align them along the aft deck. She was still at a loss for what Yedor had planned, but when she glanced around the starboard cabin walkway, she almost gasped. Jake, who had slipped out of the *Flying Spruce*'s forward deck hatch, was creeping around the side of *The Princess* with his flare gun tucked against his chest. He motioned for Anna to remain calm.

Remi was hurrying to unscrew plastic caps on the containers when he sensed something awkward about

Anna's motions. He spun around, just as Yedor hauled up his hunting rifle. Remi was quicker. He fired his Glock, a perfect kill shot, but somehow Yedor's rifle got in the way. The round slammed into his rifle's shell chamber, knocking him backward. The gun smashed into the control console.

Remi lunged for the gunwale to get a clear shot at Yedor, but as he did, Jake burst around the side of *The Princess'* cabin. This time, Remi wasn't fast enough. Jake's flare gun belched fire, and the screaming incendiary round hit Remi squarely in his throat. It exploded, eviscerating his head in a roiling ball of flames. Remi's conflagrated body toppled over the side of the boat and crashed into the sea.

Jake pulled Anna tightly in his arms and kissed her. It was only a moment, but it seemed as if they had both been waiting a lifetime. A warning cry from Yedor spun him around. Anton Sorokin lunged through the cabin hatchway with his Glock trained on Jake's head. There was nowhere to run, but in that instant of fatal resignation, something flashed in front of him. Ezra Bonner had launched himself over the breasted gunwale, much like a baseball runner diving for home plate. He crashed into Anton. The Glock sailed away as both men cartwheeled into the cockpit coaming. Ezra fell to the deck, knocked senseless. Anton staggered to his feet, wobbling across the deck; his nose broken and spilling blood. Jake spun him around, landing a crushing blow to his jaw. Anton spat blood and was about to go down when Yedor swung his disabled rifle butt like a baseball bat, crushing Anton's skull with a dull crunch. The pugnacious Russian was done. His eyes rolled back in his head, as he staggered and collapsed over the gunwale and splashed into the sea.

Anna began to shake convulsively. Jake threw his coat around her. She could barely stand. Ezra Bonner had come around and pulled himself upright against the coaming. Vladimir Chernov's face appeared in the hatchway. He had pulled himself up and was beaming now. Yedor, last man standing on the *Flying Spruce*, swelled up and snarled into the night sky.

30

Five hundred yards farther out to sea, the Losos mini-sub slid to the surface. At only about one-hundred-tons displacement, it barely broke the surface, revealing only a dome-like titanium hump. Inside the vessel, Lt. Nikita Gorke, centered his periscope on the two trawlers rocking softly in gentle swells. He flipped a different lens into place to magnify the view. Jake, Anna, Yedor and Ezra Bonner were all visible, but there was no one else in sight.

Gorke had never met Anton Sorokin, much less Remi, but he had been sent recent photos of both men. They were his contacts, and it disturbed him that neither was present. He easily recognized Anna Roman through his eyepiece. She was indeed more beautiful than the photo of her that had been sent to him, Gorke thought. He had no knowledge of her specific value, but it didn't matter; his orders were explicit. Take the girl and kill the rest.

Gorke waited for nearly five minutes, hoping that his contacts would appear. Finally, he realized that something had gone terribly wrong. Worse still, a stiff current had dragged the Losos, as well as the two trawlers, rapidly southward. Gorke's fears were confirmed when he swung his scope around, only to see the sublime glow of San Francisco rising beyond the dark Marin Headlands. Beside that were the simmering lights of the Golden Gate Bridge, threatened now by the encroachment of a dense fog bank working its way in from the sea.

Gorke knew he needed to take decisive action or Anna Roman might slip away again. He hesitated, but only for a moment, before snapping at his first mate. "Are the forward tubes charged?" he asked.

"Yes, per your order, sir," the first mate replied.

"They are dead-head, correct? No explosive charge."

"Yes, sir, but…." He was about to question the lack of explosives. Gorke cut him off, "I want to sink them, not blow them up. Ready the fish for firing," Gorke ordered. "Lock in on the bow of the larger of the two trawlers."

The mate hammered the internal "Firing Stations" button. Deep maroon lights began to flash, flooding the vessel's central corridor. Two compartments forward, safely ensconced behind a watertight hatch, a sweaty crewman ritually kissed his fingertips and laid them on the slender torpedoes in side-by-side firing tubes then slammed the doors shut. He spun the charging air valves and keyed the interlock touch-pad, connecting the torpedo's directional guidance system to the sub's targeting computer.

In the command station, Lt. Gorke peered into the eyepiece of his periscope. A thin line of sweat lingered on his upper lip.

"Sir," the first mate whispered. "The fish are loaded and locked."

Gorke nodded then turned quickly to the four combat-ready KGB operatives waiting in the forward mess space. Their faces were grimly fixed and smeared black.

"Break out the Zodiac," Gorke commanded. "Take it topside and rig for engagement."

The attack team slipped aft, brushing past the rest of the crew as if they did not exist. Gorke knew these men were prepared. He had trained them himself.

The Princess and the *Flying Spruce* were still lashed together, rolling gently on the calming sea. Jake had eased Anna down on a wooden toolbox and pulled his coat more tightly around her. Yedor was trying to raise help on the marine radio, but it had been rendered useless when his rifle slammed into it.

Jake looked at Ezra, not fully understanding how and why his mentor had found Yedor. Talk could come later, he thought. Right now, he needed a plan.

Chernov was slumped nearby, more alert now, but he was in no shape to cause problems. He surveyed the two boats then flipped an acerbic taunt at Jake. "It would be a mistake to assume that this changes anything."

Jake refused to be sucked into Chernov's mind-game. He called out to Yedor, "Can you stay with us until we can get into the Bay?"

"That I can do," the big man sang out. "The Coast Guard base is just west of Aquatic Park. We can go in there."

"That'll work," Jake shouted back, though he was apprehensively surveying the broad stretch of open water that had to be traversed before entering the bay.

Yedor was already unlashing the two trawlers, and they were just beginning to drift apart when the deadhead torpedo slammed into his bow with a great spray of water and timber. There was no explosion, but the *Flying Spruce* shuddered and heeled over sharply from the impact. Jake saw it all and lunged to look over the side of the boat, gaping at the sleek, black torpedo lodged tightly in Yedor's bow.

Yedor couldn't see the damage, but he knew he had been hit hard. "What is it?" he cried out to Jake on *The Princess*.

"It looks like a torpedo, a small one! It's run through your bow, and it's stuck there, right at the waterline!"

Yedor bolted down the lower cabin hatchway. Anna, still in shock from the killings, seemed oblivious to the torpedo hit. Jake threw a look at Chernov, who offered a smug smile.

Yedor exploded on the aft deck again. "It's run clear through both sides the hull!"

Jake called out to him, "Are you sinking?"

No. The hull's holding, but I'm taking a lot of water."

Anna was trying to process the shouts surrounding her. She called out absently, "...sinking, leaking water? Who? Where?"

Jake ignored her and shouted at Yedor again, "Can your bilge pump handle it?"

"Maybe, but I need to get to shore," Yedor responded. "I'm not sure if...." But he stopped in mid-sentence when he saw the second torpedo streaking toward them. It was just below the surface, churning out a thin wake as it streaked through the water, heading straight for *The*

Princess. Yedor bellowed at Jake, "Steer hard over to starboard! Now! Now! Another torpedo is coming in!"

Jake saw the thin wake racing toward them and jerked *The Princess'* wheel hard over. Ezra Bonner slammed into the coaming, while Anna and Chernov were almost thrown off their seats. "Full throttle!" Yedor screamed.

Jake hammered the throttles down hard, his eyes still fixed on the incoming weapon. Chernov was grim-faced, as his mind streamed with lightning-fast calculations. They were going to be hit, he reasoned. There was no way to avoid it. But at the last possible moment, Jake instinctively reacted. He spun the ship's wheel the opposite direction, hard to port. The torpedo whizzed past, missing his bow by only inches, then tore away into the darkness.

Inside the Losos mini-sub, Lt. Nikita Gorke slammed his fist against a bulkhead. "Reload!" he shouted to his crew. The first mate was still conveying orders over the intercom when Gorke's fist snagged his shirt. "Sink those boats! Do not miss again." Without another word, he clambered aft and scrambled up the conning tower ladder, disappearing out the access hatch.

The Princess was churning toward the towering arches of the Golden Gate Bridge, with the *Flying Spruce* running just a few yards off to one side. Anna had joined Jake at the helm of *The Princess*. His coat had warmed her, helping to bring her to her senses again. She wanted to do something, anything. Bonner had moved forward too, though Jake was puzzled by his abrupt silence. The old professor seemed introspective, somehow detached from the reality facing them.

Ahead, a dense mound of fog rolled in beneath the bridge, swelling around its piers and spreading fully across the entrance to the bay. Jake could see the titanium hump of the submerged min-sub slicing across the water at a slight angle behind them. "They're looking for another shot," he exclaimed. Anna was watching too, but then she saw something else. "There!" she cried out, pointing into the dark. A small Zodiac inflatable boat, powered by a lightweight outboard motor, was directly behind them, carrying a nest of black-garbed men who clung to the railing ropes. It was gaining fast. Jake searched the darkness ahead of them. The fog bank was no more than two hundred yards away now.

Yedor had seen the mini-sub and the Zodiac too. He ran his boat in beside *The Princess* and shouted over the engine roar. "Make for the fog then use your compass!"

"What about you?" Anna shouted.

Yedor grinned. "I'm going to play tag." He swung his boat away, turning back.

Lt. Nikita Gorke squatted at the bow of the inflatable. They were going flat-out, and it was a bone-jarring ride. He saw the *Flying Spruce* circling back and ordered his team to open fire.

Yedor heard the shots, as wood splintered all around him. He ducked down but remained on track. He was sweeping wide around the Zodiac, aiming for the moonlit mini-sub instead. That boat and her torpedoes would have to come first.

The Losos' first mate was bent tightly over the periscope, stunned to see Yedor's big trawler suddenly bearing down. He screamed into the intercom. "Bow firing station! Are you loaded?"

A voice crackled back, "Negative. The breech is jammed. Clearing now."

Yedor's boat was heading straight for the sub. The mate made a command decision. "Dive!" he yelled. "Dive!"

Yedor was running full ahead with the torpedo jutting through his bow like a dog with a bone. He was singing now; it was an old seaman's tune, loud and proud. The Losos was starting to sink beneath the water, but it was not fast enough. Yedor's boat crashed across the back of the slender mini-sub, buckling the titanium shell.

The first mate and his crew were upended by the impact. Framing and bracketing failed all around them as the sub's hull fractured. Water poured in, swelling around the terrified crew before they had time to react. And then the hull simply gave way, ripping nearly in half with a gaping fracture. The Losos and its crew were doomed. In seconds they were spiraling downward, only to be lost in the murky subterranean abyss.

Yedor slowed and looked back. He had lost one propeller, and the other one was vibrating badly. This was of no concern to him as he saw the great rush of bubbles spewing from the surface. He knew the mini-sub was sunk.

Though his Zodiac team was nearly a thousand yards away, Nikita Gorke could see the collision through his binoculars, and he feared the worst, certain that his crew was gone. He was infuriated now, excoriating his stealth team as he fired randomly at *The Princess*, which he knew was still out of range.

Yedor Fedin slowly turned his crippled trawler southward. A quick glance down the companionway steps told him that his cypress hull had withstood the impact of the thin-skinned mini-sub, but water was still pouring in. His pump was keeping up with the sloshing water, barely, as it lapped just over the lower floorboards. With one engine drive down and the other vibrating severely, Yedor knew his chances of catching the Zodiac and *The Princess* were slim. Still, he refused to give up. With measured hope, he shoved the remaining engine's throttle all the way down, but it was no use. The vibration threatened to shake the boat apart. Yedor pulled the throttle back and scanned the opaque sea to the south. He could only watch helplessly as *The Princess* slipped silently into the fog bank and disappeared. The Zodiac entered the enveloping mass a few moments later.

Yedor set his remaining engine at a slow idle and followed. He knew he was out of the fight.

31

The Princess inched through dense fog that afforded zero visibility. When Anna had returned to the helm, she had no choice but to slow the boat dramatically. Without the radar, she was running blind in the fog. She could hear the rush of vehicles somewhere two hundred feet above on the Golden Gate Bridge, but the billowing mist had left her disoriented and afraid. The compass helped; Anna had the boat running steadily at one hundred degrees, a course which should bring them under the bridge and close to the shore of the bay somewhere near the Marina Green.

Jake had taken up position at the forward end of the bow. He strained to see into the dense swirl of fog. Foghorns sounded mournfully, first to the east and then closer to the north. Jake listened carefully for any changing sound, but all he could hear was the gentle slap of water against the hull and the dull throbbing of *The Princess'* engines. He knew they could collide with an unseen freighter at any moment.

Farther back in the cockpit, Ezra Bonner and Vladimir Chernov sat in stoic silence. Bonner's head was ringing from his collision with Anton Sorokin. He was dizzy and nauseated, and could not help but wonder if he might have a severe concussion. Chernov's eyes were closed, but he was listening carefully, selectively categorizing groans from *The*

Princess' hull, the engine rumble, and the beat of water washing past.

Crossing the sea-lane beneath the Golden Gate Bridge was challenging even in perfect weather. Attempting the transit at night in an incapacitating fog was immensely more dangerous. Jake and Anna strained to identify the hollow, disorienting sounds that surrounded them. Chernov listened too, and his eyes snapped open when he heard the faint whine of the Zodiac's outboard motor. It was close. The motor had probably been silenced with a thick blanket, Chernov thought. He was certain that the assailants' weapons had been similarly equipped for silence and that each man would assuredly be carrying a serrated combat knife as well. Such were the tools of KGB strike teams.

Anna heard a loud slap off to her left; Jake heard it too. Was it a paddle in the water? Anna questioned. Jake theorized, correctly, that someone had just crammed a fresh magazine into the underside of an Uzi. He motioned for Anna to slow the engines still further.

When *The Princess* thumped softly against something beneath her hull, Anna glanced over the side of the boat, expecting to see a chunk of driftwood flushing up from below. Jake looked down into the water too. It took a moment for him to recognize the shape of a kelp-encrusted rock and then the gentle incline of sand. They had made land.

Jake spun around, pointing down, and whispered through the mist, "We're beached."

Anna was still unsure. She could just make out the formless shapes of other rocks and boulders stacked steeply upward. Above the wall of stones, an even darker barrier loomed skyward in the mist. It was huge, and it seemed to spread out in all directions. Anna kept the boat in gear to maintain position on the narrow beach then motioned for Jake to come back from the bow. When he slipped around the side of the cabin and dropped into the cockpit, Anna whispered to him, "We're short of the marina and the Coast Guard base."

"How short?"

"A lot," Anna posited. "Those stones out there, they form the main seawall around Fort Point. Just above that is the outer wall of the fort itself."

"Fort Point? That's barely inside the bridge. We're at least a mile from the marina and the Coast Guard station."

"More like a mile and a half, "Anna corrected.

Jake thought for a moment, but he already knew they couldn't risk going back out on the bay. The Zodiac had to be very close. "Okay, we get off here," Jake barked. "When we climb up to the fort, we can hike back down the beach. Somebody will find us."

"Yeah, like those black-faced guys in the rubber raft?" Anna said.

"Maybe not. We have to go up. They're still out there on the water, probably close."

Chernov was looking at them now. Even through the wet veil, his eyes gleamed with cold blue intensity. "You are playing a game you can't win," he cautioned. "They want the girl. The rest of us, especially me, will need to be exterminated first. There is no other outcome."

Ezra Bonner finally spoke up, soundly rejecting the Russian statesman's prognostications. "Vladimir Chernov, I know you. For a very long time I have known you. Logic rules your life. It always has. You have no use for unsupported conjecture or unfounded optimism, but you are wrong this time."

"Does the good professor have a reason for his sagacious assessment?"

"Yes. You see endings; I see new horizons. And that is the poverty of your judgment."

Chernov stewed angrily. Jake cocked his head and hissed at Bonner. "Ezra, tell me again what the hell you're doing here."

"If you mean aside from trying to keep you alive, then I should think the term *enmity* might be appropriate."

"Enmity?" Jake questioned.

"Enmity, animus, rancor, or could it be simple acrimony for the abuse of power by those entrusted to prevent abuse."

"Meaning you're no fan of Russian hegemony?"

"Not when it's been monetized and militarized just so President Dmitri Bellus can play his pernicious games on the world stage."

Jake hesitated, trying to dissect Bonner's cryptic admission, "Did I take that class, Ezra?"

"No, but you should have," Bonner snapped, "Bellus wants you dead, Jake. For no good reason other than that you have inserted yourself into his chess game. He wants to *kill* you. That's an outcome that I couldn't accept."

"That's why you did all of this?"

"Yes."

"But what about Chernov? Anna?" Jake protested.

"Vladimir is a dead man. He knows it; you should accept it."

"Anna?"

Ezra Bonner was resolute, "Dmitri Bellus will take her back to Russia. He will give her an impressive but entirely ceremonial position. In a year, maybe two, she will disappear from the public eye. By then, she will have told Bellus everything he wants to know."

"Jesus, Ezra! You're okay with that?"

Bonner's face tightened. He was resigned to Chernov and Anna's fate, and he did not answer Jake's question.

Captain Illia Lavrov had monitored the Losos mini-sub from the command center aboard the Novgorod mother ship. Coded subsonic transmissions had relayed real-time voice data, as well as visual oversight through on-board monitors and the Losos' optical interlink. Lavrov's unsettled apprehensions about the mission had been more than justified. The Losos was lost with all hands. Lavrov was furious that Nikita Gorke took it upon himself to command the KGB Zodiac team. It was a fool-hearty and ill-conceived attempt to reap personal glory.

Before she sank, the Losos' tracking telemetry had indicated to Lovrov that Gorke and the Zodiac team were pursuing the American trawler, slipping toward the bay. It was insane to think that the Americans would not detect the mini-sub. Lovrov also knew that, unless he brought the Novgorod to the surface, he had no direct communication link to the Zodiac team. They were on their own, and they would most certainly be lost if he did not act.

Captain Lavrov expelled a stream of Russian expletives then swung around to his command crew. "Bring us about, slow ahead, bearing one-five-five at fifty feet."

Jake was the first to climb past the last boulder on the steeply inclined sea wall. He reached back and took Anna's hand, helping her over the slick embankment. Bonner and Chernov were still hidden in the fog, somewhere lower on the slope. Jake could only hope that the wounded Russian could make the climb. He was about to call out when a ghostly light suddenly washed across them; it was strangely diffused, emanating from an unseen point well offshore. The light swept past then thankfully disappeared. Anna gripped Jake's arm tightly.

Jake tried to take stock of their situation. He knew that the Coast Guard base was over a mile away, with nothing but raw parkland between them. They could easily get lost in the fog. Besides, Bonner and Chernov had still not appeared, and this was of growing concern.

Jake turned away from the bay. Despite the dense fog, he was able to see the massive breastwork of Fort Point. It rose up above them, a near impenetrable edifice, broken only by a sinister array of narrow gun ports. Built between 1853 and 1861, the fort was intended to be a formidable deterrence to naval attack during the Civil War. So strong were the towering walls that it had been dubiously dubbed the Gibraltar of the West Coast. The sprawling installation, which had been meticulously preserved as a national park, was laid out as a trapezoidal fortress that most resembled the Roman Colosseum. There were three firing levels, each one open to a huge, unroofed center court, and all bristling with heavy cannon placements, including a number of ten inch behemoths that could hurl red-hot, one-hundred-thirty-pound cannon balls over two miles.

The menacing fortress was serenely silent now, dark and unattended. Jake and Anna finally spotted Ezra Bonner, who was assisting Vladimir Chernov up the steep slope. It had not been easy for either of them. Bonner landed on a large boulder, sucking in great gulps of air. Chernov was weak, but he managed to limp through the mist to lay a hand on the stone parapet. "I have read about this place," he expounded. "It was constructed, as I recall, to defend San Francisco, and to a larger extent California, from naval attacks."

"It never fired a shot," Ezra Bonner noted wearily.

"But it protected the city, did it not?"

"Yeah, it protected the city," Jake interceded tiredly.

"Then I should hope that it will protect us now," Chernov allowed with a surprising degree of hope. Jake was puzzled by the old man's comment, yet it felt entirely forthright.

Jake stood up quickly; he knew he had to act. "Let's get out of here," he barked.

Jake led the way, inching through the fog, carefully navigating the perimeter wall of Fort Point. He could hear waves beating at the base of the breakwater below them. A couple of seagulls fluttered away into the night. Anna and

Ezra Bonner supported Chernov, helping him along the uneven rock surface.

When Jake rounded the eastern façade of the fort, his feet found the spreading expanse of a gravel parking space. He stepped over a corroded anchor chain, hung low as a barrier along the edge of the lot, but he could still not see anything more than several feet in front of him. Anna found her way to his side. "I think we should go to the left."

"Left," Jake noted, could mean anything. "We could be going in circles."

Anna bristled, "It's left, that way. The park road goes out there. If we can find it, we can follow it along the coast."

Jake was still considering Anna's suggestion when he caught Chernov's eye. There was a glimmer of optimism in his face. "Excellent plan, absent a better alternative, of which I have none," Chernov wheezed with forced bravado.

Even Anna took note of the old man's tacit approval.

Jake suddenly held up a silencing hand. The light from the bay had reappeared, now atop the seawall. It swung slowly back and forth, a muted yet omnipresent specter of approaching danger. The gently wafting night breeze shifted slightly, and the sound of music rolled out of the mist. It was very faint, a pulsing throb, primitive yet compelling. Jake quickly hiked away into the fog, swiping angrily at the drifting cloud. The music grew louder. Anna jerked Jake's arm, pointing off to their right.

Jake was moving fast now, drawn to the rhythmic beat like a firefly to a flame. He pulled up sharply when a feeble light appeared overhead. Just ahead, a slender pole rose up through the mist, topped by an anemic parking lot light. Beneath it, Jake could just make out the hulking shape of a car. He inched closer. It was a vintage Dodge Challenger, bright orange but well maintained. It appeared to be a solitary vehicle, the only one in the sprawling parking lot, mournfully adrift in a sea of fog.

Anna stumbled up with Chernov in tow; it took a moment for Jake to realize Ezra Bonner wasn't with them. "Where's Ezra?" he asked.

Anna spun around to look back into the dense mist. "He was there just a minute ago."

She was about to call out, but Jake stopped her. He knew that Bonner was gone, lost somewhere in the fog. There was nothing he could do.

The dull throb of music continued to pulse from inside the parked car. Its windows were completely clouded over with condensation, but Jake could see dim lights radiating behind the glass. He slipped up to the car and jerked the front door open. A bare ass greeted him; the boy couldn't have been more than seventeen. He was too stunned to speak. The girl, torturously ensnarled in her discarded clothes, screamed at the intruders. Jake cursed and instinctively slammed the door but instantly regretted his accommodation to the testosterone-ravaged couple. He was about to rip the door open again when a spray of nine-millimeter rounds hissed through the mist, shattering the car windows and pelting the doors. It all happened in an instant. The silenced gunshots sounded more like blowgun darts, whiffing past with deadly intent. Jake hauled Anna to the ground, while Chernov dropped beside them. He was grim-faced now, certain that his life was about to end. He could hear someone, a Russian, screaming at his men, demanding that they stop shooting blindly.

Jake covered Anna as best he could. They could hear more voices in the fog, Russian, hushed and angry. Anna threw her arm up, reaching for the door handle. Jake grabbed hold too, but the car engine roared to life, and the tangerine muscle car tore away in a violent spray of gravel.

Jake was surprised, and even relieved, when a single burst of gunfire broke out again, following the sound of the car as it was swallowed up by the fog. A commanding voice screamed again, ordering the man to stop firing.

"They're shooting blind," he whispered to his group. "They're as lost as we are."

"Follow the car," Anna hissed. "The road's that way."

"Maybe," Jake cautioned as he strained to see into the mist.

"Jake, it's *that* way! Come on!" Anna clambered to her feet and stumbled after the car. Jake threw a look back, hoping to see Ezra Bonner, but as Russian voices grew louder, he grudgingly followed Anna, hauling Chernov with him. Another burst of muffled gunfire erupted, as a spray of slugs sung past. Anna was just a few yards ahead. Jake began to run, half-carrying Chernov with him.

Behind them, searchlight beams streaked obliquely into the night. Anna had pulled still farther ahead of the rest. She had turned left then right, not certain she could still see the lights of a car. She stopped and turned full circle then spotted two lights, possibly taillights; it was hard to discern the color, but they were there. She was sure of it. Before

Jake could catch her, Anna broke through the fog and ran ahead, only to slam headlong into the heavily barred entrance gate to Fort Point. The impact knocked her to the ground. She was dazed and bleeding from a gash on her forehead.

Jake stumbled up, panting for breath; he could only expel a barren exclamation, "Wrong way..."

32

Lt. Gorke and his KGB troops raced through the fog, disoriented and frustrated. Gorke pulled up and listened, but there was only the distant sound of foghorns in the bay. The car was gone, and they could no longer hear Jake's group running across the gravel.

The landside entrance to Fort Point did not require a door. Instead, the stout iron gate offered both security and a means for after-hours visitors to peek inside the open gunnery rotunda. Jake's mind was racing as he lifted Anna to her feet. "Where are we?" she asked vaguely.

"Back where we started," Jake replied. "Can you walk?"

"Yes. Yeah, I can walk," she repeated.

Jake was certain it would be fruitless to continue running blindly in the fog. He eyed the small lock that secured a chain around the entrance gate. It was surprisingly small, just a typical hardware store padlock. Jake grabbed a metal waste-can next to the doorway, lifted it overhead, and slammed it down on the lock. The mechanism popped open and fell to the ground. Jake steadied Anna, leading her and Chernov past the iron gate. He quickly swung the gate closed and carefully re-threaded the chain and slipped the broken lock back into place, setting it so that it appeared to be fully engaged. When Jake turned back, Chernov offered an accommodating smile. "The men that Dmitri Bellus has sent for the girl, they are professionals."

"KGB?"

"Most probably."

"Then it won't go well for them when they get caught."

"They don't intend to be caught."

Anna had pulled herself together, and while she was still confused from her collision with an iron gate, she was more upset by Ezra Bonner's disappearance. "Jake, what about Bonner. What happened to him?"

The reality of losing Bonner descended on Jake again. He wondered if his mentor was still stumbling around in the fog, possibly caught by the Russian hit team, or did he wandered too near the seawall, and tumbled down the rock face into the bay? None of the scenarios were acceptable, but there was no reason to think better.

Jake struggled for assurances that might assuage Anna. "Ezra is a resourceful man," he posited. "If he hasn't been caught…"

Anna sensed his uncertainty, but she let it drop. Jake had edged the group away from the gate, sinking deeper into the menacing shadows of the inner courtyard. A few feeble security lights glowed dimly and did little to dispel the gloom. All around them, they could see the open-sided gunnery bays rising up; they appeared almost like private box seats at a New York theater, symmetrically blocked off on all three levels, each occupied by a cannon and stack of steel projectiles There were even gun placements on the top of the structure, open to the night sky and weather.

For the first time in a long time, Jake and Anna were able to rest. They found a mist-shrouded visitor's bay crowded with souvenir displays and Civil War memorabilia. Anna sank onto a hand-hewn bench. Jake eased down beside her. They were too exhausted to speak.

Chernov painfully held himself upright, one hand clasped over his wound, as he peered out through a slit-like gun port in the stone wall. "I'm very afraid they will find us," he offered to no one in particular. He didn't expect to receive a response, and neither Jake nor Anna felt compelled to provide one. Chernov allowed his eyes to sink shut, his face caressed by a sibilant sea breeze wafting through the open port. The scent was so very familiar. It transcended the immediacy of his impending death, transporting him instead to haunting images from the past, each in its own way framing the complex texture of his life. Had it all been an illusion, he thought, each moment of profound joy, fear, and even exaltation, moments never fully lost, but rather held immutably captive in the deepest recesses of his mind. Was this how it was to end?

Jake's thoughts ran deep as well, but for him, the imperative of simple survival easily eclipsed any sense of regret or self-incrimination. He was a consummate pragmatist; he dealt with certainties of the moment, and allowed introspection to overtake him only when logic failed. Jake glanced sideways, peering at Anna. For better or for worse, this woman had become an inexorable part of his life, and where such an admonition would have been impossible to accept only one day before, he knew now that she had become the singular motivation of his own existence.

Anna didn't have the strength to stand, as she slumped on the bench, leaning against the cold stonework. She tried to catch her breath, but her thoughts careened back to Mikhail and his gruesome death. She was still certain that Chernov ordered his torture and execution. The fact that Anton, Remi and Oleg had turned on him, didn't change that belief as far as she was concerned. Chernov, with his appalling capacity for inhumanity, was responsible for Mikhail's murder. Nothing could change that.

Anna's hard eyes fell on the old Russian, and while she knew that she might well die that night, it gave her great consolation to know that Chernov would be departing with her. "Hey, old man," she called out softly.

Chernov shifted slightly but did not turn from the gun port. "You have observations to share, but there's no point, not any longer."

"Tell me again how you planned to defect," she demanded. "If there's no point to any of this any longer, then there's no point in lying. Tell me."

Chernov took a deep breath of cool sea air then turned toward her. He was still half-hidden in dark shadows, but his face was devoid of emotion. "What I told you, it was true. But it's not a simple matter to leave one's country of birth."

"I don't buy it. Defection for a man like you is improbable," Jake interjected.

"Did you have my father killed?" Anna asked solemnly.

"No."

"I don't believe you."

Chernov dismissed her, saying, "What you believe or disbelieve is of no consequence. But, as for the truth, I was not responsible for your father's death." Chernov paused then spoke again, more softly but with great resolve. "I had just arrived in San Francisco when I was told about the old woman, Marvina, about how she went to the cathedral, confessed to something we will never know, and took her own life. Konstantin was next, a murder this time. I asked questions, but Remi and Oleg lied to me. By the time Mikhail Roman had been killed, I suspected, but I wasn't certain."

"Is this what you want us to believe?" Jake charged.

"It is the truth."

"What about the Baikal; what about me?" Anna asked.

"That, I did know about."

"Then you wanted the rubles, the gold," Jake posited.

Chernov suddenly flared, "I wanted my freedom! *Freedom*!" He wiped spittle from the corners of his mouth. "The country that I served is gone. First the royalty, the empire, and all it stood for. Then the Soviets came, and loyalty to the party became the currency of my life. I made the choice to stay, to serve, and to hope, but hope is an ephemeral ghost. You can feel it, even taste it at times, but it's not really there." Chernov sagged, unable to project austere confidence any longer. "I am an old man. I only wanted to find peace. Nothing more."

Chernov fell silent. His words had resonated with Jake, but the old man had not mentioned Eryn. Jake felt compelled to ask, "What about Eryn? Did you have her killed?"

Chernov shook his head wearily. "No. When she came to me, I found her questions and her spirit to be utterly charming. She a captivating young woman, but I had nothing to do with her death." He paused, searching for the right words. "Dmitri Bellus knew about your fiancée and her political research. He was displeased, shall we say, and he asked that I *take care of matters*. Instead, I told her about this, about the danger surrounding her. But I suppose she found it impossible to believe the man who she sought to bring down. She didn't listen to me, or perhaps she did, but she couldn't bring herself to accept the truth. Dmitri Bellus had your fiancée killed; he orchestrated her drowning. It was always Dmitri." Chernov's incredibly clear eyes fell on Jake as he whispered softly, "I'm very sorry."

Jake absorbed Chernov's admission, and he understood. He could never be certain, but in some small way, finally, he was able to release at least a part of the searing rage that had consumed his life. If Chernov was lying, he would never really know. At the same time, Jake realized that if he was telling the truth, it would do nothing to bring Eryn back. That battle was lost. As uncertain as it appeared to be, the future suddenly loomed in front of him with even greater urgency.

Jake stood, trying to take stock of their situation. Escape appeared to be impossible, but if they could wait and hide in the old gunnery until sunrise, if they could hold out that long, the fog would dissipate and Bellus' assassins would have no choice but to retreat.

"We have to go deeper into the fort," Jake suddenly announced. "There's got to be a cellar or somewhere we can hide."

"We have to stay *here*?" Anna questioned.

"Yeah, here. That's all we've got. We can make it work. Let's go."

Chernov's head rose abruptly. He was buoyed by Jake's sense of determination and seemed invigorated by the challenge. "You should break the security lights, or at least some of them," he called out.

Jake threw a quick glance back; the old man was actually trying to help. Chernov shrugged indifferently, "This would make it more difficult for them."

"Jake nodded, acknowledging the gift of Chernov's advice. He grabbed a broom from the corner of the room and smashed the dim globe hovering in the corner. "Let's go," he hissed to the others.

Jake led the group through the next series of two adjoining bays, each containing a new diorama, a further presentation of life in a Civil War fort. He broke a second light, and was about to move on when he slammed to a stop. The shadowy figure of a tall man was suddenly right in front of them.

Anna let out a gasp. Jake brandished the broomstick, his only weapon, but when the figure failed to move or speak, he moved closer, jabbing the broom handle in the man's chest.

The mannequin shuddered, and its head fell off. It was nothing more than a lifelike prop, a crisply dressed Union commander, replete with battle awards and a waist-draped saber. Jake ignored the fallen head and quickly unsheathed the sword. It wasn't much, he thought, but it was better than a broomstick.

Chernov broke the silence with an abrupt warning, "I heard something. They're out there. They're close."

Jake took Anna's hand and moved off into the shadows. They had come to the end of the south wall of the fort. To move forward, they would have to slip across an open, fog-bound space to the north wall. "How far across is it?" he asked Anna.

"I'm not sure, a hundred feet at least. It's been a long time since I was here."

"I can't remember either," Jake noted as his eyes found the old Russian.

"Sorry. Don't look at me. I'm just a tourist," Chernov added with wry humor.

Jake couldn't help but smile. He smashed a security light with the saber and started across the veiled courtyard. Wet gravel crunched softly beneath their feet as they felt their way through the fog. Jake could not see a thing. They might as well be on the moon, he thought.

Chernov, tapping his adroit sense for danger, suddenly stopped and looked back. He didn't have time to speak before a loud creaking sound cut through the gloom. Jake and Anna heard it too. Someone had just opened the iron gate at the entrance to the fort. At first, there was only the soft moan of cold night air swirling past the stone walls surrounding them.

After only a few moments, the bleak silence was broken by the sound of footsteps, soft at first, then quicker and more pronounced. Someone was moving methodically closer. Jake, hauled the rusty saber up and pivoted to meet the advancing threat.

Anna gripped his arm and hissed, "There's only one of them. You can hear him."

Jake motioned for her to stay back as he raised the saber higher over his shoulder. He gripped the weapon tightly and prepared to strike. The spectral form of a mist-shrouded man appeared, and Ezra Bonner called out through the fog, "Jake?"

Jake checked his swing; he instantly recognized Bonner's voice.

"Ezra?" he stammered. "What the hell?"

Bonner took several steps closer and came face to face with Jake. "You're still breathing," he noted with an elemental smirk. "And this is of no small consequence."

Jake was still too stunned to speak.

"Where were you?" Anna exclaimed.

Bonner ignored her comment and kept a judicious eye on Jake, "I can extricate you from this mess. But you have to trust me, I mean *really* trust me."

Jake was confused. "What do you mean?"

Before Bonner could answer, Jake heard another set of footsteps moving out of the fog. He started to raise his sword again, but Bonner put a hand on his arm. "No," he said.

Lt. Nikita Gorke appeared next to Bonner; he was a startlingly silent presence. Gorke didn't speak, but his eyes flashed malevolently. Jake recoiled, taking a step back. "Ezra, what is this?"

"It's okay," Bonner urged. "Trust me, Jake."

Anna glared at Gorke, "He's trying to kill us!"

Gorke's four-man team appeared behind him, guns held ready.

"Ezra?" Jake repeated stridently.

Bonner seemed unmoved by Jake's evocation. "This is the way it has to be. I tried to tell you before."

"Tell me what!" Jake demanded.

Bonner raised his palms calmingly, "Jake, I understand the Russians better than you might imagine. I know Vladimir, and I know about his past. He is doomed. You have to give him to Lt. Gorke."

"What are you telling me, Ezra?"

"Life is about making bargains," Bonner announced. "For your life, to *save* your life, I made a bargain. They want Chernov."

"What about Anna!"

"Her too. I gave them both -- for you."

A sea-bound ship sounded its foghorn somewhere far out on the bay. A silent moment passed as the enormity of these revelations descended on Jake. He was speechless. His friend and mentor was willing to capitulate with the Russians in return for his life.

Bonner's eyes had filled with tears. "Jake, I had no son. You filled a void in my life."

"But you made a bargain with Dmitri Bellus!"

"Yes. I couldn't let you die, Jake. I couldn't lose you."

Jake looked deeply at Bonner and asked a simple question, "Do you want the gold too? Is that part of this?"

"No gold. It was never about that."

"Actually," Lt. Gorke growled, "That is not entirely accurate." He slid a sleek handgun from his jacket. He had remained detached from Ezra Bonner's impassioned acknowledgement, but now it was time to act. "I'm afraid *is* about the gold," he announced. "Of course, I have no direct information about this. But agencies do talk, confidences are exchanged, and secrets are revealed. It *is* about the gold, and this girl is of great importance." He shoved the gun against Anna's head. "She will be coming with us."

Jake tried to move in front of Anna, but Gorke slammed him in the face with his gun. Anna cried out. Jake slumped to one knee but struggled to his feet again, his cheek split open and spilling blood.

Gorke snapped at his men, "The old man, the girl. Take them."

Ezra Bonner could see the agony in Jake's face. He finally realized what he had done. How could he not have seen it, he thought. Jake was in love with Anna. She had set him free from Eryn O'Shea. Bonner was reeling from the horror of his betrayal. Self-doubt consumed him. It was all happening too fast. And then he heard Gorke's chilling voice again.

"Take both of them. Kill Dr. Altman."

"No!" Bonner exploded. "We had a deal"

"There is no *deal*," Gorke spat back. He barked at his men, "Kill him! Use your knife."

Infuriated, Ezra Bonner lunged for Gorke. The gun popped with a muffled shot and the old man went down; his body was still.

Anna was overwhelmed. She collapsed to the ground. Gorke saw her fall, and that brief second of inattention was all Jake needed. He brought his fist up under the Gorke's jaw, snapping his head backward. Gorke staggered, trying to regain his balance. He was disoriented but quick to recover. Enraged, he swung his handgun toward Jake.

Gorke never saw the saber as it flashed through the mist. Vladimir Chernov had found it in the dirt and somehow managed to wrap his hand around the tattered leather grip. He brought it down swiftly, severing Gorke's forearm just below the elbow, and before the stunned Russian could cry out, Chernov drove the sword deeply into his chest.

The sky above them suddenly burst open with a blinding wash of white light, as a Coast Guard helicopter appeared and sank quickly through the dense fog with its Xenon searchlight searing downward.

The pilot was on infrared instrumentation, expertly bringing the massive aircraft down quickly; its sixty-foot rotors shred the fog, whipping it downward then up again like a volcanic eruption. The chopper hit the ground hard and a heavily armed Coast Guard interdiction team sprang out.

Chernov had collapsed to the ground. Anna was covering him with her arms. Jake was stooped over Ezra Bonner's body. He rolled the old man over. Bonner groaned; he was still alive. Jake shouted for help, and the Coast Guard team swooped in.

Bonner's eyes cracked open. He forced a smile and whispered a frail apology to Jake, "I'm sorry. I couldn't let you die. I couldn't let that happen."

"I know. It's okay, Ezra. I love you."

Bonner forced a bloody smile then whispered weakly. "I was *so* wrong. Anna – you, I didn't see it. I must be getting old."

"You *are* old," Jake blurted out, forever grateful Bonner was still alive.

A young Coast Guard officer dropped down beside Jake. His gun was trained on Ezra. "Is he one of ours, or theirs?" he demanded.

Jake clutched Bonner's hand tightly, looking deeply into his eyes. "He's one of us. He's the best of us."

In the confusion of the moment, as the helicopter swooped down, the Russian KGB team had scooped up Nikita Gorke's lifeless body. They backed away, slinked into the mist, then slipped away, unseen, through the fog-shrouded gate. The remaining KGB team members would survive, and there would be no proof that they had ever been on American soil. Three hours later, their rubber Zodiac was picked up by the Novgorod. Captain Ilia Lavrov turned the massive sub back to sea, and when they passed over the continental shelf, he ordered Gorke's body-bag to be weighted and unceremoniously ejected out a torpedo tube.

The Coast Guard team had plugged an IV into Chernov's arm. He was still on the ground but was protesting vehemently, demanding to stand. Anna forced him to remain still.

At the same time, the interdiction team produced a canvas litter and began to ease Ezra Bonner into position. Jake rose up and shielded his eyes against the maelstrom of fog, wind, and dust. He could see a woman emerge from the aircraft, protectively guided forward along with another big man. As they drew closer, Jake recognized Katherine Sexton. He didn't know the man though and was surprised to see a finely oiled shotgun tucked under his arm. Liam McGeorge, the gun club master shooter, pulled up beside Katherine and respectfully removed his tweed cap.

Katherine surveyed the scene with droll deference. "Jake, you're a real screw up. Can we stipulate that?"

Jake nodded with faint smile. "Don't tell me, Katherine. You and the CIA have a little thing going on. You're one of them."

"Actually, no. My large and handsome friend here, Liam McGeorge, is most definitely CIA. Me, I'm just a lowly NSA facilitator. Russian bullshit mainly. The pay sucks, but I'm all over the patriot thing."

Liam McGeorge took a step forward, "Aye, Dr. Altman, we've all been waiting a long time for this. I am sorry about your loss, your fiancée."

"You knew her?" Jake stammered.

"We knew about her work. It helped us, more than you know. McGeorge offered a warm smile then turned to

Chernov who was looking up at him. The big Scotsman offered strong hand to the old Russian and lifted him to his feet. "Aye, sir, you should have come to us sooner. Might have spared everyone a bit of trouble, hmm?"

Chernov struggled to square himself in front of McGeorge. He had known pain before, and he knew that, this time, he would survive once again. Before he spoke, a hint of a smile spread across his weary face. He looked at Jake and Anna then turned to McGeorge. "My name is Vladimir Chernov. I am the Russian Federation Consul General to San Francisco, California. I wish to seek asylum in your country."

Liam McGeorge extended his hand. "Welcome to the United States of America, sir."

"Thank you."

McGeorge hesitated then handed the stunning shotgun to Chernov. "We never quite finished our conversation about this piece." He put an arm around his prize catch and guided him slowly away toward the waiting helicopter. The old Russian could hardly walk, but he summoned his deep pride and limped resolutely toward a new life.

McGeorge was chattering amicably about shooting and clay targets. Jake could hear him pestering Chernov. "Now about this fine shotgun," McGeorge preened. "We really need to finish our evaluation. Would it be presumptuous of me to suggest a wee shooting party? Perhaps we could pop a few rounds out on the range."

Chernov nodded with a weary but grateful smile, "Perhaps we could do that, Mr. McGeorge. Perhaps we could."

Jake watched the two old men climb into the chopper then realized Katherine was still looking at him. It was as if she was waiting for something. "Thanks," he said.

"You're welcome."

Jake cocked his head and pressed his luck, "Does this mean we can make peace over my dissertation?"

"Is it finished?"

"Jake thought for moment then he nodded slightly. "Yeah. It's finished." He suddenly threw out a question, "How did you find us, here, tonight?"

Katherine shrugged and slipped a cell phone from her coat. "Ezra," she allowed. "He made one too many calls to Moscow. We were listening."

"Is he going to be in trouble for that?"

"For horse-trading with Dmitri Bellus?"

"Yeah."

"Naw. It's hard to blame a guy for trying to protect someone he cares a lot about."

Jake nodded his silent thanks. Katherine glanced over her shoulder. She could see that Anna was watching them closely. The game had changed, forever; Katherine knew that. With regret, she turned back to Jake. "So, I guess I'm going to need to find a new shower buddy."

"Sorry about that," Jake allowed, finally understanding the unexpected depth of her admission. But he brightened quickly with the realization that Katherine was a survivor. She would be okay, in fact he was certain she would do just fine.

Katherine laid her slender fingers on Jake's shoulder and brushed dust from his baggy sweatshirt. "Are you still afraid of me, Jake?"

"No, but I might be lying."

"Goodbye, Jake," Katherine said with a deep smile. She kissed him lightly on the cheek then turned and marched back toward the aircraft.

Jake shifted his gaze to Anna. A Coast Guard crewman had given her a blanket, and she held it loosely around her shoulders. She was just standing there watching him, uncertain, hopeful. Jake moved closer and pulled the blanket more tightly around her. Her eyes were wide with relief, but there was much more. Jake touched her cheek and kissed her lips.

Several police cars pulled into the courtyard. Officers emerged but waited respectfully for Jake and Anna. The helicopter's engine wound up, and the blades ripped at the night air. Katherine, Chernov, and Liam McGeorge soared away.

Jake and Anna were left holding each other tightly amid the swirling fog.

33

The Princess bobbed easily on a tranquil sea. It was getting late, and the sun was fading over the horizon, spreading flaming orange hues across the distant edge of the world. There was no wind. Waves undulated gently, caressing *The Princess* as if it were a child in a rocking crib.

Jake took another sip from his longneck beer. He was reclining in a cheap Walmart beach chair with his head leaning comfortably against the warm cockpit coaming.

It had cost a lot to get *The Princess* fixed up. Hull planking had to be replaced. New shafts and propellers had been fitted as well, but the old trawler had lived to see another journey to sea. Jake was comforted by the sound of creaking timbers and the gentle slap of waves against the hull. He knew that darkness would be upon them soon, but he wanted one last look at the shore. It was beautiful. Low California hills were bathed in a majestic sweep of muted sunlight.

Jake lifted the hood of a tiny Weber grill sitting next to him on the cockpit deck. Smoke swirled up, followed by the sweet aroma of grilled fish. There was more than enough for the two of them, he thought.

"Anna," he called out. "I'm about to burn the damn redfish."

Anna's muffled voice called back to him from somewhere below in the cabin. He didn't really care what she had said; he just wanted to hear her voice. It was lovely, he thought, earnest and unaffected, finally hopeful again, much as it was when he first met her. The violence that had nearly destroyed them seemed more distant now. There were memories of course, still painful and never to be forgotten, but he knew that his future with Anna lay ahead, not ensnarled in a past they could not change.

Jake was pleased that Anna had decided to drop anchor just offshore; they were within a mile of the entrance to Bodega Bay. He could see the broad arc of the seaward peninsula, and farther back, the thin line of flickering lights framed the town and fishing fleet. The sky was an immense dome of emerald blue, punctuated by a million stars.

Jake took another sip of beer as Anna emerged from the cabin carrying a tray of vegetables and roll of fresh sourdough bread. She still moved like a model, Jake thought, her bare feet pattering softly across worn decking. She was wearing a baggy pair of Khaki shorts and frayed sweatshirt proclaiming, "I Escaped From Alcatraz." Her long hair shimmered in the twilight, hanging loosely over her slender shoulders. Jake couldn't help but smile. If Anna was trying to downplay her sensuality, she was doing a poor job of it. She was stunning. To hell with the fish, he mused.

Anna set the tray down and slipped into a lawn chair next to Jake. She took a sip from her own beer then settled back, relishing the slow undulation of the old hull. Though she had witnessed nightfall on the sea countless of times before, the breathtaking tableau surrounding them once again overpowered her. She breathed in the cool air and comfortably closed her eyes.

The tranquility of the moment was abruptly shattered by the bawling sound of a ship's horn. Jake and Anna looked up quickly to see Yedor Fedin's big trawler racing past. The hole through the bow had been repaired, but Yedor, in his characteristic off-kilter humor had painted a big black spot on the repaired area and added neat lettering over it, reading, "Torpedo Here."

"He's not stopping," Jake observed as Yedor sounded his horn again and streaked away.

"Nothing to stop for," Anna replied. "He lost, you won."

Jake gave Yedor a solid wave then settled back against the coaming. Anna watched him for a moment then closed her eyes again. Moments passed as the drone of Yedor's engines faded away.

"You want to eat something?" Jake asked without looking over.

"Not yet," Anna replied, her eyes still shut.

A long moment passed before Jake spoke again, "Want to smoke some weed?"

Anna smiled, "You don't smoke. Neither do I."

"Yeah, I guess that's right. Do you think maybe we should do something else?"

Anna laid her head over and peered warily at him, "Was that an offer?"

"Or I suppose we could just hang out here. You know, eat the burned fish and sing Broadway show tunes."

Anna sat up. She took Jake's hand in hers. "Do you want to talk?"

"Sure. I guess so." He paused then hoisted his bottle as if in a salute. "Ezra got out of the hospital yesterday. He will be back terrorizing graduate students before you know it."

That's good," Anna allowed. "And I suppose Vladimir Chernov is off someplace cushy with a new identity. He's probably got a bunch of agents hanging around to make sure he doesn't change his mind."

Jake took this in and mulled it over. "So, what was he? What was Vladimir Chernov really all about?

"He was a bad guy," Anna specified as she glanced over with a cocked eye.

"Yeah, but he was more than that," Jake posited. "You know, the Feds still haven't told us squat about their investigation. They should have found the mini-sub by now. They have equipment that can scan the bottom of the ocean. That's what they do."

"I don't think so," Anna noted. "The current out there is horrendous, especially down deep. It would have washed the sub out to sea."

Jake shrugged. He knew she was probably right, but he still wasn't satisfied. "Okay, so they're not going to find the mini-sub. That leaves them with nothing but the torpedo stuck through the bow of Yedor's boat."

"Kinda hard to miss something like that," Anna noted as she closed her eyes and laid her head back again.

Jake was still mulling things over in his head. "Katherine told me the tech guys pulled the torpedo apart, but it was made up of a whole bunch of black market Chinese and North Korean parts. Nothing to trace. Nothing Russian."

Anna was mildly disinterested, "Well, that's just crazy."

"Not really. The Russians wouldn't arm a stealth submarine, that's supposed to go deep into restricted waters, with anything that's traceable."

Anna thought for a long moment before speaking, "You, know. I don't really care."

"I guess I don't either, not anymore," Jake said. He realized that Anna had grown more introspective. She was holding something back. "What is it?" he asked.

"It's nothing."

"Okay."

Anna frowned. She wasn't ready to let it drop. "Jake, I said it was nothing, but that doesn't *mean* it was nothing."

"I see."

"Aw, come on, Jake. Here's the thing. You've never asked me if I knew where the Baikal sank. Not once. Why not?"

Jake thought for a moment then shrugged and tipped his beer up. "None of my business."

"I mean it," she said. "You've *never* asked." Jake gave her nothing. Anna thought for a long moment then got up and went to the control consol. She rummaged around on a shelf then returned with a book of nautical charts. She sat down again then produced a pen and began to scribble a series of numbers, separated by dash marks, on the front of the book.

"What's that," Jake asked.

"Numbers."

"I can see that."

"Do you recognize them? You've seen them before," Anna noted.

Jake frowned. "I'm good with political science, not so good with numbers."

Anna tapped the book cover. "Two numbers, then a dash, then another set of two numbers, and more."

"Fascinating."

"You saw them under there," she said, pointing to the engine hatches in the deck.

It finally dawned on Jake. "The Coast Guard numbers -- they were carved into the timber down there. Imagine that."

Anna hesitated then said, "Coast Guard numbers have seven digits, no dashes."

Jake peered closer at the numbers scrawled on the book. "Numbers, then a dash, then more numbers, blah, blah, blah. So what?"

"The numbers represent a location: latitude and longitude -- degrees, minutes, seconds. See, right there, look at the sequence."

Jake looked closer. Anna offered a faint smirk then tapped the book of nautical charts again. Jake was puzzled, but he was beginning to fit the pieces together. He slid the book over, tracing the numbers with his finger. He opened the book and scanned the reference latitudes and longitudes at the top of several pages.

"This is fun," Anna teased.

Jake checked the numbers on the cover then opened the page again. He laid his finger down and allowed it to trace and across the chart. After a moment, he stopped. For a long moment, he just stared at the chart. Without looking up, he whispered with astonishment. "The numbers, these numbers."

"Latitude and longitude," Anna added impetuously.

"They're right here."

"Really?"

"I mean they're *right* here. Right where we're anchored!" Jake sank back heavily in his chair. He had to collect his thoughts before speaking, "Did you know all along?"

"No. Not until you found the hull numbers and read them to me."

"Damn." Jake tilted his head and looked at her, "What are you going to do about it?

"Hmm. I'm not sure."

Jake suddenly sat forward, "Aw, quit messing with me. There's thirty billion dollars in gold down there!"

"Right. One hundred twenty-five feet down."

"I repeat. What are you going to do about it?"

Anna didn't answer at first. Instead, she gazed out over the sea.

"Anna?"

Finally, she turned back to Jake. "Well, okay. It's like this. I've got a friend; he's pretty smart, like a nerdy professor. And I'm thinking that between the two of us, we can find a junkyard-mean attorney who can negotiate with the Feds for us."

"You want to negotiate with the Feds? For what?"

"First we disappear for a while. Maybe Java. Definitely someplace warm -- with boats. Then we get our nasty attorney to paper up a contract that tells the government where to find *The Princess* – the rubles."

Jake was stunned. "You want to give it to the Feds?"

Anna was grinning now, "Every bit of it."

"Aw, man."

"Every bit, except for our two percent fee."

Jake fell silent. Anna could tell that his mind was roiling with mathematic calculations. "You said you were lousy with numbers," she chirped.

"Six-hundred-million dollars!" Jake expelled. "Two percent is six-hundred-million dollars!"

Anna leaned over and kissed Jake. It was meant to be an impetuous nothing, but their lips lingered tenderly together. Something hissed loudly beneath the grill hood. Jake whispered to Anna. "The fish is burning."

"Who cares," Anna quipped. "Maybe we could smoke some weed."

"We don't smoke pot," Jake noted.

Anna's lips curled into a tempting smile, "Got any other ideas?"

———————